PET SEMATARY

STEPHEN KING Photograph © Dick Dickinson

There is a reason why Stephen King is one of the bestselling writers in the world, *ever*. As George Pelecanos says: 'King's gift of storytelling is unrivalled. His ferocious imagination is unlimited.' King knows how to write stories that draw you in and are *impossible to put down*.

King is the author of more than fifty books, all of them worldwide bestsellers, including the iconic, chilling classics *Cujo*, *The Dark Half*, *Pet Sematary*, *'Salem's Lot* and *The Shining*. Many of his books and novellas have been turned into celebrated films, including *Cujo*, *Misery*, *The Shining* and *The Shawshank Redemption*.

King was the recipient of the 2003 National Book Foundation Medal for Distinguished Contribution to American Letters. He lives with his wife, novelist Tabitha King, in Maine.

HAVE YOU READ . . . ?

CUJO

Cujo is a huge Saint Bernard dog, the family's best friend and protector. Then one day Cujo gets bitten by a rabid bat . . . and the gentle giant becomes a vortex of terror, trapping those around him.

THE DARK HALF

For years, Thad Beaumont has been writing books under the pseudonym George Stark. When a journalist threatens to expose Beaumont's pen name, the author decides to go public first, killing off his pseudonym. But Stark isn't content to be dispatched that easily . . .

'SALEM'S LOT

Author Ben Mears returns to 'Salem's Lot to write a book about a house that has haunted him since childhood, only to find his isolated hometown infested with vampires. Now Ben must gather the locals to combat the terrors before it is too late.

THE SHINING

Danny is only five years old but in the words of old Mr Hallorann he is a 'shiner', aglow with psychic voltage. When his father becomes caretaker of the Overlook Hotel, Danny's visions grow out of control. Somewhere, somehow, there is an evil force in the hotel – and that too is beginning to shine . . .

'Obviously a masterpiece, probably the best super-natural novel in a hundred years' – Peter Straub

By Stephen King and published by Hodder & Stoughton

NOVELS:

Carrie
'Salem's Lot
The Shining
The Stand
The Dead Zone
Firestarter
Cujo
Cycle of the Werewolf
Christine
The Talisman (with Peter Straub)
Pet Sematary
IT
The Eyes of the Dragon
Misery
The Tommyknockers
The Dark Half
Needful Things
Gerald's Game
Dolores Claiborne
Insomnia
Rose Madder
Desperation
Bag of Bones
The Girl Who Loved Tom Gordon
Dreamcatcher
From a Buick 8
Cell
Lisey's Story
Duma Key
Under the Dome
Blockade Billy

The Dark Tower I: The Gunslinger
The Dark Tower II: The Drawing of
the Three
The Dark Tower III: The Waste Lands
The Dark Tower IV: Wizard and Glass
The Dark Tower V: Wolves of the Calla
The Dark Tower VI: Song of Susannah
The Dark Tower VII: The Dark Tower

As Richard Bachman
Thinner
The Running Man
The Bachman Books
The Regulators
Blaze

STORY COLLECTIONS:

Night Shift
Different Seasons
Skeleton Crew
Four Past Midnight
Nightmares and Dreamscapes
Hearts in Atlantis
Everything's Eventual
Just After Sunset
Stephen King Goes to the Movies
Full Dark, No Stars

NON-FICTION

Danse Macabre
On Writing (A Memoir of the Craft)

STEPHEN KING

PET SEMATARY

HODDER

A CIP catalogue record for this title is available from the British Library

ISBN 978 1 444 70813 4

Typeset in Bembo

Printed and bound in Great Britain by Clays Ltd, St Ives plc

Hodder & Stoughton policy is to use papers that are natural,
renewable and recyclable products and made from wood grown in
sustainable forests. The logging and manufacturing processes are expected
to conform to the environmental regulations of the country of origin

Hodder & Stoughton
338 Euston Road
London NW1 3BH

www.hodder.co.uk

Here are some people who have written books, telling what they did and why they did those things:

John Dean. Henry Kissinger. Adolf Hitler. Caryl Chessman. Jeb Magruder. Napoleon. Talleyrand. Disraeli. Robert Zimmerman, also known as Bob Dylan. Locke. Charlton Heston. Errol Flynn. The Ayatollah Khomeini. Gandhi. Charles Olson. Charles Colson. A Victorian Gentleman. Dr X.

Most people also believe that God has written a Book, or Books, telling what He did and why – at least to a degree – He did those things, and since most of these people also believe that humans were made in the image of God, then He also may be regarded as a person . . . or, more properly, as a Person.

Here are some people who have not written books, telling what they did . . . and what they saw:

The man who buried Hitler. The man who performed the autopsy on John Wilkes Booth. The man who embalmed Elvis Presley. The man who embalmed – badly, most undertakers say – Pope John XXIII. The twoscore undertakers who cleaned up Jonestown, carrying body-bags, spearing paper cups with those spikes custodians carry in city parks, waving away the flies. The man who cremated William Holden. The man who encased the body of Alexander the Great in gold so it would not rot. The men who mummified the Pharoahs.

Death is a mystery, and burial is a secret.

For Kirby McCauley

INTRODUCTION

STEPHEN KING

When I'm asked (as I frequently am) what I consider to be the most frightening book I've ever written, the answer I give comes easily and with no hesitation: *Pet Sematary*. It may not be the one that scares readers the most – based on the mail, I'd guess the one that does that is probably *The Shining* – but the fearbone, like the funnybone, is located in different places on different people. All I know is that *Pet Sematary* is the one I put away in a drawer, thinking I had finally gone too far. Time suggests that I had not, at least in terms of what the public would accept, but certainly I had gone too far in terms of my own personal feelings. Put simply, I was horrified by what I had written, and the conclusions I'd drawn. I've told the story of how the book came to be written before, but I guess I can tell it one more time: last time pays for all.

In the late seventies, I was invited to spend a year at my alma mater, the University of Maine, as the writer in residence, and also teach a class in the literature of the fantastic (my lecture notes for that course formed the spine of *Danse Macabre*, which was published a year or two later). My wife and I rented a house in Orrington, about twelve miles from the campus. It was a wonderful house in a wonderful rural Maine town. The only problem was the road we lived on. It was very busy, a lot of the traffic consisting of heavy tanker trucks from the chemical plant down the road.

Julio DeSanctis, who owned the store across the road from us, told me early on that my wife and I wanted to keep a close watch on our children, and on any pets our children might have. 'That road has used up a lot of animals,' Julio said, a phrase that made its way into the story. And the proof of how many animals the road had used up was in the woods, beyond our rented house. A path led up through the neighboring field to a little pet cemetery in the woods . . . only the sign on the tree just outside this charming little makeshift graveyard read PET SEMATARY. This phrase did more than just make it into the book; it became the title. There were dogs and cats buried up there, a few birds, even a goat.

Our daughter, who was eight or so at the time, had a cat named Smucky, and not long after we moved into the Orrington house, I found Smucky dead on the lawn of a house across the road. The newest animal Route 5 had used up, it seemed, was my daughter's beloved pet. We buried Smucky in the pet sematary. My daughter made the grave marker, which read SMUCKY: HE WAS OBEDIANT. (Smucky wasn't in the least obedient, of course; he was a cat, for heaven's sake.)

All seemed to be well until that night, when I heard a thumping from the garage, accompanied by weeping and popping sounds like small firecrackers. I went out to investigate and found my daughter, furious and beautiful in her grief. She had found several sheets of that blistered packing material in which fragile objects are sometimes shipped. She was jumping up and down on this, popping the blisters, and yelling, 'He was *my* cat! Let God have his own cat! Smucky was *my* cat!' Such anger, I think, is the sanest first response to grief that a thinking, feeling human being can have, and I've always loved her for that defiant cry: *Let God have his own cat!* Right on, beautiful; right on.

Our youngest son, then less than two years old, had only learned to walk, but already he was practicing his running skills. On a day not long after Smucky's demise, while we were out in the neighboring yard fooling around with a kite, our toddler took it into his head to go running toward the road. I ran after him, and damned if I couldn't hear one of those Cianbro trucks coming (Orinco, in the novel). Either I caught him and pulled him down, or he tripped on his own; to this day, I'm not entirely sure which. When you're really scared, your memory often blanks out. All I know for sure is that he is still fine and well and in his young manhood. But a part of my mind has never escaped from that gruesome *what if:* Suppose I hadn't caught him? Or suppose he had fallen in the middle of the road instead of on the edge of it?

I think you can see why I found the book which rose out of these incidents so distressing. I simply took existing elements and threw in that one terrible *what if.* Put another way, I found myself not just thinking the unthinkable, but writing it down.

There was no writing space in the Orrington house, but there was an empty room in Julio's store, and it was there that I wrote *Pet Sematary.* On a day by day basis, I enjoyed the work, and I knew I was telling a 'hot' story, one that engaged my attention and would engage the attention of readers, but when you're working day by day, you're not seeing the forest; you're only counting trees. When I finished, I let the book rest six weeks, which is my way of working, and then read it over. I found the result so startling and so gruesome that I put the book in a drawer, thinking it would never be published. Not in my lifetime, anyway.

That it was published was a case of mere circumstance. I had ended my relationship with Doubleday, the publisher of my early books, but I owed them a final novel before accounts could be closed completely. I only had one in hand that wasn't spoken for, and that one was *Pet Sematary.* I talked it over with my wife, who is my best counselor when I'm not sure how to proceed, and she told me that I should go ahead and publish the book. She thought it was good. Awful, but too good not to be read.

My early editor at Doubleday, Bill Thompson, had moved on by then (to Everest House, as a matter of fact; it was Bill who first suggested, then edited and published *Danse Macabre*), so I sent the book to Sam Vaughn, who was one of the

INTRODUCTION

editorial giants of the time. It was Sam who made the final decision – he wanted to do the book. He edited it himself, giving particular attention to the book's conclusion, and his input turned a good book into an even better one. I've always been grateful to him for his inspired blue pencil, and I've never been sorry that I did the book, although in many ways I still find it distressing and problematic.

I'm particularly uneasy about the book's most resonant line, spoken by Louis Creed's elderly neighbor, Jud. 'Sometimes, Louis,' Jud says, 'dead is better.' I hope with all my heart that that is not true, and yet within the nightmarish context of *Pet Sematary*, it seems to be. And it may be okay. Perhaps 'sometimes dead is better' is grief's last lesson, the one we get to when we finally tire of jumping up and down on the plastic blisters and crying out for God to get his own cat (or his own child) and leave ours alone. That lesson suggests that in the end, we can only find peace in our human lives by accepting the will of the universe. That may sound like corny, new-age crap, but the alternative looks to me like a darkness too awful for such mortal creatures as us to bear.

September 20, 2000

PART ONE:
THE PET SEMATARY

Jesus said to them, 'Our friend Lazarus sleeps, but I go, that I may awake him out of his sleep.'

Then the disciples looked at each other and some smiled, because they did not know Jesus had spoken in a figure. 'Lord, if he sleeps, he shall do well.'

So then Jesus spoke to them more plainly. 'Lazarus is dead, yes . . . nevertheless, let us go to him.'

– John's Gospel (paraphrase)

CHAPTER ONE

Louis Creed, who had lost his father at three and who had never known a grandfather, never expected to find a father as he entered his middle age, but that was exactly what happened . . . although he called this man a friend, as a grown man must do when he finds the man who should have been his father relatively late in life. He met this man on the evening he and his wife and his two children moved into the big white frame house in Ludlow. Winston Churchill moved in with them. Church was his daughter Eileen's cat.

The search committee at the University had moved slowly, the search for a house within commuting distance of the University had been hair-raising, and by the time they neared the place where he believed the house to be (*all the landmarks are right . . . like the astrological signs the night before Caesar was assassinated*, Louis thought morbidly), they were all tired and tense and on edge. Gage was cutting teeth and fussed almost ceaselessly. He would not sleep no matter how much Rachel sang to him. She offered him the breast even though it was off his schedule. Gage knew his dining schedule as well as she – better, maybe – and he promptly bit her with his new teeth. Rachel, still not entirely sure about this move to Maine from Chicago, where she had lived her whole life, burst into tears. Eileen joined her, apparently in some sort of mystic feminine sympathy. In the back of the station wagon, Church continued to pace restlessly as he had done for the last three days it had taken them to drive here from Chicago. His yowling from the cat-kennel had been bad, but his restless pacing after they finally gave up and set him free in the car had been almost as unnerving.

Louis himself felt a little like crying. A wild but not unattractive idea suddenly came to him: he would suggest that they go back to Bangor for something to eat while they waited for the moving van, and when his three hostages to fortune got out, he would floor the accelerator and drive away without so much as a look back, foot to the mat, the wagon's huge four-barrel carburetor gobbling expensive gasoline. He would drive south, all the way to Orlando, Florida, where he would get a job at Disney World as a medic, under a new name. But before he hit the turnpike – big old 95 southbound – he would stop by the side of the road and put the fucking cat out, too.

Then they rounded a final curve and there was the house that only he had seen up until now. He had flown out and looked at each of the seven possibles they had picked from photos once the position at the University was solidly his, and this was the one he had chosen: a big old New England colonial (but newly sided and insulated; the heating costs, while horrible enough, were not out of line in terms of consumption), three big rooms downstairs, four more up, a long shed that might be converted to more rooms later on, all of it surrounded by a luxuriant sprawl of lawn, lushly green even in this August heat.

Beyond the house was a large field for the children to play in, and beyond the field were woods that went on damn near for ever. The property abutted state lands, the realtor had explained, and there would be no development in the foreseeable future. The remains of the Micmac Indian tribe had laid claim to nearly 8,000 acres in Ludlow, and in the towns east of Ludlow, and the complicated litigation, involving the Federal government as well as that of the state, might stretch into the next century.

Rachel stopped crying abruptly. She sat up. 'Is that—'

'That's it,' Louis said. He felt apprehensive – no, he felt scared. In fact he felt *terrified*. He had mortgaged twelve years of their lives for this; it wouldn't be paid off until Eileen was seventeen, an unbelievable age.

He swallowed.

'What do you think?'

'I think it's *beautiful*,' Rachel said, and that was a huge weight off his chest – and off his mind. She wasn't kidding, he saw; it was in the way she was looking at it as they turned in the asphalted driveway that swept around to the shed in back, her eyes sweeping the blank windows, her mind already ticking away at such matters as curtains and oilcloth for the cupboards and God knew what else.

'Daddy?' Eileen said from the back seat. She had stopped crying as well. Even Gage had stopped fussing. Louis savored the silence.

'What, love?'

Her eyes, brown under darkish blonde hair in the rear-view mirror, also surveying the house: the lawn, the roof of a house seen off to the left in the distance, the big field stretching up to the woods.

'Is this home?'

'It's going to be, honey,' he said.

'*Hooray!*' she shouted, almost taking his ear off. And Louis, who could sometimes become very irritated with Eileen, decided he didn't care if he never clapped an eye on Disney World in Orlando.

He parked in front of the shed and turned off the wagon's motor.

The engine ticked. In the silence, which seemed very big after Chicago and the bustle of State Street and the Loop, a bird sang sweetly in the late afternoon.

'Home,' Rachel said softly, still looking at the house.

'Home,' Gage said complacently on her lap.

Louis and Rachel stared at each other. In the rear-view mirror, Eileen's eyes widened.

'Did you —'

'Did he —'

'Was that —'

They all spoke together, then all laughed together. Gage

took no notice; only sucked his thumb. He had been saying 'Ma' for almost a month now, and had taken a stab or two at something that might have been 'Daaa' or only wishful thinking on Louis's part.

But this, either by accident or imitation, had been a real word. *Home.*

Louis plucked Gage from his wife's lap and hugged him.

That was how they came to Ludlow.

CHAPTER TWO

In Louis Creed's memory that one moment always held a magical quality — partly, perhaps, because it really *was* magical, but mostly because the rest of the evening was so wild. In the next three hours, neither peace nor magic made an appearance.

Louis had stored the house-keys away neatly (he was a neat and methodical man, was Louis Creed) in a small manila envelope which he had labelled *Ludlow House — keys received June 29th*. He had stored the keys away for this trip in the Fairlane's glove compartment. He was absolutely sure of that. Now they weren't there.

While he hunted for them, growing increasingly irritated (and a little worried), Rachel hoisted Gage on to her hip and followed Eileen over to the tree in the field. He was checking under the seats for the third time when his daughter screamed and then began to cry.

'Louis!' Rachel called. 'She's cut herself!'

Eileen had stumbled out of the tire swing and hit a rock with her knee. The cut was shallow, but she was screaming like someone who had just lost a leg, Louis thought (a bit ungenerously). He glanced at the house across the road, where a light burned in the living room.

'All right, Eileen,' he said. 'That's enough. Those people over there will think someone's being murdered.'

'*But it hurrrts!*'

Louis struggled with his temper, and went silently back to the wagon. The keys were gone, but the first-aid kit was still in the glove compartment. He got it and came back. When Eileen saw it, she began to scream louder than ever.

7

'*No! Not the stingy stuff! I don't want the stingy stuff, Daddy! No*—'

'Eileen, it's just mecurichrome and it doesn't sing—'

'Be a big girl,' Rachel said. 'It's just—'

'*No-no-no-no-no*—'

'You want to stop that or your ass will sting,' Louis said.

'She's tired, Lou,' Rachel said quietly.

'Yeah, I know the feeling. Hold her leg out.'

Rachel put Gage down and held Eileen's leg, which Louis painted with mecurichrome in spite of her increasingly hysterical wails.

'Someone just came out on the porch of that house across the street,' Rachel said. She picked Gage up. He had started to crawl away through the grass.

'Wonderful,' Louis muttered.

'Lou, she's—'

'Tired, I know.' He capped the mecurichrome and looked grimly at his daughter. 'There. And it didn't hurt a bit. Fess up, Ellie.'

'*It does! It does hurt! It hurrr*—'

His hand itched to slap her and he grabbed his leg hard.

'Did you find the keys?' Rachel asked.

'Not yet,' Louis said, snapping the first-aid kit closed and getting up. 'I'll—'

Gage began to scream. He was not fussing or crying but really screaming, writhing in Rachel's arms.

'What's wrong with him?' Rachel cried, thrusting him almost blindly at Louis. It was, he supposed, one of the advantages of having married a doctor – you could shove the kid at your husband when the kid seemed to be dying. 'Louis! what's—'

The baby was grabbing frantically at his neck, screaming wildly. Louis flipped him over and saw an angry white knob rising on the side of Gage's neck. And there was also something on the strap of his jumper, something fuzzy, squirming weakly.

Eileen, who had been quieting, began to scream again: '*Bee!*

Bee! BEEEEEE!' She jumped back, tripped over the same protruding rock on which she had already come a cropper, sat down hard, and began to cry again in mingled pain, surprise, and fear.

I'm going crazy, Louis thought wonderingly. *Wheeeeee!*

'Do something, Louis! Can't you do something?'

'Got to get the stinger out,' a voice behind them drawled. 'That's the ticket. Get the stinger out and put some baking soda on it. Bump'll go down.' But the voice was so thick with Downeast accent that for a moment Louis's tired, confused mind refused to translate the dialect: *Got t'get the stinga out 'n put some bakin' soda on't. 'T'll go daown.*

He turned and saw an old man of perhaps seventy – a hale and healthy seventy – standing there on the grass. He wore a biballs over a blue chambray shirt that showed his thickly folded and wrinkled neck. His face was sunburned and he was smoking an unfiltered cigarette. As Louis looked at him, the old man pinched the cigarette out between his thumb and forefinger and pocketed it neatly. He held out his hands and smiled crookedly, a smile Louis liked at once – and he was not a man who 'took' to people.

'Not to tell you y'business, doc,' he said, and that was how Louis met Judson Crandall, the man who should have been his father.

CHAPTER THREE

He had watched them arrive from across the street, and had come across to see if he could help when it seemed they were 'in a bit of a tight', as he put it.

While Louis held the baby on his shoulder, Crandall stepped near, looked at the swelling on Gage's neck, and reached out with one blocky, twisted hand. Rachel opened her mouth to protest – his hand looked terribly clumsy and almost as big as Gage's head – but before she could say a word the old man's fingers had made a single decisive movement, as apt and deft as the fingers of a man walking cards across his knuckles or sending coins into conjurer's limbo. And the stinger lay in his palm.

'Big 'un,' he remarked. 'No prize-winner, but it'd do for a ribbon, I guess.' Louis burst out laughing.

Crandall regarded him with that crooked smile and said, 'Ayuh, she's a corker, ain't she?'

'What did he say, Mommy?' Eileen asked wonderingly, and then Rachel burst out laughing, too. Of course it was terribly impolite, but somehow it was okay. Crandall pulled out a deck of Chesterfield Kings, poked one into the seamed corner of his mouth, nodded at them pleasantly as they laughed – even Gage was chortling now, in spite of the swelling of the bee-sting – and popped a wooden match alight with his thumbnail. *The old have their tricks*, Louis thought. *Small ones, but some of them are good ones.*

He stopped laughing and held out the hand that wasn't supporting Gage's bottom – Gage's decidedly damp bottom. 'I'm pleased to meet you, Mr—'

'Jud Crandall,' he said, and shook. 'You're the doc, I guess.'

'Yes. Louis Creed. This is my wife, Rachel, my daughter Ellie, and the kid with the bee-sting is Gage.'

'Nice to know all of you.'

'I didn't mean to laugh . . . that is, we didn't mean to laugh . . . it's just that we're . . . a little tired.'

That – the understatement of it – caused him to giggle again. He felt totally exhausted.

Crandall nodded. 'Course you are,' he said, which came out: *Coss you aaa*. He glanced at Rachel. 'Why don't you take your little boy and your daughter over to the house for a minute, Missus Creed? We can put some bakin' soda on a washrag and cool that off some. My wife would like to say hello, too. She don't get out too much. Arthritis got bad the last two or three years.'

Rachel glanced at Louis, who nodded.

'That would be very kind of you, Mr Crandall.'

'Oh, I just answer to Jud,' he said.

There was a sudden loud honk, a motor winding down, and then the big blue moving van was turning – lumbering – into the driveway.

'Oh Christ, and I don't know where the keys are,' Louis said.

'That's okay,' Crandall said. 'I got a set. Mr and Mrs Cleveland – they that lived here before you – gave me a set, oh, must have been fourteen, fifteen years ago. They lived here a long time. Joan Cleveland was my wife's best friend. She died two years ago. Bill went to that old folks' apartment complex over in Orrington. I'll bring 'em back over. They belong to you now, anyway.'

'You're very kind, Mr Crandall,' Rachel said gratefully.

'Not at all,' he said. 'Lookin' forward to having young 'uns around again.' Except that the sound of this, as exotic to their Midwestern ears as a foreign language, was *youwuns*. 'You just want to watch 'em around the road, Missus Creed. Lots of big trucks on that road.'

Now there was the sound of slamming doors as the moving men hopped out of the cab and came toward them.

Ellie had wandered away a little and now she said: 'Daddy, what's this?'

Louis, who had started to meet the moving men, glanced back. At the edge of the field, where the lawn stopped and high summer grass took over, a path about four feet wide had been cut, smooth and close. It wound up the hill, curved through a low stand of bushes and a copse of birches, and out of sight.

'Looks like a path of some kind,' Louis said.

'Oh, ayuh,' Crandall said, smiling. 'Tell you about it sometime, missy. You want to come over and we'll fix your baby brother up?'

'Sure,' Ellie said, and then with a certain hopefulness: 'Does baking soda sting?'

CHAPTER FOUR

Crandall brought back the keys, but by then Louis had found his set. There was a space at the top of the glove compartment and the small envelope had slipped down into the wiring. He fished it out and let the movers in. Crandall gave him the extra set. They were on an old, tarnished fob. Louis thanked him and slipped them absently into his pocket, watching the movers take in boxes and dressers and bureaus and all the other things they had collected over the ten years of their marriage. Seeing them this way, out of their accustomed places, diminished them. *Just a bunch of stuff in boxes*, he thought, and suddenly he felt sad and depressed – he guessed he was feeling what people called homesickness.

'Uprooted and transplanted,' Crandall said suddenly beside him, and Louis jumped a little.

'You sound like you know the feeling,' he said.

'No, actually I don't.' Crandall lighted a cigarette. Pop! went the match, flaring brightly in the first early evening shadows. 'My dad built that house across the way. Brought his wife there, and she was taken with child there, and that child was me, born in the very year 1900.'

'That makes you—'

'Eighty-three,' Crandall said, and Louis was mildly relieved that he didn't add *years young*, a phrase he cordially detested.

'You look a lot younger than that.'

Crandall shrugged. 'Anyway, I've always lived there. I joined up when we fought the Great War, but the closest I got to Europe was Bayonne, New Jersey. Nasty place. Even in 1917 it was a nasty place. I was just as glad to come back here. Got married to my Norma, put in my time on the railroad, and here we still are. But I've seen a lot of life right here in Ludlow. I sure have.'

The moving men stopped by the shed entrance, holding the box spring that went under the big double bed he and Rachel shared. 'Where do you want this, Mr Creed?'

'Upstairs. Just a minute, I'll show you.' He started toward them, then paused for a moment and glanced back at Crandall.

'You go on,' Crandall said, smiling. 'I'll see how y'folks're makin' out. Send 'em back over and get out of your way. But movin' in's mighty thirsty work. I usually sit out on my porch about nine and have a couple of beers. In warm weather I like to watch the night come on. Sometimes Norma joins me. You come over, if you've a mind.'

'Well, maybe I will,' Louis said, not intending to at all. The next thing would be an informal (and free) diagnosis of Norma's arthritis on the porch. He liked Crandall, liked his crooked grin, his offhand way of talking, his Yankee accent, which was not hard-edged at all, but so soft it was almost a drawl. A good man, Louis thought, but doctors became leery of people fast. It was unfortunate, but. Sooner or later even your best friends wanted medical advice. And with old people there was no end to it. 'But don't look for me, or stay up – we've had a hell of a day.'

'Just so long as you know you don't need no engraved invitation,' Crandall said, and there was something in the man's crooked grin that made Louis feel that Crandall knew exactly what Louis was thinking.

He watched the old guy for a moment before joining the movers. Crandall walked straight and easily, like a man sixty instead of over eighty. Louis felt that first faint tug of affection.

CHAPTER FIVE

By nine o'clock the movers were gone. Ellie and Gage, both exhausted, were sleeping in their new rooms, Gage in his crib, Ellie on a mattress on the floor surrounded by a foothill of boxes: her billions of Crayolas, whole, broken and blunted, her Sesame Street posters, her picture books, her clothes, and heaven knew what else. And of course Church was with her, also sleeping and growling rustily in the back of his throat. That just about seemed the closest the big tom could come to purring.

Rachel had prowled the house restlessly with Gage in her arms earlier, second-guessing the places where Louis had told the movers to leave things, getting them to rearrange, change, restack. Louis had not lost their check; it was still in his breast pocket, along with the five ten-dollar bills he had put aside for a tip. When the van was finally emptied, he handed both the check and the cash over, nodded at their thanks, signed the bill of receipt and stood on the porch, watching them head back to their big truck. He supposed they would probably lay over in Bangor and have a few beers to lay the dust. A couple of beers would go down well right now. That made him think of Jud Crandall again.

He and Rachel sat at the kitchen table, and he saw the circles under her eyes. 'You,' he said, 'go to bed.'

'Doctor's orders?' she asked, smiling a little.

'Yeah.'

'Okay,' she said, standing. 'I'm beat. And Gage is apt to be up in the night. You coming?'

He hesitated. 'I don't think so, just yet. That old fella across the street—'

'Road. You call it a road, out in the country. Or if you're Judson Crandall, I guess you call it a *rud*.'

'Okay, across the *rud*. He invited me over for a beer. I think I'm going to take him up on it. I'm tired, but I'm too jived-up to sleep.'

Rachel smiled. 'You'll end up getting Norma Crandall to tell you where it hurts and what kind of mattress she sleeps on.'

Louis laughed, thinking how funny – funny and scary – it was, the way wives could read their husbands' minds after a while.

'He was here when we needed him,' he said. 'I can do him a favor, I guess.'

'Barter system?'

He shrugged, unwilling and unsure how to tell her that he had taken a liking to Crandall on short notice. 'How's his wife?'

'Very sweet,' Rachel said. 'Gage sat on her lap. I was surprised, because he's had a hard day and you know he doesn't take very well to new people on short notice under the best of circumstances. And she had a dolly she let Eileen play with.'

'How bad would you say her arthritis is?'

'Quite bad.'

'In a wheel chair?'

'No . . . but she walks very slowly, and her fingers. . .' Rachel held her own slim fingers up and hooked them into claws to demonstrate. Louis nodded. 'Anyway, don't be late, Lou. I get the creeps in strange houses.'

'It won't be strange for long,' Louis said, and kissed her.

CHAPTER SIX

Louis came back later feeling small. No one asked him to examine Norma Crandall; when he crossed the street (*rud*, he reminded himself, smiling), the lady had already retired for the night. Jud was a vague silhouette behind the screens of the enclosed porch. There was the comfortable squeak of a rocker on old linoleum. Louis knocked on the screen door, which rattled companionably against its frame. Crandall's cigarette glowed like a large, peaceable firefly in the summer darkness. From a radio, low, came the voice of a Red Sox game, and all of it gave Louis Creed the oddest feeling of coming home.

'Doc,' Crandall said. 'I thought that was you.'

'Hope you meant it about the beer,' Louis said, coming in.

'Oh, about beer I never lie,' Crandall said. 'A man who lies about beer makes enemies. Sit down, doc. I put an extra couple on ice, just in case.'

The porch was long and narrow, furnished with rattan chairs and sofas. Louis sank into one and was surprised at how comfortable it was. At his left hand was a tin pail filled with ice-cubes and a few cans of Black Label. He took one.

'Thank you,' he said, and opened it. The first two swallows hit his throat like a blessing.

'More'n welcome,' Crandall said. 'I hope your time here will be a happy one, doc.'

'Amen,' Louis said.

'Say! If you want crackers or somethin', I could get some. I got a wedge of rat that's just about ripe.'

'A wedge of *what*?'

'Rat cheese.' Crandall sounded faintly amused.

'Thanks, but just the beer will do me.'

17

'Well then, we'll just let her go.' Crandall belched contentedly.

'Your wife gone to bed?' Louis asked, wondering why he was opening the door like this.

'Ayuh. Sometimes she stays up. Sometimes she don't.'

'Her arthritis quite painful, is it?'

'You ever see a case that wasn't?' Crandall asked.

Louis shook his head.

'I guess it's tolerable,' Crandall said. 'She don't complain much. She's a good old girl, my Norma.' There was a great and simple weight of affection in his voice. Out on Route 15, a tanker truck droned by, one so big and long that for a moment Louis couldn't see his house across the road. Written on the side, just visible in the last light, was the word ORINCO.

'One hell of a big truck,' Louis commented.

'Orinco's near Orrington,' Crandall said. 'Chemical fertilizer fact'ry. They come and go, all right. And the oil tankers and the dump trucks, and the people who go to work in Bangor or Brewer and come home at night.' He shook his head. 'That's the one thing about Ludlow I don't like anymore. That frigging road. No peace from it. They go all day and night. Wake Norma up sometimes. Hell, wake *me* up sometimes, and I sleep like a goddam log.'

Louis, who thought this strange Maine landscape almost eerily quiet after the constant roar of Chicago, only nodded his head.

'One day soon the Arabs will pull the plug and they'll be able to grow African violets right down the yellow line,' Crandall said.

'You might be right.' Louis tilted his can back and was surprised to find it empty.

Crandall laughed. 'You just grab yourself one to grow on, doc.'

Louis hesitated and then said, 'All right, but just one more. I have to be getting back.'

'Sure you do. Ain't moving a bitch?'

'It is,' Louis agreed, and then for a time they were silent. The silence was a comfortable one, as if they had known each other for a long time. This was a feeling about which Louis had read in books, but which he had never experienced until now. He felt ashamed of his casual thoughts about free medical advice earlier.

On the road a semi roared by, its running lights twinkling like earthstars.

'That's one mean road all right,' Crandall repeated thoughtfully, almost vaguely, and then turned to Louis. There was a peculiar little smile on his seamed mouth. He poked a Chesterfield into one corner of the smile and popped a match with his thumbnail. 'You remember the path there your little girl commented on?'

For a moment Louis didn't; Ellie had commented on a whole catalogue of things before finally collapsing for the night. Then he did remember. That wide mown path winding up through the copse of trees and over the hill.

'Yes, Ido. You promised to tell her about it sometime.'

'I did, and I will,' Crandall said. 'That path goes up into the woods about a mile and a half. The local kids around Route 15 and Middle Drive keep it nice, because they use it. Kids come and go . . . there's a lot more moving around than there used to be when I was a boy; then you picked a place out and stuck to it. But they seem to tell each other, and every spring a bunch of them mows that path. They keep it nice all the summer long. They know it's up there. Not all of the adults in town know it's there – a lot of them do, of course, but not all, not by a long chalk – but all of the kids do. I'd bet on it.'

'Know what's there?'

'The pet cemetery,' Crandall said.

'Pet cemetery,' Louis repeated, bemused.

'It's not as odd as it prob'ly sounds,' Crandall said, smoking and rocking. 'It's the road. It uses up a lot of animals, that road does. Dogs and cats, mostly, but that ain't all. One of those big Orinco trucks run down the pet raccoon the Ryder children used to keep. That was back – Christ, must have been in '73, maybe earlier. Before the state made keeping a 'coon or even a denatured skunk illegal, anyway.'

'Why did they do that?'

'Rabies,' Crandall said. 'Lot of rabies in Maine now. There was a big old St Bernard went rabid downstate a couple of years ago and killed four people. That was a hell of a thing. Dog hadn't had his shots. If those foolish people had seen that dog had had its shots, it never would have happened. But a 'coon or a skunk, you can vaccinate it twice a year and still it don't always take. But that 'coon the Ryder boys had, that was what the oldtimers used to call a "sweet 'coon". It'd waddle right up to you – gorry, wa'n't he fat! – and lick your face like a dog. Their dad even paid a vet to spay him and declaw him. *That* must have cost him a country fortune!

'Ryder, he worked for IBM in Bangor. They went out to Colorado five years ago . . . or maybe it was six. Funny to think of those two almost old enough to drive. Were they broken up over that 'coon? I guess they were. Matty Ryder cried so long his mom got scared and wanted to take him to the doctor. I s'pose he's over it now, but they never forget. When a good animal gets run down in the road, a kid never forgets.'

Louis's mind turned to Ellie as he had last seen her tonight, fast asleep with Church purring rustily on the foot of the mattress.

'My daughter's got a cat,' he said. 'Winston Churchill. We call him Church for short.'

'Do they climb when he walks?'

'I beg your pardon?' Louis had no idea what he was talking about.

'He still got his balls, or has he been fixed?'

'No,' Louis said. 'No, he hasn't been fixed.'

In fact there had been some trouble over that back in

Chicago. Rachel had wanted to get Church spayed; had even made the appointment with the vet. Louis cancelled it. Even now he wasn't really sure why. It wasn't anything as simple or as stupid as equating his masculinity with that of his daughter's tom, nor even his resentment at the idea that Church would have to be castrated to make sure that the fat housewife next door wouldn't need to be troubled with twisting down the lids of her plastic garbage cans so Church couldn't paw them off and investigate what was inside – both of those things had been part of it, but most of it had been a vague but strong feeling that it would destroy something in Church that he himself valued – that it would put out the go-to-hell look in the cat's green eyes. Finally he had pointed out to Rachel that they were moving to the country, and it shouldn't be a problem. Now here was Judson Crandall, pointing out that part of country living in Ludlow consisted of dealing with Route 15, which was very busy, and asking him if the cat was fixed. Try a little irony, Dr Creed – it's good for your blood.

'I'd get him fixed,' Crandall said, crushing his smoke between his thumb and forefinger. 'A fixed cat don't tend to wander as much. But if it's all the time crossing back and forth, its luck will run out, and it'll end up there with the Ryder kids' 'coon and little Timmy Dessler's cocker spaniel and Missus Bradleigh's parakeet. Not that the parakeet got run over in the road, you understand. It just went feet up one day.'

'I'll take it under advisement,' Louis said.

'You do that,' Crandall said, and stood up. 'How's that beer doing? I believe I'll go in for a slice of old Mr Rat after all.'

'Beer's gone,' Louis said, also standing, 'and I ought to go, too. Big day tomorrow.'

'Starting in at the University?'

Louis nodded. 'The kids don't come back for two weeks, but by then I ought to know what I'm doing, don't you think?'

21

'Yeah, if you don't know where the pills are, I guess you'll have trouble.' Crandall offered his hand and Louis shook it, mindful again of the fact that old bones pained easily. 'Come on over any evening,' he said. 'Want you to meet my Norma. Think she'd enjoy you.'

'I'll do that,' Louis said. 'Nice to meet you, Jud.'

'Same goes both ways. You'll settle in. May even stay a while.'

'I hope we do.'

Louis walked down the crazy-paved path to the shoulder of the road and had to pause while yet another truck, this one followed by a line of five cars headed in the direction of Bucksport, passed by. Then, raising his hand in a short salute, he crossed the street (*road*, he reminded himself again) and let himself into his new house.

It was quiet with the sounds of sleep. Ellie appeared not to have moved at all, and Gage was still in his crib, sleeping in typical Gage fashion, spreadeagled on his back, a bottle within easy reach. Louis paused there looking in at his son, his heart abruptly filling with a love for the boy so strong that it seemed almost dangerous. He supposed part of it was simply an emotional displacement for all the familiar Chicago places and Chicago faces that were now gone, erased so efficiently by the miles that they might never have been at all. *There's a lot more moving around than there used to be . . . used to be you picked a place out and stuck to it.* There was some truth in that.

He went to his son, and because there was no one there, not even Rachel, to see him do it, he kissed his fingers and then pressed them lightly and briefly to Gage's cheek through the bars of the crib.

Gage clucked and turned over on his side.

'Sleep well, baby,' Louis said.

He undressed quietly and slipped into his half of the double bed that was for now just a mattress on the floor. He felt the strain of the day beginning to pass. Rachel didn't stir. Unpacked boxes bulked ghostly in the room.

Just before sleep, Louis hiked himself up on one elbow and looked out of the window. Their room was at the front of the house, and he could look across the road at the Crandall place. It was too dark to see shapes – on a moonlit night it would not have been – but he could see the cigarette ember over there. *Still up*, he thought. *He'll maybe be up for a long time. The old sleep poorly. Perhaps they stand watch.*

Against what?

Louis was thinking about that when he slipped into sleep. He dreamed he was in Disney World, driving a bright white van with a red cross on the side. Gage was beside him, and in the dream Gage was at least ten years old. Church was on the white van's dashboard, looking at Louis with his bright green eyes, and out on Main Street by the 1890s train station, Mickey Mouse was shaking hands with the children clustered around him, his big white cartoon gloves swallowing their small, trusting hands.

CHAPTER SEVEN

The next two weeks were busy ones for the family. Little by little Louis's new job began to shake down for him (how it would be when ten thousand students, Many of them drug and liquor abusers, some afflicted with social diseases, some anxious about grades or depressed about leaving home for the first time, a dozen of them – girls, mostly – anorexic . . . how it would be when all of them converged on the campus at once would be something else again). And while Louis began getting a handle on his job as head of University Medical Services, Rachel began to get a handle on the house. As she was doing so, something happened which Louis had only dared to hope for – she fell in love with the place.

Gage was busy taking the bumps and spills that went with getting used to his new environment, and for a while his night-time schedule was badly out of whack, but by the middle of their second week in Ludlow he had begun to sleep through again. Only Ellie, with the prospect of beginning kindergarten in a new place before her, seemed always over-excited and on a hairtrigger. She was apt to go into prolonged giggling fits or periods of almost menopausal depression or temper-tantrums at the drop of a word. Rachel said she would get over it when she saw that school was not the great red devil she had made it out to be in her own mind, and Louis thought she was right. Most of the time, Ellie was what she had always been – a dear.

His evening beer or two with Jud Crandall became something of a habit. Around the time Gage began sleeping through again, Louis began bringing his own six-pack over every second or third night. He met Norma Crandall, a sweetly pleasant woman who had rheumatoid arthritis – filthy old rheumatoid arthritis, which kills so much of what could be good in the old ages of men and women who are otherwise healthy – but her attitude was good. She would not surrender to the pain; there would be no white flags. Let it take her if it could. Louis thought she might have another five to seven productive if not terribly comfortable years ahead of her.

Going completely against his own established customs, he examined her at his own instigation, inventoried the prescriptions her own doctor had given her, and found them to be completely in order. He felt a nagging disappointment that there was nothing else he could do or suggest for her, but her Dr Weybridge had things as under control as they were ever going to be for Norma Crandall – barring some sudden breakthrough, which was possible but not to be counted upon. You learned to accept, or you ended up in a small room writing letters home with Crayolas.

Rachel liked her, and they had sealed their friendship by exchanging recipes the way small boys trade baseball cards: Norma Crandall's deep-dish apple pie for Rachel's beef stroganoff. Norma was taken with both of the Creed children – particularly with Ellie, who, she said, was going to be 'an old-time beauty'. At least, Louis told Rachel that night in bed, Norma hadn't said Ellie was going to grow into a real sweet 'coon. Rachel laughed so hard she broke explosive wind, and then both of them laughed so long and loudly they woke up Gage in the next room.

The first day of kindergarten arrived. Louis, who felt pretty well in control of the infirmary and the medical support facilities now (besides, the infirmary was currently dead empty; the last patient, a summer student who had broken her leg on the Union steps, had been discharged a week before), took the day off. He stood on the lawn beside Rachel with Gage in his arms, as the big yellow bus made the turn from Middle Drive and lumbered to a stop in front of their house. The doors at the front folded open; the babble and squawk of many children drifted out on the mild September air.

Ellie cast a strange, vulnerable glance back over her shoulder, as if to ask them if there might not yet be time to abort this inevitable process now, and perhaps what she saw on the faces of her parents convinced her that the time was gone, and everything which would follow this first day was simply inevitable – like the progress of Norma Crandall's arthritis. She turned away from them and mounted the steps of the bus. The doors folded shut with a gasp of dragon's breath. The bus pulled away. Rachel burst into tears.

'Don't, for Christ's sake,' Louis said. He wasn't crying. Only damn near. 'It's only half a day.'

'Half a day is bad enough,' Rachel answered in a scolding voice, and began to cry harder. Louis held her, and Gage slipped an arm comfortably around each parent's neck. When Rachel cried, Gage usually cried, too. Not this time. *He has us to himself*, Louis thought, *and he damn well knows it*.

They waited with some trepidation for Ellie to return, drinking too much coffee, speculating on how it was going for her. Louis went out into the back room that was going to be his study and messed about idly, moving papers from one place to another but not doing much else. Rachel began lunch absurdly early.

When the phone rang at quarter past ten, Rachel raced for it and answered with a breathless 'Hello?' before it could ring a second time. Louis stood in the doorway between his office and the kitchen, sure it would be Ellie's teacher telling them that she had decided Ellie couldn't take it, and the stomach of public education had found her indigestible and was spitting her back. But it was only Norma Crandall, calling to tell them that Jud had picked the last of the corn and they were welcome to a dozen ears if they wanted it. Louis went over with a shopping bag and scolded Jud for not letting him help pick it.

'Most of it ain't worth a tin shit anyway,' Jud said.

'You spare that kind of talk while I'm around,' Norma said. She came out on the porch with iced tea on an antique Coca-Cola tray.

'Sorry, my love.'

'He ain't sorry a bit,' Norma said to Louis, and sat down with a wince.

'Saw Ellie get on the bus,' Jud said, lighting a Chesterfield.

'She'll be fine,' Norma said. 'They almost always are.' *Almost*, Louis thought morbidly.

But Ellie *was* fine. She came home at noon smiling and sunny, her blue first-day-of-school dress belling gracefully around her scabbed shins (and there was a new scrape on one knee to marvel over), a picture of what might have been two children or perhaps two walking gantries in one hand, one shoe untied, one ribbon missing from her hair, shouting: 'We sang *Old MacDonald!* Mommy! Daddy! We sang *Old MacDonald!* Same one as in the Carstairs Street School!'

Rachel glanced over at Louis, who was sitting in the windowseat with Gage on his lap. The baby was almost asleep. There was something sad in Rachel's glance, and although she looked away quickly, Louis felt a moment of terrible panic. *We're really going to get old*, he thought. *It's really true. No one's going to make an exception for us. She's on her way . . . and so are we.*

Ellie ran over to him, trying to show him her picture, her new scrape, and tell him about *Old MacDonald* and Mrs Berryman all at the same time. Church was twining in and out between her legs, purring loudly, and Ellie was somehow, almost miraculously, not tripping over him.

'Shh,' Louis said, and kissed her. Gage had gone to sleep, unmindful of all the excitement. 'Just let me put the baby to bed and then I'll listen to everything.'

He took Gage up the stairs, walking through hot slanting

September sunshine, and as he reached the landing, such a premonition of horror and darkness struck him that he stopped – stopped cold – and looked around in surprise, wondering what could possibly have come over him. He held the baby tighter, almost clutching him, and Gage stirred uncomfortably. Louis's arms and back had broken out in great rashes of gooseflesh.

What's wrong? he wondered, confused and frightened. His heart was racing; his scalp felt cool and abruptly too small to cover his skull; he could feel the surge of adrenalin behind his eyes. Human eyes really did bug out when fear was extreme, he knew; they did not just widen but actually *bulged* as blood-pressure climbed and the hydrostatic pressure of the cranial fluids increased. *What the hell is it? Ghosts? Christ, it really feels as if something just brushed by me in this hallway, something I almost saw.*

Downstairs the screen door whacked against its frame.

Louis Creed jumped, almost screamed, and then laughed. It was simply one of those psychological cold-pockets people sometimes passed through – no more, no less. A momentary fugue. They happened, that was all. What had Scrooge said to the ghost of Jacob Marley? *You may be no more than an underdone bit of potato. There's more gravy than grave to you.* And that was more correct – physiologically as well as psychologically – than Charles Dickens had probably known. There were no ghosts, at least not in his experience. He had pronounced two dozen people dead in his career and had never once felt the passage of a soul.

He took Gage into his room and laid him in his crib. As he pulled the blanket up over his son, though, a shudder twisted up his back and he thought suddenly of his Uncle Frank's showroom. No new cars there, no televisions with all the modern features, no dishwashers with glass fronts so you could watch the magical sudsing action. Only boxes with their lids up, a carefully hidden spotlight over each. His mother's brother was an undertaker.

Good God, what gave you the horrors? Let it go! Dump it!
He kissed his son and went down to listen to Ellie tell about her first day at big kids' school.

CHAPTER EIGHT

That Saturday, after Ellie had completed her first week of school and just before the college kids came back to campus, Jud Crandall came across the road and walked over to where the Creed family sat on their lawn. Ellie had gotten off her bike and was drinking a glass of iced tea. Gage was crawling in the grass, examining bugs, perhaps even eating a few; Gage was not particular where his protein came from.

'Jud,' Louis said, getting up. 'Let me get you a chair.'

'No need.' Jud was wearing jeans, an open-throated work-shirt, and a pair of green boots. He looked at Ellie. 'You still want to see where yon path goes, Ellie?'

'Yes!' Ellie said, getting up immediately. Her eyes sparkled. 'George Buck at school told me it was the pet cemetery, and I told Mommy, but she said to wait for you because you knew where it was.'

'I do, too,' Jud said. 'If it's okay with your folks, we'll take us a stroll up there. You'll want a pair of boots, though. Ground's a bit squishy in places.'

Ellie rushed into the house.

Jud looked after her with amused affection. 'Maybe you'd like to come, too, Louis.'

'I would,' Louis said. He looked at Rachel. 'You want to come, honey?'

'What about Gage? I thought it was a mile.'

'I'll put him in the Gerrypack.'

Rachel laughed. 'Okay . . . but it's your back, mister.'

They started off ten minutes later, all of them but Gage wearing boots. Gage sitting up in the Gerrypack and looking at every-

30

thing over Louis's shoulder, goggle-eyed. Ellie ranged ahead
constantly, chasing butterflies and picking flowers.

The grass in the back field was almost waist-high and now
there was golden-rod, that late-summer gossip that comes to
tattle on autumn every year. But there was no autumn in the
air today; today the sun was still all August, although calendar
August was almost two weeks gone. By the time they had
reached the top of the first hill, walking strung-out along the
mown path, there were big patches of sweat under Louis's
arms.

Jud paused. At first Louis thought it might be because the
old man was winded – then he saw the view that had opened
out behind them.

'Pretty up here,' Jud said, putting a piece of timothy grass
between his teeth. Louis thought he had just heard the quintes-
sential Yankee understatement.

'It's *gorgeous*,' Rachel breathed, and then turned to Louis,
almost accusingly. 'How come you didn't tell me about this?'

'Because I didn't know it was here,' Louis said, and was a
little ashamed. They were still on their own property; he had
just never found time to climb the hill at the back of the house
until today.

Ellie had been a good way ahead. Now she came back,
also gazing with frank wonder. Church padded at her heels.

The hill was not a high one, but it did not need to be. To
the east, heavy woods blocked any view, but looking this way,
west, the land fell away in a golden and dozy late summer
dream. Everything was still, hazed, silent. There was not even
an Orinco tanker on the highway to break the quiet.

It was the river-valley they were looking into, of course;
the Penobscot where loggers had once floated their timber
from the north-east down to Bangor and Derry. But they
were south of Bangor and a bit north of Derry here. The river
flowed wide and peacefully, as if in its own deep dream. Louis
could make out Hampden and Winterport on the far side, and
over here he fancied he could trace the black, river-paralleling

snake of Route 15 nearly all the way to Bucksport. They looked over the river, its lush hem of trees, the roads, the fields. The spire of the North Ludlow Baptist Church poked through one canopy of old elms, and to the right he could see the square brick sturdiness of Ellie's school.

Overhead, white clouds hung suspended, moving toward a horizon the color of faded denim. And everywhere were the late summer fields, used up at the end of the cycle, dormant but not dead, an incredible tawny color.

'Gorgeous is the right word,' Louis said finally.

'They used to call it Prospect Hill back in the old days,' Jud said. He put a cigarette in the corner of his mouth but did not light it. 'There's a few that still do, but now that younger people have moved into town, it's mostly been forgot. I don't think there's very many people that even come up here. It don't look like you could see much because the hill's not very high. But you can see —' He gestured with one hand and fell silent.

'You can see everything,' Rachel said in a low, awed voice. She turned to Louis. 'Honey, do we *own* this?'

And before Louis could answer, Jud said: 'It's part of the property, oh yes.'

Which wasn't, Louis thought, quite the same thing.

It was cooler in the woods, perhaps by as much as eight or ten degrees. The path, still wide and occasionally marked with flowers in pots or in coffee cans (most of them wilted), was now floored with dry pine needles. They had gone about a quarter of a mile, moving downhill now, when Jud called Ellie back.

'This is a good walk for a little girl,' Jud said kindly, 'but I want you to promise your mom and dad that if you come up here, you'll always stay on the path.'

'I promise,' Ellie said promptly. 'Why?'

He glanced at Louis, who had stopped to rest. Toting Gage, even in the shade of these old pines and spruces, was heavy work. 'Do you know where you are?' Jud asked Louis.

Louis considered and rejected answers: Ludlow, North Ludlow, behind my house, between Route 15 and Middle Drive. He shook his head.

Jud jerked a thumb back over his shoulder. 'Plenty of stuff that way,' he said. 'That's town. This way, nothing but woods for fifty miles or more. The North Ludlow Woods they call it here, but it hits a little corner of Orrington, then goes over to Rockford. Ends up going on to those state lands I told you about, the ones the Indians want back. I know it sounds funny to say your nice little house there on the main road, with its phone and electric lights and cable TV and all, is on the edge of a wilderness, but it is.' He looked back at Ellie. 'All I'm saying is that you don't want to get messing around in these woods, Ellie. You might lose the path and God knows where you might end up then.'

'I won't, Mr Crandall.' Ellie was suitably impressed, even awed, but not afraid, Louis saw. Rachel, however, was looking at Jud uneasily, and Louis felt a little uneasy himself. It was, he supposed, the city-bred's almost instinctive fear of the woods. Louis hadn't held a compass in his hands since Boy Scouts, twenty years before, and his memories of how to find your way by things like the North Star or which side of the trees moss grew on were as vague as his memories of how to tie a sheepshank or a half-hitch.

Jud looked them over and smiled a little. 'Now, we ain't lost nobody in these woods since 1934,' he said. 'At least, nobody local. The last one was Will Jeppson. No great loss; except for Stanny Bouchard, I guess Will was the biggest tosspot this side of Bucksport.'

'You said nobody local,' Rachel remarked in a voice that was not quite casual, and Louis could read her mind: *We're not local. At least, not yet.*

Jud paused and then nodded. 'We do lose one of the tourists every two or three years, because they think you can't get lost right off the main road. But we never lost even one of them for good, Missus. Don't you fret.'

'Are there moose?' Rachel asked apprehensively, and Louis smiled. If Rachel wanted to fret, she would jolly well fret.

'Well, you might see a moose,' Jud said, 'but he wouldn't give you any trouble, Rachel. During mating season they get a little irritated, but otherwise they do no more than look. Only people they take after out of their rutting time are people from Massachusetts. I don't know why that's so, but it is.' Louis thought the man was joking, but could not be sure; Jud looked utterly serious. 'I've seen it time and time again. Some fella from Saugus or Milton or Weston up a tree, yelling about a herd of moose, every damn one of 'em as big as a motor-home. Seems like moose can *smell* Massachusetts on a man or a woman. Or maybe it's just all those new clothes from L. L. Bean's they smell, I dunno. I'd like to see one of those animal husbandry students from the college do a paper on it, but I s'pose none ever will.'

'What's rutting time?' Ellie asked.

'Never mind,' Rachel said. 'I don't want you up here unless you're with a grown-up, Ellie.' Rachel moved a step closer to Louis.

Jud looked pained. 'I didn't want to scare you, Rachel. You or your daughter. No need to be scared in these woods. This is a good path; it gets a little buggy in the spring and it's a little sloppy all the time – except for '55, which was the driest summer I can remember – but hell, there isn't even any poison ivy or poison oak, which there is at the back of the schoolyard, and you want to stay away from it, Ellie, if you don't want to spend three weeks of your life takin' starch baths.'

Ellie covered her mouth and giggled.

'It's a *safe* path,' Jud said earnestly to Rachel, who still didn't look convinced. 'Why, I bet even Gage could follow it, and the town kids come up here a lot, I already told you that. They keep it nice. Nobody tells them to; they just do it. I wouldn't want to spoil that for Ellie.' He bent over her and winked. 'It's like many other things in life, Ellie. You keep on the path and all's well. You get off it and the next thing you know you're lost if you're not lucky. And then someone has to send out a searchin' party.'

They walked on. Louis began to get a dull cramp of pain in his back from the baby-carrier. Every now and then Gage would grab a double handful of his hair and tug enthusiastically or administer a cheerful kick to Louis's kidneys. Late mosquitoes cruised around his face and neck, making their eye-watering hum.

The path curved down, bending in and out between very old firs, and then cut widely through a brambly, tangled patch of undergrowth. The going *was* soupy here, and Louis's boots squelched in mud and some standing water. At one point they stepped over a marshy bit using a pair of good-sized tussocks as stepping-stones. That was the worst of it. They started to climb again and the trees reasserted themselves. Gage seemed to have magically put on ten pounds, and the day had, with some similar magic, suddenly warmed up ten degrees. Sweat poured down Louis's face.

'How you doing, hon?' Rachel asked. 'Want me to carry him for a while?'

'No, I'm fine,' he said, and it was true, although his heart was larruping along at a good speed in his chest. He was more used to prescribing physical exercise than he was to doing it.

Jud was walking with Ellie by his side, her lemon-yellow slacks and red blouse bright splashes of color in the shady brown-green gloom.

'Lou, does he really know where he's going, do you think?' Rachel asked in a low, slightly worried tone.

'Sure,' Louis said.

Jud called back cheerily over his shoulder: 'Not much further now . . . You bearin' up, Louis?'

My God, Louis thought, *the man's well past eighty but I don't think he's even broken a sweat.*

'I'm fine,' he called back a little aggressively. Pride probably would have led him to say the same thing even if he had felt the onset of a coronary. He grinned, hitched the straps of the Gerrypack up a bit, and went on.

They topped the second hill, and then the path sloped through a head-high swatch of bushes and tangled under-brush. It narrowed and then, just ahead, Louis saw Ellie and Jud go under an arch made of old weatherstained boards. Written on these in faded black paint, only just legible, were the words PET SEMATARY. He and Rachel exchanged an amused glance and stepped under the arch, instinctively reach-ing out and grasping each other's hand as they did so, as if they had come here to be married.

For the second time that morning Louis was surprised into wonder.

There was no carpet of needles here. Here was an almost perfect circle of mown grass, perhaps as large as forty feet in diameter. It was bounded by thickly interlaced underbrush on three sides and an old blowdown on the fourth, a jackstraw-jumble of fallen trees that looked both sinister and dangerous. A man trying to pick his way through that or climb over it would do well to put on a steel jock before making the try, Louis thought. The clearing was crowded with markers, obvi-ously made by children from whatever materials they could beg or borrow – the slats of crates, scrapwood, pieces of beaten tin. And yet, seen against the perimeter of low bushes and straggly trees that fought for living space and sunlight here, the very fact of their clumsy manufacture seemed to emphasize what symmetry they had, and the fact that humans were responsible for what was here. The forested backdrop lent the place a crazy sort of profundity, a charm that was not Christian but pagan.

'It's lovely,' Rachel said, not sounding as if she meant it.

'*Wow!*' Ellie cried.

Louis unshouldered Gage and pulled him out of the baby-carrier so he could crawl. His back sighed with relief.

Ellie ran from one monument to the next, exclaiming over each. Louis followed her while Rachel kept an eye on the baby. Jud sat down cross-legged, his back against a protruding rock, and smoked.

Louis noticed that the place did not just *seem* to have a sense of order, a pattern; the memorials had been arranged in rough concentric circles.

SMUCKY THE CAT, one crate-board marker proclaimed. The hand was childish but careful. HE WAS OBEDIANT. And below this: 1971–1974. A little way around the outer circle he came to a piece of natural slate with a name written on it in fading but perfectly legible red paint: BIFFER. And below this a bit of verse that made Louis grin. *Biffer, Biffer, a helluva sniffer/Until he died he made us richer.*

'Biffer was the Desslers' cocker spaniel,' Jud said. He had dug a bald place in the earth with the heel of his shoe and was carefully tapping all his ashes into it. 'Got run over by a dumpster last year. Ain't that some poime?'

'It is,' Louis agreed.

Some of the graves were marked with flowers, some fresh, most old, not a few almost totally decomposed. Over half of the painted and penciled inscriptions Louis tried to read had faded away to partial or total illegibility. Others bore no discernible mark at all, and Louis guessed that the writing on these might have been done with chalk or crayon.

'Mom!' Ellie yelled. 'Here's a goldfishie! Come and see!'

'I'll pass,' Rachel said, and Louis glanced at her. She was standing by herself, outside the outermost circle, looking more uncomfortable than ever. Louis thought: *Even here she's upset.* She never had been easy around the appearances of death (not, he supposed, that anyone really was), probably because of her sister. Rachel's sister had died very young, and it had left a scar which Louis had learned early in their marriage not to touch. Her name had been Zelda, and it had been spinal meningitis. Her dying had probably been long and painful and ugly, and Rachel would have been at an impressionable age.

If she wanted to forget it, he thought there could be no harm in that.

Louis tipped her a wink, and Rachel smiled gratefully at him.

Louis looked up. They were in a natural clearing. He supposed that explained how well the grass did; the sun could get through. Nevertheless, it would have taken watering and careful tending. That meant cans of water lugged up here, or maybe Indian pumps, even heavier than Gage in his Gerrypack, carried on small backs. He thought again that it was an odd thing for children to have kept up for so long. His own memory of childhood enthusiasms – reinforced by his dealings with Ellie – was that they tended to burn like newsprint, fast . . . hot . . . and quick to die.

But they *had* kept it up for a long time; Jud was right about that. It became obvious as he cut across the circle toward its approximate center. Moving inward, the pet graves became older; fewer and fewer of the inscriptions could be read, but those that could yielded a rough timeline extending into the past. Here was TRIXIE, KILT ON THE HIGHWAY SEPT 15, 1968. In the same circle was a wide flat board planted deep in the earth. Frost and thaw had warped it and canted it to one side, but Louis could still make out IN MEMORY OF MARTA OUR PET RABIT DYED MARCH 1 1965. A row further in was GEN. PATTON (OUR! GOOD! DOG!, the inscription amplified), who had died in 1958; and Polynesia (who would have been a parrot, if Louis remembered his Doctor Dolittle aright), who had squawked her last 'Polly want a cracker' in the summer of 1953. There was nothing readable in the next two rows, and then, still a long way in from the center, chiseled roughly on a piece of sandstone, was HANNAH THE BEST DOG THAT EVER LIVED 1929– 1939. Although sandstone was relatively soft – and as a result the inscription was now little more than a ghost – Louis found it hard to conceive of the hours some child must have spent impressing those nine words on the stone. The commitment of love and grief seemed to him staggering; this was something parents did not even do for their own parents, or for their children if they died young.

'Boy, this does go back some,' he said to Jud, who had strolled over to join him.

Jud nodded. 'Come here, Louis. Want to show you something.'

They walked to a row only three back from the center. Here the circular pattern, perceived as an almost haphazard coincidence in the outer rows, was very evident. Jud stopped before a small piece of slate that had fallen over. Kneeling carefully, the old man set it up again.

'Used to be words here,' Jud said. 'I chiseled 'em myself, but it's worn away now. I buried my first dog here. Spot. He died of old age in 1914, the year the Great War began.'

Bemused by the thought that here was a graveyard that went further back than many graveyards for people, Louis walked toward the center and examined several of the markers. None of them were readable, and most had been almost reclaimed by the forest floor. The grass had almost entirely overgrown one, and when he set it back up, there was a small tearing, protesting sound from the earth. Blind beetles scurried over the section he had exposed. He felt a small chill and thought: *Boot Hill for animals. I'm not sure I really like it.*

'How far do these go back?'

'Gorry, I don't know,' Jud said, putting his hands deep in his pockets. 'Place was here when Spot died, of course. I had a whole gang of friends in those days. They helped me dig the hole for Spot. Digging here ain't that easy, either — ground's awful stony, you know, hard to turn. And I helped them sometimes.' He pointed here and there with a horny finger. 'That there was Pete LaVassuer's dog, if I remember right, and there's three of Albion Groatley's barncats buried right in a row there.

'Old man Fritchie kept racing pigeons. Me and Al Groatley and Carl Hannah buried one of them that a dog got. He's right there.' He paused thoughtfully. 'I'm the last of that bunch left, you know. All dead now, my gang. All gone.'

Louis said nothing, only stood looking at the pet graves with his hands in his pockets.

'Ground's stony,' Jud repeated. 'Couldn't plant nothing here but corpses anyway, I guess.'

Across the way, Gage began to cry thinly, and Rachel brought him over, toting him on her hip. 'He's hungry,' she said. 'I think we ought to go back, Lou.' *Please, okay?* her eyes asked.

'Sure,' he said, answering her eyes. He shouldered the Gerrypack again and turned around so Rachel could pop Gage in. 'Ellie! Hey Ellie, where are you?'

'There she is,' Rachel said, and pointed toward the blowdown. Ellie was climbing as if the blowdown was a bastard cousin to the monkeybars at school.

'Oh, honey, you want to come down off there!' Jud called over, alarmed. 'You stick your foot in the wrong hole and those old trees shift, you'll break your ankle.'

Ellie jumped down. 'Ow!' she cried, and came toward them, rubbing her hip. The skin wasn't broken, but a stiff, dead branch had torn her slacks.

'You see what I mean,' Jud said, ruffling her hair. 'Old blowdown like this, not even someone wise about the woods will try to climb over it if he can go around. Trees that all fall down in a pile get mean. They'll bite you if they can.'

'Really?' Ellie asked.

'Really,' Louis said before Jud could answer.

Jud amplified. 'They're piled up like straws, you see. And if you was to step on the right one, they might all come down in an avalanche.'

Ellie looked at Louis. 'Is that true, daddy?'

'I think so, hon.'

'Yuck!' She looked back at the blowdown and yelled: 'You tore my pants, you cruddy trees!'

All three of the grown-ups laughed. The blowdown did

not. It merely sat whitening in the sun as it had done for decades. To Louis it looked like the skeletal remains of some long-dead monster, something slain by a parfait good and gentil knight, perchance. A dragon's bones, left here in a giant cairn.

It occurred to him even then that there was something too convenient about that blowdown and the way it stood between the pet cemetery and the depths of woods beyond, woods to which Jud Crandall later sometimes referred absently as 'the Indian woods'. Its very randomness seemed too artful, too perfect, for the work of nature. It—

Then Gage grabbed his ear and twisted it, crowing happily, and Louis forgot all about the blowdown in the woods beyond the pet cemetery. It was time to go home.

CHAPTER NINE

Ellie came to him the next day, looking troubled. Louis was working on a model in his tiny study. This one was a 1917 Rolls-Royce Silver Ghost; 680 pieces, over fifty moving parts. It was nearly done, and he could almost imagine the liveried chauffeur, direct descendant of eighteenth and nineteenth century English coachmen, sitting imperially behind the wheel.

He had been model-crazy since his tenth year. He had begun with a First World War Spad that his Uncle Carl had bought him, had worked his way through most of the Revell airplanes, and had moved on to bigger and better things in his teens and twenties. There had been a boats-in-bottles phase and a war-machines phase and even a phase in which he had built guns so realistic it was hard to believe they wouldn't fire when you pulled the trigger – Colts and Winchesters and Lugers, even a Buntline Special. Over the last five years or so it had been the big cruise-ships. A model of the *Lusitania* and one of the *Titanic* sat on his shelves at his University office, and the *Andrea Doria*, completed just before they left Chicago, was currently cruising the mantelpiece in their living room. Now he had moved on to classic cars, and if previous patterns held true, he supposed it would be four or five years before the urge to do something new struck him. Rachel looked on this, his only real hobby, with a wifely indulgence that held, he supposed, some elements of contempt; even after ten years of marriage she probably thought he would grow out of it. Perhaps some of this attitude came from her father, who believed just as much now as at the time Louis and Rachel had married that he had gotten an asshole for a son-in-law.

Maybe, he thought, *Rachel is right. Maybe I'll just wake up one morning at the age of thirty-seven, put all these models up in the attic, and take up hang-gliding.*

Meanwhile, Ellie looked serious.

Far away, drifting in the clear air, he could hear that perfect Sunday morning sound of churchbells calling worshippers.

'Hi dad,' she said.

'Hello, pumpkin. Wass happenin'?'

'Oh, nothing,' she said, but her face said differently; her face said that plenty was up, and none of it was so hot, thank you very much. Her hair was freshly washed and fell loose to her shoulders. In this light it was still more blonde than the brown it was inevitably becoming. She was wearing a dress, and it occurred to Louis that his daughter almost always put on a dress on Sundays, although they did not attend church. 'What are you building?'

Carefully gluing on a mudguard, he told her. 'Look at this,' he said, carefully handing her a hubcap. 'See those linked R's? That's a nice detail, huh? If we fly back to Shytown for Thanksgiving and we get on an L-1011, you look out at the jet engines and you'll see those same R's.'

'Hubcap, big deal.' She handed it back.

'Please,' he said. 'If you own a Rolls-Royce, you call that a wheel covering. If you're rich enough to own a Rolls, you can strut a little. When I make my second million, I'm going to buy myself one. Rolls-Royce Corniche. Then when Gage gets carsick, he can throw up on to real leather.' *And just by the way, Ellie, what's on your mind?* But it didn't work that way with Ellie. You didn't ask things right out. She was wary of giving too much of herself away. It was a trait Louis admired.

'Are we rich, Daddy?'

'No,' he said, 'but we're not going to starve, either.'

'Michael Burns at school says all doctors are rich.'

'Well, you tell Michael Burns at school that lots of doctors *get* rich, but it takes twenty years . . . and you don't get rich running a University infirmary. You get rich being a specialist.

A gynecologist or a pediatrist or a neurologist. They get rich quicker. For utility infielders like me it takes longer.'

'Then why don't you be a specialist, Daddy?'

Louis thought of his models again, and the way he had one day just not wanted to build any more warplanes, the way he had likewise gotten tired of Tiger Tanks and gun emplacements, the way he had come to believe (almost overnight, it seemed in retrospect) that building boats in bottles was pretty dumb; and then he thought of what it would be like to spend your whole life inspecting children's feet for hammertoe or putting on the thin Latex gloves so you could grope along some woman's vaginal canal with one educated finger, feeling for bumps and/or lesions.

'I just wouldn't like it,' he said.

Church came into the office, paused, inspected the situation with his bright green eyes. He leaped silently on to the windowsill and appeared to go to sleep.

Ellie glanced at him and frowned, which struck Louis as exceedingly odd. Usually Ellie looked at Church with an expression of love so soppy it was almost painful. She began to walk around the office, looking at various models, and in a voice that was nearly casual, she said: 'Boy, there were a lot of graves up in the Pet Sematary, weren't there?'

Ah, here's the nub, Louis thought, but did not look around; after examining his instructions, he began putting the carriage-lamps on the Rolls.

'There were,' he said. 'Better than a hundred, I'd say.'

'Daddy, why don't pets live as long as people?'

'Well, some animals do live about as long,' he said, 'and some live much longer. Elephants live a very long time, and there are some sea turtles so old that people really don't know *how* old they are . . . or maybe they do, and they just can't believe it.'

Ellie dismissed these simply enough. 'Elephants and sea turtles aren't *pets*. *Pets* don't live very long *at all*. Michael Burns says that every year a dog lives, it's like nine of our years.'

'Seven,' Louis corrected automatically. 'I see what you're getting at, honey, and there's some truth to it. A dog who lives to be twelve is an old dog. See, there's this thing called *metabolism*, and what metabolism seems to do is tell time. Oh, it does other stuff, too — some people can eat a lot and stay thin because of their metabolism, like your mother. Other people — me, for instance — just can't eat as much without getting fat. Our metabolisms are different, that's all. But what metabolism seems to do most of all is to serve living things as a kind of body-clock. Dogs have a fairly rapid metabolism. The metabolism of human beings is much slower. We live to be about seventy-two, most of us. And believe me, seventy-two years is a very long time.'

Because Ellie looked really worried, he hoped he sounded more sincere than he actually felt. He was thirty-five, and it seemed to him that those years had passed as quickly and ephemerally as a momentary draft under a door. 'Sea turtles, now, have an even slower metabo—'

'What about cats?' Ellie asked, and looked at Church again.

'Well, cats live as long as dogs,' he said, 'mostly, anyway.' This was a lie, and he knew it. Cats lived violent lives and often died bloody deaths, always just below the usual range of human sight. Here was Church, dozing in the sun (or appearing to), Church who slept peacefully on his daughter's bed every night, Church who had been so cute as a kitten, all tangled up in a ball of string. And yet Louis had seen him torture a bird with a broken wing, his green eyes sparkling with curiosity and — yes, Louis would have sworn it — cold delight; Church who brought Rachel his infrequent kills to be admired: a mouse, a bug, and once a large rat, probably caught in the alley between their apartment house and the next. The rat had been so bloody and gore-flecked that Rachel, then in her sixth month with Gage, had had to run into the bathroom and vomit. Violent lives, violent deaths. A dog got them and ripped them open instead of just chasing them like the bumbling, easily-fooled dogs in the TV cartoons, or another tom got them, or a poisoned bait, or a passing car. Cats were the gangsters of the animal world, living outside the law and often dying there. There were a great many of them who never grew old by the fire.

But those were maybe not things to tell your five-year-old daughter, who was for the first time examining the facts of death.

'I mean,' he said, 'Church is only three now, and you're five. He might still be alive when you're fifteen, a sophomore in high school. And that's a long time away.'

'It doesn't seem long to me,' Ellie said, and now her voice trembled. 'Not long at *all*.'

Louis gave up the pretense of working on his model and gestured for her to come. She sat on his lap and he was again struck by her beauty, which was emphasized now by her emotional upset. She was dark-skinned, almost Levantine. Tony Benton, one of the doctors he had worked with in Chicago, used to call her the Indian princess.

'Honey,' he said, 'if it was up to me, I'd let Church live to be a hundred. But I don't make the rules.'

'Who does?' she asked, and then, with infinite scorn: 'God, I suppose.'

Louis stifled the urge to laugh. It was too serious.

'God or somebody,' he said. 'Clocks run down, that's all I know. There are no guarantees, babe.'

'I don't want Church to be like all those dead pets!' she burst out, suddenly tearful and furious. 'I don't want Church to ever be dead! He's my cat! He's not God's cat! Let God have his own cat! Let God have all the damn old cats He wants, and kill them all! Church is *mine*!'

There were footsteps across the kitchen, and Rachel looked in, startled. Ellie was now weeping against Louis's chest. The horror had been articulated; it was out; its face had been drawn and could be regarded. Now, even if it could not be changed, it could at least be wept over.

'Ellie,' he said, rocking her. 'Ellie, Ellie, Church isn't dead; he's right over there, sleeping.'

'But he *could* be,' she wept. 'He *could* be, any time.'

He held her and rocked her, believing, rightly or wrongly, that Ellie wept for the very intractability of death, its imperviousness to argument or to a little girl's tears; that she wept over its cruel unpredictability; and that she wept because of the human being's wonderful, deadly ability to translate symbols into conclusions that were either fine and noble or blackly terrifying. If all those animals had died and been buried, then Church could die

any time!

and be buried; and if that could happen to Church, it could happen to her mother, her father, her baby brother. To herself. Death was a vague idea; the Pet Sematary was real. In the texture of those rude markers were truths which even a child's hands could feel.

It would be easy to lie at this point, the way he had lied earlier about the life-expectancy of tom cats. But a lie would be remembered later and perhaps finally totted up on the report-card all children hand in to themselves on their parents. His own mother had told him such a lie, an innocuous one about women finding babies in the dewy grass when they really wanted them, and innocuous as the lie had been, Louis had never forgiven himself for believing it — or his mother for telling it.

'Honey,' he said, 'it happens. It's a part of life.'

'It's a *bad* part!' she cried. 'It's a really *bad* part!'

There was no answer for this. She wept. Eventually, he supposed, her tears would stop. It was a necessary first step on the way to making an uneasy peace with a truth that was never going to go away.

He held his daughter and listened to churchbells on Sunday morning, floating across the September fields; and it was some time after her tears had stopped before he realized that, like Church, she had gone to sleep.

★

He put her up in her bed and then came downstairs to the kitchen, where Rachel was beating cake batter with far too much vigor. He mentioned his surprise that Ellie should just cork off like that in the middle of the morning; it wasn't like her.

'No,' Rachel said, setting the bowl down on the counter with a decisive thump. 'It isn't, but I think she was awake most of last night. I heard her tossing around, and Church cried to go out around three. He only does that when she's restless.'

'Why would she—'

'Oh, you know why!' Rachel said angrily. 'That damned pet cemetery is why! It really upset her, Lou. It was the first cemetery of *any* kind for her, and it just . . . upset her. I don't think I'll write your friend Jud Crandall any thank-you notes for *that* little hike.'

All at once he's *my* friend, Louis thought, bemused and distressed at the same time.

'Rachel—'

'And I don't want her going up there again.'

'Rachel, what Jud said about the path is true.'

'It's not the *path* and you know it,' Rachel said. She picked up the bowl again and began beating the cake batter even faster. 'It's that damned *place*. It's unhealthy. Kids going up there and tending the graves, keeping the path . . . fucking *morbid* is what it is. Whatever disease the kids in this town have got, I don't want Ellie to catch it.'

Louis stared at her, nonplussed. He more than half-suspected that one of the things which had kept their marriage together when it seemed as if each year brought the news that two or three of their friends' marriages had collapsed was their respect of the mystery; the half-grasped but never spoken-of idea that maybe, when you got right down to the place where the cheese binds, there was no such *thing* as marriage, no such thing as union – each soul stood alone and ultimately defied rationality. That was the mystery. And no matter how well you thought you knew your partner, you occasionally ran into blank walls or fell into pits. And sometimes (rarely, thank God) you ran into a full-fledged pocket of alien strangeness, something like the clear-air turbulence that can buffet an airliner for no reason at all. An attitude or belief which you had never suspected, one so peculiar (at least to you) that it seemed nearly psychotic. And then you trod lightly, if you valued your marriage and your peace of mind; you tried to remember that anger at such discovery was the province of fools who really believed it was possible for one mind to really know another.

'Honey, it's just a pet cemetery,' he said.

'The way she was crying in there just now,' Rachel said, gesturing toward the door to his office with a batter-covered spoon, 'do you think it's just a pet cemetery to *her*? It's going to leave a scar, Lou. No. She's not going up there anymore. It's not the path, it's the *place*. Here she is already thinking Church is going to die.'

For a moment Louis had the crazy impression that he was still talking to Ellie; she had simply donned stilts, one of her mother's dresses, and a very clever, very realistic Rachel mask. Even the expression was the same; set and a bit sullen, but wounded beneath.

He groped, because suddenly the issue seemed large to him, not a thing to be simply passed over in deference to that mystery . . . or that aloneness. He groped because it seemed to him that she was missing something so large it nearly filled the landscape, and you couldn't do that unless you were deliberately closing your eyes to it.

'Rachel,' he said, 'Church *is going* to die.'

She stared at him angrily. 'That is hardly the point,' she said, enunciating each word carefully, speaking as one might speak to a backward child. 'Church is not going to die today, or tomorrow—'

'I tried to tell her that—'

'Or the day after *that*, or probably for *years*—'

'Honey, we can't be sure of th—'

49

'Of course we *can!*' she shouted. 'We take good care of him, he's not going to *die*, no one is going to *die* around here, and so why do you want to go and get a little girl all upset about something she can't understand until she's much older?'

'Rachel, listen.'

But Rachel had no intention of listening. She was blazing. 'It's bad enough to try and cope with a death — a pet or a friend or a relative — when it happens, without turning it into a . . . a goddam tourist attraction . . . a F-F-Forest Lawn for a-animals . . .' Tears were running down her cheeks.

'Rachel,' he said, and tried to put his hands on her shoulders. She shrugged them off in a quick, hard gesture.

'Never mind,' she said. 'It's no good talking to you. You don't have the slightest idea what I'm talking about.'

He sighed. 'I feel like I fell through a hidden trapdoor and into a giant Mixmaster,' he said, hoping for a smile. He got none; only her eyes, locked on his, black and blazing. She was furious, he realized; not just angry, but absolutely furious. 'Rachel,' he said suddenly, not fully sure what he was going to say until it was out, 'how did *you* sleep last night?'

'Oh boy,' she said scornfully, turning away, but not before he had seen a wounded flicker in her eyes. 'That's really intelligent. *Really* intelligent. You never change, Louis. When something isn't going right, blame Rachel, right? Rachel's just having one of her weird emotional reactions.'

'That's not fair.'

'No?' She took the bowl of cake batter over to the far counter by the stove and set it down with another bang. She began to grease a cake tin, her lips pressed tightly together.

He said patiently, 'There's nothing wrong with a child finding out something about death, Rachel. In fact, I'd call it a necessary thing. Ellie's reaction — her crying — that seemed perfectly natural to me. It—'

'Oh, it *sounded* natural,' Rachel said, whirling on him again. 'It sounded *very* natural to hear her weeping her heart out over her cat which is perfectly fine—'

'Stop it,' he said. 'You're not making any sense.'

'I don't want to discuss it any more.'

'Yes, but we're going to,' he said, angry himself now. 'You had your at-bats, how about giving me mine?'

'She's not going up there any more. And as far as I'm concerned, the subject is closed.'

'Ellie has known where babies come from since last year,' Louis said deliberately. 'We got her the Myers book and talked to her about it, do you remember that? We both agreed that children ought to know where they come from.'

'That has nothing to do with —'

'It does, though!' he said roughly. 'When I was talking to her in my office, about Church, I got thinking about my mother, and how she spun me that old cabbage-leaf story when I asked her where women got babies. I've never forgotten that lie. I don't think children ever forget the lies their parents tell them.'

'Where babies come from has nothing to do with a goddam pet cemetery!' Rachel cried at him, and what her eyes said to him was *Talk about the parallels all night and all day, if you want to, Louis; talk until you turn blue, but I won't accept it.*

Still, he tried.

'The pet cemetery upset her because it's a concretization of death. She knows about babies; that place up in the woods just made her want to know something about the other end of things. It's perfectly natural. In fact, I think it's the most natural thing in the w—'

'*Will you stop saying that!*' She screamed suddenly — really screamed, and Louis recoiled, startled. His elbow struck the open bag of flour on the counter. It tumbled off the edge and struck the floor, splitting open. Flour puffed up in a dry white cloud.

'Oh, fuck,' he said dismally.

In an upstairs room, Gage began to cry.

'That's nice,' she said, also crying now. 'You woke the baby up, too. Thanks for a nice, quiet, stressless Sunday morning.'

She started by him and Louis put a hand on her arm, angry now in spite of himself. After all, she was the one who had wakened Gage. She had wakened him yelling like that. 'Let me ask you something,' he said, 'because I know that anything – literally *anything* – can happen to physical beings. As a doctor I know that. Do you want to be the one to explain to her what happened if her cat gets distemper or leukemia – cats are very prone to leukemia, you know – or if he gets run over in that road? Do you want to be the one, Rachel?'

'Let me go,' she nearly hissed. The anger in her voice, however, was overmatched by the hurt and bewildered terror in her eyes: *I don't want to talk about this, Louis, and you can't make me*, that look said. 'Let me go, I want to get Gage before he falls out of his cr—'

'Because maybe you *ought* to be the one,' he said. 'You can tell her we don't talk about it, nice people don't talk about it, they just bury it – oops! but don't say buried, you'll give her a complex.'

'*I hate you!*' Rachel sobbed, and tore away from him.

Then he was of course sorry and it was of course too late. 'Rachel—'

She pushed by him roughly, crying harder. 'Leave me alone. You've done enough.' She paused in the kitchen doorway, turning toward him, the tears coursing down her cheeks. 'I don't want this discussed in front of Ellie any more, Lou. I mean it. There's nothing natural about death. *Nothing.* You as a doctor should know *that.*'

She whirled and was gone, leaving Louis in the empty kitchen, which still vibrated with their argument. At last he went to the pantry to get the broom. As he swept he reflected on the last thing she had said, and on the enormity of this difference of opinion, which had gone undiscovered for so long. Because, as a doctor, he knew that death was, except perhaps for childbirth, the most natural thing in the world. Taxes were not so sure; human conflicts were not; the conflicts of society were not; boom and bust were not. In the end there was only the clock, and the markers, which became eroded and nameless in the passage of time. Even sea turtles and the giant sequoias had to buy out someday.

'Zelda,' he said aloud. 'Christ, that must have been bad for her.'

The question was, did he just let it ride, or try to do something about it?

He tilted the dustpan over the wastebasket and flour slid out with a soft *foom*, powdering the cast-out cartons and used-up cans.

CHAPTER TEN

'Hope Ellie didn't take it too hard,' Jud Crandall said that night, and not for the first time Louis thought that the man had a peculiar – and rather uncomfortable – ability to put his finger gently on whatever the sore spot was.

He and Jud and Norma Crandall now sat on the Crandalls' porch in the cool of the evening, drinking iced tea instead of beer. On 15, going-home-after-the-weekend traffic was fairly heavy; people recognizing that every good late-summer weekend now might be the last one, Louis supposed. Tomorrow he took up his full duties at the U of M infirmary. All day yesterday and today students had been arriving, filling apartments in Orono and dorms on campus, making beds, renewing acquaintances, and no doubt groaning over another year of eight o'clock classes and commons food. Rachel had continued to be cool to him – no, freezing was more like it – and when he went back across the road tonight he knew that she would already be in bed, Gage sleeping with her more than likely, the two of them so far over to her side that the baby would be in danger of falling off. His half of the bed would have grown to three quarters, all of it looking like a big, sterile desert.

'I said I hoped—'

'Sorry,' Louis said. 'Woolgathering. She was a little upset, yeah. How did you guess that?'

'Seen 'em come and go, like I said.' Jud took his wife's hand gently, and grinned at her. 'Haven't we, dear?'

'Packs and packs of them,' Norma Crandall said. 'We love the children.'

'Sometimes that pet cemetery is their first eyeball-to-eyeball

54

with death,' Jud said. 'They see people die on TV, but they know that's pretend, like the old Westerns they used to have at the movies on Saturday afternoons. On TV and in the Western movies they just hold their stomachs or their chests and fall over. Place up on that hill seems a lot more real to most of 'em than all those movies and TV shows put together, don't you know.'

Louis nodded, thinking: *Tell my wife that, why don't you.*

'Some kids it don't affect at all, at least not so you can see it, although I'd guess most of 'em kinda . . . kinda take it home in their pockets to look over later, like all the other stuff they collect. Most of 'em are fine. But some . . . you remember the little Symonds boy, Norma?'

She nodded. Ice chattered softly in the glass she held. Her glasses hung on her chest, and the headlights of a passing car illuminated the chain briefly. 'He had *such* nightmares,' she said. 'Dreams about corpses coming out of the ground and I don't know whatall. Then his dog died – ate some poisoned bait was all anyone in town could figure, wasn't it, Jud?'

'Poison bait,' Jud said, nodding. 'That's what most people thought, ayuh. That was 1925. Billy Symonds was maybe ten then. Went on to become a State Senator. Ran for the US House of Representatives later on, but he lost. That was just before Korea.'

'He and some of his friends had a funeral for the dog,' Norma remembered. 'It was just a mongrel, but he loved it well. I remember his parents were a little against the burying, because of the bad dreams and all, but it went off fine. Two of the bigger boys made a coffin, didn't they, Jud?'

Jud nodded and drained his iced tea. 'Dean and Dana Hall,' he said. 'Them and that other kid Billy chummed with – I can't remember his first name, but I'm sure he was one of the Bowie kids. You remember the Bowies that used to live up on Middle Drive in the old Brochette house, Norma?'

'Yes!' Norma said, as excited as if it had happened yesterday, and perhaps in her mind, it seemed that way. 'It was a Bowie! Alan, or Burt—'

'Or maybe it was Kendall,' Jud agreed. 'Anyways, I remember they had a pretty good argument about who was going to be pallbearers. The dog wasn't very big, and so there wasn't room but for two. The Hall boys said they ought to be the ones to do it since they made the coffin, and also because they were twins – sort of a matched set, y'see. Billy said they didn't know Bowser – that was the dog – well enough to be the pallbearers. "My dad says only close friends get to be pallbearers," was his argument, "not jest any *carpenter*."' Jud and Norma both laughed at this, and Louis grinned. He found himself wishing that Rachel could be here.

'They was just about ready to fight over it when Mandy, Billy's sister, fetched out fourth volume of the *Encyclopedia Britannica*,' Jud said. 'Her dad, Stephen, was the only doctor this side of Bangor and that side of Bucksport in those days, Louis, and they was the only family in Ludlow that could afford a set of encyclopedia.'

'They were also the first to have electric lights,' Norma broke in.

'Anyway,' Jud resumed, 'Mandy come out all aflukin', head up and tail over the splashboard, as my mom used to say, all of eight years old, petticoats flyin', that big book in her arms. Billy and the Bowie kid – I think it must have been Kendall, him that crashed and burned up in Pensacola where they was trainin' fighter pilots in early 1942 – they was getting ready to take on the Hall twins over the privilege of toting that poor old poisoned mutt up to the boneyard.'

Louis started giggling. Soon he was laughing out loud. He could feel the day-old residue of tension left from the bitter argument with Rachel beginning to loosen.

'So she says, "Wait! Wait! Looka this!" And they all stop and look. And goddam if she ain't—'

'Jud,' Norma said warningly.

'Sorry, dear; I get carried away yarning, you know that.'

'I guess you do,' she said.

'And darned if she ain't got that book open to FUNERALS, and there's a picture of Queen Victoria getting her final send-off and *bon voyage*, and there are about forty-seven people on each side of her coffin, some sweatin' and strainin' to lift the bugger, some just standin' around in their funeral coats and ruffled collars like they was waitin' for someone to call post-time at the racetrack. And Mandy says, "When it's a cer-emonial funeral of state, you can have as many as you want! The book says so!"'

'That solved it?' Louis asked.

'That did the trick. They ended up with about twenty kids, and damn if they didn't look just like the picture Mandy had found, except maybe for the ruffles and tall hats. Mandy took charge, she did. Got 'em lined up and gave each of 'em a wildflower — a dandelion or a lady's slipper or a daisy — and off they went. By the Gee, I always thought the country missed a bet when Mandy Symonds never got voted to the United Nations.' He laughed and shook his head. 'Anyway, that was the end of Billy Symonds's bad dreams about the pet sematary. He mourned his dog and finished his mourning and got on. Which is what we all do, I guess.'

Oh yeah? Louis thought again of Rachel's near-hysteria.

'Your Ellie will get over it,' Norma said, and shifted pos-ition. 'You must be thinking that death is all we talk about around here, Louis. Jud and I are getting on, but I hope neither of us has gotten to the gore-crow stage yet—'

'No, of course not, don't be silly,' Louis said.

'—but it's not such a bad idea to be on nodding acquaint-ance with it. These days . . . I don't know . . . no one wants to talk about it or think about it, it seems. They took it off the TV because they thought it might hurt the children some way — hurt their minds — and people want closed coffins so they don't have to look at the remains or say goodbye . . . it just seems like people want to forget it.'

'And at the same time they brought in the cable TV with

all those movies showing people—' Jud looked at Norma and cleared his throat. '—showing people doing what people usually do with their shades pulled down,' he finished. 'Queer how things change from one generation to the next, isn't it?'

'Yes,' Louis said. 'I suppose it is.'

'Well, we come from a different time,' Jud said, sounding almost apologetic. 'We was on closer terms with death. We saw the flu epidemic after the Great War, and mothers dying with child, and children dying of infection and fevers that it seems like doctors just wave a magic wand over these days. In the time when me and Norma was young, if you got cancer, why, that was your death-warrant, right there. No radiation treatments back in the 1920s! Two wars, murders, suicides . . .'

He fell silent for a moment.

'We knew it as a friend and as an enemy,' he said finally. 'My brother Pete died of a burst appendix in 1912, back when Taft was President. He was just fourteen and he could hit a baseball farther than any kid in town. In those days you didn't need to take a course in college to study death, hot-spice or whatever they call it. In those days it came into the house and said howdy and sometimes it took supper with you and sometimes you could feel it bite your ass.'

This time Norma didn't correct him; instead she nodded silently.

Louis stood up, stretched. 'I have to go,' he said. 'Big day tomorrow.'

'Yes, the merry-go-round starts up for you tomorrow, don't it?' Jud said, also standing. Jud saw Norma was also trying to get up and gave her a hand. She rose with a grimace.

'Bad tonight, is it?' Louis asked.

'Not so bad,' she said.

'Put some heat on it when you go to bed.'

'I will,' Norma said. 'I always do. And Louis . . . don't fret about Ellie. She'll be too busy gettin' to know her new friends this fall to worry much about that old place. Maybe someday all of 'em'll go up and repaint some of the signs, or pull weeds, or plant flowers. Sometimes they do, when the notion takes them. And she'll feel better about it. She'll start to get that nodding acquaintance.'

Not if my wife has anything to say about it.

'Come on over tomorrow night and tell me how it went, if you get the chance,' Jud said. 'I'll whop you at cribbage.'

'Well, maybe I'll get you drunk first,' Louis said. 'Double-skunk you.'

'Doc,' Jud said with great sincerity, 'the day I get double-skunked at cribbage would be the day I'd let a quack like you treat me.'

He left on their laughter and crossed the road to his own house in the late summer dark.

Rachel was sleeping with the baby, curled up on her side of the bed in a fetal, protective position. He supposed she would get over it. There had been other arguments and times of coldness in their marriage, but this one was surely the worst of the lot. He felt sad and angry and unhappy all at the same time, wanting to make it up but not sure how, not even sure the first move should come from him. It was all so pointless; only a capful of wind somehow blown up to hurricane proportions by a trick of the mind. Other fights and arguments, yes, sure, but only a few as bitter as the one over Ellie's tears and questions. He supposed it didn't take a great many blows like that before the marriage sustained some sort of structural damage . . . and then one day, instead of reading it in a note from a friend ('Well, I suppose I ought to tell you before you hear it from someone else, Lou; Maggie and I are splitting . . .') or in the newspaper, it was you.

He undressed to his shorts quietly and set the alarm for six a.m. Then he showered, washed his hair, shaved, and crunched up a Rolaid before brushing his teeth – Norma's iced tea had given him acid indigestion. Or maybe it was coming home and seeing Rachel way over on her side of the bed. Territory is that which defines all else, hadn't he read that in some college history course?

Everything done, the evening put neatly away, he went to bed . . . but couldn't sleep. There was something else, something that nagged at him. The last two days went around and around in his head as he listened to Rachel and Gage breathing nearly in tandem. GEN. PATTON. HANNAH THE BEST DOG THAT EVER LIVED. MARTA OUR PET RABIT. Ellie, furious. *I don't want Church to ever be dead! . . . He's not God's cat! Let God have his own cat!* Rachel equally furious. *You as a doctor should know . . .* Norma Crandall saying *It just seems like people want to forget it . . .* And Jud, his voice somehow terribly sure, terribly certain, a voice from another age: *Sometimes it took supper with you and sometimes you could feel it bite your ass.*

And that voice merged with the voice of his mother, who had lied to Louis Creed about sex at four but told him the truth about death at twelve, when his cousin Ruthie had been killed in a stupid car accident. She had been crushed in her father's car by a kid who had found the keys in a Public Works Department payloader and decided to take it for a cruise and then found out he didn't know how to stop it. The kid suffered only minor cuts and contusions; his Uncle Carl's Fairlane was demolished. *She can't be dead,* he had replied in answer to his mother's bald statement. He had heard the words but he couldn't seem to get the sense of them. *What do you mean, she's dead? What are you talking about?* And then, as an afterthought: *Who's going to bury her?* For although Ruthie's father, Louis's uncle, was an undertaker, he couldn't imagine that Uncle Carl would possibly be the one to do it. In his confusion and mounting fear, he had seized upon this as the most important question. It was a genuine conundrum, like who cut the town barber's hair.

I imagine that Donny Donahue will do it, his mother replied. Her eyes were red-rimmed; most of all she had looked tired. His mother had looked almost ill with weariness. *He's your*

Uncle's best pal in the business. Oh, but Louis . . . sweet little Ruthie . . . I can't stand to think she suffered . . . pray with me, will you, Louis? Pray with me for Ruthie. I need you to help me.

So they had gotten down on their knees in the kitchen, he and his mother, and they prayed, and it was the praying that finally brought it home to him; if his mother was praying for Ruthie Hodge's *soul*, then it meant that her *body* was gone. Before his closed eyes rose a terrible image of Ruthie coming to his thirteenth birthday party with her decaying eyeballs hanging on her cheeks and blue mould growing in her red hair, and this image provoked not just sickening horror but an awful doomed love.

He cried out in the greatest mental agony of his life, '*She can't be dead! MOMMA SHE CAN'T BE DEAD I LOVE HER!*'

And his mother's reply, like a tomb door swinging shut for ever on gritty, rusted hinges, her voice flat and yet full of images: dead fields under a November wind, scattered rose-petals brown and turning up at the edges, empty pools scummed with algae, rot, decomposition, dust:

She is, my darling. I'm sorry, but she is. Ruthie is gone.

Louis shuddered, thinking: Dead is dead, what else do you need?

Suddenly Louis knew what it was he had forgotten to do, why he was still awake on this night before the first day of his new job, hashing over old griefs.

He got up, headed for the stairs, and suddenly detoured down the hall to Ellie's room. She was sleeping peacefully, mouth open, wearing her blue baby-doll pajamas that she had really outgrown. *My God, Ellie*, he thought, *you're sprouting like corn*. Church lay between her splayed ankles, also dead to the world. *You should pardon the pun.*

Downstairs there was a bulletin board on the wall by the phone with various messages, memos and bills tacked to it. Written across the top in Rachel's neat caps was THINGS TO PUT OFF AS LONG AS POSSIBLE. Louis got the telephone book, looked up a number, and jotted it on a blank memo sheet. Below the number he wrote: *Quentin L. Jolander, DVM – call for appointment re Church – if Jolander doesn't neuter animals, he will refer.*

He looked at the note, wondering if it was time, knowing that it was. Something concrete had to come out of all this bad feeling, and he had decided sometime between this morning and tonight – without even knowing he was deciding – that he didn't want Church crossing the road any more if he could help it.

His old feelings on the subject rose up in him, the idea that it would lessen the cat, turn him into a fat old tom before his time, content to just sleep on the radiator until someone put something into his dish. He didn't want Church like that. He liked Church the way he was, lean and mean.

Outside in the dark, a big semi droned by on 15, and that decided him. He tacked the memo up and went to bed.

CHAPTER ELEVEN

The next morning at breakfast, Ellie saw the new memo on the bulletin board and asked him what it meant.

'It means he's going to have a very small operation,' Louis said. 'He'll probably have to stay over at the vet's for one night afterwards. And when he comes home, he'll stay in our yard and not want to roam around so much.'

'Or cross the road?' Ellie asked.

She may be only five, Louis thought, *but she's sure no slouch.* 'Or cross the road,' he agreed.

'Yay!' Ellie said, and that was the end of the subject.

Louis, who had been prepared for a bitter and perhaps hysterical argument about Church being out of the house for even one night, was mildly stunned by the ease with which she had acquiesced. And he realized how worried she must have been. Perhaps Rachel had not been entirely wrong about the effect the Pet Sematary had had on her, after all.

Rachel herself, who was feeding Gage his breakfast egg, shot him a grateful approving look, and Louis felt something loosen in his chest. The look told him that the chill was over; this particular hatchet had been buried. For ever, he hoped.

Later, after the big yellow schoolbus had gobbled Ellie up for the morning, Rachel came to him, put her arms around his neck and kissed his mouth gently. 'You were very sweet to do that,' she said, 'and I'm sorry I was such a bitch.'

Louis returned her kiss, feeling a little uncomfortable nonetheless. It occurred to him that the *I'm sorry I was such a bitch* statement, while by no means a standard, was not exactly something he'd never heard before, either. It usually came after Rachel had gotten her way.

Gage, meanwhile, had toddled unsteadily over to the front door and was looking out of the lowest pane of glass at the empty road. 'Bus,' he said, hitching nonchalantly at his sagging diapers. 'Ellie-bus.'

'He's growing up fast,' Louis said.

Rachel nodded. 'Too fast to suit me, I think.'

'Wait until he's out of diapers,' Louis said. 'Then he can stop.'

She laughed and it was all right between them again; completely all right. She stood back, made a minute adjustment to his tie, and looked him up and down critically.

'Do I pass muster, Sarge?' he asked.

'You look very nice.'

'Yeah, I know. But do I look like a heart-surgeon? Two hundred thousand dollar a year man?'

'No, just like old Lou Creed,' she said, and giggled. 'The rock and roll animal.'

Louis glanced at his watch. 'The rock and roll animal has got to put on his boogie shoes and go,' he said.

'Are you nervous?'

'Yeah, a little.'

'Don't be,' she said. 'It's sixty-seven thousand dollars a year for putting on Ace bandages, prescribing for the flu and for hangovers, giving girls the pill—'

'Don't forget the crab-and-louse lotion,' Louis said, smiling again. One of the things that had surprised him on his first tour of the infirmary had been the supplies of Quell, which seemed to him enormous — more fitted to an army base infirmary than to one on a middle-sized University campus.

Miss Charlton, the head nurse, had smiled cynically. 'Off-campus apartments in the area are pretty tacky. You'll see.'

He supposed he would.

'Have a good day,' she said, and kissed him again, lingeringly. But when she pulled away she was mock-stern. 'And for Christ's sake remember that you're an *administrator*, not an intern or a second-year resident!'

'Yes, doctor,' Louis said humbly, and they both laughed again. For a moment he thought of asking: *Was it Zelda, babe? Is that what's got under your skin? Is that the zone of low pressure? Zelda and how she died?* But he wasn't going to ask her that, not now. As a doctor he knew a lot of things, and while the fact that death was just as natural as childbirth might be the greatest of them, the fact that you don't monkey with a wound that has finally started to heal was far from the least of them.

So instead of asking, he only kissed her again and went out.

It was a good start, a good day. Maine was putting on a late summer show, the sky was blue and cloudless, the temperature pegged at an utterly perfect seventy-two degrees. Rolling to the end of the driveway and checking for traffic, Louis mused that so far he hadn't seen so much as a trace of the fall foliage that was supposed to be so spectacular. But he could wait.

He pointed the Honda Civic they had picked up as a second car toward the University and let it roll. Rachel would call the vet this morning, they would get Church fixed, and that would put this whole nonsense of Pet Semataries (it was funny how that misspelling got into your head and began to seem right) and death-fears behind them. There was no need to be thinking about death on a beautiful September morning like this one.

Louis turned on the radio and dialed until he found Huey Lewis and the News belting out 'Working for a Living'. He turned up the radio and sang along – not well, but with lusty enjoyment.

CHAPTER TWELVE

The first thing he noticed turning into the University grounds was how suddenly and spectacularly the traffic swelled. There was car traffic, bike traffic, joggers in gym shorts. He had to stop quickly to avoid two of the joggers, coming from the direction of Dunn Hall toward the athletic grounds beyond the field-house. Louis braked hard enough to lock his shoulder-belt and honked. He was always annoyed at the way joggers (bicyclers had the same irritating habit) seemed to automatically assume that their responsibility lapsed completely the moment they began to run. They were, after all, *exercising*. One of them gave Louis the finger without even looking around. Louis sighed and drove on.

The second thing he noticed was that the ambulance was gone from its slot in the small infirmary parking lot, and that gave him a nasty start. The infirmary was equipped to treat almost any illness or accident on a short-term basis; there were three well-equipped examination-and-treatment rooms opening off the big foyer, and beyond this were two wards with fifteen beds each. But there was no operating theater, nor anything even resembling one. In case of serious accidents, there was the ambulance, which would rush an injured or seriously ill person to the Eastern Maine Medical Center. Steve Masterton, the physician's assistant who had given Louis his first tour of the facility, had shown Louis the log from the previous two academic years with justifiable pride; there had only been thirty-eight ambulance runs in that time, not bad when you considered that the student population here was over ten thousand and the total University population was almost seventeen thousand.

And here he was, on his first real day of work, with the ambulance gone.

He parked in the slot headed with a freshly-painted sign reading RESERVED FOR DR CREED, and hurried in.

He found Charlton, a graying little woman of about fifty, in the first examining room, taking the temperature of a girl who was wearing jeans and a halter top. The girl had gotten a bad sunburn not too long ago, Louis observed; the peeling was well advanced.

'Good morning, Joan,' he said. 'Where's the ambulance?'

'Oh, we had a real tragedy, all right,' Charlton said, taking the thermometer out of the student's mouth and reading it. 'Steve Masterton came in this morning at seven and saw a great big puddle under the engine and the front wheels. Radiator let go. They hauled it away.'

'Great,' Louis said, but he felt relieved nonetheless. At least it wasn't out on a run, which was what he had first feared. 'When do we get it back?'

Joan Charlton laughed. 'Knowing the University Motor Pool,' she said, 'it'll come back around December 15th wrapped in Christmas ribbon.' She glanced at the student.

'You've got half a degree of fever,' she said. 'Take two aspirins and stay out of bars and dark alleys.'

The girl got down. She gave Louis a quick appraising glance and then went out.

'Our first customer of the new semester,' Charlton said sourly. She began to shake the thermometer down with brisk snaps.

'You don't seem too pleased about it.'

'I know the type,' she said. 'Oh, we get the other type too – athletes who go on playing with bone chips and tendonitis and everything else because they don't want to be benched, they got to be macho men, not let the team down, even if they're jeopardizing pro careers later on. Then you've got little Miss Half-Degree of Fever—' She jerked her head toward the window, where Louis could see the girl with the peeling sunburn walking in the direction of the Gannett-Cumberland-Androscoggin complex of dorms. In the examining room the girl had given the impression of someone who did not feel well at all but was trying not to let on. Now she was walking briskly, her hips swinging prettily, noticing and being noticed.

'Your basic college hypochondriac.' Charlton dropped the thermometer into a sterilizer. 'We'll see her two dozen times this year. Her visits will be more frequent before each round of prelims. A week or so before finals she'll be convinced she has either mono or pneumonia. Bronchitis is the fall-back position. She'll get out of four or five tests – the ones where the instructors are wimps, to use the word they use – and get easier makeups. They always get sicker if they know the prelim or final is going to be an objective test rather than an essay exam.'

'My, aren't we cynical this morning,' Louis said. He was, in fact, a little nonplussed.

She tipped him a wink that made him grin. 'I don't take it to heart, doctor. Neither should you.'

'Where's Stephen now?'

'In your office, answering mail and trying to figure out the latest ton of updates from Blue Cross-Blue Shield,' she said.

Louis went in. Charlton's cynicism not withstanding, he felt comfortably in harness.

Looking back on it, Louis would think – when he could bear to think about it at all – that the nightmare really began when they brought the dying boy, Victor Pascow, into the infirmary around ten that morning.

Until then, things were very quiet. At nine, half an hour after he arrived, the two candy-stripers who would be working the nine-to-three shift came in. Louis gave them each a doughnut and cup of coffee and talked to them for about fifteen minutes, outlining their duties and, what was perhaps more important, what was beyond the scope of their duties. Then Charlton took over. As she led them out of Louis's office,

Louis heard her ask: 'Either of you allergic to shit or puke? You'll see a lot of both here.'

'Oh God,' Louis murmured, and covered his eyes. But he was smiling. A tough old babe like Charlton was not always a liability.

Louis began filling out the long Blue Cross-Blue Shield forms, which amounted to a complete inventory of drug-stock and medical equipment ('Every year,' Steve Masterton said in an aggrieved voice. 'Every goddam year the same thing. Why don't you write down COMPLETE HEART TRANSPLANT FACILITY, APPROX. VALUE 8 MILLION DOLLARS, Louis? That'll foozle 'em!'), and he was totally engrossed, thinking only marginally that a cup of coffee would go down well, when Masterton screamed from the direction of the foyer-waiting room: '*Louis! Hey, Louis get out here! We got a mess!*'

The near-panic in Masterton's voice got Louis going in a hurry. He bolted out of his chair almost as though he had, in some subconscious way, been expecting this. A shriek, as thin and sharp as a shard of broken glass, arose from the direction of Masterton's shout. It was followed by a sharp slap and Charlton saying, 'Stop that or get the hell out of here! Stop it *right now!*'

Louis burst into the waiting room and was first only conscious of the blood — there was a lot of blood. One of the candy-stripers was sobbing. The other, pale as cream, had put her fisted hands to the corners of her mouth, pulling her lips into a big revolted grin. Masterton was kneeling down, trying to hold the head of the boy sprawled on the floor.

Steve looked up at Louis, eyes grim and wide and frightened. He tried to speak. Nothing came out.

People were congregating at the Student Medical Center's big glass doors, peering in, their hands cupped around their faces to butt out the glare. Louis's mind conjured up an insanely appropriate image: sitting in the living room as a boy of no more than six with his mother in the morning before she went to work, watching the television. Watching the old *Today* show, with Dave Garroway. People were outside, gaping in at Dave and Frank Blair and good old J. Fred Muggs. He looked around and saw other people standing at the windows. He couldn't do anything about the doors, but—

'Shut the drapes,' he snapped at the candy-striper who had screamed.

When she didn't move immediately, Charlton slapped her can. 'Do it, girl!'

The candy-striper got in gear. A moment later green drapes were jerked across the windows. Charlton and Steve Masterton moved instinctively between the boy on the floor and the doors, cutting off the view as best they could.

'Hard stretcher, Doctor?' Charlton asked.

'If we need it, get it.' Louis said, squatting beside Masterton. 'I haven't even had a chance to look at him.'

'Come on,' Charlton said to the girl who had closed the drapes. She was pulling the corners of her mouth with her fists again, making that humorless, screaming grin. She looked at Charlton and moaned, 'Oh, ag.'

'Yeah, *oh, ag* is right. Come on.' She gave the girl a hard yank and got her moving, her red-and-white-pinstriped skirt swishing against her legs.

Louis bent over his first patient at the University of Maine in Orono.

He was a young man, age approximately twenty, and it took Louis less than three seconds to make the only diagnosis that mattered: the young man was going to die. Half of his head was crushed. His neck had been broken. One collarbone jutted from his swelled and twisted right shoulder. From his head, blood and a yellow, pussy fluid seeped sluggishly into the carpet. Louis could see the man's brain, whitish-gray and pulsing through a shattered section of skull. It was like looking through a broken window. The incursion was perhaps five centimeters wide; if he had had a baby in his skull, he could almost have birthed it, like Zeus delivering from his forehead.

That he was still alive at all was incredible. In his mind suddenly he heard Jud Crandall saying *sometimes you could feel it bite your ass*. And his mother: *dead is dead*. He felt a crazy urge to laugh. Dead was dead, all right. That's affirmative, good buddy.

'Holler for the ambulance,' he snapped at Masterton. 'We—'

'Louis, the ambulance is—'

'Oh *Christ*,' Louis said, slapping his own forehead. He shifted his gaze to Charlton. 'Joan, what do you do in a case like this? Call Campus Security or the EMMC?'

Joan looked flustered and upset, an extreme rarity with her, Louis guessed. But her voice was composed enough as she replied. 'Doctor, I don't know. We've never had a situation like this before in my time at the Medical Center.'

Louis thought as fast as he could. 'Call the campus police. We can't wait for EMMC to send out their own ambulance. If they have to, they can take him up to Bangor in one of the fire engines. At least it has a siren, flashers. Go do it, Joan.'

She went, but not before he caught her deeply sympathetic glance and interpreted it. This young man, who was deeply tanned and well-muscled – perhaps from a summer working on a roadcrew somewhere, or painting houses, or giving tennis lessons – and dressed now only in red gym shorts with white piping, was going to die no matter what they did. He would be just as dead even if their ambulance had been parked out front with the motor idling when the patient was brought in.

Incredibly, the dying man was moving. His eyes fluttered and opened. Blue eyes, the irises ringed with blood. They stared vacantly around, seeing nothing. He tried to move his head and Louis exerted pressure to keep him from doing so, mindful of the broken neck. The terrible cranial trauma did not preclude the possibility of pain.

The hole in his head, oh Christ, the hole in his head.

'What happened to him?' he asked Steve, aware that it was, under the circumstances, a stupid and pointless question. The question of a bystander. But the hole in the man's head confirmed his status; a bystander was all he was. 'Did the police bring him?'

'Some students brought him in a blanket sling. I don't know what the circumstances were.'

There was what happened next to be thought of. That was his responsibility, too. 'Go out and find them,' Louis said. 'Take them around to the other door. I want them handy, but I don't want them to see any more of this than they already have.'

Masterton, looking relieved to be away from what was happening in here, went to the door and opened it, letting in a babble of excited, curious, confused conversation. Louis could also hear the warble of a police siren. Campus Security was here, then. Louis felt a kind of miserable relief.

The dying man was making a gurgling sound in his throat. He tried to speak. Louis heard syllables – phonetics, at least – but the words themselves were slurred and unclear.

Louis leaned over him and said, 'You're going to be all right, fella.' He thought of Rachel and Ellie as he said it and his stomach gave a great, unlovely lurch. He put a hand over his mouth and stifled a burp.

'Caaa,' the young man said. '*Gaaaaaa*—'

Louis looked around and saw he was momentarily alone with the dying man. Dimly he could hear Joan Charlton yelling at the candy-stripers that the hard stretcher was in the supply closet off Room Two. Louis doubted if they knew Room Two from a frog's gonads; it was, after all, their first day on the job. They had gotten a hell of an introduction to the world of medicine. The green wall-to-wall carpet was now soaked a muddy purple in an expanding circle around the young man's ruined head; the leakage of intercranial fluid had, mercifully, stopped.

'In the Pet Sematary,' the young man croaked . . . and he began to grin. This grin was remarkably like the mirthless, hysterical grin of the candy-striper who had closed the drapes.

Louis stared down at him, at first refusing to credit what

he had heard. Then he thought he must have had an auditory hallucination. *He made some more of those phonetic sounds and my subconscious made them into something coherent; cross-patched the sounds into my own experience*, he thought. But that was not what had happened, and a moment later he was forced to know it. A swooning, mad terror struck him and his flesh began to creep avidly, seeming to actually *move* up and down his arms and along his belly in waves . . . but even then he simply refused to believe it. Yes, the syllables had been on the bloody lips of the man on the carpet as well as in Louis's ears, but that only meant the hallucination had been visual as well as auditory.

'What did you say?' he whispered.

And this time, as clear as the words of a speaking parrot or a crow whose tongue had been split, the words were unmistakable: 'It's not the real Sematary . . .' The eyes were vacant, not seeing, rimmed with blood; the mouth, grinning the large grin of a dead carp.

Horror rolled through Louis, gripping his warm heart in its cold hands, squeezing. It reduced him, made him less and less, until he felt like taking to his heels and running from this bloody, twisted, speaking head on the floor of the infirmary waiting room. He was a man with no deep religious training, no bent toward the superstitious or the occult. He was ill-prepared for this . . . whatever it was.

Fighting the urge to run with everything in him, he forced himself to lean even closer. 'What did you say?' he asked a second time.

The grin. That was bad.

'The soil of a man's heart is stonier, Louis,' the dying man whispered. 'A man grows what he can . . . and tends it.'

Louis, he thought, hearing nothing with his conscious mind after his own name. *Oh my God he called me by my name.*

'Who are you?' Louis asked in a trembling, papery voice. 'Who are you?'

'Injun bring my fish.'

'How did you know my—'

'Keep clear, us. Know—'

'You—'

'*Caa*,' the young man said, and now Louis fancied he could smell death on his breath, internal injuries, lost rhythm, failure, ruin.

'What?' A crazy urge came to shake him.

'*Gaaaaaaaa*—'

The young man in the red gym shorts began to shudder all over. Suddenly he seemed to freeze with every muscle locked. His eyes lost their vacant expression momentarily and seemed to find Louis's eyes. Then everything let go at once. Louis thought he would, must, speak again. Then the eyes resumed their vacant expression . . . and began to glaze. He was dead.

Louis sat back, vaguely aware that all his clothes were sticking to him; he was drenched with sweat. Darkness bloomed, spreading a wing softly over his eyes, and the world began to swing sickeningly sideways. Recognizing what was happening, he half-turned from the dead man, thrust his head down between his knees, and pressed the nails of his left thumb and left forefinger into his gums hard enough to bring blood.

After a moment the world began to clear again.

CHAPTER THIRTEEN

Then the room filled up with people, as if they were all only actors, waiting for their cue. This only added to Louis's feeling of unreality and disorientation – the strength of these feelings, which he had studied in psychology classes but never actually experienced, frightened him badly. It was, he supposed, the way a person would feel shortly after someone had slipped a powerful dose of LSD into his drink.

Like a play staged only for my benefit, he thought. The room is first conveniently cleared so the dying Sybil can speak a few lines of oblique prophecy to me and me alone, and as soon as he's dead, everyone comes back.

The candy-stripers bungled in, one on each end of the hard stretcher, the one they used for people with spinal or neck injuries. Joan Charlton followed them, saying that the campus police were on their way. The young man had been struck by a car while jogging. Louis thought of the joggers who had run in front of his car that morning and his guts rolled.

Behind Charlton came Steve Masterton with two Campus Security cops. 'Louis, the people who brought Pascow in are . . .' He broke off and said sharply, 'Louis, are you all right?'

'I'm okay,' he said, and got up. Faintness washed over him again and then withdrew. He groped. 'Pascow is his name?'

One of the campus cops said, 'Victor Pascow, according to the girl he was jogging with.'

Louis glanced at his watch and subtracted two minutes. From the room where Masterton had sequestered the people who had brought Pascow in, he could hear a girl sobbing wildly. Welcome back to school, little lady, he thought. Have a nice semester. 'Mr Pascow died at 10:09 a.m.,' he said.

75

One of the cops wiped the back of his hand across his mouth.

Masterton said again, 'Louis, are you really okay? You look *terrible*.'

Louis opened his mouth to answer, and one of the candy-stripers abruptly dropped her end of the hard stretcher and ran out, vomiting down the front of her pinafore. A phone began to ring. The girl who had been sobbing now began to scream the dead man's name – 'Vic! Vic! Vic!' – over and over. Bedlam. Confusion. One of the cops was asking Charlton if they could have a blanket to cover him up and Charlton was saying she didn't know if she had the authority to requisition one and Louis found himself thinking of a line from Maurice Sendak: 'Let the wild rumpus start!'

Those rotten giggles rose in his throat again, and somehow he managed to bottle them up. Had this Pascow really said the words Pet Sematary? Had this Pascow really spoken his name? Those were the things that were knocking him off-kilter, the things that had sent him wobbling out of orbit. But already his mind seemed to be wrapping those few moments in a protective film – sculpting, changing, disconnecting. Surely he had said something else (if he had indeed spoken at all), and in the shock and unhappy passion of the moment, Louis had misinterpreted it. More likely, Pascow had only mouthed sounds, as he had at first thought.

Louis groped for himself, for that part of himself that had caused the administration to give him this job over the other fifty-three applicants for the position. There was no one in command here, no forward motion; the room was full of milling people.

'Steve, go give that girl a trank,' he said, and just saying the words made him feel better. It was as if he were in a rocket-ship under power now, pulling away from a tiny moon-let. Said moonlet being, of course, that irrational moment when Pascow had spoken. He had been hired to take charge; he was going to do it.

'Joan. Give the cop a blanket.'

'Doctor, we haven't inventoried—'

'Give it to him anyway. Then check on that candy-striper.' He looked at the other girl, who still held her end of the hard stretcher. She was staring at Pascow's remains with a kind of hypnotized fascination. 'Candy-striper!' Louis said harshly, and her eyes jerked away from the body.

'W-W-Wh—'

'What's the other girl's name?'

'W-Who?'

'The one who puked,' he said with deliberate harshness.

'Juh-Juh-Judy. Judy DeLessio.'

'Your name?'

'Carla.' Now the girl sounded a little more steady.

'Carla, you go check on Judy. And get that blanket. You'll find a pile of them in the little utility closet off Examining Room One. Go, all of you. Let's look a little professional here.'

They got moving. Very shortly the screaming in the other room quieted. The phone, which had stopped ringing, now began again. Louis pushed the HOLD button without picking the receiver up off its cradle.

The older campus cop looked more together, and Louis spoke to him: 'Who do we notify? Can you give me a list?'

The cop nodded and said, 'We haven't had one of these in six years. It's a bad way to start the semester.'

Louis punched one of the unlighted buttons on the phone and started making his calls without bothering to check who he had on hold.

CHAPTER FOURTEEN

Things did not slow down until nearly four that afternoon, after Louis and Richard Irving, the head of Campus Security, made a statement to the press. The young man, Victor Pascow, had been jogging with two friends, one of them his fiancée. A car driven by Tremont Withers, twenty-three, of Haven, Maine, had come up the road leading from the Lengyll Women's Gymnasium toward the center of campus at an excessive speed. Withers's car had struck Pascow and driven him into a tree. Pascow had been brought to the infirmary in a blanket by his friends and two passers-by. He had died minutes later. Withers was being held pending charges of reckless driving, driving under the influence, and vehicular manslaughter.

The editor of the campus newspaper asked if he could say that Pascow had died of head injuries. Louis, thinking of that broken window through which the brain itself could be seen, said he would rather let the Penobscot County coroner announce the cause of death. The editor then asked if the four young people who had brought Pascow to the infirmary in the blanket might not have inadvertently caused his death.

'No,' Louis replied, glad to have the chance to absolve the four of them, who had acted quickly and compassionately, of blame. 'Not at all. Unhappily, Mr Pascow was, in my opinion, mortally wounded upon being struck.'

There were other questions – a few – but that answer really ended the press conference. Now Louis sat in his office (Steve Masterton had gone home an hour before, immediately following the press conference, to catch himself on the evening news, Louis suspected) trying to pick up the shards of the day

– or maybe he was just trying to cover what had happened, to paint a thin coating of routine over it. He and Charlton were going over the cards in the 'front file' – those students who were pushing grimly through their college years in spite of some disability. There were twenty-three diabetics in the front file, fifteen epileptics, fourteen paraplegics, and assorted others: students with leukemia, students with cerebral palsy and muscular dystrophy, blind students, two mute students, and one case of sickle cell anemia, which Louis had never even seen.

Perhaps the lowest point of the afternoon had come just after Steve left. Charlton came in and laid a pink memo slip on Louis's desk. *Bangor Carpet will be here at 9:00 tomorrow*, it read.

'Carpet?' he had asked.

'It will have to be replaced,' she said apologetically. 'No way it's going to come out, Doctor.'

Of course. At that point Louis had gone into the dispensary and taken a Tuinal – what his first med school roommate had called Tooners. 'Hop up on the Toonerville Trolley, Louis,' he'd say, 'and I'll put on some Creedence.' More often than not Louis had declined the ride on the fabled Toonerville, and that was maybe just as well; his roomie had flunked out halfway through his third semester, and had ridden the Toonerville Trolley all the way to Vietnam as a medical corpsman. Louis sometimes pictured him over there, stoned to the eyeballs, listening to Creedence do 'Run Through the Jungle'.

But he needed something. If he was going to have to see that pink slip about the carpet on his note-minder board every time he glanced up from the front file spread out in front of them, he needed one.

He was cruising fairly well when Mrs Baillings, the night nurse, poked her head in and said, 'Your wife, Dr Creed. Line one.'

Louis glanced at his watch and saw it was nearly five thirty; he had meant to be out of here an hour and a half ago.

'Okay, Nancy. Thanks.'

He picked up the phone and punched line one. 'Hi, honey. Just on my—'

'Louis, are you all right?'

'Yeah. Fine.'

'I heard about it on the news. Lou, I'm so sorry.' She paused a moment. 'It was the radio news. They had you on, answering some question. You sounded fine.'

'Did I? Good.'

'Are you sure you're all right?'

'Yes, Rachel. I'm fine.'

'Come home,' she said.

'Yes,' he said. Home sounded good to him.

CHAPTER FIFTEEN

She met him at the door, and his jaw dropped. She was wearing the net bra he liked, a pair of semi-transparent panties, and nothing else.

'You look delicious,' he said. 'Where are the kids?'

'Missy Dandridge took them. We're on our own until eight-thirty . . . which gives us two and a half hours. Let's not waste it.'

She pressed against him. He could smell faint, lovely scent – was it attar of roses? His arms went around her; first around her waist, and then his hands found her buttocks as her tongue danced lightly over his lips and then into his mouth, licking and darting.

At last their kiss broke and he asked her a bit hoarsely: 'Are you for dinner?'

'Dessert,' she said, and then began to rotate her lower body slowly and sensuously against his groin and abdomen. 'But I promise you you don't have to eat anything you don't like.'

He reached for her but she slipped out of his arms and took his hand. 'Upstairs first,' she said.

She drew him an extremely warm bath, then undressed him slowly and shooed him into the water. She donned the slightly rough sponge-glove that usually hung unused on the shower-head, soaped his body gently, then rinsed it. He could feel the day – this horrible first day – slipping slowly off him. She had gotten quite wet, and her panties clung like a second skin.

Louis started to get out of the tub, and she pushed him back gently.

'What—'

Now the sponge-glove gripped him gently — gently but with almost unbearable friction, moving slowly up and down.

'Rachel—' Sweat had broken all over him, and not just from the heat of the bath.

'Shush.'

It seemed to go on almost eternally — he would near climax and the hand in the sponge-glove would slow, almost stop. Then it didn't stop but squeezed, loosened, squeezed again, until he came so strongly that he felt his eardrums bulge.

'My God,' he said shakily when he could speak again. 'Where did you learn *that*?'

'Girl Scouts,' she said primly.

She had made a stroganoff which had been simmering during the bathtub episode, and Louis, who would have sworn at four o'clock that he would next want to eat sometime around Halloween, ate two helpings.

After, she led him upstairs again.

'Now,' she said, 'let's see what you can do for *me*.'

All things considered, Louis thought he rose to the occasion quite well.

Afterward, Rachel dressed in her old blue pajamas. Louis pulled on a flannel shirt and nearly shapeless corduroy pants — what Rachel called his grubs — and went after the kids.

Missy Dandridge wanted to know about the accident, and Louis sketched it in for her, giving her less than she would probably read in the Bangor *Daily News* the following day. He didn't like doing it — it made him feel like the most rancid sort of gossip — but Missy would accept no money for sitting, and he was grateful to her for the evening he and Rachel had shared.

Gage was fast asleep before Louis had gotten the mile between Missy's house and their own, and Ellie was yawning and glassy-eyed. He put Gage into fresh diapers, poured him into his sleeper-suit, and popped him into his crib. Then he read Ellie a story-book. As usual, she clamored for *Where the*

Wild Things Are, being a veteran wild thing herself. Louis convinced her to settle for *The Cat in the Hat.* She was asleep five minutes after he carried her up and Rachel tucked her in.

When he came downstairs again, Rachel was sitting in the living room with a glass of milk. A Dorothy Sayers mystery was open on one long thigh.

'Louis, are you really all right?'

'Honey, I'm fine,' he said. 'And thanks. For everything.'

'We aim to please,' she said with a curving, slight smile. 'Are you going over to Jud's for a beer?'

He shook his head. 'Not tonight. I'm totally bushed.'

'I hope I had something to do with that.'

'I think you did.'

'Then grab yourself a glass of milk, doctor, and let's go to bed.'

He thought perhaps he would lie awake, as he often had when he was interning and days that were particularly hairy would play over and over in his mind. But he slid smoothly toward sleep, as if on a slightly inclined, frictionless board. He had read somewhere that it takes the average human being just seven minutes to turn off all the switches and uncouple from the day. Seven minutes for conscious and subconscious to revolve, like the trick wall in an amusement park haunted house. Something a little eerie in that.

He was almost there when he heard Rachel say, as if from a great distance: '— day after tomorrow.'

'Ummmmmm?'

'Jolander. The vet. He's taking Church the day after tomorrow.'

'Oh.' Church. Treasure your *cojones* while you got 'em, Church, old boy, he thought, and then he slipped away from everything, down a hole, sleeping deeply and without dreams.

CHAPTER SIXTEEN

Something woke him much later, a crash loud enough to cause him to sit up in bed, wondering if Ellie had fallen on to the floor or if maybe Gage's crib had collapsed. Then the moon sailed out from behind a cloud, flooding the room with cold white light, and he saw Victor Pascow standing in the doorway. The crash had been Victor Pascow throwing open the door.

He stood there with his head grotesquely bashed in behind the left temple. The blood had dried on his face in maroon stripes like Indian war-paint. His collarbone jutted whitely. He was grinning.

'Come on, doctor,' Pascow said. 'We got places to go.'

Louis looked around. His wife was a vague bump under her yellow comforter, sleeping deeply. He looked back at Pascow, who was dead but somehow not dead. Yet Louis felt no fear. He realized why almost at once.

It's a dream, he thought, and it was only in his relief that he realized he had been frightened after all. *The dead do not return; it is physiologically impossible. This young man is in an autopsy drawer in Bangor with the pathologist's tattoo — a Y-cut stitched back up — on him. The pathologist probably tossed his brain into his chest-cavity after taking a tissue sample and filled up the skull cavity with brown paper to prevent leaking — simpler than trying to fit the brain back into the skull like a jigsaw piece into a puzzle.* Uncle Carl, father of the unfortunate Ruthie, had told him that pathologists did that, and all sorts of other random information that he supposed would give Rachel, with her death-phobia, the screaming horrors. But Pascow was not here; no way, baby. Pascow was in a refrigerated locker with a tag around his toe. *And he is most certainly not wearing those red jogging shorts in there.*

Yet the compulsion to get up was strong. Pascow's eyes were upon him.

He threw back the covers and swung his feet on to the floor. The hooked rug – a wedding present from Rachel's grandmother long ago – pressed cold nubbles into the balls of his feet. The dream had a remarkable reality. It was so real that he would not follow Pascow until Pascow had turned and begun to go back down the stairs. The compulsion to follow was strong, but he did not want to be touched, even in a dream, by a walking corpse.

But he *did* follow. Pascow's jogging shorts glimmered.

They crossed the living room, dining room, kitchen. Louis expected Pascow to turn the lock and then lift the latch on the door which connected the kitchen to the shed where he garaged the station wagon and the Civic, but Pascow did no such thing. Instead of opening the door, he simply passed through it. And Louis, watching, thought with mild amazement: *Is that how it's done? Remarkable! Anyone could do that!*

He tried it himself – and was a little amused to meet only unyielding wood. Apparently he was a hard-headed realist, even in his dreams. Louis twisted the knob on the Yale lock, lifted the latch, and let himself into the shed-garage. Pascow was not there. Louis wondered briefly if Pascow had just ceased to exist. Figures in dreams often did just that. So did locations – first you were standing nude by a swimming pool with a raging hard-on, discussing the possibilities of wife-swapping with, say, Roger and Missy Dandridge, then you blinked and you were climbing the side of a Hawaiian volcano. Maybe he had lost Pascow because this was the beginning of Act II.

But when Louis emerged from the garage he saw him again, standing in the faint moonlight at the back of the lawn – at the head of the path.

Now fear came, entering softly, sifting through the hollow places of his body and filling them up with dirty smoke. He didn't want to go up there. He halted.

Pascow glanced back over his shoulder, and in the moonlight his eyes were silver. Louis felt a hopeless crawl of horror in his belly. That jutting bone, those dried clots of blood. But it was hopeless to resist those eyes. This was apparently a dream about being hypnotized, being dominated . . . being unable to change things, perhaps, the way he had been unable to change the fact of Pascow's death. You could go to school for twenty years and you still couldn't do a thing when they brought a guy in who had been rammed into a tree hard enough to open a window in his skull. They might as well have called a plumber, a rainmaker, or the Man from Glad.

And even as these thoughts passed through his mind, he was drawn forward on to the path. He followed the jogging shorts, as maroon in this light as the dried blood on Pascow's face.

He didn't like this dream. Oh God, not at all. It was too real. The cold nubbles in the rug, the way he had not been able to pass through the shed door when a person could (or should) be able to walk through doors and walls in any self-respecting dream . . . and now the cool brush of dew on his bare feet, and the feel of the night wind, just a breath of it, on his body, which was naked except for his Jockey shorts. Once under the trees, fir needles stuck to the soles of his feet . . . another little detail that was just a bit more real than it needed to be.

Never mind. Never mind. I am home in my own bed. It's just a dream, no matter how vivid, and like all other dreams, it will seem ridiculous in the morning. My waking mind will discover its inconsistencies.

The small branch of a dead tree poked his bicep rudely and he winced. Up ahead, Pascow was only a moving shadow, and now Louis's terror seemed to have crystallized into a bright

sculpture in his mind: *I am following a dead man into the woods,
I am following a dead man up to the Pet Sematary, and this is no
dream. God help me*, this is no dream. *This is* happening.

They walked down the far side of the wooded hill. The
path curved in lazy S-shapes between the trees, and then
plunged into the underbrush. No boots now. The ground
dissolved into cold jelly under his feet, grabbing and holding,
letting go only reluctantly. There were ugly sucking noises.
He could feel the mud oozing between his toes, trying to
separate them.

He tried desperately to hold on to the dream idea.

It wouldn't wash.

They reached the clearing and the moon sailed free of
its reef of clouds again, bathing the graveyard with ghastly
effulgence. The leaning markers — bits of board and tin cans
that had been cut with a father's tinsnips and then hammered
into rude squares, chipped chunks of shale and slate — stood
out with three-dimensional clarity, casting shadows perfectly
black and defined.

Pascow stopped near SMUCKY THE CAT HE WAS
OBEDIANT and turned back toward Louis. The horror, the
terror; he felt these things would grow in him until his body
blew apart under their soft yet implacable pressure. Pascow
was grinning. His bloody lips were wrinkled back from his
teeth and his healthy road-crew tan in the moon's bony light
had become overlaid with the white of a corpse about to be
sewn into its winding shroud.

He lifted one arm and pointed. Louis looked in that direction and moaned. His eyes grew wide, and he crammed his
knuckles against his mouth. There was coolness on his cheeks
and he realized that, in the extremity of his terror, he had
begun to weep.

The deadfall from which Jud Crandall had called Ellie in
alarm had become a heap of bones. The bones were moving.
They writhed and clicked together, mandibles and femurs and
ulnas and molars and incisors; he saw the grinning skulls of

humans and animals. Fingerbones clittered. Here the remains of a foot flexed its pallid joints.

Ah, it was moving; it was *creeping*—

Pascow was walking toward him now, his bloody face grim in the moonlight, and the last of Louis's coherent mind began to slip away in a yammering, cyclic thought: *You got to scream yourself awake doesn't matter if you scare Rachel Ellie Gage wake the whole household the whole neighborhood got to scream yourself awake screamscreamscreamyourselfawakeawakeawake*—

But only a thin whisper of air would come. It was the sound of a little kid sitting on a stoop somewhere and trying to teach himself to whistle.

Pascow came closer and then spoke.

'The door must not be opened,' Pascow said. He was looking down at Louis, because Louis had fallen to his knees. He was no longer grinning. A look was on his face which Louis at first mistook for compassion. It wasn't really compassion at all; only a dreadful kind of patience. Still he pointed at the moving pile of bones. 'Don't go beyond, no matter how much you feel you need to, Doctor. The barrier was not made to be broken. Remember this: there is more power here than you know. *It* is old, and always restless. Remember.'

Louis tried again to scream. He could not.

'I come as a friend,' Pascow said, but was *friend* actually the word Pascow had used? Louis thought not. It was as if Pascow had spoken in a foreign language which Louis could understand through some dream-magic . . . and *friend* was as close to whatever word Pascow had actually used that Louis's struggling mind could come. 'Your destruction and the destruction of all you love is very near, Doctor.' He was close enough for Louis to be able to smell death on him.

Pascow, reaching for him.

The soft, maddening click of the bones.

Louis began to overbalance in his effort to get away from that hand. His own hand struck a monument and tilted it into the earth. Pascow's face, leaning down, filled the sky.

'Doctor – *remember.*'

Louis tried to scream, and the world whirled away – but still he heard the click of moving bones in the moonlit crypt of the night.

CHAPTER SEVENTEEN

It takes the average human seven minutes to go to sleep, but, according to *Hand's Human Physiology*, it takes the same average human fifteen to twenty minutes to wake up, as if sleep is a pool from which emerging is more difficult than entering. When the sleeper wakes, he or she comes up by degrees, from deep sleep to light sleep to what is sometimes called 'waking sleep', a state in which the sleeper can hear sounds and will even respond to questions without being aware of it later . . . except perhaps as fragments of dream.

Louis heard the click and rattle of bones, but gradually this sound became sharper, more metallic. There was a bang. A yell. More metallic sounds . . . something rolling? *Sure*, his drifting mind agreed. *Roll dem bones.*

He heard his daughter, calling: 'Get it, Gage! Go get it!'

This was followed by Gage's crow of delight, and was the sound on which Louis opened his eyes and saw the ceiling of his own bedroom.

He held himself perfectly still, waiting for the reality, the good reality, the *blessed* reality, to come home all the way.

All a dream. No matter how terrible, how real, it had all been a dream. Only a fossil in the mind under his mind.

The metallic sound came again. It was one of Gage's toy cars being rolled along the upstairs hall.

'Get it, Gage!'

'*Get it!*' Gage yelled. '*Get-it-get-it-get-it!*'

Thumpa-thumpa-thumpa. Gage's small bare feet thundering along the hallway runner. He and Ellie were giggling.

Louis looked to his right. Rachel's side of the bed was

empty, the covers thrown back. The sun was well up. He glanced at his watch and saw it was nearly eight o'clock. Rachel had let him oversleep, probably on purpose.

Ordinarily this would have irritated him, but this morning it did not. He drew in a deep breath and let it out, content for the moment to lie here with a bar of sunlight slanting in through the window, feeling the unmistakable texture of the real world. Dustmotes danced in the sunlight.

Rachel called upstairs: 'Better come down and get your snack and go out for the bus, El!'

'Okay!' The louder clack–clack of her feet. 'Here's your car, Gage. I got to go to school.'

Gage began to yell indignantly. Although it was garbled – the only clear words being *Gage, car, geddit*, and *Ellie-bus* – his text seemed clear enough: Ellie should stay. Public education could go hang for the day.

Rachel's voice again: 'Give your dad a shake before you come down, El.'

Ellie came in, her hair done up in a ponytail, wearing her red dress.

'I'm awake, babe,' he said. 'Go on and get your bus.'

'Okay, Daddy.' She came over, kissed his slightly scruffy cheek, and bolted for the stairs.

The dream was beginning to fade, to lose its coherency. A damn good thing, too.

'Gage!' he yelled. 'Come give your dad a kiss!'

Gage ignored this. He was following Ellie downstairs as rapidly as he could, yelling, '*Get it! Get-it-get-it-GET-IT!!*' at the top of his lungs. Louis caught just a glimpse of his sturdy little kid's body, clad only in diapers and rubber pants.

Rachel called up again: 'Louis, was that you? You awake?'

'Yeah,' he said, sitting up.

'Told you he was!' Ellie called. 'I'm goin'. Bye!' The slam of the front door and Gage's outraged bellow punctuated this.

'One egg or two?' Rachel called.

Louis pushed back the blankets and swung his feet out on

to the nubs of the hooked rug, ready to tell her he'd skip the eggs, just a bowl of cereal and he'd run . . . and the words died in his throat.

His feet were filthy with dirt and fir needles.

His heart leaped up in his throat like a crazy jack-in-the-box. Moving fast, eyes bulging, teeth clamped unfeelingly on his tongue, he kicked the covers all the way back. The foot of the bed was littered with needles. The sheets were mucky and dirty.

'Louis?'

He saw a few errant fir needles on his knees, and suddenly he looked at his right arm. There was a scratch there on the bicep, a fresh scratch, exactly where the dead branch had poked him . . . in the dream.

I'm going to scream. I can feel it.

And he could, too; it was roaring up from inside, nothing but a big cold bullet of fear. Reality shimmered. Reality – *the real reality*, he thought – was those needles; the filth on the sheets; the bloody scratch on his bare arm.

I'm going to scream and then I'll go crazy and I won't have to worry about it any more—

'Louis?' Rachel was coming up the stairs. 'Louis, did you go back to sleep?'

He grappled for himself in those two or three seconds; he fought grimly for himself just as he had done in those moments of roaring confusion after Pascow had been brought into the Medical Center, dying, in a blanket. He won. The thought which tipped the scales was that she must not see him this way, his feet muddy and coated with needles, the blankets tossed back on to the floor to reveal the muck-splashed ground sheet.

'I'm awake,' he called cheerfully. His tongue was bleeding from the sudden, involuntary bite he had given it. His mind swirled, and somewhere deep inside, away from the action, he wondered if he had always been within touching distance of such mad irrationalities; if everyone was.

'One egg or two?' She had stopped on the second or third riser. Thank God.

'Two,' he said, barely aware of what he was saying. 'Scrambled.'

'Good for you,' she said, and went back downstairs again.

He closed his eyes briefly in relief, but in the darkness he saw Pascow's silver eyes. His eyes flew open again. Louis began to move rapidly, putting off any further thought. He jerked the bedclothes off the bed. The blankets were okay. He separated out the two sheets, balled them up, took them into the hallway, and dumped them down the laundry chute.

Almost running, he entered the bathroom, jerked the shower handle on, and stepped under water so hot it was nearly scalding, unmindful. He washed the dirt from his feet and legs.

He began to feel better, more in control. Drying off, it struck him that this was how murderers must feel when they believe they have gotten rid of all the evidence. He began to laugh. He went on drying himself, but he also went on laughing. He couldn't seem to stop.

'Hey, up there!' Rachel called. 'What's so funny?'

'Private joke,' Louis called back, still laughing. He was frightened, but the fright didn't stop the laughter. The laughter came, rising from a belly that was as hard as stones mortared into a wall. It occurred to him that shoving the sheets down the laundry chute was absolutely the best thing he could have done. Missy Dandridge came in five days a week to vacuum, clean and do the laundry. Rachel would never see those sheets at all until she put them back on the bed – clean. He supposed it was possible that Missy would mention it to Rachel, but he didn't think so. She would probably whisper to her husband that the Creeds were playing some strange sex-game that involved mud and fir needles instead of body paints.

This thought made Louis laugh all the harder.

The last of the giggles and chuckles dried up as he was dressing, and he realized that he felt a little better. How that could be he didn't know, but he did. The room looked normal now except for the stripped bed. He had gotten rid of the poison. Maybe evidence was actually the word he was looking for, but in his mind it felt like poison.

Perhaps this is what people do with the inexplicable, he thought. This is what they do with the irrational that refuses to be broken down into the normal causes and effects that run the Western world. Maybe this is how the mind copes with the flying saucer you saw hovering silently over your back field one morning, the rain of frogs, the hand from under the bed that stroked your bare foot in the dead of night: there was a giggling fit, or a crying fit . . . and since it was its own inviolable self and would not break down, you simply passed terror intact, like a kidney stone.

Gage was in his chair, eating and decorating the table with Special K. He was decorating the plastic mat under his high chair with Special K, and apparently shampooing with Special K.

Rachel came out of the kitchen with his eggs and a cup of coffee. 'What was the big joke, Lou? You were laughing like a loon up there. Scared me a little.'

Louis opened his mouth with no idea of what he was going to say, and what came out was a joke he had heard the week before at the corner market down the road, something about a Jewish tailor who bought a parrot whose only line was 'Ariel Sharon jerks off.'

By the time he finished, Rachel was laughing, too – so was Gage, for that matter.

Fine. Our hero has taken care of all the evidence, to wit: the muddy sheets and the loony laughter in the bathroom. Our hero will now read the morning paper – or at least look at it – putting the seal of normality on the morning.

So thinking, Louis opened the paper.

That's what you do, all right, he thought with immeasurable relief. *You pass it like a stone and that's the end of it . . . unless there comes a campfire some night with friends when the wind is high and the talk turns to inexplicable events. Because on campfire night when the wind is high, talk is cheap.*

He ate his eggs. He kissed Rachel and Gage. He glanced at the square, white-painted laundry cabinet at the foot of the chute only as he left. Everything was okay. It was another knockout of a morning. Late summer showed every sign of just going on for ever, and everything was okay. He glanced at the path as he backed the car out of the garage, but that was okay, too. Never turned a hair. You passed it like a stone.

Everything was okay until he had gotten ten miles down the road, and then the shakes hit him so hard that he had to pull off Route 2 and into the morning-deserted parking lot of Sing's, the Chinese restaurant not far from the Eastern Maine Medical Center – where Pascow's body would have been taken. The EMMC, that was, not Sing's. Vic Pascow was never going to eat another helping of moo goo gai pan, ha-ha.

The shakes twisted his body, rippled it, had their way with it. Louis felt helpless and terrified – not terrified of anything supernatural, not in this bright sunshine, but simply terrified of the possibility that he might be losing his mind. It felt as if a long, invisible wire was being twirled through his body.

'No more,' he said. 'Please, no more.'

He fumbled for the radio and got Joan Baez singing about diamonds and rust. Her sweet, cool voice soothed him, and by the time she had finished, Louis felt that he could drive on.

When he got to the Medical Center, he called hello to Charlton and then ducked into the bathroom, believing that he must look like hell. Not so. He was a little hollow under the eyes, but not even Rachel had noticed that. He slapped some cold water on his face, dried off, combed his hair, and went into his office.

Steve Masterton and the Indian doctor, Surrendra Hardu,

were in there, drinking coffee and continuing to go over the front file.

'Morning, Lou,' Steve said.

'Morning.'

'Let's hope it is not like last morning,' Hardu said.

'That's right, you missed all the excitement.'

'Surrendra had plenty of excitement himself last night,' Masterton said, grinning. 'Tell him, Surrendra.'

Hardu polished his glasses, smiling. 'Two boys bring in their lady-friend around one o'clock in the morning,' he said. 'She is very happily drunk; celebrating the return to University, you understand. She has cut one thigh quite badly, and I tell her it will be at least four stitches, no scar. Stitch away, she tells me, and so I do, bending over like this —'

Hardu demonstrated, salaaming over an invisible thigh. Louis began to grin, sensing what was coming.

'And as I am suturing, she vomits on my head.'

Masterton broke up. So did Louis. Hardu smiled calmly, as if this had happened to him thousands of times in thousands of lives.

'Surrendra, how long have you been on duty?' Louis asked, when the laughter died.

'Since midnight,' Hardu said. 'I am just leaving. But I wanted to stay long enough to say hello again.'

'Well, hello,' Louis said, shaking his small, brown hand, 'now go home and go to sleep.'

'We're almost through with the front file,' Masterton said. 'Say hallelujah, Surrendra.'

'I decline,' Hardu said, smiling. 'I am not a Christian.'

'Then sing the chorus of "Instant Karma", or something.'

'May you both shine on,' Hardu said, still smiling, and glided out the door.

Louis and Steve Masterton looked after him for a moment, silent, then at each other. Then they both burst out laughing. To Louis, no laugh had ever felt so good . . . so normal.

'Just as well we got the file finished up,' Steve said. 'Today's the day we put the welcome mat out for the dope pushers.'

Louis nodded. The first of the drug salesmen would begin arriving at ten. As Steve liked to crack, Wednesday might be Prince Spaghetti Day, but at UMO, every Tuesday was D-Day. The D stood for Darvon, the all-time favorite.

'A word of advice, O Great Boss,' Steve said. 'I don't know what these guys were like out in Chicago, but around here they'll stoop to just about anything from all-expenses paid hunting junkets into the Allagash in November to free bowling at Family Fun Lanes in Bangor. I had one guy try to give me one of those inflatable Judy dolls. Me! And I'm only a PA! If they can't sell you drugs, they'll drive you to them.'

'Should have taken it.'

'Nah, she was a redhead. Not my type.'

'Well, I agree with Surrendra,' Louis said. 'Just as long as it's not like yesterday.'

CHAPTER EIGHTEEN

When the rep from Upjohn didn't turn up promptly at ten, Louis gave in and called the Registrar's Office. He spoke with a Mrs Stapleton, who said she would send over a copy of Victor Pascow's records immediately. When he hung up, the Upjohn guy was there. He didn't try to give Louis anything, only asked him if he had any interest in buying a season's ticket to the New England Patriots' games at a discount.

'Nope,' Louis said.

'I didn't think you would,' the Upjohn guy said glumly, and left.

At noon, Louis walked up to the Bear's Den and got a tuna fish sandwich and a Coke. He brought them back to his office, and ate lunch while going over Pascow's records. He was looking for some connection with himself or with North Ludlow, where the Pet Sematary was . . . a vague belief, he supposed, that there must be some sort of rational explanation even for such a weird occurrence as this. Maybe the guy had grown up in Ludlow – had, maybe, even buried a dog or a cat up there.

He didn't find the connection he was looking for. Pascow was from Bergenfield, New Jersey, and had come to UMO to study electrical engineering. In those few typed sheets, Louis could see no possible connection between himself and the young man who had died in the reception room – other than the mortal one, of course.

He sucked the last of the Coke out of his cup, listening to the straw crackle in the bottom, and then tossed all his trash into the wastebasket. Lunch had been light, but he had eaten it with good appetite. Nothing wrong there, anyway . . . and not much wrong with the way he felt, really. Not now. There had been no recurrence of the shakes, and now even that morning's horror began to seem more like a nasty, pointless surprise, dreamlike itself, of no consequence.

He drummed his fingers on his blotter, shrugged, and picked up the phone again. He dialed the EMMC and asked for the morgue.

After he was connected with the Pathology Clerk he identified himself and said, 'You have one of our students there, a Victor Pascow—'

'Not any more,' the voice at the other end said. 'He's gone.'

Louis's throat closed. At last he managed. 'What?'

'His body was flown back to his parents late last night. Guy from Brookings-Smith Mortuary came and took custody. They put him on Delta, uh . . .' Papers riffling. 'Delta Flight 109. Where did you think he went? Out dancing at the Show Ring?'

'No,' Louis said. 'No, of course not. It's just . . .' It was just what? What the Christ was he doing pursuing this, anyway? There was no sane way to deal with it. It had to be let go, marked off, forgotten. Anything else was asking for a lot of pointless trouble. 'It's just that it seemed very quick,' he finished lamely.

'Well, he was autopsied yesterday afternoon—' That faint riffle of papers again – 'at around 3:20, by Dr Rynzwyck. By then his father had made all the arrangements. I imagine the body got to Newark by two in the morning.'

'Oh. Well, in that case—'

'Unless one of the carriers screwed up and sent it somewhere else,' the Pathology Clerk said brightly. 'We've had that happen, you know, although never with Delta. Delta's actually pretty good. We had a guy who died on a fishing trip way up in Aroostook County, in one of those little towns that just have a couple of map coordinates for a name. Asshole strangled on a pop-top while he was chugging a can of beer. Took his buddies two days to buck him out of the wilderness and you know that by then it's a toss-up whether or not the Forever Goop will take. But they shoved it in and hoped for the best. Sent him home to Grand Falls, Minnesota, in the cargo compartment of some airliner. But there was a screw-up. They shipped him first to Miami, then to Des Moines, then to Fargo, North Dakota. Finally somebody wised up, but by then another three days had gone by. Nothing took. They might as well have injected him with Kool-Aid instead of Jaundaflo. The guy was totally black and smelled like a spoiled pork roast. That's what I heard, anyway. Six baggage handlers got sick.'

The voice on the other end of the line laughed heartily.

Louis closed his eyes and said, 'Well, thank you—'

'I can give you Dr Rynzwyck's home phone if you want it, Doctor, but he usually plays golf up in Orono in the morning.' That hearty laugh again.

'No,' Louis said. 'No, that's okay.'

He hung up the telephone. *Let that put paid to it*, he thought. *When you were having that crazy dream, or whatever it was, Pascow's body was almost certainly in a Bergenfield funeral home. That closes it off; let that be the end of it.*

Driving home that afternoon, a simple explanation of the filth at the foot of the bed finally occurred to him, flooding him with relief.

He had experienced an isolated incident of sleepwalking, brought on by the unexpected and extremely upsetting happenstance of having a student mortally injured and then dying in his infirmary during his first real day on the job.

It explained everything. The dream had seemed extremely real because large parts of it *were* real – the feel of the carpet, the cold dew and, of course, the dead branch that had scratched his arm. It explained why Pascow had been able to walk through the door and he had not.

A picture rose in his mind, a picture of Rachel coming downstairs last night and catching him bumping against the back door, trying in his sleep to walk through it. The thought made him grin. It would have given her a hell of a turn, all right.

With the sleepwalking hypothesis in mind, he was able to analyze the causes of the dream – and he did so with a certain eagerness. He had walked to the Pet Sematary because it had become associated with another moment of recent stress. It had in fact been the cause of a serious argument between him and his wife . . . and also, he thought with growing excitement, it was associated in his mind with his daughter's first real encounter with the idea of death – something his own subconscious must have been grappling with last night when he went to bed.

Damn lucky I got back to the house okay – I don't even remember that part. Must have come back on autopilot.

It was a good thing he had. He couldn't imagine what it would have been like to have wakened up this morning by the grave of Smucky the Cat, disoriented, covered with dew, and probably scared shitless – as Rachel would have been, undoubtedly.

But it was over now.

Put paid to it, Louis thought with immeasurable relief. *Yes, but what about the things he said when he was dying?* his mind tried to ask, and Louis shut it up fast.

That evening, with Rachel ironing and Ellie and Gage sitting in the same chair, both of them engrossed with *The Muppet Show*, Louis told Rachel casually that he believed he might go for a short walk – get a little air.

'Will you be back in time to help me put Gage to bed?' she asked without looking up from her ironing. 'You know he goes better when you're there.'

'Sure,' he said.

'Where you going, daddy?' Ellie asked, not looking away from the TV. Kermit was about to be punched in the eye by Miss Piggy.

'Just out back, hon.'

'Oh.'

Louis went out.

Fifteen minutes later he was in the Pet Sematary, looking around curiously and coping with a strong feeling of *déjà vu*. That he had been here was beyond doubt: the little grave marker put up to honor the memory of Smucky the Cat was knocked over. He had done that when the vision of Pascow approached, near the end of what he could remember of the dream. Louis righted it absently and walked over to the deadfall.

He didn't like it. The memory of all these weather-whitened branches and dead trees turning into a pile of bones still had the power to chill. He forced himself to reach out and touch one. Balanced precariously on the jackstraw pile, it rolled and fell, bouncing down the side of the heap. Louis jumped back a step.

He walked along the deadfall, first to the left, then to the right. On both sides the underbrush closed in so thickly as to be impenetrable. Nor was it the kind of brush you'd try to push your way through – not if you were smart, Louis thought. There were lush masses of poison ivy growing close to the ground (all his life Louis had heard people boast that they were immune to the stuff, but Louis knew that almost no one really was) and further in were some of the biggest, most wicked-looking thorns he had ever seen.

Louis strolled back to the rough center of the deadfall. He looked at it, hands stuck in the back pockets of his jeans.

You're not going to try to climb that, are you?

Not me, boss. Why would I want to do a stupid thing like that?

Great. Had me worried for just a minute there, Lou. Looks like a good way to land in your own infirmary with a broken ankle, doesn't it?

Sure does! Also, it's getting dark.

Sure that he was all together and in total agreement with himself, Louis began to climb the deadfall.

He was halfway up when he felt it shift under his feet with a peculiar creaking sound.

Roll dem bones, Doc.

When the pile shifted again, Louis began to clamber back down. The tail of his shirt had pulled out of his pants.

He reached solid ground without incident and dusted crumbled bits of bark off his hands. He walked back to the head of the path which would return him to his house – to his children who would want a story before bed, to Church, who was enjoying his last day as a card-carrying tom cat and ladykiller, to tea in the kitchen with his wife after the kids were down.

He surveyed the clearing again before leaving, struck by its green silence. Tendrils of groundfog had appeared from nowhere and were beginning to wind around the markers. Those concentric circles . . . as if, all unknowing, the childish hands of North Ludlow's generations had built a kind of scale-model Stonehenge.

But, Louis, is this all?

Although he had gotten only the barest glimpse over the top of the deadfall before the shifting sensation had made him nervous, he could have sworn there was a path beyond, leading deeper into the woods.

No business of yours, Louis. You've got to let this go.

Okay, boss.

Louis turned and headed home.

He stayed up that night an hour after Rachel went to bed, reading a stack of medical journals he had already been through, refusing to admit that the thought of going to bed – going to sleep – made him nervous. He had never had an episode of somnambulism before, and there was no way to be sure it was an isolated incident . . . until it did or didn't happen again.

He heard Rachel get out of bed and then she called down softly, 'Lou? Hon? You coming up?'

'Just was,' he said, turning out the lamp over his study desk and getting up.

It took a good deal longer than seven minutes to shut the machine down that night. Listening to Rachel draw the long, calm breaths of deep sleep beside him, the apparition of Victor Pascow seemed less dreamlike. He would close his eyes and see the door crashing open and there he was, Our Special Guest Star, Victor Pascow, standing there in his jogging shorts, pallid under his summer tan, his collar-bone poking up.

He would slide down toward sleep, think about how it would be to come fully, coldly awake in the Pet Sematary, to see those roughly concentric circles lit by moonlight, to have to walk back, awake, along the path through the woods. He would think these things and then snap fully awake again.

It was sometime after midnight when sleep finally crept up on his blind side and bagged him. There were no dreams. He woke up promptly at seven-thirty, to the sound of cold autumn rain beating against the window. He threw the sheets back with some apprehension. The groundsheet on his bed was flawless. No purist would describe his feet, with their hammer-toes and their rings of heel-calluses, that way, but they were at least clean.

Louis caught himself whistling in the shower.

CHAPTER NINETEEN

Missy Dandridge kept Gage while Rachel ran Winston Churchill to the vet's office. That night Ellie stayed awake until after eleven, complaining querulously that she couldn't sleep without Church and calling for glass after glass of water. Finally Louis refused to let her have any more on the grounds that she would wet the bed. This caused a crying tantrum of such ferocity that Rachel and Louis stared at each other blankly, eyebrows raised.

'She's scared for Church,' Rachel said. 'Let her work it out, Lou.'

'She can't keep it up at that pitch for long,' Louis said. 'I hope.'

He was right. Ellie's hoarse, angry cries became hitches and hiccups and moans. Finally there was silence. When Louis went up to check on her, he found she was sleeping on the floor with her arms wrapped tightly around the cat-bed that Church hardly even deigned to sleep in.

He removed it from her arms, put her back in bed, brushed her hair back from her sweaty brow gently, kissed her. On impulse he went into the small room that served as Rachel's office, wrote a quick note in large block letters on a sheet of paper – I WILL BE BACK TOMORROW, LOVE, CHURCH – and pinned it to the cushion on the bottom of the cat-bed. Then he went into his bedroom, looking for Rachel. Rachel was there. They made love and fell asleep in each other's arms.

Church returned home on the Friday of Louis's first full week of work; Ellie made much of him, used part of her allowance to buy him a box of cat treats, and nearly slapped Gage once for trying to touch him. This made Gage cry in a way mere parental discipline could never have done. Receiving a rebuke from Ellie was like receiving a rebuke from God.

Looking at Church made him feel sad. It was ridiculous, but that didn't change the emotion. There was no sign of Winnie Church's former feistiness. No more did he walk like a gunslinger; now his walk was the slow, careful walk of the convalescent. He allowed Ellie to hand-feed him. He showed no sign of wanting to go outside, not even to the garage. He had changed. Perhaps it was ultimately for the better that he had changed.

Neither Rachel nor Ellie seemed to notice.

CHAPTER TWENTY

Indian summer came and went. Brazen color came into the trees, rioted briefly, and then faded. After one cold, driving rain in mid-October, the leaves started to fall. Ellie began to arrive home laden with Halloween decorations she had made at school and entertained Gage with the story of the Headless Horseman. Gage spent that evening babbling happily about somebody named Itchybod Brain. Rachel got giggling and couldn't stop. It was a good time for them, that early autumn.

Louis's work at the University had settled into a demanding but pleasant routine. He saw patients, he attended meetings of the Council of Colleges, he wrote the obligatory letters to the student newspaper, advising the University's co-ed students of the confidentiality of the infirmary's treatment for VD and exhorting the student population to get flu boosters, as the A-type was apt to be prevalent again that winter. He sat on panels. He chaired panels. During the second week in October he went to the New England conference on College and University Medicine in Providence and presented a paper on the legal ramifications of student treatment. Victor Pascow was mentioned in his paper under the fictitious name 'Henry Montez'. The paper was well-received. He began working up the infirmary budget for the next academic year.

His evenings fell into a routine: kids after supper, a beer or two with Jud Crandall later. Sometimes Rachel came over with him if Missy was available to sit for an hour, and sometimes Norma joined them, but mostly it was just Louis and Jud. Louis found the old man as comfortable as an old slipper, and he would talk about Ludlow history going back three hundred years, almost as though he had lived all of it. He talked but never rambled. He never bored Louis, although he had seen Rachel yawning under her hand on more than one occasion.

He would cross the road to his house again before ten on most evenings, and, like as not, he and Rachel would make love. Never since the first year of their marriage had they made love so often, and never so successfully and pleasurably. Rachel said she believed it was something in the artesian well-water; Louis opted for the Maine air.

The nasty death of Victor Pascow on the first day of the fall semester began to fade in the memory of the student body and in Louis's own; Pascow's family no doubt still grieved. Louis had spoken to the tearful, mercifully face-less voice of Pascow's father on the telephone; the father had only wanted assurance that Louis had done everything he could, and Louis had assured him that everyone involved had. He did not tell him of the confusion, the spreading stain on the carpet, and how his son had been dead almost from the instant he was brought in, although these were things that Louis thought he himself would never forget. But for those to whom Pascow was only a casualty, he had already dimmed.

Louis still remembered the dream and the sleepwalking incident that had accompanied it, but it now seemed almost as if it had happened to someone else, or on a television show he had once watched. His one trip to a massage parlor in Chicago six years ago seemed like that now; they were equally unimportant, side-trips which held a false resonance, like sounds produced in an echo-chamber.

He did not think at all about what the dying Pascow had or had not said.

There was a hard frost on Halloween night. Louis and Ellie began trick-or-treating at the Crandalls'. Ellie cackled satisfyingly, pretended to ride her broom around Norma's kitchen, and was duly pronounced 'Just the cutest thing I ever saw . . . isn't she, Jud?'

Jud agreed that she was and lit a cigarette. 'Where's Gage, Louis? Thought you'd have him dressed up, too.'

They had indeed planned on taking Gage around – Rachel in particular had been looking forward to it because she and Missy Dandridge had whomped together a sort of bug-costume with twisted coathangers wrapped in crepe paper for feelers – but Gage had come down with a troublesome bronchial cold, and after listening to his lungs, which sounded a bit rattly, and consulting the thermometer outside the window, which read only forty degrees at six o'clock, Louis had nixed it. Rachel, although disappointed, had agreed.

Ellie had promised to give Gage some of her candy, but the exaggerated quality of her sorrow made Louis wonder if she wasn't just a bit glad that Gage wouldn't be along to slow her down . . . or steal part of the limelight.

'Poor Gage,' she had said in tones usually reserved for those suffering terminal illness. Gage, unaware of what he was missing, sat on the sofa watching *Zoom* with Church snoozing beside him.

'Ellie-witch,' Gage said without a great deal of interest, and went back to the TV.

'Poor Gage,' Ellie said again, fetching another sigh. Louis thought of crocodile tears and grinned. Ellie grabbed his hand and started pulling him. 'Let's go, Daddy. Let's go-let's go-let's go.'

'Gage has got a touch of the croup,' he said to Jud now.

'Well, that's a real shame,' Norma said, 'but it will mean more to him next year. Hold out your bag, Ellie . . . whoops!'

She had taken an apple and a bite-sized Snickers bar out of the treat-bowl on the table, but both of them had fallen from her hand. Louis was a little shocked at how clawlike that hand looked. He bent over and picked up the apple as it rolled across the floor. Jud got the Snickers and dropped it into Ellie's bag.

'Oh, let me get you another apple, honey,' Norma said. 'That one will bruise.'

'It's fine,' Louis said, trying to drop it into Ellie's bag, but Ellie stepped away, holding her bag protectively shut.

'I don't want a bruised apple, Daddy,' she said, looking at her father as if he might have gone mad. 'Brown spots . . . *yuck*!'

'Ellie, that's damned impolite!'

'Don't scold her for telling the truth, Louis,' Norma said. 'Only children tell the whole truth, you know. That's what makes them children. The brown spots *are* yucky.'

'Thank you, Mrs Crandall,' Ellie said, casting a vindicated eye on her father.

'You're very welcome, honey,' Norma said.

Jud escorted them out to the porch. Two little ghosts were coming up the walk, and Ellie recognized them both as friends from school. She took them back to the kitchen, and for a moment Jud and Louis were alone on the porch.

'Her arthritis had gotten worse,' Louis said.

Jud nodded and pinched out his cigarette over an ashtray. 'Yeah. It's come down harder on her every fall and winter, but this is the worst it's ever been.'

'What does her doctor say?'

'Nothing. He can't say nothing, because Norma hasn't been back to see him.'

'What? Why not?'

Jud looked at Louis, and in the light cast by the headlamps of the station wagon waiting for the ghosts, he looked oddly defenseless. 'I'd meant to ask you this at a better time, Louis, but I guess there isn't no good time to impose on a friendship. Would you examine her?'

From the kitchen, Louis could hear the two ghosts *boooing* and Ellie going into her cackles – which she had been practicing all week – again. It all sounded very fine and Halloweenish.

'What else is wrong with Norma?' he asked. 'Is she afraid of something else, Jud?'

'She's been having pains in her chest,' Jud said in a low voice. 'She won't go see Dr Weybridge any more. I'm a little worried.'

'Is Norma worried?'

Jud hesitated and then said, 'I think she's scared. I think that's why she doesn't want to go to the doctor. One of her oldest friends, Betty Coslaw, died in the EMMC just last week. Cancer. She and Norma were of an age. She's scared.'

'I'd be happy to examine her,' Louis said. 'No problem at all.'

'Thanks, Louis,' Jud said gratefully. 'If we catch her one night, gang up on her, I think—'

Jud broke off, head cocking quizzically to one side. His eyes met Louis's.

Later on Louis couldn't remember exactly how he felt just then, or exactly how one emotion slipped into the next. Trying to analyze it only made him feel dizzy. All he could remember for sure was that curiosity changed swiftly into a feeling that somewhere something had gone badly wrong. His eyes met Jud's, both unguarded. It was a moment before he could find a way to act.

'*Hoooo-hoooo,*' the Halloween ghosts in the kitchen chanted. '*Hooo-hooo.*' And then suddenly the h-sound was gone and the cry rose louder, genuinely frightening: '*oooo-OOOOOO—*'

And then one of the ghosts began to scream.

'*Daddy!*' Ellie's voice was wild and tight with alarm. '*Daddy! Missus Crandall fell down!*'

'Ah, Jesus,' Jud almost moaned.

Ellie came running out on to the porch, her black dress flapping. She clutched her broom in one hand. Her green face, now pulled long in dismay, looked like the face of a pygmy wino in the last stages of alcohol poisoning. The two little ghosts followed her, crying.

Jud lunged through the door, amazingly spry for a man of over eighty. No, more than spry. Again, almost lithe. He was calling his wife's name.

Louis bent and put his hands on Ellie's shoulders. 'Stay right here on the porch, Ellie. Understand?'

'Daddy, I'm scared,' she whispered.

The two ghosts barreled past them and ran down the walk, candy-bags rattling, screaming their mother's name.

Louis ran down the front hall and into the kitchen, ignoring Ellie, who was calling for him to come back.

Norma lay on the hilly linoleum by the table in a litter of apples and small Snickers bars. Apparently, going down, she had caught the bowl with her hand and had overturned it. It lay nearby like a small Pyrex flying saucer. Jud was chafing one of her wrists, and he looked up at Louis with a strained face.

'Help me, Louis,' he said. 'Help Norma. She's dying, I think.'

'Move to one side,' Louis said. He knelt and one knee came down on a Spy, crushing it. He felt juice bleed through the knee of his old cords, and the cidery smell of apple suddenly filled the kitchen.

Here it is, Pascow all over again, Louis thought, and then shoved the thought out of his mind so fast it might have been on wheels.

He felt for her pulse and got something that was weak, thready, and rapid – not really a beat but only simple spasming. Extreme arrhythmia, well on the way to full cardiac arrest. *You and Elvis Presley, Norma*, he thought.

He opened her dress, exposing a creamy-yellow silk slip. Moving with his own rhythm now, he turned her head to one side and began administering CPR.

'Jud, listen to me,' he said. Heel of the left hand one-third of the way up the breastbone – four centimeters above xyphoid process. Right hand gripping the left wrist, bracing, lending pressure. Keep it firm, but let's take it easy on the old ribs;

no need to panic yet. And for Christ's sake, don't collapse the old lungs.

'I'm here,' Jud said.

'Take Ellie,' he said. 'Go across the street. Carefully – don't get hit by a car. Tell Rachel what's happened. Tell her I want my bag. Not the one in the study, the one on the high shelf in the upstairs bathroom. She'll know the one. Tell her to call Bangor MedCu and to send an ambulance.'

'Bucksport's closer,' Jud said.

'Bangor's faster. Go. Don't you call; let Rachel do that. I need that bag.' *And once she knows the situation here*, Louis thought, *I don't think she'll bring it over.*

Jud went. Louis heard the screen door bang. He was alone with Norma Crandall and the smell of apples. From the living room came the steady tick of the seven-day clock.

Norma suddenly uttered a long, snoring breath. Her eyelids fluttered. And Louis was suddenly doused with a cold, horrid certainty.

She's going to open her eyes . . . oh Christ she's going to open her eyes and start talking about the Pet Sematary.

But she only looked at Louis with a muddled sort of recognition and then her eyes closed again. Louis was ashamed of himself and this stupid fear that was so unlike him. At the same time he felt hope and relief. There had been some pain in her eyes, but not agony. His first guess was that this had not been a grave seizure.

Louis was breathing hard now, and sweating. No one but TV paramedics could make CPR look easy. A good steady closed-chest massage popped a lot of calories, and the webbing between his arms and shoulders would ache tomorrow.

'Can I do anything?'

He looked around. A woman dressed in slacks and a brown sweater stood hesitantly in the doorway, one hand clutched into a fist between her breasts. The mother of the ghosts, Louis thought. His snap judgment was that she was scared but not helpless.

'No,' he said, and then: 'Yes. Wet a cloth, please. Wring it out. Put it on her forehead.'

She moved to do it. Louis looked down. Norma's eyes were open again.

'Louis, I fell down,' she whispered. 'Think I fainted.'

'You've had some sort of coronary event,' Louis said. 'Doesn't look too serious. Now relax and don't talk, Norma.'

He rested for a moment, then took her pulse again. The beat was too fast. She was doing what Dr Tucker at the University of Chicago Med School had once called Morse-coding: her heart would beat regularly, then run briefly in a series of beats that was almost but not quite fibrillation, and then begin to beat regularly again. Beat-beat-beat, WHACK/ WHACK/WHACK, beat-beat-beat-beat-beat. It was not good, but it was marginally better than cardiac arrhythmia.

The woman came over with the cloth and put it on Norma's forehead. She stepped away uncertainly. Jud came back in with Louis's bag.

'Louis?'

'She's going to be fine,' Louis said, looking at Jud but actually speaking to Norma. 'MedCu coming?'

'Your wife is calling them,' Jud said. 'I didn't stay around.'

'No . . . hospital,' Norma whispered.

'Yes, hospital,' Louis said. 'Five days' observation, medica-tion, then home with your feet up, Norma my girl. And if you say anything else, I'll make you eat all these apples. Cores and all.'

She smiled wanly, then closed her eyes again.

Louis opened his bag, rummaged, found the Isodil, and shook one of the pills, so tiny it would have fitted easily on the moon of one fingernail, into the palm of his hand. He recapped the bottle and pinched the pill between his fingers.

'Norma, can you hear me?'

'Yes.'

'Want you to open your mouth. You did your trick, now you get your treat. I'm going to put a pill under your tongue. Just a small one. I want you to hold it there until it dissolves.

It's going to taste a little bitter, but never mind that. All right?'

She opened her mouth. Stale denture breath wafted out, and Louis felt a moment of aching sorrow for her, lying here on her kitchen floor in a litter of apples and Halloween candy. It occurred to him that once she had been seventeen, her breasts eyed with great interest by the young men of the neighborhood, all her teeth her own, and the heart under her shirtwaist a tough little pony-engine.

She settled her tongue over the pill and grimaced a little. The pill tasted a little bitter, all right. It always did. But she was no Victor Pascow, beyond help and beyond reach. He thought Norma was going to live to fight another day. Her hand groped in the air and Jud took it gently.

Louis got up then, found the overturned bowl, and began to pick up the treats. The woman, who introduced herself as Mrs Storey from down the road, helped him and then said she thought she better go back to the car. Her two boys were frightened.

'Thank you for your help, Mrs Storey,' Louis said.

'I didn't do anything,' she said flatly. 'But I'll go down on my knees tonight and thank God you were here, Dr Creed.'

Louis waved a hand, embarrassed.

'That goes for me, too,' Jud said. His eyes found Louis's and held them. They were steady. He was in control again. His brief moment of confusion and fear had passed. 'I owe you one, Louis.'

'Get off it,' Louis said, and tipped a finger toward Mrs Storey as she left. She smiled and waved back. Louis found an apple and began to eat it. The Spy was so sweet that his tastebuds cramped momentarily . . . but that was not a totally unpleasurable sensation. *Won one tonight, Lou*, he thought, and worked on the apple with relish. He was ravenous.

'I do, though,' Jud said. 'When you need a favor, Louis, you see me first.'

'All right,' Louis said. 'I'll do that.'

★

The ambulance from Bangor MedCu arrived twenty minutes later. As Louis stood outside watching the orderlies load Norma into the back, he saw Rachel looking out the living-room window. He waved to her. She lifted a hand in return.

He and Jud stood together and watched the ambulance pull away, lights flashing, siren silent.

'Guess I'll go on up to the hospital now,' Jud said.

'They won't let you see her tonight, Jud. They'll want to run an EXG on her and then put her in intensive care. No visitors for the first twelve hours.'

'Is she going to be okay, Louis? Really okay?'

Louis shrugged. 'No one can guarantee that. It *was* a heart attack. For whatever it's worth, I think she's going to be fine. Maybe better than ever, once she gets on some medication.'

'Ayuh,' Jud said, lighting a Chesterfield.

Louis smiled and glanced at his watch. He was amazed to see it was only ten minutes to eight. It seemed that a great deal more time had gone by.

'Jud, I want to go get Ellie so she can finish her trick-or-treating.'

'Yeah, course you do.' This came out *Coss y'do*. 'Tell her to get all the treats she can, Louis. I guess she's had her trick for the evening.'

'I guess she has at that,' Louis said.

Ellie was still in her witch costume when Louis got home. Rachel had tried persuade her into her nightie, but Ellie had resisted, holding out for the possibility that the game, suspended because of heart attack, might yet be played out. When Louis told her to put her coat back on, Ellie whooped and clapped.

'It's going to be awfully late for her, Louis.'

'We'll take the car,' he said. 'Come on, Rachel. She's been looking forward to this for a month.'

'Well . . .' She smiled. Ellie saw it and shouted again. She ran for the coat closet. 'Is Norma all right?'

'I think so.' He felt good. Tired, but good. 'It was a small one. She's going to have to be careful, but when you're seventy-five you have to recognize that your pole-vaulting days are done, anyway.'

'It's lucky you were there. Almost God's providence.'

'I'll settle for luck.' He grinned as Ellie came back. 'You ready, Witch Hazel?'

'I'm ready,' she said. 'Come on–come on–come on!'

On the way home with half a bag of candy an hour later (Ellie protested when Louis finally called a halt, but not too much; she was tired), his daughter startled him by saying: 'Did I make Missus Crandall have the heart attack, Daddy? When I wouldn't take the apple with the bruise on it?'

Louis looked at her, startled, wondering where children got such funny, half-superstitious ideas. Step on a crack, break your mother's back. Loves-me-loves-me-not. Daddy's stomach, Daddy's head, smile at midnight, Daddy's dead. That made him think of the Pet Sematary again, and those crude circles. He wanted to smile at himself and was not quite able.

'No, honey,' he said. 'When you were in with those two ghosts—'

'Those weren't ghosts, just the Buddinger twins.'

'Well, when you were in with them, Mr Crandall was telling me that his wife had been having little chest pains. In fact, you might have been responsible for saving her life, or at least for keeping it from being much worse.'

Now it was Ellie's turn to look startled.

Louis nodded. 'She needed a doctor, honey. I'm a doctor. But I was only there because it was your night to go trick-or-treating.'

Ellie considered this for a long time and then nodded. 'But she'll probably die anyway,' she said matter-of-factly. 'People who have heart attacks usually die. Even if they live, pretty soon they have another one and another one until . . . boom!'

'And where did you learn these words of wisdom, may I ask?'

Ellie only shrugged – a very Louis-like shrug, he was amused to see.

She allowed him to carry in her bag of candy – an almost ultimate sign of trust – and Louis pondered her attitude. The thought of Church's death had brought on near-hysteria. But the thought of grandmotherly Norma Crandall dying . . . that Ellie seemed to take calmly, a matter of course, as given. What had she said? Another one and another one, until . . . *boom!*

The kitchen was empty, but Louis could hear Rachel moving around upstairs. He set Ellie's candy down on the counter and said, 'It doesn't necessarily work that way, Ellie. Norma's heart attack was a very small one, and I was able to administer the treatment right away. I doubt if her heart was damaged much at all. She—'

'Oh, I know,' Ellie agreed, almost cheerfully. 'But she's old, and she'll die pretty soon anyway. Mr Crandall, too. Can I have an apple before I go to bed, daddy?'

'No,' he said, looking at her thoughtfully. 'Go up and brush your teeth, babe.'

Did anyone really think they understood kids? he wondered.

When the house was settled and they were in bed, Rachel asked softly: 'Was it very bad for Ellie, Lou? Was she upset?'

No, he thought. She knows old people croak at regular intervals, just like she knows to let the grasshopper go when it spits . . . like she knows that if you stumble on number thirteen when you're skipping rope that your best friend will die . . . like she knows that you put the graves in diminishing circles up in the Pet Sematary . . .

'Nope,' he said. 'She handled herself very well. Let's go to sleep, Rachel, okay?'

That night, as they slept in their house and as Jud lay wakeful in his, there was another hard frost. The wind rose in the early morning, ripping most of the remaining leaves, which were now an uninteresting brown, from the trees.

The wind awoke Louis and he started up on his elbows,

mostly asleep and confused. There were steps on the stairs . . . slow, dragging steps. Pascow had come back. Only now, he thought, two months had passed. When the door opened he would see a rotting horror, the jogging shorts caked with mould, the flesh fallen away in great holes, the brain decayed to paste. Only the eyes would be alive . . . hellishly bright and alive. Pascow would not speak this time; his vocal cords would be too decayed to produce sounds. But his eyes . . . they would beckon him to come.

'No,' he breathed, and the steps died out.

He got up, went to the door, and pulled it open, his lips drawn back in a grimace of fear and resolution, his flesh cringing. Pascow would be there, and with his raised arms he would look like a long-dead conductor about to call for the first thundering phrase of *Walpurgisnacht*.

No such thing, as Jud might have said. The landing was empty . . . silent. There was no sound but the wind. Louis went back to bed and slept.

CHAPTER TWENTY-ONE

The next day Louis called the intensive care unit at the EMMC. Norma's condition was still listed as critical; that was standard operating procedure for the first twenty-four hours following a heart attack. Louis got a cheerier assessment from Weybridge, her doctor, however. 'I wouldn't even call it a minor myocardial infarction,' he said. 'No scarring. She owes you a hell of a lot, Dr Creed.'

On impulse, Louis stopped by the hospital later that week with a bouquet of flowers, and found that Norma had been moved to a semi-private room downstairs – a very good sign. Jud was with her.

Norma exclaimed over the flowers, and buzzed a nurse for a vase. Then she directed Jud until they were in water, arranged to her specifications, and placed on the dresser in the corner.

'Mother's feeling ever s'much better,' Jud said dryly after he had fiddled with the flowers for the third time.

'Don't be smart, Judson,' Norma said.

Jud offered a comic salute. 'No, ma'am.'

At last Norma looked at Louis. 'I want to thank you for what you did,' she said with a shyness that was utterly unaffected and thus doubly touching. 'Jud says I owe you my life.'

Embarrassed, Louis said: 'Jud exaggerates.'

'Not very damn much, he don't,' Jud said. He squinted at Louis, almost smiling but not quite. 'Didn't your mother tell you never to slip a thank-you, Louis?'

She hadn't said anything about that, at least not that Louis could remember, but he believed she had said something once about false modesty being half the sin of pride.

'Norma,' he said, 'anything I could do, I was pleased to do.'

'You're a dear man,' Norma said. 'You take this man of mine out somewhere and let him buy you a glass of beer. I'm feeling sleepy again, and I can't seem to get rid of him.'

Jud stood up with alacrity. 'Hot damn! I'll go for that, Louis. Quick, before she changes her mind.'

The first snow came a week before Thanksgiving. They got another four inches on November 20th, but the day before the holiday itself was clear and blue and cold. Louis took his family to Bangor International Airport and saw them off on the first leg of their trip back to Chicago for a reunion with Rachel's people.

'It's not right,' Rachel said for perhaps the twentieth time since discussions on this matter had commenced in earnest a month ago. 'I don't like thinking of you rattling around the house alone on Thanksgiving Day. That's supposed to be a family holiday, Louis.'

Louis shifted Gage, who looked gigantic and wide-eyed in his first big-boy parka, to his other arm. Ellie was at one of the big windows, watching an Air Force helicopter take off.

'I'm not exactly going to be crying in my beer,' Louis said. 'Jud and Norma are going to have me over for turkey and all the trimmings. Hell, I'm the one who feels guilty. I've never liked these big holiday group gropes anyway. I start drinking in front of some football game at three in the afternoon and fall asleep at seven and the next day it feels like the Dallas Cowgirls are dancing around and yelling boola-boola inside my head. I just don't like sending you off with the two kids.'

'I'll be fine,' she said. 'Flying first-class, I feel like a princess. And Gage will sleep on the flight from Logan to O'Hare.'

'You hope,' he said, and they both laughed.

The flight was called, and Ellie scampered over. 'That's us, Mommy. Come on–come on–come on. They'll leave without us.'

'No, they won't.' Rachel said. She was clutching her three pink boarding cards in one hand. She was wearing her fur coat, some fake stuff that was a luxuriant brown . . . probably supposed to look like muskrat, Louis thought. Whatever *it* was supposed to look like, it made *her* look absolutely lovely.

Perhaps something of what he felt showed in his eyes, because she hugged him impulsively, semi-crushing Gage between them. Gage looked surprised but not terribly upset.

'Louis Creed, I love you,' she said.

'Mom-*eee*,' Ellie said, now in a fever of impatience. 'Come on—come on—c—'

'Oh, all right,' she said. 'Be good, Louis.'

'Tell you what,' he said, grinning. 'I'll be careful. Say hello to your folks, Rachel.'

'Oh, you,' she said, and wrinkled her nose at him. Rachel was not fooled; she knew perfectly well why Louis was skipping this trip. 'Fun-*nee*.'

He watched them enter the boarding ramp and disappear from sight for the next week. He already felt homesick and lonely for them. He moved over to the window where Ellie had been, hands stuffed in his coat pockets, watching the baggage-handlers loading the hold.

The truth was simple. Not only Mr but Mrs Irwin Goldman of Lake Forest had disliked Louis from the beginning. He came from the wrong side of the tracks, but that was just for starters. Worse, he fully expected their daughter, who had been catered to with an almost religious dedication for the first eighteen years of her life and sent to the best schools money could buy, to support him while he went to medical school, where he would almost surely flunk out.

Louis could have handled all this, in fact had been doing so. Then something had happened which Rachel did not know about and never would . . . not from Louis, anyway. Irwin Goldman had offered to pay Louis's entire tuition through med school. The price of this 'scholarship' (Goldman's word) was that Louis should break off his engagement with Rachel at once.

Louis Creed had not been at the optimum time of life to deal with such an outrage, but such melodramatic proposals (or bribes, to call a spade a spade) are rarely made to those who *are* at an optimum time – which might be around the age of eighty-five. He was tired, for one thing. He was spending eighteen hours a week in classes, another twenty hitting the books, another fifteen waiting tables in a deep-dish pizza joint down the block from the Whitehall Hotel. He was also nervous. Mr Goldman's oddly jovial manner that evening had contrasted completely with his previous cold behavior, and Louis thought that when Goldman invited him into the study for a cigar, a look had passed from him to his wife. Later – much later, when time had lent a little perspective – Louis would reflect that horses must feel much the same free-floating anxiety when they smell the first smoke of a prairie fire. He began expecting Goldman to reveal at any moment that he knew Louis had been sleeping with his daughter.

When Goldman instead made his incredible offer – even going so far as to take his checkbook from the pocket of his smoking jacket like a rake in a Noël Coward farce and wave it in Louis's face – Louis had blown up. He accused Goldman of trying to keep his daughter like an exhibit in a museum, of having no regard for anyone but himself, and of being an overbearing, thoughtless bastard. It would be a long time before he would admit to himself that part of his rage had been relief.

All of these little insights into Irwin Goldman's character, though true, had no redeeming touch of diplomacy in them. Any semblance of Noël Coward departed; if there was humor in the rest of the conversation, it was of a much more vulgar sort. Goldman told him to get out, and that if he ever saw Louis on his doorstep again, he would shoot him like a yellow dog. Louis told Goldman to take his checkbook and plug up his ass with it. Goldman said he had seen bums in the gutter who had more potential than Louis Creed. Louis told Goldman he could shove his goddam BankAmericard and his American Express Gold Card right up beside his checkbook.

None of this had been a promising first step toward good relations with the future in-laws.

In the end, Rachel had brought them around (after each man had had a chance to repent of the things he had said, although neither of them had ever changed his mind in the slightest about the other). There was no more melodrama, certainly no dismally theatrical from-this-day-forward-I-have-no-daughter scene. Goldman would have probably suffered through his daughter's marriage to the Creature from the Black Lagoon before denying her. Nevertheless, the face rising above the collar of Irwin Goldman's morning coat on the day Louis married Rachel had greatly resembled the faces sometimes seen carved on Egyptian sarcophagi. Their wedding present had been a six-place setting of Spode china and a microwave oven. No money. For most of Louis's harum-scarum med school days, Rachel had worked as a clerk in a women's apparel store. And from that day to this day, Rachel only knew that things had been and continued to be 'tense' between her husband and her parents . . . particularly between Louis and her father.

Louis could have gone to Chicago with his family, although the University schedule would have meant flying back three days earlier than Rachel and the kids. Still, that was no great hardship. On the other hand, four days with Im-Ho-Tep and his wife the Sphinx would have been.

The children had melted his in-laws a good deal, as children often do. Louis suspected he himself could have completed the rapprochement simply by pretending he had forgotten that evening in Goldman's study. It wouldn't even matter that Goldman knew he was pretending. But the fact was (and he at least had the guts to be up front about it with himself) he did not quite want to make the rapprochement. Ten years was a long time, but it was not quite long enough to take away the slimy taste that had come into his mouth when, in

Goldman's study over glasses of brandy, the old man had opened one side of that idiotic smoking jacket and removed the checkbook residing within. Yes, he had felt relief that the nights – five of them in all – that he and Rachel had spent in his narrow, sagging apartment bed had not been discovered, but that surprised disgust had been quite its own thing, and the years between then and now had not changed it.

He could have come, but he preferred to send his father-in-law his grandchildren, his daughter, and a message.

The Delta 727 pulled away from the rampway, turned . . . and he saw Ellie at one of the front windows, waving frantically. Louis waved back, smiling, and then someone – Ellie or Rachel – hiked Gage into the window. Louis waved, and Gage waved back – perhaps seeing him, perhaps only imitating Ellie.

'Fly my people safe,' he muttered, then zipped his coat and went out to the parking lot. Here the wind whined and zoomed with force enough to almost tear his hunter's cap off his head, and he clapped a hand to it. He fumbled with his keys to unlock the driver's side door of his car and then turned as the jet rose beyond the terminal building, its nose tilted upward into the hard blue, its turbos thundering.

Feeling very lonely indeed now – ridiculously close to tears – Louis waved again.

He was still feeling blue that evening when he recrossed Route 15 after a couple of beers with Jud and Norma – Norma had drunk a glass of wine, something she was allowed, even encouraged to have, by Dr Weybridge. They had moved into the kitchen tonight in deference to the season.

Jud had stoked up the small Marek stove and they had sat around it, the beer cold, the heat good, and Jud had talked about how the Micmac Indians had staved off a British landing at Machias two hundred years ago. In those days the Micmacs had been pretty fearsome, he said, and then added that he guessed there were a few state and Federal land-lawyers who thought they still were.

It should have been a fine evening, but Louis was aware

of the empty house waiting for him. Crossing the lawn and feeling the frost crunching under his shoes, he heard the telephone begin to ring in the house. He broke into a run, got through the front door, sprinted through the living room (knocking over a magazine stand), and then slid across the kitchen to the phone, his frosty shoes skidding over the linoleum. He snared the phone.

'Hello?'

'Louis?' Rachel's voice, a little distant, but absolutely fine. 'We're here. We made it. No problems.'

'Great!' he said, and sat down to talk to her, thinking: *I wish to God you were here.*

CHAPTER TWENTY-TWO

The Thanksgiving dinner Jud and Norma put on was a fine one. When it was over, Louis went home feeling full and sleepy. He went upstairs to the bedroom, relishing the quiet a little, flipped off his loafers and lay down. It was just after three o'clock, the day outside lit with thin, wintry sunshine.

I'll just doze a little, he thought, and then fell fast asleep.

It was the bedroom extension that woke him up. He groped for it, trying to pull himself together, disoriented by the fact that it was almost dark outside. He could hear the wind whining around the corners of the house and the faint, husky mutter of the furnace.

'Hello,' he said. It would be Rachel, calling from Chicago again to wish him a happy Thanksgiving. She would put Ellie on and Ellie would talk and then Gage would get on and Gage would babble and how the hell had he managed to sleep all afternoon when he had meant to watch the football game—

But it wasn't Rachel. It was Jud.

'Louis? 'Fraid maybe you've got a little spot of trouble.'

He swung out of bed, still trying to scrub the sleep out of his mind. 'Jud? What trouble?'

'Well, there's a dead cat over here on our lawn,' Jud said. 'I think it might be your daughter's.'

'Church?' Louis asked. There was a sudden sinking in his belly. 'Are you sure, Jud?'

'No, I ain't one hundred per cent sure,' Jud said, 'but it sure looks like him.'

'Oh. Oh shit. I'll be right over, Jud.'

'All right, Louis.'

He hung up and just sat there for a minute longer. Then

127

he went in and used the bathroom, put his shoes on, and went downstairs.

Well, maybe it isn't Church. Jud himself said he wasn't a hundred per cent sure. Christ, the cat doesn't even want to go upstairs anymore unless someone carries him . . . why would he cross the road?

But in his heart he felt sure that it *was* Church . . . and if Rachel called this evening as she almost certainly would, what was he going to say to Ellie?

Crazily, he heard himself saying to Rachel: *I know that anything, literally* anything, *can happen to physical beings. As a doctor I know that . . . do you want to be the one to explain to her what happened if he gets run over in the road?* But he hadn't really believed anything was going to happen to Church, had he?

He remembered one of the guys he played poker with, Wickes Sullivan, asking him once how he could get horny for his wife and not get horny for the naked women he saw day in and day out. Louis had tried to explain to him that it wasn't the way people imagined in their fantasies — a woman coming in to get a pap smear or to learn how to give herself a breast self-examination didn't suddenly drop a sheet and stand there like Venus on the half-shell. You saw a breast, a vulva, a thigh. The rest was draped in a sheet, and there was a nurse in attendance, more to protect the doctor's reputation than anything else. Wicky wasn't buying it. A tit is a tit, was Wicky's thesis, and a twat was a twat. You should either be horny all the time or none of the time. All Louis could respond was that your wife's tit was *different*.

Just like your family's supposed to be different, he thought now. Church wasn't supposed to get killed because he was inside the magic circle of the family. What he hadn't been able to make Wicky understand was that doctors compartmentalized just as cheerfully and blindly as anyone else. A tit wasn't a tit unless it was your wife's tit. In the office, another woman's tit wasn't a tit, it was a case. You could stand up in front of a medical colloquium and cite leukemia figures in children until you were blue in the face and still not believe it if one of your own kids got a call on the Bone-Phone. My kid? My kid's cat, even? Doctor, you must be joking.

Never mind. Take this one step at a time.

But that was hard when he remembered how hysterical Ellie had gotten at the prospect of Church someday dying.

Stupid fucking cat, why did we ever have to get a fucking cat, anyway?

But he wasn't fucking any more. That was supposed to keep him alive.

'Church?' he called, but there was only the furnace, muttering and muttering, burning up dollars. The couch in the living room, where Church now spent most of his time, was empty. He was not lying on any of the radiators. Louis rattled the cat's dish, the one thing absolutely guaranteed to bring Church running if he was in earshot, but no cat came running this time . . . or ever would again, he was afraid.

Reluctantly, he put on his coat and hat, and started for the door. Then he came back. Giving in to what his heart told him, he opened the cupboard under the sink and squatted down. There were two kinds of plastic bags in there – small white ones for the household trash-baskets and big green garbage can liners. Louis took one of the latter. Church had gotten larger since he had been fixed.

He poked the bag into one of the side pockets of his jacket, not liking the slick, cool way the plastic felt under his fingers. Then he let himself out the front door and crossed the street to Jud's house.

It was about five-thirty. Twilight was ending. The landscape had a strange dead look. The remainder of sunset was a strange orange line on the horizon across the river. The wind howled straight down Route 15, numbing Louis's cheeks and whipping away the white plume of his breath. He shuddered, but not from the cold. It was a feeling of aloneness that made him shudder. It was strong and persuasive. There seemed no way to concretize it with a metaphor. It was faceless. He just felt by himself, untouched and untouching.

He saw Jud across the road, bundled up in his big green duffle-coat, his face lost in the shadow cast by the fur-fringed hood. Standing on his frozen lawn, he looked like a piece of statuary, just another dead thing in this twilit landscape where no bird sang.

Louis started across, and then Jud moved – waved him back. Shouted something Louis could not make out over the pervasive whine of the wind. He stepped back, realizing suddenly that the wind's whine had deepened and sharpened. A moment later an air-horn blatted and an Orinco truck roared past close enough to make his pants and jacket flap. Damned if he hadn't almost walked right out in front of the thing.

This time he checked both ways before crossing. There was only the tanker's tail lights, dwindling into the twilight.

'Thought that 'Rinco truck was gonna get you,' Jud said. 'Have a care, Louis.' Even this close, Louis couldn't see Jud's face, and the uncomfortable feeling persisted that this could have been anyone . . . anyone at all.

'Where's Norma?' he asked, still not looking down at the sprawled bundle of fur by Jud's foot.

'Went to the Thanksgiving church service,' he said. 'She'll stay to the supper, I guess, although I don't think she'll eat nothing.' The wind gusted, shifting the hood back momentarily and Louis saw that it was indeed Jud – who else would it have been? 'It's mostly an excuse for a hen-paaa-ty,' Jud said. 'They don't eat much but sanwidges after the big meal at noon. She'll be back around eight.'

Louis knelt down to look at the cat. *Don't let it be Church*, he wished fervently, as he turned it over gently with gloved fingers. *Let it be someone else's cat, let Jud be wrong.*

But of course it was Church. The cat was in no way mangled or disfigured, as if he had been run over by one of the big tankers or semis that cruised Route 15 (*just what was that Orinco truck doing out on Thanksgiving?* he wondered randomly). Church's eyes were half-open, as glazed as green marbles. A small flow of blood had come from his mouth, which was also open. Not a great deal of blood; just enough to stain the white bib on his chest.

'Yours, Louis?'

'Mine,' he agreed, and sighed.

He was aware for the first time that he had loved Church – maybe not as fervently as Ellie, but in his own absent way. In the weeks following his castration, Church had changed, had gotten fat and slow, had established a routine that took him between Ellie's bed, the couch and his dish but rarely out of the house. Now, in death, he looked to Louis like the old Church. The mouth, so small and bloody, filled with needle-sharp cat's teeth, was frozen in a shooter's snarl. The dead eyes seemed furious. It was as if, after the short and placid stupidity of his life as a neuter, Church had rediscovered his real nature in dying.

'Yeah, it's Church,' he said. 'I'll be damned if I know how I'm going to tell Ellie about it.'

Suddenly he had an idea. He would bury Church up in the Pet Sematary with no marker or any of that foolishness. He would say nothing to Ellie on the phone tonight about Church; tomorrow he would mention casually that he hadn't seen Church around; the day after he would suggest that perhaps Church had wandered off. Cats did that sometimes. Ellie would be upset, sure, but there would be none of the finality . . . no reprise of Rachel's upsetting refusal to deal with death . . . just a withering away . . .

Coward, part of his mind pronounced.

Yes . . . no argument. But who needs this hassle?

'Loves that cat pretty well, doesn't she?' Jud asked.

'Yes,' Louis said absently. Gently, he moved Church's head. The cat had begun to stiffen, but the head still moved much more easily than it should have. Broken neck. Yeah. Given that, he thought he could reconstruct what had happened. Church had been crossing the road – for what reason God alone knew – and a car or truck had hit him, breaking his neck and throwing him aside on to Jud Crandall's lawn. Or perhaps the cat's neck had been broken when he struck the frozen ground. It didn't matter. Either way the remains remained the same. Church was dead.

He glanced up at Jud, about to tell him his conclusions, but Jud was looking away toward that fading orange line of light at the horizon. His hood had fallen back halfway, and his face seemed thoughtful and stern . . . harsh, even.

Louis pulled the green garbage bag out of his pocket and unfolded it, holding it tightly to keep the wind from whipping it away. The brisk crackling sound of the bag seemed to bring Jud back to this here and now.

'Yes, I guess she loves it pretty well,' Jud said. His use of the present tense felt slightly eerie . . . the whole setting, with the fading light, the cold and the wind, struck him as eerie and gothic.

Here's Heathcliff out on the desolate moors, Louis thought, grimacing against the cold. *Getting ready to pop the family cat into a Hefty Bag. Yowza.*

He grabbed Church's tail, spread the mouth of the bag, and lifted the cat. He pulled a disgusted, unhappy face at the sound the cat's body made coming up *rrriiippp* as he pulled it out of the frost it had set into. The cat seemed almost unbelievably heavy, as if death had settled into it like a physical weight. *Christ, he feels like a bucket of sand.*

Jud held the other side of the bag and Louis dropped Church in, glad to be rid of that strange, unpleasant weight.

'What are you going to do with it now?' Jud asked. His face looked almost carved inside the hood. But his eyes held Louis's own strongly.

'Put him in the garage, I guess,' Louis said. 'Bury him in the morning.'

'In the Pet Sematary?'

Louis shrugged. 'Suppose so.'

'Going to tell Ellie?'

'I . . . I'll have to mull that one over, a while.'

Jud was quiet a moment longer, and then he seemed to reach a decision. 'Wait here a minute or two, Louis.'

Jud moved away, with no apparent thought that Louis might not want to wait just a minute on this bitter night. He moved away with assurance and that lithe ease that was so strange in a man of his age. And Louis found he had nothing to say anyway. He didn't feel much like himself. He watched Jud go, quite content to stand here.

He raised his face into the wind after the door had clicked closed, the garbage bag with Church's body in it riffling between his feet.

Content.

Yes; he was. For the first time since they had moved to Maine he felt that he was in his place, that he was home. Standing here by himself in the eerie afterglow of the day, standing on the rim of winter, he felt unhappy and yet oddly exhilarated and strangely whole – whole in a way he had not been, or could not remember feeling that he had been, since childhood.

Something gonna happen here, Bubba. Something pretty weird, I think.

He tilted his head back and saw cold winter stars in a blackening sky.

How long he stood like that he did not know, although it could not have been long in terms of seconds and minutes. Then a light flickered on Jud's porch, bobbed, approached the porch door, and descended the steps. It was Jud behind a big four-cell flashlight. In his other hand he held what Louis at first thought was a large X . . . and then he saw that it was a pick and shovel.

He handed the shovel to Louis, who took it in his free hand.

'Jud, what the hell are you up to? We can't bury him tonight.'

'Yeah, we can. And we're gonna.' Jud's face was lost behind the glaring circle of the flashlight.

'Jud, it's dark. It's late. And cold—'

'Come on,' Jud said. 'Let's get it done.'

Louis shook his head and tried to begin again, but the words came hard – the words of explanation and reason. They seemed so meaningless against the low shriek of the wind, the seedling bed of stars in the black.

'It can wait till tomorrow when we can see—'

'Does she love the cat?'

'Yes, but—'

Jud's voice, soft and somehow logical: 'And do you love her?'

'Of course I love her, she's my dau—'

'Then come on.'

Louis went.

Twice – maybe three times – on the walk up to the Pet Sematary that night Louis tried to talk to Jud, but Jud didn't answer. Louis gave up. That feeling of contentment, odd under the circumstances but a pure fact, persisted. It seemed to come from everywhere. Even the steady ache in his muscles from carrying Church in one hand and the shovel in the other was a part of it. The wind, deadly cold, numbing exposed skin, was a part of it; it wound steadily in the trees. Once they got into the woods, there was no snow to speak of. The bobbing light of Jud's flash was a part of it, glowing like some primitive torch borne deeper and deeper into the woods. He felt the pervasive, undeniable, magnetic presence of some secret. Some dark secret.

The shadows fell away and there was a feeling of space. Snow shone pallidly.

'Rest here,' Jud said, and Louis set the bag down. He wiped sweat off his forehead with his arm. *Rest* here? But they *were* here. He could see the markers in the moving, aimless sweep of Jud's light as Jud sat down in the thin snow and put his face between his arms.

'Jud? Are you all right?'

'Fine. Need to catch my breath a bit, that's all.'

Louis sat down next to him and deep-breathed half a dozen times.

'You know,' he said, 'I feel better than I have in maybe six years. I know that's a crazy thing to say when you're burying your daughter's cat, but it's the flat truth, Jud. I feel good.'

Jud breathed deeply once or twice himself. 'Yeah, I know,' he said. 'It is that way once in a while. You don't pick your times for feeling good, any more than you do for the other. And the place has something to do with it, too, but you don't want to trust that. Heroin makes dope-addicts feel good when they're putting it in their arms, but all the time it's poisoning them. Poisoning their bodies and poisoning their way of thinking. This place can be like that, Louis, and don't you ever forget it. I hope to God I'm doing right. I think I am, but I can't be sure. Sometimes my head gets muddled. It's senility coming, I think.'

'I don't know what you're talking about.'

'This place has power, Louis. Not so much here, but . . . the place we're going.'

'Jud—'

'Come on,' Jud said, and was on his feet again. The flashlight's beam illuminated the deadfall. Jud was walking toward it. Louis suddenly remembered his episode of somnambulism. What was it Pascow had said in the dream that had accompanied it?

Don't go beyond, no matter how much you feel you need to, Doctor. The barrier was not made to be broken.

But now, tonight, that dream or warning or whatever it had been seemed years rather than months distant. Louis felt fine and fey and alive, ready to cope with anything, and yet full of wonder. It occurred to him that *this* was very much like a dream.

Then Jud turned toward him, the hood seeming to surround a blankness, and for one moment Louis imagined that it was

Pascow himself who now stood before him, that the shining light would be reversed, trained on a grinning, gibbering skull framed in fur, and his fear returned like a dash of cold water.

'Jud,' he said, 'we can't climb over that. We'll each break a leg and then probably freeze to death trying to get back.'

'Just follow me,' Jud said. 'Follow me and don't look down. Don't hesitate and don't look down. I know the way through, but it has to be done quick and sure.'

Louis began to think that perhaps it *was* a dream, that he had simply never awakened from his afternoon nap. *If I was awake*, he thought, *I'd no more head up that deadfall than I'd get drunk and go skydiving. But I'm going to do it. I really think I am. So . . . I must be dreaming. Right?*

Jud angled slightly left, away from the center of the deadfall. The flash's beam centered brightly on the jumbled heap of

(*bones*)

fallen trees and old logs. The circle of light grew smaller and even brighter as they approached. Without the slightest pause, without even a brief scan to assure himself that he was in the right place, Jud started up. He did not scramble; he did not climb bent over, the way a man will climb a rocky hillside or a sandy slope. He simply mounted, as if climbing a set of stairs. A man climbing stairs doesn't bother to look down because he knows where each stair will be. Jud climbed like a man who knows exactly where his next step is coming from.

Louis followed in the same way.

He did not look down or search for footholds. It came to him with a strange but total surety that the deadfall could not harm him unless he allowed it to. It was a piece of utter assholery, of course; like the stupid confidence of a man who believes it's safe to drive when totally shitfaced as long as he's wearing his St Christopher medallion.

But it worked.

There was no pistol-shot snap of an old branch giving way, no sickening plunge, into a hole lined with jutting, weather-whitened splinters, each one ready to cut and gore and mangle.

His shoes (Hush Puppy loafers; hardly recommended for climbing deadfalls) did not slip on the old dry moss which had overgrown many of the fallen trees. He pitched neither forward nor backward. The wind sang wildly through the fir trees all around them.

For a moment he saw Jud standing on top of the deadfall, and then he began down the far side, calves dropping out of sight, then thighs, then hips and waist. The light bounced randomly off the whipping branches of the trees on the other side of the . . . the barrier. Yes, that's what it was, why try to pretend it wasn't? The barrier.

Louis reached the top himself and paused there momentarily, right foot planted on an old fallen tree that was canted up at a thirty-five-degree angle, left foot on something springier — a mesh of old fir branches? He didn't look down to see, but only switched the heavy trashbag with Church's body in it from his right hand to his left, exchanging it for the lighter shovel. He turned his face up into the wind and felt it sweep past him in an endless current, lifting his hair. It was so cold, so clean . . . *so constant*.

Moving casually, almost sauntering, he started down again. Once a branch that felt to be the thickness of a brawny man's wrist snapped loudly under his foot, but he felt no concern at all — and his plunging foot was stopped firmly by a heavier branch some four inches down. Louis hardly staggered. He supposed that now he could understand how company commanders in the First World War had been able to stroll along the top of the trenches with bullets snapping all around them, whistling 'Tipperary'. It was crazy, but the very craziness made it tremendously exhilarating.

He walked down, looking straight ahead at the bright circle of Jud's light. Jud was standing there, waiting for him. Then he reached the bottom, and the exhilaration flared up in him like a shot of coal-oil on embers.

'We made it!' He shouted. He put the shovel down and clapped Jud on the shoulder. He remembered crossing a railroad trestle on a dare as a boy; he remembered climbing an apple tree to the top fork where it swayed in the wind like a ship's mast. He had not felt so young or so viscerally alive in twenty years or more. 'Jud, we made it!'

'Did you think we wouldn't?' Jud asked.

Louis opened his mouth to say something – *Think we wouldn't? We're damn lucky we didn't kill ourselves!* – and then he shut it again. He had never really questioned at all, not from the moment Jud approached the deadfall. And he was not worried about getting back over again.

'I guess not,' he said.

'Come on. Got a piece to walk yet. Three miles, I guess.'

They walked. The path did indeed go on. In places it seemed very wide, although the moving light revealed little clearly; it was mostly a feeling of space, that the trees had drawn back. Once or twice Louis looked up and saw stars wheeling between the massed dark border of trees. Once something loped across the path ahead of them, and the light picked up the reflection of greenish eyes – there and then gone.

At other times the path closed in until underbrush scratched stiff fingers across the shoulders of Louis's coat. He switched the bag and the shovel more often, but the ache in his shoulders was now constant. He fell into a rhythm of walking and became almost hypnotized with it. There was power here, yes, he felt it. He remembered a time when he had been a senior in high school and he, his girl and some other couple had gone way out in the boonies and had ended up necking at the end of a dead-end dirt road near a power-station. They hadn't been there long before Louis's girl said that she wanted to go home, or at least to another place, because all of her teeth (all the ones with fillings, anyway, and that was most of them) were aching. Louis had been glad to leave himself. The air around the power-station made him feel nervous and too awake. This was like that, but it was stronger. Stronger but not unpleasant at all. It was—

Jud had stopped at the base of a long slope and Louis ran into him.

Jud turned toward him. 'We're almost where we're going now,' he said calmly. 'This next bit is like the deadfall – you got to walk steady and easy. Just follow me, and don't look down. You felt us going downhill?'

'Yes.'

'This is the edge of what the Micmacs used to call Little God Swamp. The fur traders who came through called it Dead Man's Bog, and most of them who came once and got out never came again.'

'Is there quicksand?'

'Oh, ayuh, quicksand aplenty! Streams that bubble up through a big deposit of quartz sand left over from the glacier. Silica-sand, we always called it, although there's probably a proper name for it.'

Jud looked at him, and for a moment Louis thought he saw something bright and not completely pleasant in the old man's eyes. It was strong and charged, as the air around the power-station had been on that long-ago school night. It struck Louis as distinctly unpleasant.

Then Jud shifted the flashlight and that look was gone.

'There's a lot of funny things down this way, Louis. The air's heavier . . . more electrical . . . or somethin'.'

Louis started.

'What's wrong?'

'Nothing,' Louis said.

'You might see St Elmo's fire, what the sailors call foo-lights. It makes funny shapes, but it's nothing. If you should see some of those shapes and they bother you, just look the other way. You may hear sounds like voices, but they are the loons down south toward Prospect. The sound carries. It's funny.'

'Loons?' Louis said doubtfully. 'This time of year?'

'Oh, ayuh,' Jud said again, and his voice was terribly bland and totally unreadable. For a moment Louis wished desperately he could see the old man's face again. That look——

'Jud, where are we going? What the hell are we doing out here in the back of the beyond?'

'I'll tell you when we get there.' Jud turned away. 'Mind the tussocks.'

They began to walk again, stepping from one broad hummock to the next. Louis did not feel for them. His feet seemed to find them automatically, with no effort from him. He slipped only once, his left shoe breaking through a thin scum of ice and dipping into cold and somehow slimy standing water. He pulled it out quickly and went on, following Jud's bobbing light. That light, floating through the woods, brought back memories of the pirate tales he had liked to read as a boy. Evil men off to bury gold doubloons by the dark of the moon . . . and of course one of them would be tumbled into the pit on top of the chest, a bullet in his heart, because the pirates had believed – or so the authors of these lurid tales solemnly attested – that the dead comrade's ghost would remain there to guard the swag.

Except it's not treasure we've come to bury. Just my daughter's castrated cat.

He felt wild laughter bubble up inside and stifled it.

He did not hear any 'sounds like voices', nor did he see any St Elmo's fire, but after stepping over half a dozen tussocks, he looked down and saw that his feet, calves, knees and lower thighs had disappeared into a groundfog that was perfectly smooth, perfectly white, and perfectly opaque. It was like moving through the world's lightest drift of snow.

The air seemed to have a quality of light in it now, and it was warmer, he would have sworn it. He could see Jud before him, moving steadily along, the blunt end of the pick hooked over his shoulder. The pick enhanced the illusion of a man intent on burying treasure.

That crazy sense of exhilaration persisted, and he suddenly wondered if maybe Rachel was trying to call him; if, back in the house, the phone was ringing and ringing, making its rational, prosaic sound. If—

He almost walked into Jud's back again. The old man had stopped in the middle of the path. His head was cocked to one side. His mouth was pursed and tense.

'Jud? What's—'

'Shhh!'

Louis hushed, looking around uneasily. Here the ground mist was thinner, but he still couldn't see his own shoes. Then he heard crackling underbrush and breaking branches. Something was moving out there – something big.

He opened his mouth to ask Jud if it was a moose (*bear* was the thought that actually crossed his mind) and then he closed it again. *The sound carries*, Jud had said.

He cocked his head to one side in unconscious imitation of Jud, unaware that he was doing it, and listened. The sound seemed at first distant, then very close; moving away and then moving ominously toward them. Louis felt sweat break on his forehead and begin to trickle down his chapped cheeks. He shifted the Hefty Bag with Church's body in it from one hand to the other. His palm had dampened and the green plastic now seemed greasy, wanting to slide through his fist. Now the thing out there seemed so close that Louis expected to see its shape at any moment, rising up on two legs, perhaps, blotting out the stars with some unthought-of, immense and shaggy body.

Bear was no longer what he was thinking of.

Now he didn't know just *what* he was thinking of.

Then it moved away and disappeared.

Louis opened his mouth again, the words *What was that?* already on his tongue. Then a shrill, maniacal laugh came out of the darkness, rising and falling in hysterical cycles, loud, piercing, chilling. To Louis it seemed that every joint in his body had frozen solid and that he had somehow gained weight, so much weight that if he turned to run he would plunge down and out of sight in the swampy ground.

The laughter rose, split into dry cackles like some rottenly friable chunk of rock along many fault-lines; it reached the pitch of a scream, then sank into a guttural chuckling noise that might have become sobs before it faded out altogether.

Somewhere there was a drip of water and above them, like a steady river in a bed of sky, the monotonous whine of the wind. Otherwise, Little God Swamp was silent.

Louis began to shudder all over. His flesh – particularly that of his lower belly – began to creep. Yes, creep was the right word; his flesh actually seemed to be moving on his body. His mouth was totally dry. There seemed to be no spit at all left in it. Yet that feeling of exhilaration persisted, an unshakable lunacy.

'What in Christ's name?' he whispered hoarsely to Jud.

Jud turned to look at him, and in the dim light Louis thought the old man looked a hundred and twenty. There was no sign of that odd, dancing light in his eyes now. His face was drawn and there was stark terror in his eyes. But when he spoke, his voice was steady enough. 'Just a loon,' he said. 'Come on. Almost there.'

They went on. The tussocks became firm ground again. For a few moments Louis had a sensation of open space, although that dim glow in the air had now faded and it was all he could do to make out Jud's back three feet in front of him. Short grass stiff with frost was under foot. It broke like glass at every step. Then they were in the trees again. He could smell aromatic fir, feel needles. Occasionally a twig or a branch scraped against him.

Louis had lost all sense of time or direction, but they did not walk long before Jud stopped again and turned toward him.

'Steps here,' he said. 'Cut into rock. Forty-two or forty-four, I disremember which. Just follow me. We get to the top and we're there.'

He began to climb again, and again Louis followed.

The stone steps were wide enough, but the sense of the ground dropping away was unsettling. Here and there his shoe gritted on a strew of pebbles and stone fragments.

. . . Twelve . . . thirteen . . . fourteen . . .

The wind was sharper, colder, quickly numbing his face. *Are we above the treeline?* he wondered. He looked up and saw a billion stars, cold lights in the darkness. Never in his life had the stars made him feel so completely small, infinitesimal, without meaning. He asked himself the old question – *is there anything intelligent out there?* – and instead of wonder, the thought brought a horrid cold feeling, as if he had asked himself what it might be like to eat a handful of squirming bugs.

. . . Twenty-six . . . twenty-seven . . . twenty-eight . . .

Who carved these, anyway? Indians? The Micmacs? Were they tool-bearing Indians? I'll have to ask Jud. 'Tool-bearing Indians' made him think of 'fur-bearing animals', and that made him think of that thing that had been moving near them in the woods. One foot stumbled and he raked a gloved hand along the rock wall to his left for balance. The wall felt old, chipped and channeled and wrinkled. *Like dry skin that's almost worn out,* he thought.

'You all right, Louis?' Jud murmured.

'I'm okay,' he said, although he was nearly out of breath and his muscles throbbed from the weight of Church in the bag.

. . . Forty-two . . . forty-three . . . forty-four . . .

'Forty-five,' Jud said. 'I've forgot. Haven't been up here in twelve years, I guess. Don't suppose I'll ever have a reason to come again. Here . . . up you come.'

He grabbed Louis's arm and helped him up the last step.

'We're here,' Jud said.

Louis looked around. He could see well enough; the starlight was dim but adequate. They were standing on a rocky, rubble-strewn plate of rock which slid out of the thin earth directly ahead like a dark tongue. Looking the other way, he could see the tops of the fir trees they had come through in order to reach the steps. They had apparently climbed to the top of some weird, flat-topped mesa, a geological anomaly that would have seemed far more normal in Arizona or New

Mexico. Because the grassed-over top of the mesa, or hill, or truncated mountain, or whatever it was, was bare of trees, the sun had melted the snow here. Turning back to Jud, Louis saw dry grasses bending before the steady wind that blew coldly in his face, and saw that it was a hill, and not an isolated mesa. Ahead of them the ground rose again toward trees. But this flatness was so obvious, and so odd in the context of New England's low and somehow tired hills—

Tool-bearing Indians, his mind suddenly spoke up.

'Come on,' Jud said, and led him twenty-five yards toward the trees. The wind blew hard up here, but it felt clean. Louis saw a number of shapes just under the gloom cast by the trees – trees which were the oldest, tallest firs he had ever seen. The whole effect of this high, lonely place was emptiness – but an emptiness which vibrated.

The dark shapes were cairns of stones.

'Micmacs sanded off the top of the hill here,' Jud said. 'No one knows how, no more than anyone knows how the Mayans built their pyramids. And the Micmacs have forgot themselves, just like the Mayans have.'

'Why? Why did they do it?'

'This was their burying ground,' Jud said. 'I brought you here so you could bury Ellie's cat here. The Micmacs didn't discriminate, you know. They buried their pets right alongside their owners.'

This made Louis think of the Egyptians, who had gone that one better: they had slaughtered the pets of royalty, so that the souls of the pets might go along to whatever afterlife there might be with the soul of the master. He remembered reading about the slaughter of more than ten thousand pets and domestic animals following the decease of one pharaoh's daughter – included in the tally had been six hundred pigs, and two thousand peacocks. The pigs had been scented with attar of roses, the dead lady's favorite perfume, before their throats were cut.

And they built pyramids, too. No one knows for sure what the

Mayan pyramids are for — navigation and chronography, some say, like Stonehenge — but we know damn well what the Egyptian pyramids were and are great monuments to death, the world's biggest gravestones. Here lies Ramses II. He Was Obedient, Louis thought, and uttered a wild, helpless cackle.

Jud looked at him, unsurprised.

'Go on and bury your animal,' he said. 'I'm gonna have a smoke. I'd help you, but you got to do it yourself. Each buries his own. That's the way it was done then.'

'Jud, what's this all about? Why did you bring me here?'

'Because you saved Norma's life,' Jud said, and although he sounded sincere — and Louis was positive he believed himself sincere — he had a sudden, overpowering sense that the man was lying . . . or that he was being lied to and was then passing the lie on to Louis. He remembered that look he had seen, or thought he had seen, in Jud's eye.

But up here, none of that seemed to matter. The wind mattered more, pushing freely around him in that steady river, lifting his hair from his brow and off his ears.

Jud sat down with his back against one of the trees, cupped his hands around a match and lit a Chesterfield.

'You want to rest a bit before you start?'

'No, I'm okay,' Louis said. He could have pursued the questions, but he found he didn't really care to. This felt wrong but it also felt right, and he decided to let that be enough . . . for now. There was really only one thing he needed to know. 'Will I really be able to dig him a grave? The soil looks thin.' Louis nodded toward the place where the rock pushed out of the ground at the edge of the steps.

Jud nodded slowly. 'Ayuh,' he said. 'Soil's thin, all right. But soil deep enough to grow grass is generally deep enough to bury in, Louis. And people have been burying here for a long, long time. You won't find it any too easy, though.'

Nor did he. The ground was stony and hard, and very quickly he saw that he was going to need the pick to dig the grave deep enough to hold Church. So he began to alternate, first using the pick to loosen the hard earth and stones, then the shovel to dig out what he had loosened. His hands began to hurt. His body began to warm up again, and he felt a strong and unquestionable need to do a good job. He began to hum under his breath, something he sometimes did when suturing a wound. Sometimes the pick would strike a rock hard enough to flash sparks, and the shiver would travel up the wooden haft to vibrate in his hands. He could feel blisters forming on his palms and didn't care, although he was, like most doctors, usually careful of his hands. Above and around him, the wind sang and sang, playing a three-note melody.

Counterpointing this he heard the soft drop and chunk of rock. He looked over his shoulder and saw Jud, hunkered down and pulling out the bigger rocks he had dug up, making a heap of them.

'For your cairn,' he said when he saw Louis looking.

'Oh,' Louis said, and went back to work.

He made the grave about two feet wide and three feet long – a Cadillac of a grave for a damn cat, he thought – and when it was perhaps thirty inches deep and the pick was flashing sparks up from almost every stroke, he tossed it and the shovel aside and asked Jud if it was okay.

Jud got up and took a cursory look. 'Seems fine to me,' he said. 'Anyway, it's what you think that counts.'

'Will you tell me now what this is about?'

Jud smiled a little. 'The Micmacs believed this hill was a magic place,' he said. 'Believed this whole forest, from the swamp on north and east, was magic. They made this place, and they buried their dead here, away from everything else. Other tribes steered clear of it – the Penobscots said these woods were full of ghosts. Later on the fur trappers started saying pretty much the same thing. I suppose some of them saw the foo-fire in Little God Swamp and thought they were seeing ghosts.'

Jud smiled and Louis thought: *That isn't what you think at all.*

146

'Later on, not even the Micmacs themselves would come here. One of them claimed he saw a Wendigo here, and that the ground had gone sour. They had a big pow-wow about it . . . or so I heard the tale in my green years, Louis, but I heard it from that old tosspot Stanny B. – which is what we all called Stanley Bouchard – and what Stanny B. didn't know, he'd make up.'

Louis, who knew only that the Wendigo was supposed to be a spirit of the north country, said: 'Do you think the ground's gone sour?'

Jud smiled – or at least, his lips slanted. 'I think it's a dangerous place,' he said softly, 'but not for cats or dogs or pet hamsters. Go on and bury your animal, Louis.'

Louis lowered the Hefty Bag into the hole and slowly shovelled the dirt back in. He was cold now, and tired. The patter of the earth on the plastic was a depressing sound, and while he did not regret coming up here, that sense of exhilaration was fading and he had begun to wish the adventure over. It was a long walk back home.

The pattering sound muffled, then stopped – there was only the *whump* of dirt on more dirt. He scraped the last bit into the hole with the blade of his shovel (there's never enough, he thought, recalling something his undertaker uncle had said to him at least a thousand years ago, never enough to fill the hole up again) and then turned to Jud.

'Your cairn,' Jud said.

'Look, Jud, I'm pretty tired and—'

'It's Ellie's cat,' Jud said, and his voice, although soft, was implacable. 'She'd want you to do it right.'

Louis sighed. 'I suppose she would,' he said.

It took another ten minutes to pile up the rocks Jud handed him, one by one. When it was done, there was a low, conical pile of stones on Church's grave, and Louis did indeed feel a small, tired pleasure. It looked right, somehow, rising with the others in the starlight. He supposed Ellie would never see it – the thought of taking her through that patch of swamp where there was quicksand would make Rachel's hair turn white – but he had seen it, and it was good.

'Most of these have fallen over,' he said to Jud, standing and brushing at the knees of his pants. He was seeing more clearly now, and in several places he could make out distinctly the scattered strews of loose stones. But Jud had seen to it that he built his own cairn only from stones taken from the grave he himself had dug.

'Ayuh,' Jud said. 'Told you: the place is old.'

'Are we done now?'

'Ayuh.' He clapped Louis on the shoulder. 'You did good, Louis. I knew you would. Let's go home.'

'Jud—' he began again, but Jud only grabbed the pick and walked off toward the steps. Louis got the shovel, had to trot to catch up, and then saved his breath for walking. He looked back once, but the cairn marking the grave of his daughter's cat Winston Churchill had melted into the shadows and he could not pick it out.

We just ran the film backwards, Louis thought tiredly as they emerged from the woods and into the field overlooking his own house some time later. He did not know how much later; he had taken off his watch when he had lain down to doze that afternoon, and it would still be there on the windowsill by his bed. He only knew that he was beat, used up, done in. He could not remember feeling so kicked-dog weary since his first day on Chicago's rubbish-disposal crew one high-school summer sixteen or seventeen years ago.

They came back the same way they had gone, but he could remember very little about the trip. He stumbled on the deadfall, he remembered that: lurching forward and thinking absurdly of *Peter Pan* – *oh Jesus, I lost my happy thoughts and down I come* – and then Jud's hand had been there, firm and hard, and a few moments later they had been trudging past the final resting places of Smucky and Trixie and Marta Our

Pet Rabit and on to the path he had once walked not only with Jud but with his whole family.

It seemed that in some weary way he had pondered the dream of Victor Pascow, the one which had resulted in his somnambulistic episode, but any connection between that night walk and this had eluded him. It had also occurred to him that the whole adventure had been dangerous – not in any melodramatic, Wilkie Collins sense, but in a very real one. That he had outrageously blistered his hands while in a state that was nearly somnambulistic was really the least of it. He could have killed himself on the deadfall. Both of them could have. It was hard to square such behavior with sobriety. In his current exhaustion, he was willing to ascribe it to confusion and emotional upset over the death of a pet the whole family had loved.

And after a time, there they were, home again.

They walked toward it together, not speaking, and stopped again in Louis's driveway. The wind moaned and whined. Wordlessly, Louis handed Jud his pick.

'I best get across,' Jud said at last. 'Louella Bisson or Ruthie Perks will be bringin' Norma home and she'll wonder where the hell I am.'

'Do you have the time?' Louis asked. He was surprised that Norma wasn't home yet; in his muscles it seemed to him that midnight must have struck.

'Oh, ayuh,' Jud said. 'I keep the time as long as I'm dressed and then I let her go.'

He fished a watch out of his pants pocket and flicked the scrolled cover back from its face.

'It's gone eight-thirty,' he said, and snapped the cover closed again.

'Eight-thirty?' Louis repeated stupidly. 'That's all?'

'How late did you think it was?' Jud asked.

'Later than that,' Louis said.

'I'll see you tomorrow, Louis,' Jud said, and began to move away.

'Jud?'

He turned toward Louis, mildly questioning.

'Jud, what did we do tonight?'

'Why, we buried your daughter's cat.'

'Is that all we did?'

'Nothing but that,' Jud said. 'You're a good man, Louis, but you ask too many questions. Sometimes people have to do things that just seem right. That seem right in their hearts, I mean. And if they do those things and then end up not feeling right, full of questions and sort of like they got indigestion, only inside their heads instead of in their guts, they think they made a mistake. Do you know what I mean?'

'Yes,' Louis said, thinking that Jud must have been reading his mind as the two of them walked downhill through the field and toward the houselights.

'What they don't think is that maybe they should be questioning those feelings of doubt before they question their own hearts,' Jud said, looking at him closely. 'What do you think, Louis?'

'I think,' Louis said slowly, 'that you might be right.'

'And the things that are in a man's heart, it don't do him much good to talk about those things, does it?'

'Well—'

'No,' Jud said, as if Louis had simply agreed. 'It don't.' And in his calm voice that was so sure and so implacable, in that voice that somehow put the chill through Louis, he said: 'They are secret things. Women are supposed to be the ones good at keeping secrets, and I guess they do keep a few, but any woman who knows anything at all would tell you she's never really seen into any man's heart. The soil of a man's heart is stonier, Louis — like the soil up there in the old Micmac burying ground. Bedrock's close. A man grows what he can . . . and he tends it.'

'Jud—'

'Don't question, Louis. Accept what's done and follow your heart.'

'But—'

'But nothing. *Accept what's done, Louis, and follow your heart.* We did what was right at this time . . . at least, I hope to Christ it was right. Another time it could be wrong – wrong as hell.'

'Will you at least answer one question?'

'Well, let's hear what it is, and then we'll see.'

'How did you know about that place?' This question had also occurred to Louis on the way back, along with the suspicion that Jud himself might be part Micmac – although he did not look like it; he looked as if every one of his ancestors had been one hundred per cent card-carrying Anglos.

'Why, from Stanny B.,' he said, looking surprised.

'He just told you?'

'No,' Jud said. 'It isn't the kind of place you just tell somebody about. I buried my dog Spot up there when I was ten. He was chasing a rabbit and he run on some rusty barbed wire. The wounds infected and it killed him.'

There was something wrong about that, something that didn't fit with something Louis had been previously told, but he was too tired to puzzle out the discontinuity. Jud said no more; only looked at him from his inscrutable old man's eyes.

'Goodnight, Jud,' Louis said.

'Goodnight.'

The old man crossed the road, carrying his pick and shovel.

'Thanks!' Louis called impulsively.

Jud didn't turn; only raised one hand to indicate he had heard.

And in the house, suddenly, the telephone began to ring.

Louis ran, wincing at the aches that flared in his upper thighs and lower back, but by the time he had gotten into the warm kitchen, the phone had already rung six or seven times. It stopped ringing just as he put his hand on it. He picked it up anyway and said hello, but there was only the open hum.

That was Rachel, he thought, *I'll call her back.*

151

STEPHEN KING

But suddenly it seemed like too much work to dial the number, to dance clumsily with her mother — or worse, her checkbook-brandishing father — to be passed on to Rachel . . . and then to Ellie. Ellie would still be up, of course; it was an hour earlier in Chicago. Ellie would ask him how Church was doing.

Great, he's fine. Got hit by an Orinco truck. Somehow I'm absolutely positive it was an Orinco truck. Anything else would lack dramatic unity, if you know what I mean. You don't? Well, never mind. The truck killed him but didn't mark him up hardly at all. Jud and I planted him up in the old Micmac burying ground — sort of an annex to the Pet Sematary, if you know what I mean. Amazing walk. I'll take you up there sometime and we'll put flowers by his marker — excuse me, his cairn. After the quicksand's frozen over, that is, and the bears go to sleep for the winter.

He let go of the telephone, crossed to the sink and filled it with hot water. He removed his shirt and washed. He had been sweating like a pig in spite of the cold, and a pig was exactly what he smelled like.

There was some left-over meatloaf in the refrigerator. Louis cut it into slabs, put them on a slice of Roman Meal bread, and added two thick rounds of Bermuda onion. He contemplated this for a moment and then doused it liberally with ketchup before slamming down another slice of bread. If Rachel and Ellie had been around, they would have wrinkled their noses in identical gestures of distaste — yuck, gross.

Well, you missed it, ladies, Louis thought with undeniable satisfaction, and gobbled his sandwich. It tasted great. *Confucius say he who smell like pig eat like wolf,* he thought, and smiled. He chased the sandwich with several long swallows of milk directly from the carton — another habit Rachel frowned on strenuously — and then he went upstairs, undressed, and got into bed without even washing his teeth. His aches and pains had faded to one low throb that was almost comforting.

His watch was there, where he had left it, and he looked at it. Ten minutes of nine. It really was incredible. Already

152

the whole thing seemed like a dream – another sleep-walking incident.

Louis turned off the light, turned over on his side, and slept.

He woke up sometime after three the next morning and shuffled to the bathroom. He was standing there urinating, blinking owlishly in the bright white fluorescent bathroom light, when the discrepancy suddenly showed up in his mind, and his eyes widened – it was as if two pieces of something which should have fitted together perfectly had instead thudded against one another and rebounded.

Tonight Jud had told him that his dog had died when he was ten – had died of infection after being scraped up in a snarl of rusty barbed wire. But on the late summer day when all of them had walked up to the Pet Sematary together, Jud said that his dog had died of old age and was buried there – he had even pointed out the marker, although the years had worn the inscription away.

Louis flushed the toilet, turned out the light, and went back to bed. Something else was wrong, as well – and in a moment he had it. Jud had been born with the century, and that day at the Pet Sematary he had told Louis his dog had died during the first year of the Great War. That would have been when Jud was fourteen, if he had meant when the war actually started in Europe. When he was seventeen, if he had meant when America entered the war.

But tonight he had said Spot died when he, Jud, was ten.

Well, he's an old man, and old men get confused in their memories, he thought uneasily. *He's said himself that he's noticed signs of increasing forgetfulness – groping for names and addresses that used to come to him easily, sometimes getting up in the morning and having no memory of the chores he planned to do just the night before. For a man of his age he's getting off pretty goddamned light . . . senility's probably too strong a word for it in Jud's case; forgetfulness is actually better, more accurate. Nothing too surprising about a man forgetting the age of a dog that died some seventy years ago. Or the circumstances in which it died, for that matter. Forget it, Louis.*

But he wasn't able to fall asleep again right away; for a long while he lay awake, too conscious of the empty house and the wind that whined around the eaves outside it.

At some point he slept without even being aware that he had gone over the edge; it must have been so, because as he slipped away, it seemed to him that he heard bare feet slowly climbing the stairs and that he thought, *let me alone, Pascow, let me alone, what's done is done and what's dead is dead* – and the steps faded away.

And although a great many other inexplicable things happened as that year darkened, Louis was never bothered by the specter of Victor Pascow again, either waking or dreaming.

CHAPTER TWENTY-THREE

He awoke at nine the next morning. Bright sunshine streamed in the bedroom's east windows. The telephone was ringing. Louis reached up and snared it. 'Hello?'

'Hi!' Rachel said. 'Did I wake you up? Hope so.'

'You woke me up, you bitch,' he said, smiling.

'Ooooh, such nasty language, you bad old bear,' she said. 'I tried to call you last night. Were you over at Jud's?'

He hesitated for only the tiniest fraction of a moment.

'Yes,' he said. 'Had a few beers. Norma was up at some sort of Thanksgiving supper. I thought about giving you a ring, but . . . you know.'

'Yes,' she said. 'I do know.'

They chatted a while. Rachel updated him on her family, something he could have done without, although he took a small, mean satisfaction in her news that her father's bald spot seemed to be expanding at a faster rate.

'You want to talk to Gage?' Rachel asked.

Louis grinned. 'Yeah, I guess so,' he said. 'Don't let him hang up the phone like he did the other time.'

Much rattling at the other end. Dimly he heard Rachel cajoling the kid to say Hi, Daddy.

At last Gage said, 'Hi, Dayee.'

'Hi, Gage,' Louis said cheerfully. 'How you doing? How's your life? Did you pull over your grandda's pipe-rack again? I certainly hope so. Maybe this time you can ruin his stamp collection as well.'

Gage babbled on happily for thirty seconds or so, interspersing his gobbles and grunts with a few recognizable words from his growing vocabulary – *Mommee, Ellie, Grandda, Granma, car*

155

(pronounced in the best Yankee tradition as *kaaaaaaaa*, Louis was amused to note), *twuck*, and *shit*.

At last Rachel pried the phone away from him, to Gage's wail of indignation and Louis's measured relief – he loved his son and missed him like mad, but holding a conversation with a not–quite–two–year–old was a little bit like trying to play cribbage with a lunatic; the cards kept going everywhere and sometimes you found yourself pegging backwards.

'So how's everything there?' Rachel asked.

'Okay,' Louis said, with no hesitation at all this time – but he was aware he had crossed a line, back when Rachel had asked him if he had gone over to Jud's last night and he told her he had. In his mind he suddenly heard Jud Crandall saying: *The soil of a man's heart is stonier, Louis . . . a man grows what he can . . . and he tends it.* 'Well . . . a little dull, if you want to know the God's honest. Miss you.'

'You actually mean to tell me you're not enjoying your vacation from this sideshow?'

'Oh, I like the quiet,' he admitted, 'sure. But it gets strange after the first twenty–four hours or so.'

'Can I talk to Daddy?' It was Ellie, in the background.

'Louis? Ellie's here.'

'Okay, put her on.'

He talked to Ellie for almost five minutes. She prattled on about the doll Granma had gotten her, about the trip she and Grandda had taken to the stockyards ('Boy, do they *stink*, Daddy,' Ellie said, and Louis thought: *Your grandda's no rose, either, sweetie*), about how she had helped make bread, and about how Gage had gotten away from Rachel while she was changing him. Gage had run down the hallway and pooped right in the doorway leading into Grandda's study (*atta boy, Gage!* Louis thought, a big grin spreading over his face).

He actually thought he was going to get away – at least for this morning – and was getting ready to ask Ellie for her mother again so he could say goodbye to her when Ellie asked, 'How's Church, Daddy? Does he miss me?'

The grin faded from Louis's mouth, but he answered readily and with the perfect note of off-handed casualness: 'He's fine, I guess. I gave him the left-over beef stew last night and then put him out. Haven't seen him this morning, but I just woke up.'

Oh boy, you would have made a great murderer − cool as a cucumber. Dr Creed, when did you last see the deceased? He came in for supper. Had a plate of beef stew, in fact. I haven't seen him since then.

'Well, give him a kiss for me.'

'Yuck, kiss your own cat,' Louis said, and Ellie giggled.

'You want to talk to Mummy again, Daddy?'

'Sure. Put her on.'

Then it was over. He talked to Rachel for another couple of minutes; the subject of Church was not touched upon. He and his wife exchanged love-you's and Louis hung up.

'That's that,' he said to the empty, sunny room, and maybe the worst thing about it was that he didn't feel bad, didn't feel guilty, at all.

CHAPTER TWENTY-FOUR

Steve Masterton called around nine-thirty and asked if Louis would like to come up to the University and play some racquetball – the place was deserted, he said gleefully, and they could play the whole goddam day if they wanted to.

Louis could understand the glee – when the University was in session, the wait-list for a racquetball court was sometimes two days long – but he declined all the same, telling Steve he wanted to work on an article he was writing for *The Magazine of College Medicine*.

'You sure?' Steve asked. 'All work and no play makes Jack a dull boy, you know.'

'Check me later,' Louis said. 'Maybe I'll be up for it.'

Steve said he would and hung up. Louis had told only a half-lie this time; he did plan to work on his article, which concerned itself with treating contagious ailments such as chicken-pox and mononucleosis in the infirmary environment, but the main reason he had turned down Steve's offer was that he was a mass of aches and pains. He had discovered this as soon as he finished talking to Rachel and went into the bathroom to brush his teeth. His back muscles creaked and groaned, his shoulders were sore from lugging the cat in that damned garbage bag, and the hamstrings in the back of his knees felt like guitar strings tuned three octaves past their normal pitch. *Christ*, he thought, *and you had the stupid idea you were in some kind of shape.* He would have looked cute trying to play racquetball with Steve, lumbering around like an arthritic old man.

And speaking of old men, he hadn't made that hike into the woods the night before by himself; he had gone with a guy who was closing in on eighty-five. He wondered if Jud was hurting as badly as he was this morning.

He spent an hour and a half working on his article, but it did not march very well. The emptiness and the silence began to get on his nerves, and at last he stacked his yellow legal pads and the offprints he had ordered from Johns Hopkins on the shelf above his typewriter, put on his parka, and crossed the road.

Jud and Norma weren't there, but there was an envelope tacked to the porch door with his name written across the front of it. He took it down and opened the flap with his thumb.

Louis,

The good wife and me are off to Bucksport to do some shopping and to look at a Welsh dresser at the Emporium Galorium that Norma's had her eye on for about a hundred years, it seems like. Probably we'll have a spot of lunch at McLeod's while we're there and come back in the late afternoon. Come on over for a beer or two tonight, if you want.

Your family is your family, I don't want to be no 'buttinsky', but if Ellie were my daughter, I wouldn't rush to tell her that her cat got killed on the highway — why not let her enjoy her holiday?

By the way, Louis, I wouldn't talk about what we did last night, either, not around North Ludlow. There are other people who know about that old Micmac burying ground, and there are other people in town who have buried their animals there . . . you might say it's another part of the 'Pet Sematary'. Believe it or not, there is even a bull buried up there! Old Zack McGovern, who used to live out on the Stackpole Road, buried his prize bull Hanratty in the Micmac burying ground back in 1967 or '68. Ha, ha! He told me that he and his two boys had taken that bull out there and I laughed until I thought I would rupture myself! But people around here don't like to talk about it, and they don't like people they consider to be 'outsiders' to know about it, not because some of these old superstitions go back three hundred years or more (although they do), but because they sort of believe in those superstitions, and they think any 'outsider' who knows that they do must be laughing at them. Does that make any sense? I suspect it doesn't, but nevertheless that's how it is. So just do me a favor and keep shut on the subject, will you?

We will talk more about this, probably tonight, and by then you will understand more, but in the meantime I want to tell you that you did yourself proud. I knew you would.

Jud

PS Norma doesn't know what this note says — I told her something different — and I would just as soon keep it that way if it's all the same to you. I've told Norma more than one lie in the fifty-eight years we've been married, and I'd guess that most men tell their wives a smart of lies, but you know, most of them could stand before God and confess them without dropping their eyes from His.

Well, drop over tonight and we'll do a little boozing.

J.

Louis stood on the top step leading to Jud and Norma's porch — now bare, its comfortable rattan furniture stored to wait for another spring — frowning over this note. Don't tell Ellie the cat had been killed — he hadn't. Other animals buried there? Superstitions going back three hundred years?

. . . and by then you will understand more.

He touched this line lightly with his finger, and for the first time allowed his mind to deliberately turn back to what they had done the night before. It was blurred in his memory, it had the melting, cotton-candy texture of dreams, or of waking actions performed under a light haze of drugs. He could recall climbing the deadfall, and the odd, brighter quality of light in the bog — that and the way it had felt ten or twenty degrees warmer there — but all of it was like the conversation you had with the anesthetist just before he or she put you out like a light.

and I'd guess most men tell their wives a smart of lies . . .

Wives and daughters as well, Louis thought — but it was eerie in the way Jud seemed almost to know what had transpired this morning, both on the telephone and in his own head.

Slowly, he refolded the note, which had been written on a sheet of lined paper like that in a schoolboy's Blue Horse tablet, and put it back into the envelope. He put the envelope into his hip pocket and crossed the road again.

CHAPTER TWENTY-FIVE

It was around one o'clock that afternoon when Church came back like the cat in the nursery rhyme. Louis was in the garage, where he had been working off and on for the last six weeks on a fairly ambitious set of shelves; he wanted to put all of the dangerous garage-stuff like bottles of windshield-wiper fluid, anti-freeze, and sharp tools on these shelves, where they would be out of Gage's reach. He was hammering in a nail when Church strolled in, his tail high. Louis did not drop the hammer or even slam his thumb – his heart jogged in his chest but did not leap; a hot wire seemed to glow momentarily in his stomach and then cool immediately, like the filament of a lightbulb that glows overbrightly for a moment and then burns out. It was as if, he told himself later, he had spent that entire sunny post-Thanksgiving Friday morning waiting for Church to come back; as if he had known in some deeper, more primitive part of his mind what their night-hike up to the Micmac burying ground had meant all along.

He put the hammer down carefully, spat the nails he had been holding in his mouth back into his palm and then dumped them into the pockets of his workman's apron. He went to Church and picked the cat up.

Live weight, he thought with a kind of sick excitement. *He weighs what he did before he was hit. This is live weight. He was heavier in the bag. He was heavier when he was dead.*

His heart took a bigger jog this time – almost a leap – and for a moment the garage seemed to swim in front of his eyes.

Church laid his ears back and allowed himself to be held. Louis carried him out into the sunlight and sat down on the back steps. The cat tried to get down then, but Louis stroked him and held him on his lap. His heart seemed to be taking regular jogs now.

He probed gently into the heavy ruff of fur at Church's neck, remembering the sick, boneless way Church's head had swivelled on his broken neck the night before. He felt nothing now but good muscle and tendon. He held the cat up and looked at its muzzle closely. What he saw there caused him to drop the cat on to the grass quickly and to cover his face with one hand, his eyes shut. The whole world was swimming now, and tottery, sick vertigo – it was the sort of feeling he could remember from the bitter end of long drunks, just before the puking started.

There was dried blood caked on Church's muzzle, and caught in his long whiskers were two tiny shreds of green plastic. Bits of Hefty Bag.

We will talk more about this and by then you will understand more . . .

Oh Christ, he understood more than he wanted to right now.

Give me a chance, Louis thought, and I'll understand myself right into the nearest mental asylum.

He let Church into the house, got his blue dish, and opened a Tuna and Liver Cat Dinner. As he spooned the graybrown mess out of its can, Church purred unevenly and rubbed back and forth along Louis's ankles. The feel of the cat caused Louis to break out in gooseflesh, and he had to clench his teeth grimly to keep from kicking it away. Its furry sides felt somehow too slick, too thick – in a word, loathsome. Louis found he didn't care if he never touched Church again.

When he bent and put the dish on the floor, Church streaked past him to get it, and Louis could have sworn he smelled sour earth – as if it had been ground into the cat's fur.

He stood back, watching the cat eat. He could hear it smacking – had Church smacked over his food that way

163

before? Perhaps he had, and Louis had just never noticed it. Either way, it was a disgusting sound. Gross, Ellie would have said.

Abruptly Louis turned and went upstairs. He started at a walk, but by the time he got to the top of the stairs, he was almost running. He undressed, tossing all of his clothes in the laundry hamper although he had put them on fresh from the underwear out that morning. He drew himself a hot bath, as hot as he could take it, and plopped in.

The steam rose around him, and he could feel the hot water working on his muscles, loosening them. The hot bath was also working on his head, loosening that. By the time the water had begun to cool, he was feeling dozy and pretty much all right again.

The cat came back, just like the cat in the nursery rhyme, all right, so what, big deal.

It had all been a mistake. Hadn't he thought to himself yesterday evening that Church looked remarkably whole and unmarked for an animal that had been struck by a car?

Think of all the woodchucks and cats and dogs you've seen strewn all over the highway, he thought, *their bodies burst, their guts everywhere. Tech-ni-color, as Loudon Wainwright says on that record about the dead skunk.*

It was obvious now. Church had been struck hard and stunned. The cat he had carried up to Jud's old Micmac burying ground had been unconscious, not dead. Didn't they say cats had nine lives? Thank God he hadn't said anything to Ellie! She wouldn't ever have to know how close Church had come.

The blood on his mouth and ruff . . . the way his neck turned . . .

But he was a doctor, not a vet. He had made a misdiagnosis, that was all. It had hardly been under the best circumstances for close examination, squatting on Jud's lawn in twenty-degree temperatures, the light almost gone from the sky. And he had been wearing gloves. That could have—

A bloated, misshapen shadow rose on the tiled bathroom

wall, like the head of a small dragon or of some monstrous snake; something touched his bare shoulder lightly and skidded. Louis jerked upward galvanically, splashing water out of the tub and soaking the bathmat. He turned, cringing back at the same time, and stared into the muddy yellow-green eyes of his daughter's cat, who was perched on the lowered seat of the toilet.

Church was swaying slowly back and forth as if drunk. Louis watched it, his body crawling with revulsion, a scream barely held back in his mouth by his clamped teeth. Church had never looked like this – had never *swayed*, like a snake trying to hypnotize its prey – not before he was fixed, and not afterward. For the first and last time he played with the idea that this was a different cat, one that just looked like Ellie's, a cat that had just wandered into his garage while he was putting up those shelves, and that the real Church was still buried under that cairn on the bluff in the woods. But the markings were the same . . . and the one ragged ear . . . and the paw that had that funny chewed look. Ellie had slammed that paw in the back door of their little suburban house when Church was little more than a kitten.

It was Church, all right.

'Get out of here,' Louis whispered hoarsely at it.

Church stared at him a moment longer – God, his eyes were different, somehow they were different – and then leaped down from the toilet seat. He landed with none of the uncanny grace cats usually display. He staggered awkwardly, haunches thudding against the tub, and then he was gone.

It, Louis thought. *Not he; it. Remember, it's been spayed.*

He got out of the tub and dried off quickly, jerkily. He was shaved and mostly dressed when the phone rang, shrill in the empty house. When it sounded, Louis whirled, eyes wide, hands going up. He lowered them slowly. His heart was racing. His muscles felt full of adrenalin.

It was Steve Masterton, checking back about racquetball, and Louis agreed to meet him at the Memorial Gym in an

STEPHEN KING

hour. He could not really afford the time, and racquetball was the last thing in the world he felt like right now, but he had to get out. He wanted to get away from the cat, that weird cat which had no business being here at all.

He was hurrying now. He tucked in his shirt quickly, stuffed a pair of shorts and T-shirt and a towel into his zipper bag, and trotted down the stairs.

Church was lying on the fourth riser from the bottom. Louis tripped over the cat and almost fell. He managed to grab the banister and barely save himself from what could have been a nasty fall.

He stood at the bottom of the stairs, breathing in snatches, his heart racing, the adrenalin whipping unpleasantly through his body.

Church stood up, stretched . . . and seemed to grin at him.

Louis left. He should have put the cat out, he knew that, but he didn't. At that particular moment he didn't think he could bring himself to touch it.

CHAPTER TWENTY-SIX

Jud lit a cigarette with a wooden kitchen match, shook it out, and tossed the stub into a tin ashtray with a barely readable Jim Beam advertisement painted on its bottom.

'It was Stanley Bouchard who told me about the old Micmac burying ground,' he repeated to Louis.

They were in Jud's kitchen. Barely touched glasses of beer stood before them on the checked oilcloth that covered the kitchen table. Behind them, the barrel of range-oil clamped to the wall gurgled three times, deliberately, and was still. Louis had caught a pick-up supper with Steve: submarine sandwiches in the mostly deserted Bear's Den. He had found out early that if you asked for a hoagie or a grinder or a gyro in Maine, they didn't know what you were talking about. Ask for a sub or a Wop-burger and you were in business. With some food in him, Louis began to feel better about Church's return, felt that he had things more in perspective, but he was still not anxious to return to his dark, empty house where the cat could be – let's face it, gang – anywhere at all.

Norma had sat with them for quite a while, watching TV and working on a sampler that showed the sun going down behind a small county meeting-house. The cross on the roof-tree was silhouetted black against the setting sun. Something to sell, she said, at the church sale the week before Christmas. Always a big event. Her fingers moved well, pushing the needle through the cloth, pulling it up through the steel circle. Her arthritis was barely noticeable tonight. Louis supposed it might be the weather, which had been cold but very dry. She had recovered nicely from her heart attack, and on that evening some ten weeks before a second heart attack would kill her, he thought that she looked less haggard and actually younger. On that evening he could see the girl she had been.

At quarter to ten she had said goodnight and now he sat here with Jud, who had ceased speaking and seemed only to be following his cigarette smoke up and up, like a kid watching a barber-pole to see where the stripes go.

'Stanny B.,' Louis prompted gently.

Jud blinked, seemed to come back to himself. 'Oh, ayuh,' he said. 'Everyone in Ludlow – round Bucksport and Prospect and Orrington, too, I guess – just called him Stanny B. That year my dog Spot died – 1910, I mean, the first time he died – Stanny was already an old man, and more than a little crazy. There was others around these parts that knew the Micmac burying ground was there, but it was Stanny B. I heard it from, and he knew about it from his father and his father before him. A whole family of proper Canucks, they were.'

Jud laughed and sipped his beer.

'I can still hear him talking in that broken English of his. He found me sitting behind the livery stable that used to stand on Route 15 – except it was just the Bangor-Bucksport Road back then – right about where the Orinco plant is now. Spot wasn't dead but he was going, and my dad sent me away to check on some chickenfeed, which old Yorky sold back then. We didn't need chickenfeed any more than a cow needs a blackboard, and I knew well enough why he sent me down there.'

'He was going to kill the dog?'

'He knew how tenderly I felt about Spot, so he sent me away while he did it. I saw about the chickenfeed and while old Yorky set it out for me I went around the back and sat down on the old grindstone that used to be there and just bawled.'

Jud shook his head slowly and gently, still smiling a little.

'And along comes old Stanny B.,' he said. 'Half the people in town thought he was soft, and the other half thought he might be dangerous. His grandfather was a big fur-trapper and trader in the early 1800s. Stanny's grandda would go all the way from the Maritimes to Bangor and Derry, sometimes as far south as Skowhegan to buy pelts, or so I've heard. He drove a big wagon covered with rawhide strips like something out of a medicine show. He had crosses all over it, for he was a proper Christian and would preach on the Resurrection when he was drunk enough – this is what Stanny said, he loved to talk about his grandda – but he had pagan Indian signs all over it as well, because he believed that all Indians, no matter what the tribe, belonged to one big tribe: that lost one of Israel the Bible talks about. He said he believed all Indians were hellbound, but that their magic worked because they were Christians all the same, in some queer, damned way.

'Stanny's grandda bought from the Micmacs and did a good business with them long after most of the other trappers and traders had given up or gone West because he traded with them at a fair price and because, Stanny said, he had the whole Bible by heart, and the Micmacs liked to hear him speak the words the blackrobes had spoken to them before.'

He fell silent. Louis waited.

'The Micmacs told Stanny B.'s grandda about the burying ground which they didn't use any more because the Wendigo had soured the ground, and about Little God Swamp, and the steps, and all the rest. The Wendigo story, now, that is something you could hear in those days all over the north country. It was a story they had to have, the same way I guess we have to have some of our Christian stories. Norma would damn me for a profaner if she heard me say that, but Louis, it's true. Sometimes, if the winter was long and hard and the food was short, there were north country Indians who would finally get down to the bad place where it was starve or . . . or do something else.'

'Cannibalism?' Louis asked.

Jud shrugged. 'Maybe. Maybe they'd pick out someone who was old and used up, and then there would be stew for a while. And the story they worked out would be that the

Wendigo had walked through their village or encampment while they were sleepin' and touched them. And the Wendigo was supposed to give those it touched a taste for the flesh of their own kind.'

Louis nodded. 'Getting around the taboo by saying in effect that the devil made them do it.'

'Sure. I guess. My own guess is that the Micmacs round here had to do it at some point and buried the bones of whoever they ate – one or two or maybe even ten or a dozen – up there in their burying ground.'

'And then decided the ground had gone sour,' Louis muttered.

'So here's Stanny B., come out in the back of the livery to get his jug, I guess,' Jud said, 'already half-crocked, he was. His grandfather was worth maybe a million dollars when he died – or so people said – and Stanny B. was nothing but the local rag-man. He asked me what was wrong, and I told him. He saw I'd been bawling, and he told me there was a way it could be fixed up, if I was brave and sure I wanted it fixed up.

'I said I'd give anything to have Spot well again, and I asked him if he knew a vet that could do it. "Don't know no vet, me," Stanny said, "but I know how to fix your dog, boy. You go home now and tell your dad to put that dog in a grain-sack, him, but you ain't gonna bury him, no! You gonna drag him up to the Pet Sematary and you gonna put him in the shade by that big deadfall. Then you gonna come back and say it's done."

'I asked him what good that would do, and Stanny told me to stay awake that night and come out when he threw a stone against my window. "And it be midnight, boy, so if you forget Stanny B. and go to sleep, Stanny B. gonna forget you, and it's goodbye dog, him, let him go straight to Hell!"'

Jud looked at Louis and lit another cigarette.

'It went just the way Stanny set it up. When I got back, my dad said he'd put a bullet in Spot's head to spare him any more suffering. I didn't even have to say anything about the Pet Sematary; my dad asked me if I didn't think Spot would want me to bury him up there, and I said I guessed he would. So off I went, dragging my dog in a grain-sack. My dad asked me if I wanted help and I said no, because I remembered what Stanny B. said.

'I laid awake that night, for ever; seemed like. You know how time is for kids. It would seem to me I must have stayed awake right around until morning and then the clock would only chime ten, or eleven. A couple of times I almost nodded off, but each time I snapped wide awake again. It was almost as if someone had shaken me and said, *Wake up, Jud! Wake up!* Like something wanted to make sure I stayed awake.'

Louis raised his eyebrows at that and Jud shrugged, as if to say he knew it was crazy, all right.

'When the clock in the downstairs hall chimed twelve, I got right up and sat there dressed on my bed with the moon shinin' in the window. Next I know, the clock is chimin' the half-hour, then one o'clock, and still no Stanny B. He's forgot all about me, that dumb Frenchman, I think to myself, and I'm gettin' ready to take my clothes off again, when these two pebbles whap off the window, damn near hard enough to break the glass. One of them did put a crack in a pane, but I never noticed it until the next morning, and my mother didn't see it until the next winter, and by then she thought the frost done it. Lucky for me.

'I just about flew across to that window and heaved it up. It grated and rumbled against the frame, the way they only seem to do when you're a kid and you want to get out after midnight—'

Louis laughed even though he could not remember ever having wanted to get out of the house at some dark hour after midnight when he was a boy of ten. Still, if he had wanted to, he was sure that windows which had never creaked in the daytime would creak then.

'I figured my folks must have figured burglars were trying

to break in, but when my heart quieted down I could hear my dad still sawing wood in the bedroom on the first floor. I looked out and there was Stanny B., standing in our driveway and looking up, swaying like there was a high wind when there wasn't so much as a puff of breeze. I don't think he ever would have come, Louis, except that he'd gotten to that stage of drunkenness where you're as wide awake as an owl with diarrhea and you just don't give a care about anything. And he sort of yells up at me – only I guess he thought he was whispering, "You comin' down, boy, or am I comin' up to get you?"

'"Shh," I says, scared to death now that my dad will wake up and give me the whopping of my young life. "What'd you say?" Stanny says, even louder than before. If my parents had been around on the road side of this house, Louis, where we are now, I would have been a goner. But they had the bedroom that belongs to Norma and me now, with the river view.'

'I bet you got down those stairs in one hell of a hurry,' Louis said. 'Have you got another beer, Jud?' He was already two past his usual limit, but tonight that seemed okay. Tonight that seemed almost mandatory.

'I do, and you know where they're kept,' Jud said, and lit a fresh smoke. He waited until Louis was seated again. 'No, I wouldn't have dared to try the stairs. They went past my parents' bedroom. I went down the ivy trellis, hand over hand just as quick as I could. I was some scared, I can tell you, but I think I was more scared of my dad just then than I was of going up to the Pet Sematary with Stanny B.'

He crushed out his smoke.

'We went up there, the two of us, and I guess Stanny B. must have fallen down half a dozen times if he fell down once. He was really far gone; smelled like he'd fallen into a vat of corn. One time he damn near put a stick through his throat. But he had a pick and shovel with him. When we got to the Pet Sematary, I kind of expected he'd sling me the pick and shovel and just pass out while I dug the hole.

'Instead, he seemed to sober up a little. He told me we was goin' on, up over the deadfall and deeper into the woods, where there was another burial place. I looked at Stanny, who was so drunk he could barely keep his feet, and I looked at that deadfall, and I said, "You can't climb that, Stanny B., you'll break your neck."

'And he said, "I ain't gonna break my neck, me, and neither are you. I can walk and you can lug your dog." And he was right. He sailed up over that deadfall just as smooth as silk, never even looking down, and I lugged Spot all the way up there, although he must have weighed thirty-five pounds or so and I only went about ninety myself. I want to tell you, though, Louis, I was some sore and sprung the next day. How do *you* feel today?'

Louis didn't answer; only nodded. The beer was working on him and he was glad for it.

'We walked and we walked,' Jud said. 'It seemed to me like we was gonna walk for ever. The woods were spookier in those days. More birds calling from the trees, and you didn't know what any of them was. Animals moving around out there. Deer, most likely, but back then there were moose, too, and bears, and catamounts. I dragged Spot. After a while I started to get the funny idea that old Stanny B. was gone and I was following an Indian and somewhere further along he'd turn around, all grinning and black-eyed, his face streaked up with that stinking paint they made from bear-fat, that he'd have a tommyhawk made out of a wedge of slate and a hake of ashwood all tied together with rawhide, and he'd grab me by the back of the neck and whack off my hair – along with the top of my skull. Stanny wasn't staggerin' or fallin' any more, he just walked straight and easy, with his head up, and that sort of helped to feed the idea. But when we got to the edge of the Little God Swamp and he turned around to talk to me, I seen it was Stanny, all right, and the reason he wasn't staggerin' or fallin' any more was because he was scared. Scairt himself sober, he did.

'He told me the same things I told you last night, about the loons, and the St Elmo's fire, and how I wasn't to take any notice of anything I saw or heard. Most of all, he said, don't speak to anything if it should speak to you. Then we started across the swamp. And I did see something. I ain't going to tell you what, only that I've been up there maybe five times since that time when I was ten, and I've never seen anything like it again. Nor will I, Louis, because my trip to the Micmac burial place last night was my last trip.'

I'm not sitting here believing all of this, am I? Louis asked himself almost conversationally – the three beers helped him to sound conversational, at least to his own mind's ear. *I am not sitting here believing this story of old Frenchmen and Indian burying grounds and something called the Wendigo and pets that come back to life, am I? For Christ's sake, the cat was stunned, that's all, a car hit it and stunned it, no big deal. This is a senile old man's maunderings.*

Except that it wasn't, and Louis knew it wasn't, and three beers were not going to cure that knowing, and thirty-three beers wouldn't.

Church had been dead, that was one thing; he was alive now and that was another; there was something fundamentally different, fundamentally *wrong* about him, and that was a third. Something had happened. Jud had repaid what he saw as a favor . . . but the medicine available at the Micmac burying ground was perhaps not such good medicine, and Louis now saw something in Jud's eyes that told him the old man knew it. Louis thought of what he had seen – or thought he had seen – in Jud's eyes the night before. That capering, gleeful thing. He remembered thinking that Jud's decision to take Louis and Ellie's cat on that particular night journey had not entirely been Jud's own.

If not his, then whose? his mind asked. And because he had no answer, Louis swept the uncomfortable question away.

'I buried Spot and built the cairn,' Jud went on flatly, 'and by the time I was done, Stanny B. was fast asleep. I had to shake the hell out of him to get him going again, but by the time we got down those forty-four stairs—'

'Forty-five,' Louis murmured.

Jud nodded. 'Yeah, that's right, ain't it? Forty-five. By the time we got down those forty-five stairs, he was walking as steady as if he was sober again. We went back through the swamp and the woods and over the deadfall and finally we crossed the road and we was at my house again. It seemed to me like ten hours must have gone past, but it was still full dark.

"What happens now?" I ask Stanny B. "Now you wait and see what may happen," Stanny says, and off he walks, staggering and lurching again. I imagine he slept out in the back of the livery that night, and as things turned out, my dog Spot outlived Stanny B. by two years. His liver went bad and poisoned him, and two little kids found him out the back of the livery on July Fourth, 1912, stiff as a poker.

'But me, that night, I just climbed back up the ivy and got into bed and fell asleep almost as soon as my head touched the pillow.

'Next morning I didn't get up until almost nine o'clock, and then my mother was calling me. My dad worked on the railroad, and he would have been gone since six.' Jud paused, thinking. 'My mother wasn't just calling me, Louis. She was *screaming* for me.'

Jud went to the fridge, got himself a Miller's, and opened it on the drawer-handle below the breadbox and toaster. His face looked yellow in the overhead light, the color of nicotine. He drained half his beer, uttered a belch like a gunshot, and then glanced down the hall toward the room where Norma slept. He looked back at Louis.

'This is hard for me to talk about,' he said. 'I have turned it over in my mind, years and years, but I've never told anyone about it. Others knew what had happened, but they never talked to me about it. The way it is about sex, I guess. I'm telling you, Louis, because you've got a different kind of pet now. Not necessarily a dangerous one, but . . . different. Do you find that's true?'

Louis thought of Church jumping awkwardly off the toilet seat, his haunches thudding against the side of the tub; he thought of those muddy eyes that were almost but not quite stupid staring into his own.

At last he nodded.

'When I got downstairs, my mother was backed into a corner in the pantry between our icebox and one of the counters. There was a bunch of white stuff on the floor – curtains she'd been meaning to hang. Standing in the doorway of the pantry was Spot, my dog. There was dirt all over him, and mud splashed clear up his legs. The fur on his belly was filthy, all knotted and snarled. He was just standing there – not growling or nothing – just standing there, but it was pretty clear that he had backed her into a corner, whether he meant to or not. She was in terror, Louis. I don't know how you felt about your parents, but I know how I felt about mine: I loved them both dearly. Knowing I'd done something to put my own mother in terror kind of took away any joy I might have felt when I saw Spot standing there. I didn't even seem to feel surprised that he was there.'

'I know the feeling,' Louis said. 'When I saw Church this morning, I just . . . it seemed like something that was—' He paused a moment. *Perfectly natural?* Those were the words that came immediately to mind, but they were not the right words. '—Like something that was *meant.*'

'Yes,' Jud said. He lit a fresh cigarette. His hands were shaking the smallest bit. 'And my mother seen me there, still in my underwear, and she screams at me, "Feed your dog, Jud, your dog needs to be fed, get him out of here before he messes the curtains!"'

'So I found him some scraps and called him, and at first he didn't come, at first it was like he didn't know his own name, and I almost thought, Well, this ain't Spot at all, it's some stray that *looks* like Spot, that's all—'

'*Yes!*' Louis exclaimed so abruptly that he startled himself.

Jud nodded. 'But the second or third time I called him, he came. He sort of *jerked* toward me, and when I led him out on to the porch, damned if he didn't run right into the side of the door and just about fall over. He ate the scraps, though; just wolfed them down. By then I was over my first fright, and was starting to get an idea of what had happened. I got on my knees and hugged him, I was so glad to see him. For just one second it scared me to be hugging him, and – I think I must have imagined this, but – I thought he growled. For just a second. Then he licked my face, and . . .'

Jud shuddered and finished his beer.

'Louis, his tongue was *cold*. Being licked by Spot was like getting rubbed up the side of your face with a dead carp.'

For a moment neither of them spoke and then Louis said, 'Go on.'

'He ate and when he was done, I got an old tub we kept for him out from under the back porch and I gave him a bath. Spot always hated to have a bath, usually it took both me and my dad to do it, and we'd end up with our shirts off and our pants soaked, my dad cussing and Spot looking sort of ashamed, the way dogs do. And more likely than not he'd roll around in the dirt right after and then go over by my mother's clothesline to shake off and put dirt all over the sheets she had hung and she'd scream at both of us that she was going to shoot that dog for a stranger before she got much older.

'But that day Spot just sat in the tub and let me wash him. He never moved at all. I didn't like it. It was like . . . like washing meat. I got an old piece of towel after I gave him his bath and dried him all off. I could see all the places where the barbed wire had hooked him – there was no fur in any of those places, and the flesh looked dimpled in. It is the way an old wound looks after it's been healed five years and more, if you've ever seen one of those.'

Louis nodded. In his line of work, he had seen such things

from time to time. The wound never seemed to fill in completely, and that made him think of graves and his days as an undertaker's apprentice, and how there was never enough dirt to fill them in again.

'Then I saw his head. There was another of those dimples there, but the fur had grown back white in a little circle. It was near his ear.'

'Where your father shot him,' Louis said.

Jud nodded and said, 'Ayuh.'

'Shooting a man or an animal in the head isn't as sure-fire as it sounds, Jud. There are would-be suicides in vegetable wards getting fed through tubes or walking around today right as rain who didn't know that a bullet can strike the skull-plate and travel right around it in a semi-circle, exiting the other side without ever penetrating the brain. I personally saw one case where a fellow shot himself above the right ear and died because the bullet went around his head and tore open his jugular vein on the other side . . . in his neck. That bullet-path looked like a county road-map.'

Jud smiled and nodded. 'I remember reading somethin' like that in one of Norma's newspapers, the *Star* or the *Enquirer*, one of those. But if my pop said Spot was gone, Louis, he was gone.'

'All right,' Louis said.

'Was your daughter's cat gone?'

'I sure thought he was,' Louis said.

'You got to do better than that. You're a doctor.'

'You make it sound like "You got to do better than that, Louis, you're God." I'm not God. It was dark—'

'Sure, it was dark, and his head swivelled on his neck like it was full of ball bearings, and when you moved him, he *pulled* out of the frost, Louis — sounded like a piece of sticky-tape comin' off a letter. Live things don't do that. You only stop meltin' the frost under where you're layin' when you're dead.'

In the other room, the clock struck ten-thirty.

'What did your father say when he came home and saw the dog?' Louis asked curiously.

'I was out in the driveway, shooting marbles in the dirt, more or less waitin' for him. I felt like I always felt when I'd done something wrong and knew I was probably gonna get a spankin'. He come in through the gateposts about eight o'clock, wearin' his bib overalls and his pillow-tick cap ... you ever seen one of those?'

Louis nodded, then stifled a yawn with the back of his hand.

'Yeah, gettin' late,' Jud said. 'Got to finish this up.'

'It's not that late,' Louis said. 'I'm just a few beers ahead of my usual pace. Go on, Jud. Take your time. I want to hear this.'

'My dad had an old lard-tin he kept his dinner in,' Jud said, 'and he come in through the gate swingin' it, empty, by the handle, you know. Whistlin' somethin'. It was gettin' dark but he seen me there in the gloom and he says, "Hi there, Judkins!" like he would do, and then "Where's your—"

'He got that far and then here comes Spot out of the dark, not runnin' like he usually did, ready to jump all over him he was so glad to see him, but just walkin', waggin' his tail, and my dad dropped that lard-bucket and stepped back. I don't know b'what he would have turned tail and run except his back hit the picket fence and then he just stood there, looking at the dog. And when Spot did jump up, dad just caught his paws and held them, like you might hold a lady's hands you was gettin' ready to dance with. He looked at the dog for a long time and then he looked at me, and he said, "He needs a bath, Jud. He stinks of the ground you buried him in." And then he went in the house.'

'What did you do?' Louis asked.

'Gave him another bath. He just sat there in the tub and took it again. And when I went in the house my mother had gone to bed, even though it wasn't even nine o'clock. My dad said, "We got to talk, Judkins." And I sat down across from him and he talked to me like a man for the first time in my life, with the smell of the honeysuckle coming across the road from what's your house now and the smell of the wild roses from our own house.' Jud Crandall sighed. 'I had always thought it would be good to have him talk to me that way, but it wasn't. It wasn't a bit good. All this tonight, Louis – it's like when you look into a mirror that's been set up right across from another mirror and you can see yourself going down a whole hall of mirrors. How many times has this story been passed along, I wonder? A story that's just the same, except for the names? And that's like the sex-thing too, isn't it?'

'Your dad knew all about it?'

'Ayuh. "Who took you up there, Jud?" he asked me, and I told him. He just nodded like it was what he would have expected. I guess it prob'ly was, although I found out later that there were six or eight people in Ludlow at that time that could have taken me up there. I guess he knew that Stanny B. was the only one crazy enough to have told me.'

'Did you ask him why he didn't take you, Jud?'

'I did,' Jud said. 'Somewhere during that long talk I did ask him that. And he said it was a bad place, by and large, and that it didn't often do anything good for people who had lost their animals or for the animals themselves. He asked me if I liked Spot the way he was, and do you know, Louis, I had the hardest time answering that . . . and it's important that I tell you my feelings on that, because sooner or later you're going to ask me why I led you up there with your daughter's cat if it was a bad thing to do. Isn't that so?'

Louis nodded. What was Ellie going to think about Church when she got back? That had been much on his mind while he and Steve Masterton had been playing racquetball that afternoon.

'Maybe I did it because kids need to know that sometimes death is better,' Jud said with some difficulty. 'That's somethin' your Ellie don't know, and I got a feelin' that maybe she don't know because your wife don't know. Now, you go ahead and tell me if I'm wrong, and we'll leave it.'

Louis opened his mouth, then closed it again.

Jud went on, now speaking very slowly, appearing to move from word to word as they had moved from hummock to hummock in Little God Swamp the night before.

'I've seen it happen over the years,' he said. 'I guess I told you that Lester Morgan buried his prize bull up there. Black Angus bull named Hanratty. Ain't that a silly name for a bull? Died of some sort of ulcer inside and Lester dragged him all the way up there on a sledge. How he did it — how he got over the deadfall there I dunno — but it's said that what you want to do, you can. And at least as far as that burying ground goes, I'd say it's true.

'Well, Hanratty came back, but Lester shot him dead two weeks later. That bull turned mean, really mean. But he's the only animal I ever heard of that did. Most of them just seem . . . a little stupid . . . a little slow . . . a little . . .'

'A little dead?'

'Yeah,' Jud said. 'A little dead. A little strange. Like they had been . . . somewhere . . . and came back . . . but not all the way. Now, your daughter isn't going to know that, Louis. Not that her cat was hit by a car, and killed, and came back. So you could say you can't teach a child a lesson unless the child knows there's a lesson to be learned. Except . . .'

'Except sometimes you can,' Louis said, more to himself than to Jud.

'Yes,' Jud agreed. 'Sometimes you can. She's going to know that something is wrong and that Church was better before. Maybe she'll learn something about what death really is, which is where the pain stops and the good memories begin. Not the end of life, but the end of pain. You don't tell her those things; she will figure them out on her own.

'And if she's anything like me, she'll go on loving her pet. It won't turn vicious, or bite, or anything like that. She'll go on loving it . . . but she'll draw her own conclusions . . . and she'll breathe a sigh of relief when it finally dies.'

'That's why you took me up there,' Louis said. He felt better now. He had an explanation. It was a little diffuse, and it relied more upon the logic of the nerve-endings than the logic of the rational mind, but under the circumstances, he found he could accept that. And it meant he could forget the expression he thought he had seen on Jud's face briefly last night – that dark, capering glee. 'Okay, that's —'

Abruptly, almost shockingly, Jud covered his face with both hands. For one moment Louis thought he had been struck by a sudden pain and he half-rose, concerned, until he saw the convulsive heave of the chest and he realized that the old man was struggling not to cry.

'That's why, but it ain't why,' he said in a strangled, choked voice. 'I did it for the same reason Stanny B. did it, and for the same reason Lester Morgan did it. Lester took Linda Lavesque up there after her dog got run over in the road. He took her up there even though he had to put his goddam bull out of its misery for chasing kids through its pasture like it was mad. He did it anyway, he did it *anyway*, Louis,' Jud almost moaned, 'and what the *Christ* do you make of that!'

'Jud, what are you talking about?' Louis asked, alarmed.

'Lester did it and Stanny did it for the same reason I did it. You do it because it gets hold of you. You do it because that burial place is a secret place and you want to share the secret and when you find a reason that seems good enough, why . . .' Jud took his hands away from his face and looked at Louis with eyes that seemed incredibly ancient, incredibly haggard. 'Why then you just go ahead and do it. You make up reasons . . . they seem like good reasons . . . but mostly you do it because you want to. Or because you have to. My dad, he didn't take me up there because he'd heard about it but he'd never *been*. Stanny B. had been up there . . . and he took me . . . and seventy years go by . . . and then . . . all at once . . .'

Jud shook his head and coughed dryly into the palm of his hand.

'Listen,' he said. 'Listen, Louis. Lester's bull was the only damn animal I ever knew of that turned really mean. I b'lieve that Missus Lavesque's little chow might have bit the postman once, after, and I heard a few other things . . . animals that got a little nasty . . . but Spot was always a good dog. He always smelled like dirt, it didn't matter how many times you washed him, he always smelled like dirt, but he was a good dog. My mother would never touch him afterwards, but he was a good dog just the same. But Louis, if you was to take your cat out tonight and kill it, I would never say a word.

'That place . . . all at once it gets hold of you . . . and you make up the sweetest-smelling reasons in the world . . . but I could have been wrong, Louis. That's all I'm saying. Lester could have been wrong. Stanny B. could have been wrong. Hell, I ain't God, either. But bringing the dead back to life . . . that's about as close to playing God as you can get, ain't it?'

Louis opened his mouth again, then closed it again. What would have come out would have sounded wrong, wrong and cruel: *Jud, I didn't go through all of that just to kill the damn cat again.*

Jud drained his beer and then put it carefully aside with the other empties. 'I guess that's it,' he said. 'I am talked out.'

'Can I ask you one other question?' Louis asked.

'I guess so,' Jud said.

Louis said: 'Has anyone ever buried a *person* up there?'

Jud's arm jerked convulsively; two of the beer-bottles fell off the table, and one of them shattered.

'Christ on His throne,' he said to Louis. '*No!* And who ever would? You don't even want to talk about such things, Louis!'

'I was just curious,' Louis said uneasily.

'Some things it don't pay to be curious about,' Jud Crandall said, and for the first time he looked really old and infirm to

Louis Creed; standing somewhere in the neighborhood of his own freshly prepared grave.

And later, at home, something else occurred to him about how Jud had looked at that moment.

He had looked like he was lying.

CHAPTER TWENTY-SEVEN

Louis didn't really know he was drunk until he got back in his own garage.

Outside there was starlight and a chilly rind of moon. Not enough light to cast a shadow, but enough to see by. Once he got in the garage, he was blind. There was a light-switch somewhere, but he was damned if he could remember any-more just where it was. He felt his way along slowly, shuffling his feet, his head swimming, anticipating a painful crack on the knee or a toy that he would stumble over, frightening himself with its crash, perhaps falling over himself. Ellie's little Schwinn with its red training wheels. Gage's Crawly-Gator.

Where was the cat? Had he left him in?

Somehow he sailed off course and ran into the wall. A splinter whispered into one palm and he cried out 'Shit!' to the darkness, realizing after the word was out that it sounded more scared than mad. The whole garage seemed to have taken a stealthy half-turn. Now it wasn't just the light-switch; now he didn't know where the fuck *anything* was, and that included the door into the kitchen.

He began walking again, moving slowly, his palm stinging. *This is what it would be like to be blind*, he thought, and that made him think of a Stevie Wonder concert he and Rachel had gone to — when? six years ago? As impossible as it seemed, it had to be. She had been pregnant with Ellie then. Two guys had led Wonder to his synthesizer, guiding him over the cables that snaked across the stage so he wouldn't stumble. And later, when he had gotten up to dance with one of the back-up singers, she had led him carefully to a clear place on the floor. He had danced well, Louis remembered thinking.

He had danced well, but he had needed a hand to lead him to the space where he could do it.

How about a hand right now to lead me to my kitchen door? he thought . . . and abruptly shuddered.

If a hand came out of the darkness now to lead him, how he would scream — scream and scream and scream.

He stood still, heart thudding. *Come on*, he told himself. *Stop this shit, come on, come on—*

Where was that fucking cat?

Then he *did* slam into something, the rear bumper of his Civic, and the pain sang up his body from his barked shin, making his eyes water. He grabbed his leg and rubbed it, standing one-legged like a heron, but at least he knew where he was now, the geography of the garage fixed firmly in his mind again, and besides, his night-vision was coming, good old visual purple. He had left the cat in, he remembered that now, hadn't really wanted to touch it, to pick it up and put it out and—

And that was when Church's hot, furry body oiled against his ankle like a low eddy of hot water, followed by its loathsome tail, curling against his calf like a clutching snake, and then Louis did scream; he opened his mouth wide and screamed.

CHAPTER TWENTY-EIGHT

'*Daddy!*' Ellie screamed.

She ran up the jetway toward him, weaving in and out between deplaning passengers like a quarterback on a keeper play. Most of them stood aside, grinning. Louis was a little embarrassed by her ardor, but he felt a large, stupid grin spreading across his own face just the same.

Rachel was carrying Gage in her arms, and he saw Louis when Ellie shouted. '*Dayeee!*' he yelled exuberantly, and began to wriggle in Rachel's arms. She smiled (a trifle wearily, Louis thought) and set him on his feet. He began to run after Ellie, his sturdy legs pumping busily. '*Dayee! Dayee!*'

Louis had time to notice that Gage was wearing a jumper he had never seen before – it looked like more of Grandda's work to Louis. Then Ellie hurtled into him and shinnied up him like a tree.

'Hi, Daddy!' she bellowed, and smacked his cheek so heartily that his ear actually rang for the next fifteen minutes.

'Hi, hon,' he said, and bent over to catch Gage. He pulled him up into the crook of his arm and hugged them both. 'I'm glad to see you back.'

Rachel came up then, her travelling bag and pocket-book slung over one arm, Gage's diaper bag (I'LL BE A BIG BOY SOON was printed on the side, a sentiment probably more meant to cheer up the parents than the diaper-wearing child) slung over the other. She looked like a professional photographer at the end of a long, gruelling assignment.

Louis bent between his two kids and planted a kiss on her mouth. 'Hi.'

'Hi, doc,' she said, and smiled.

'You look beat.'

'I *am* beat. We got as far as Boston with no problem. We changed planes with no problem. We took off with no problem. But as the plane is banking over the city, Gage looks down and says, "Pretty, pretty," and then whoopses all over himself.'

Louis groaned. 'Oh, Jesus.'

'I got him changed in the toilet,' she said. 'I don't think it's a virus, or anything. He was just airsick.'

'Come on home,' Louis said. 'I've got chilli on the stove.'

'*Chilli! Chilli!*' Ellie screamed in Louis's ear, transported with delight and excitement.

'*Chiwwi! Chiwwi!*' Gage screamed in Louis's other ear, which at least equalized the ringing.

'Come on,' Louis said. 'Let's get your suitcases and blow this joint.'

'Daddy, how's Church?' Ellie asked as he set her down. It was a question Louis had expected, but not Ellie's suddenly anxious face, and the deep worry-line that appeared between her dark blue eyes. Louis frowned, then glanced at Rachel.

'She woke up screaming over the weekend,' Rachel said quietly. 'She had a nightmare.'

'I dreamed that Church got run over,' Ellie said.

'Too many turkey sandwiches after the big day, that's my guess,' Rachel said. 'She had a bout of diarrhea, too. Set her mind at rest, Louis, and let's get out of this airport. I've seen enough airports in the last week to last me for at least five years.'

'Why, Church is fine, honey,' Louis said slowly.

Yes, he's fine. He lies around the house all day long and looks at you with those strange, muddy eyes – as if he'd seen something that had blasted away most of whatever intelligence a cat has. He's just great. I put him out with a broom at night because I don't like to touch him. I just kind of sweep at him with it and he goes. And the other day when I opened the door, Ellie, he had a mouse – or what was left of it. He'd strewed the guts hell to breakfast. And speaking of breakfast, I skipped mine that morning. Otherwise—

'He's just fine.'

'Oh,' Ellie said, and that furrow between her eyes smoothed out. 'Oh, that's good. When I had that dream, I was sure he was dead.'

'Were you?' Louis asked, and smiled. 'Dreams are funny, aren't they?'

'*Dweems!*' Gage hollered – he had reached that parrot-stage that Louis remembered from Ellie's development. '*Dweeeeeems!*' He gave Louis's hair a tug hearty enough to make his eyes water.

'Come on, gang,' Louis said, and they started down to the baggage area.

They had gotten as far as the car in the parking lot when Gage began saying 'Pretty, pretty,' in a strange, hiccupping voice. This time he whoopsed all over Louis, who had put on his new pair of double-knit slacks for the plane-meeting occasion. Apparently Gage thought *pretty* was the code-word for *I've got to throw up now, so sorry, stand clear.*

It turned out to be a virus after all.

By the time they had driven the seventeen miles from the Bangor airport to their house in Ludlow, Gage had begun to show signs of fever and had fallen into an uncomfortable doze. Louis backed into the garage, and out of the corner of his eye he saw Church slink along one wall, tail up, strange eyes fixed on the car. He disappeared into the dying glow of the day, and a moment later Louis saw another disembowelled mouse lying beside a stack of four summer tires – he had had the snows put on while Rachel and the kids were gone. The mouse's innards glowed pink and raw in the garage's gloom. Its head was missing.

Louis got out quickly and purposely bumped against the pile of tires, which were stacked up like black checkers. The top two fell over and covered the mouse. 'Ooops,' he said.

'You're a spaz, Daddy,' Ellie said, not unkindly.

'That's right,' Louis said with a kind of hectic cheer. He felt a little like saying *Pretty, pretty* and blowing his groceries all over everything. 'Daddy's a spaz.' He could not remember Church ever killing a single mouse before his queer resurrection; he sometimes cornered them and played with them in that deadly cat way that ultimately ended in destruction, but he or Ellie or Rachel had always intervened before the end. And once cats were fixed, he knew, few of them would do more than give a mouse an interested stare, at least as long as they were well-fed.

'Are you going to stand there dreaming or help me with this kid?' Rachel asked. 'Come back from Planet Mongo, Dr Creed. Earth-people need you.' She sounded tired and irritable.

'I'm sorry, babe,' Louis said. He came around to get Gage, who was now as hot as the coals in a banked stove.

So only the three of them ate Louis's famous South Side Chilli that night; Gage reclined on the living-room sofa, feverish and apathetic, drinking a bottle filled with lukewarm chicken-broth and watching a cartoon show on TV.

After dinner Ellie went to the garage door and called Church. Louis, who was doing the dishes while Rachel unpacked upstairs, hoped the cat wouldn't come, but he did – he came walking in his new slow lurch, and he came almost at once, as if he – as if *it* – had been lurking out there. *Lurking.* The word came immediately to mind.

'Church!' Ellie cried. 'Hi, Church!' She picked the cat up and hugged it. Louis watched out of the corner of his eye; his hands, which had been groping on the bottom of the sink for any left-over silverware, were still. He saw Ellie's happy face change slowly to puzzlement. The cat lay quiet in her arms, its ears laid back, its eyes on hers.

After a long moment – it seemed *very* long to Louis – she put Church down. The cat padded away toward the dining room without looking back. *Executioner of small mice*, Louis thought randomly. *Christ, what did we do that night?*

He tried honestly to remember but it already seemed far away, dim and distant, like the messy death of Victor Pascow on the floor of the infirmary's reception room. He could remember carriages of wind passing in the sky, and the white glimmer of snow in the back field which rose to the woods. That was all.

'Daddy?' Ellie said in a low, subdued voice.

'What, Ellie?'

'Church smells funny.'

'Does he?' Louis asked, his voice carefully neutral.

'Yes!' Ellie said, distressed. 'Yes, he does! He never smelled funny before! He smells like . . . he smells like *ka-ka!*'

'Well, maybe he rolled in something bad, honey,' Louis said. 'Whatever that bad smell is, he'll lose it.'

'I certainly *hope* so,' Ellie said in a comical dowager's voice. She walked off.

Louis found the last fork, washed it and pulled the plug. He stood at the sink, looking out into the night while the soapy water ran down the drain with a thick chuckling sound.

When the sound from the drain was gone he could hear the wind outside, thin and wild, coming from the north, bringing down winter, and he realized he was afraid, simply, stupidly afraid, the way you are afraid when a cloud suddenly sails across the sun and somewhere you hear a ticking sound you can't account for.

'A hundred and *three*?' Rachel asked. 'Jesus, Lou! Are you sure?'

'It's a virus,' Louis said. He tried not to let Rachel's voice, which seemed almost accusatory, grate on him. She was tired. It had been a long day for her, she had crossed half the country with her kids today, here it was eleven o'clock, and the day wasn't over yet. Ellie was deeply asleep in her room. Gage was on their bed in a state that could best be described as semi-conscious. Louis had started him on Liquiprin an hour ago. 'The aspirin will bring his fever down by morning, hon.'

'Aren't you going to give him ampicillin, or anything?'

Patiently, Louis said, 'If he had the flu or a strep infection, I would. He doesn't. He's got a virus, and that stuff doesn't do doodly-squat for viruses. It would just give him the runs and dehydrate him more.'

'Are you *sure* it's a virus?'

'Well, if you want a second opinion,' Louis snapped, 'be my guest.'

'You don't have to shout at me!' Rachel shouted.

'I wasn't shouting!' Louis shouted back.

'You *were*,' Rachel began, 'you *were* shuh-shuh-shouting—' And then her mouth began to quiver and she put a hand up to her face. Louis saw there were deep gray-brown pockets under her eyes and felt badly ashamed of himself.

'I'm sorry,' he said, and sat down beside her. 'Christ, I don't know what's the matter with me. I apologize, Rachel.'

'Never complain, never explain,' she said, smiling wanly. 'Isn't that what you told me once? The trip was a strain. And I've been afraid you'd hit the roof when you looked in Gage's dresser drawers. I guess maybe I ought to tell you now, while you're feeling sorry for me.'

'What's to hit the roof about?'

She smiled wanly. 'My mother and father bought him ten new outfits. He was wearing one of them today.'

'I noticed he had on something new,' he said shortly.

'I noticed you noticing,' she replied, and pulled a comic scowl that made him laugh, although he didn't feel much like laughing. 'And six new dresses for Ellie.'

'Six dresses!' he said, strangling the urge to yell. He was suddenly furious – sickly furious and hurt in a way he couldn't explain. 'Rachel, *why*? Why did you let him do that? We don't need . . . we can buy . . .'

He ceased. His rage had made him inarticulate, and for a moment he saw himself carrying Ellie's dead cat through the woods, shifting the plastic bag from one hand to the other . . . and all the while Irwin Goldman, that dirty old fuck from Lake

192

Forest, had been busy trying to buy his daughter's affection by unlimbering the world-famous checkbook and the world-famous fountain pen.

For one moment he felt himself on the verge of shouting: *He bought her six dresses and I brought her goddam cat back from the dead, so who loves her more?*

He clamped down on the words. He would never say anything like that. *Never.*

She touched his neck gently. 'Louis,' she said. 'It was both of them together. Please try to see. *Please.* They love the children, and they don't see them much. And they're getting *old.* Louis, you'd hardly recognize my father. Really.'

'I'd recognize him,' Louis muttered.

'Please, honey. Try to see. Try to be kind. It doesn't hurt you.'

He looked at her for a long time. 'It does, though,' he said finally. 'Maybe it shouldn't, but it does.'

She opened her mouth to reply, and then Ellie called out from her room: '*Daddy! Mommy! Somebody!*'

Rachel started to get up, and Louis pulled her back down. 'Stay with Gage. I'll go.' He thought he knew what the trouble was. But he had put the cat out, damn it; after Ellie had gone to bed he had caught it in the kitchen sniffing around its dish and had put it out. He didn't want the cat sleeping with her. Not any more. Odd thoughts of disease, mingled with memories of Uncle Carl's funeral parlor, had come to him when he thought of Church sleeping on Ellie's bed.

She's going to know that something's wrong and Church was better before.

He had put the cat out but when he went in, Ellie was sitting up in bed, more asleep than awake, and Church was spread out on the counterpane, a batlike shadow. The cat's eyes were open and stupidly gleaming in the light from the hall.

'Daddy, put him out,' Ellie almost groaned. 'He stinks *so bad.*'

'Shhh, Ellie, go to sleep,' Louis said, astounded by the calmness of his own voice. It made him think of the morning after his sleepwalking incident, the day after Pascow had died. Getting to the infirmary and ducking into the bathroom to look at himself in the mirror, convinced that he must look like hell. But he had looked pretty much all right. It was enough to make you wonder how many people were going around with dreadful secrets bottled up inside.

It's not a secret, goddammit! It's just the cat!

But Ellie was right. It stank to high heaven.

He took the cat out of her room and carried it downstairs, trying to breathe through his mouth. There were worse smells; shit was worse, if you wanted to be perfectly blunt. A month ago they'd had a go-round with the septic tank, and as Jud had said when he came over to watch Puffer and Sons pump the tank, 'That ain't Chanel Number Five, is it Louis?' The smell of a gangrenous wound – what old Doctor Bracermunn at med school had called 'hot flesh' – was worse, too. Even the smell which came from the Civic's catalytic converter when it had been idling in the garage for a while was worse.

But this smell was pretty damn bad. And how had the cat gotten in, anyway? He had put it out earlier, sweeping it out with the broom while all three of them – his people – were upstairs. This was the first time he had actually held the cat since the day it had come back, almost a week ago. It lay hotly in his arms, like a quiescent disease, and Louis wondered: *What bolthole did you find, you bastard?*

He thought suddenly of his dream that night – Pascow simply passing through the door between the kitchen and the garage.

Maybe there was no bolthole. Maybe it had just passed through the door, like a ghost.

'Bag that,' he whispered aloud, and his voice was slightly hoarse.

Louis became suddenly sure that the cat would begin to struggle in his arms, that it would scratch him. But Church lay totally still, radiating that stupid heat and that dirty stink, looking at Louis's face as if he could read the thoughts going on behind Louis's eyes.

He opened the door and tossed the cat out into the garage, maybe a little too hard. 'Go on,' he said. 'Kill another mouse, or something.'

Church landed awkwardly, his hindquarters bunching beneath him and then collapsing. It seemed to shoot Louis a look of green, ugly hate. Then it strolled drunkenly off and was gone.

Christ, Jud, he thought, *but I wish you'd kept your mouth shut.*

He went to the sink and washed his hands and forearms vigorously, as if scrubbing for an operation. *You do it because it gets hold of you . . . you make up reasons . . . they seem like good reasons . . . but mostly you do it because once you've been up there, it's your place, and you belong to it . . . and you make up the sweetest-smelling reasons in the world . . .*

No, he couldn't blame Jud. He had gone of his own free will and he couldn't blame Jud.

He turned off the water and began to dry his hands and arms. And suddenly the towel stopped moving and he stared straight ahead, looking out into the little piece of night framed in the window over the sink.

Does that mean it's my place now? That it's mine, too?

No. Not if I don't want it to be.

He slung the towel over the rack and went upstairs.

Rachel was in bed, the covers pulled up to her chin, and Gage was tucked in neatly beside her. She looked at Louis apologetically. 'Would you mind, hon? Just for tonight? I'd feel better having him with me. He's so *hot*.'

'No,' Louis said. 'That's fine. I'll pull out the hide-a-bed downstairs.'

'You really don't mind?'

'No. It won't hurt Gage, and it'll make you feel better.' He paused, then smiled. 'You're going to pick up his virus, though. That comes almost guaranteed. I don't suppose that changes your mind, does it?'

She smiled back and shook her head. 'What was Ellie fussing about?'

'Church. She wanted me to take Church away.'

'*Ellie* wanted Church taken *away*? That's a switch.'

'Yeah, it is,' Louis agreed, and then added: 'She said he smelled bad, and I did think he was a little fragrant. Maybe he rolled in a pile of someone's mulch, or something.'

'That's too bad,' Rachel said, rolling over on her side. 'I really think Ellie missed Church as much as she missed you.'

'Uh-huh,' Louis said. He bent and kissed her mouth softly. 'Go to sleep, Rachel.'

'I love you, Lou. I'm glad to be home. And I'm sorry about the couch. We'll do something tomorrow night, okay? Make some whoopee?'

'Sure,' Louis said, and turned out the light.

Downstairs, he stacked the couch cushions, pulled out the hide-a-bed, and tried to prepare himself mentally for a night of having the rod under the thin mattress dig into the small of his back. The bed was sheeted, at least; he wouldn't have to make it up from scratch. Louis got two blankets from the top shelf in the front hall closet and spread them on the bed. He began to undress, then paused.

You think he's in again? Fine. Take a walk around and have a look. Like you told Rachel, it won't hurt. May even help. And checking to make sure all the doors are on the latch won't even catch you a virus.

He took a deliberate tour of the entire downstairs, checking the locks on doors and windows. He had done everything right the first time, and Church was nowhere to be seen.

'There,' he said. 'Let's see you get in tonight, you dumb cat.' He followed this with a mental wish that Church would freeze his balls off. Except that Church of course no longer had any.

He switched off the lights and got into bed. The rod started to press into his back almost immediately, and Louis was thinking he would be awake half the night when he fell asleep. He fell asleep resting uncomfortably on his side in the hide-a-bed but when he woke up he was—

—*in the burying ground beyond the Pet Sematary again. This time he was alone. He had killed Church himself this time, and then had decided for some reason to bring him back to life a second time. God knew why: Louis didn't. He had buried Church deeper this time, though, and Church couldn't dig his way out. Louis could hear the cat crying somewhere under the earth, making a sound like a weeping child. The sound came up through the pores of the ground, through its stony flesh; the sound and the smell, that awful sickish-sweet smell of rot and decay. Just breathing it in made his chest feel heavy, as if a weight was on it.*

The crying . . . the crying . . .

. . . the crying was still going on . . .

. . . and the weight was still on his chest.

'*Louis!*' It was Rachel, and she sounded alarmed. '*Louis, can you come?*'

She sounded more than alarmed; she sounded scared, and the crying had a choked, desperate quality to it. It was Gage.

He opened his eyes and stared into Church's greenish-yellow eyes. They were less than four inches from his own. The cat was on his chest, neatly curled up there like something from an old wives' tale of breath-stealing. The stink came off it in slow, noxious waves. It was purring.

Louis uttered a cry of disgust and surprise. He shot both hands out in a primitive warding-off gesture. Church thumped off the bed, landed on its side, and walked away in that stumbling lurch.

Jesus! Jesus! It was on me! Oh God, it was right on me!

His disgust could not have been greater if he had awakened to find a spider in his mouth. For a moment he thought he was going to throw up.

'*Louis!*'

He pushed the blankets back and stumbled to the stairs. Faint light spilled from their bedroom. Rachel was standing at the head of the stairs in her nightgown.

'Louis, he's vomiting again ... choking on it ... I'm scared.'

'I'm here,' he said, and came up to her, thinking: *It got in. Somehow it got in. From the cellar, probably. Maybe there's a broken cellar window. In fact there must be a broken window down there. I'll check it tomorrow when I get home. Hell, before I go to work. I'll—*

Gage stopped crying and began to make an ugly, gargling, choking sound.

'*Louis!*' Rachel screamed.

Louis moved fast. Gage was on his side and vomit was trickling out of his mouth on to an old towel Rachel had spread beside him. He was vomiting, yes, but not enough. Most of it was inside, and Gage was blushing with the onset of asphyxiation.

Louis grabbed the boy under the arms, aware in a distant way of how hot his son's armpits were under the Dr Denton suit, and put him up on his shoulder as if to burp him. Then Louis snapped himself backward, jerking Gage with him. Gage's neck whiplashed. He uttered a loud bark that was not quite a belch, and an amazing flag of almost solid vomit flew from his mouth and spattered on the floor and the dresser. Gage began to cry again, a solid, bawling sound that was music to Louis's ears. To cry like that you had to be getting an unlimited supply of oxygen.

Rachel's knees buckled and she collapsed on to the bed, head supported in her hands. She was shaking violently.

'He almost died, didn't he, Louis? He almost ch-ch-ch— oh my *God*—'

Louis walked around the room with his son in his arms. Gage's cries were tapering off to whimperings; he was already almost asleep again.

'The chances are fifty-to-one he would have cleared it himself, Rachel. I just gave him a hand.'

'But he was close,' she said. She looked up at him, and her white-ringed eyes were stunned and unbelieving. 'Louis, he was so *close*.'

Suddenly he remembered her shouting at him in the sunny kitchen: *He's not going to DIE, no one is going to DIE around here . . .*

'Honey,' Louis said, 'we're all close. All the time.'

It was milk that had almost surely caused the fresh round of vomiting. Gage had awakened around midnight, she said, an hour or so after Louis had gone to sleep, with his 'hungry cry', and Rachel had gotten him a bottle. She had drowsed off again herself while he was still taking it. About an hour later, the choking spell began.

No more milk, Louis said, and Rachel had agreed, almost humbly. No more milk.

Louis got back downstairs at around quarter of two and spent fifteen minutes hunting up the cat. During his search, he found the door which communicated between kitchen and basement standing ajar, as he suspected he would. He remembered his mother telling him about a cat that had gotten quite good at pawing open old-fashioned latches, such as the one on their cellar door. The cat would just climb the edge of the door, she'd said, and pat the thumb plate of the latch with its paw until the door opened. A cute enough trick, Louis thought, but not one he intended to allow Church to practice often. There was, after all, a lock on the cellar door, too. He found Church dozing under the stove and tossed him out of the front door without ceremony. On his way back to the hide-a-bed, he closed the cellar door again.

And this time shot the bolt.

CHAPTER TWENTY-NINE

In the morning, Gage's temperature was almost normal. His cheeks were chapped, but otherwise he was bright-eyed and full of beans. All at once, in the course of a week it seemed, his meaningless gabble had turned into a slew of words; he would imitate almost anything you said. What Ellie wanted him to say was shit.

'Say shit, Gage,' Ellie said over her oatmeal.

'Shit-Gage,' Gage responded agreeably over his own cereal. Louis allowed the cereal only on condition that Gage ate it with only a little sugar. And, as usual, Gage seemed to be shampooing with it rather than actually eating it.

Ellie dissolved into giggles.

'Say farts, Gage,' she said.

'Farz-Gage,' Gage said, grinning through the oatmeal spread across his face. 'Farz-n-shit.'

Ellie and Louis broke up. It was impossible not to.

Rachel was not so amused. 'That's enough vulgar talk for one morning, I think,' she said, handing Louis his eggs.

'Shit-n-farz-n-farz-n-shit,' Gage sang cheerily, and Ellie hid her giggles in her hands. Rachel's mouth twitched a little, and Louis thought she was looking a hundred per cent better in spite of her broken rest. A lot of it was relief, Louis supposed. Gage was better and she was home.

'Don't say that, Gage,' Rachel said.

'Pretty,' Gage said as a change of pace, and threw up all the cereal he had eaten into his bowl.

'Oh, *gross-OUT*!' Ellie screamed, and fled the table.

Louis broke up completely then. He couldn't help it. He laughed until he was crying, and cried until he was laughing again. Rachel and Gage stared at him as if he had gone crazy.

No, Louis could have told them. *I've been crazy, but I think I'm going to be all right now. I really think I am.*

He didn't know if it was over or not but it *felt* over; perhaps that would be enough.

And for a while, at least, it was.

CHAPTER THIRTY

Gage's virus hung on for a week, then cleared up. A week later he came down with a bout of bronchitis. Ellie also caught this, and then Rachel; during the period before Christmas, the three of them went around hacking like very old and wheezy hunting dogs. Louis didn't catch it, and Rachel seemed to hold this against him.

The final week of classes at the University was a hectic one for Louis, Steve, Surrendra, and Charlton. There was no flu — at least not yet — but plenty of bronchitis and several cases of mononucleosis and walking pneumonia. Two days before classes broke for Christmas, six moaning, drunken fraternity boys were brought in by their concerned friends. There were a few moments of confusion gruesomely reminiscent of the Pascow affair. All six of the damned fools had crammed into one medium-length toboggan (the sixth had actually been sitting on the shoulders of the tail-man, from what Louis could piece together) and had set off to ride the toboggan down the hill above the Steam Plant. Hilarious. Except that, after gaining a lot of speed, the toboggan had wandered off-course and struck one of the Civil War cannons. The score was two broken arms, a broken wrist, a total of seven broken ribs, a concussion, plus contusions far too numerous to count. Only the boy riding on the shoulders of the tail-ender had escaped completely unscathed. When the toboggan hit the cannon, this fortunate soul flew over it and landed head first in a snowbank. Cleaning up the human wreckage hadn't been fun, and Louis had scored all of the boys liberally with his tongue as he stitched and bandaged and stared into pupils, but telling Rachel about it later, he had laughed almost until he cried.

Rachel had looked at him strangely, not understanding what was so funny, and Louis couldn't tell her: it had been a stupid accident, and people had been hurt, but they would all walk away from it. His laughter was partly relief, but it was partly triumph, too – won one today, Louis.

The cases of bronchitis in his own family began to clear up around the time that Ellie's school broke for the holidays on December 16th, and the four of them settled down to spend a happy and old-fashioned country Christmas. The house in North Ludlow, which had seemed so strange on that day in August when they pulled into the driveway (strange and even hostile, what with Ellie cutting herself out back and Gage getting stung by a bee at almost the same time), had never seemed more like home.

After the kids were finally asleep on Christmas Eve, Louis and Rachel stole downstairs from the attic like thieves, their arms full of brightly colored boxes – a set of Matchbox racers for Gage, who had recently discovered the joys of toy cars, a Barbie and Ken for Ellie, a Turn 'n Go, an oversized trike, doll clothes, a play oven with a light-bulb inside, other stuff.

The two of them sat side by side in the glow of lights from the tree, fussing the stuff together, Rachel in a pair of silk lounging pajamas, Louis in his robe. He could not remember a more pleasant evening. There was a fire in the fireplace, and every now and then one or the other of them would rise and throw in another chunk of split birch.

Winston Churchill brushed by Louis once and he pushed the cat away with an almost absent feeling of distaste – that smell. Later he saw Church try to settle down next to Rachel's leg and Rachel also gave him a push and an impatient 'Scat!' A moment later Louis saw his wife rubbing her palm on one silk-clad thigh, the way you sometimes do when you feel you might have touched something nasty or germy. He didn't think Rachel was even aware she was doing it.

Church ambled over to the brick hearth and collapsed in front of the fire gracelessly. He had no grace at all now, it seemed; he had lost it all on that night Louis rarely allowed himself to think about any more. And he had lost something else as well. Louis had been aware of it, but it had taken him a full month to pinpoint it exactly. The cat never purred any more, and he used to have one of the loudest motors going, particularly when he was sleeping. There had been nights when he'd had to get up and close Ellie's door so he could get to sleep himself.

Now the cat slept like a stone. Like the dead.

No, he reminded himself, there was one exception. The night he had awakened on the hide-a-bed with Church curled up on his chest like a stinking blanket . . . Church had been purring that night. He had been making some sound, anyway.

But as Jud Crandall had known – or guessed – it had not been all bad. Louis found a broken window down in the cellar behind the furnace, and when the glazier fixed it, he had saved them bucks in wasted heating oil. For calling his attention to the broken pane, which he might not have discovered for weeks – even months, maybe – he supposed he even owed Church a vote of thanks.

Ellie no longer liked Church to sleep with her, that was true, but sometimes when she was watching TV she would let the cat hop up on her lap and go to sleep (but just as often, he thought, hunting through the bag of plastic widgets that were supposed to hold Ellie's Bat-Cycle together, she would push him down after a few minutes, saying, 'Go on, Church, you stink.'); she fed him regularly and with love, and even Gage was not above giving old Church an occasional tail-tug . . . more in the spirit of friendliness than in one of meanness, Louis was convinced; he was like a tiny monk yanking a furry bell-rope. At these times Church would crawl lackadaisically under one of the radiators where Gage couldn't get him,

We might have noticed more differences with a dog, Louis thought, *but cats are such goddam independent animals, anyway. Independent and odd. Fey, even.* It didn't surprise him that the old Egyptian queens and pharaohs had wanted their cats mummified and popped into their triangular tombs with them in order to serve as spirit guides in the next world. Cats were weird.

'How you doing with that Bat-Cycle, Chief?'

He held out the finished product. 'Ta-da!'

Rachel pointed at the bag, which still had three or four plastic widgets in it. 'What are those?'

'Spares,' Louis said, smiling guiltily.

'You better hope they're spares. The kid will break her rotten little neck.'

'That comes later,' Louis said maliciously. 'When she's twelve and showing off on her new skateboard.'

She groaned. 'Come on, doc, have a heart!'

Louis stood up, put his hands on the small of his back, and twisted his torso. His spine crackled. 'That's all the toys.'

'And they're all together. Remember last year?' She giggled and Louis smiled. Last year seemingly everything they'd gotten had to be assembled, and they'd been up until almost four o'clock Christmas morning, both of them finishing grouchy and out of sorts. And by mid-afternoon of Christmas, Ellie had decided the boxes were more fun than the toys.

'*Gross-OUT!*' Louis said, imitating Ellie.

'Well, come on to bed,' Rachel said, 'and I'll give you a present early.'

'Woman,' Louis said, drawing himself up to his full height, 'that is mine by right.'

'Don't you *wish*,' she said, and laughed through her hands. In that moment she looked amazingly like Ellie . . . and like Gage.

'Just a minute,' he said. 'There's one other thing I gotta do.'

He hurried into the front hall closet and brought back one of his boots. He removed the fire-screen from in front of the dying fire.

'Louis, what are you—'

'You'll see.'

On the left side of the hearth the fire was out and there was a thick bed of fluffy gray ashes. Louis stamped the boot into them, leaving a deep track. Then he tromped the boot down on the outer bricks, using it like a big rubber stamp.

'There,' he said, after he had put the boot away in the closet again. 'You like?'

Rachel was giggling again. 'Louis, Ellie's going to go *nuts*.'

During the last two weeks of school, Ellie had picked up a disquieting rumor around kindergarten, to wit, that Santa Claus was really parents. This idea had been reinforced by a rather skinny Santa at the Bangor Mall, whom Ellie had glimpsed in the Deering Ice Cream Parlor a few days ago. Santa had been sitting on a counter stool, his beard pulled to one side so he could eat a cheeseburger. This had troubled Ellie mightily (it seemed to be the cheeseburger, somehow, even more than the false beard), in spite of Rachel's assurances that the department store and Salvation Army Santas were really 'helpers', sent out by the real Santa, who was far too busy completing the inventory and reading children's last-minute letters up north to be boogying around the world on public relations jaunts.

Louis replaced the fire-screen carefully. Now there were two clear boot-tracks in their fireplace, one in the ashes and one on the brick outer hearth. They both pointed toward the Christmas tree, as if Santa had hit bottom on one foot and immediately stepped out to leave the goodies assigned to the Creed household. The illusion was perfect unless you happened to notice that they were both left feet . . . and Louis doubted if Ellie was that analytical.

'Louis Creed, I love you,' Rachel said, and kissed him.

'You married a winner, baby,' Louis said, smiling sincerely. 'Stick with me and I'll make you a star.'

'You'll make me, that's for sure.'

They started for the stairs. He pointed at the card table Ellie had set up in front of the TV. There were oatmeal cookies and two Ring-Dings on it. Also a can of Micheloeb. FOR

YOU, SANNA, the note said in Ellie's large, stick-like printing. 'You want a cookie or a Ring-Ding?'

'Ring-Ding,' she said, and ate half of it. Louis popped the tab on the beer and drank half of it.

'A beer this late is going to give me acid indigestion,' he said.

'Crap,' she said good-humoredly. 'Come on, doc.'

Louis put down the can of beer and suddenly grasped the pocket of his robe as if he had forgotten something – although he had been aware of that small packet of weight all evening long.

'Here,' he said. 'For you. You can open it now. It's after midnight. Merry Christmas, babe.'

She turned the little box, wrapped up in silver paper and tied with wide satiny-blue ribbon, in her hands. 'Louis, what is it?'

He shrugged. 'Soap. Shampoo sample. I forget, exactly.'

She opened it on the stairs, saw the Tiffany box and squealed. She pulled out the cotton batting, and then just stood there, her mouth slightly agape.

'Well?' he asked anxiously. He had never bought her a real piece of jewelry before and he was nervous. 'Do you like it?'

She took it out, draped the fine gold chain over her tented fingers, and held the tiny sapphire up to the hall light. It twirled lazily, seeming to shoot off cool blue rays.

'Oh Louis, it's so damn beautiful—' He saw she was crying a little and felt both touched and alarmed.

'Hey, babe, don't do that,' he said. 'Put it on.'

'Louis, we can't afford – you can't afford—'

'Shhh,' he said. 'I socked some money away off and on since last Christmas . . . and it wasn't as much as you might think.'

'How much was it?'

'I'll never tell you that, Rachel,' he said solemnly. 'An army of Chinese torturers couldn't get it out of me. Two thousand dollars.'

'*Two thousand – !*' She hugged him so suddenly and so tightly that he almost fell down the stairs. 'Louis, you're *crazy!*'

'Put it on,' he said again.

She did. He helped her with the clasp, and then she turned around to look at him. 'I want to go up and look at it,' she said. 'I think I want to *preen*.'

'Preen away,' he said. 'I'll put out the cat and get the lights.'

'When we make it,' she said, looking directly into his eyes, 'I want to take everything off except this.'

'Preen in a hurry, then,' Louis said, and she laughed.

He grabbed Church and draped him over his arm – he didn't bother much with the broom these days. He supposed he had almost gotten used to the cat again. He went toward the entryway door, turning off lights as he went. When he opened the door communicating between the kitchen and garage, an eddy of cold air swirled around his ankles.

'Have a merry Christmas, Ch—'

He broke off. Lying on the welcome mat was a dead crow, a big one. Its head had been mangled. One wing had been ripped off and lay behind the body like a charred piece of paper. Church immediately squirmed out of Louis's arms and began to nuzzle the frozen corpse eagerly. As Louis watched, the cat's head darted forward, its ears laid back, and before he could turn his head, Church had ripped out one of the crow's milky, glazed eyes.

Church strikes again, Louis thought a little sickly, and turned his head – not, however, before he had seen the bloody, gaping socket where the crow's eye had been. *Shouldn't bother me, shouldn't, I've seen worse, oh yeah, Pascow, for instance, Pascow was worse, a lot worse—*

But it *did* bother him. His stomach turned over. The warm build of sexual excitement had suddenly deflated. *Christ, that bird's damn near as big as he is. Must have caught it with its guard down. Way, way down.*

This would have to be cleaned up. Nobody needed this sort of present on Christmas morning. And it was his responsibility, wasn't it? Sure was. His and nobody else's. He had recognized that much in a subconscious way even on the evening of his family's return, when he had purposely spilled the tires over the tattered body of the mouse Church had killed.

The soil of a man's heart is stonier, Louis.

This thought was so clear, so somehow three-dimensional and auditory that Louis jerked a little, as if Jud had materialized at his shoulder and spoken aloud.

A man grows what he can . . . and tends it.

Church was still hunched greedily over the dead bird. He was working at the other wing now. There was a tenebrous rustling sound as Church pulled it back and forth, back and forth. Never get it off the ground, Orville. That's right, Wilbur, fucking bird's just as dead as dogshit, might as well feed it to the cat, might as well—

Louis suddenly kicked Church, kicked him hard. The cat's hindquarters rose and came down splayfooted. It walked away, sparing him another of its greenish, ugly glances. 'Eat me,' Louis hissed at it, catlike himself.

'Louis?' Rachel's voice came faintly from their bedroom. 'Coming to bed?'

'Be right there,' he called back. *I've just got this little mess to clean up, Rachel, okay? Because it's my mess.* He fumbled for the switch that controlled the garage light. He went quickly back to the cupboard under the kitchen sink and got a green Hefty Bag . . . the similarity to that other night was not lost on him. He took the bag back into the garage and took the shovel down from its nail on the garage wall. He shoveled up the crow and dropped it into the bag. Then he shoveled up the severed wing and slipped that in. He tied a knot in the top of the bag and dropped it into the trashbin on the far side of the Civic. By the time he finished, his ankles were growing numb.

Church was standing by the garage doorway. Louis made

a threatening gesture at the cat with the shovel, and it was gone like an eddy of water.

Upstairs, Rachel was lying on her bed, wearing nothing but the sapphire on its chain . . . as promised. She smiled at him lazily. 'What took you so long, Chief?'

'The light over the sink was out,' Louis said. 'I changed the bulb.'

'Come here,' she said, and tugged him gently toward her. Not by the hand. 'He knows if you've been sleeping,' she sang softly; a little smile curved up the corners of her lips. 'He knows if you're awake . . . oh my, Louis dear, what's this?'

'Something that just woke up, I think,' Louis said, slipping off his robe. 'Maybe we ought to see if we can get it to sleep before Santa comes, what do you think?'

She rose on one elbow; he felt her breath, warm and sweet.

'He knows if you've been bad or good . . . so be good . . . for goodness' sake . . . have you been a good boy, Louis?'

'I think so,' he said. His voice was not quite steady.

'Let's see if you taste as good as you look,' she said. 'Mmmmm . . .'

It seemed that he did.

The sex was good, but Louis did not find himself simply slipping off afterwards as he usually did when the sex was good – slipping off easy with himself, his wife, his life. He lay in the darkness of Christmas morning, listening to Rachel's breathing slow and deep, and he thought about the dead bird on the doorstep. Church's Christmas present to him.

Keep me in mind, Dr Creed. I was alive and then I was dead and now I'm alive again. I've made the circuit and I'm here to tell you that you come out the other side with your purr-box broken and a taste for the hunt. I'm here to tell you that a man grows what he can and tends it. Don't forget that, Dr Creed. I'm part of what your heart will grow now, there's your wife and your daughter and your son . . . and there's me. Remember the secret, and tend your garden well.

At some point, Louis slept.

CHAPTER THIRTY-ONE

So their winter passed. Ellie's faith in Santa Claus was restored – temporarily at least – by the footprints in the hearth. Gage opened his presents splendidly, pausing every now and then to munch a particularly tasty-looking piece of wrapping paper. And that year, *both* kids had decided by mid-afternoon that the boxes were more fun than the toys.

The Crandalls came over on New Year's Eve for Rachel's eggnog, and Louis found himself mentally examining Norma. She had a pale and somehow transparent look that he had seen before. His grandmother would have said Norma was beginning to 'fail', and that was perhaps not such a bad word for it. All at once her hands, so swollen and misshapen by arthritis, seemed covered with liver-spots. Her hair looked thinner. The Crandalls went home around ten, and the Creeds saw the New Year in together in front of the TV. It was the last time Norma was in their house.

Most of Louis's semester break was sloppy and rainy. In terms of heating costs, he was grateful for the protracted thaw, but the weather was still depressing and dismal. He worked around the house, building bookshelves and cupboards for his wife. By the time classes resumed on January 23rd, Louis was happy to go back to the University.

The flu finally arrived – a fairly serious outbreak of it struck the campus less than a week after the spring semester had begun, and he had his hands full – he found himself working ten and sometimes twelve hours a day and going home utterly whipped . . . but not really unhappy.

The warm spell broke on January 29th with a roar. There was a blizzard followed by a week of numbing sub-zero weather. Louis was checking the mending broken arm of a young man who was hoping desperately — and fruitlessly, in Louis's opinion — that he would be able to play baseball that spring when one of the candy-stripers poked her head in and told him his wife was on the telephone.

Louis went into his office to take the call. Rachel was crying, and he was instantly alarmed. *Ellie*, he thought. *She's fallen off her sled and broken her arm. Or fractured her skull.* He thought with alarm of the crazed fraternity boys and their toboggan.

'It isn't one of the kids, is it?' he asked. 'Rachel?'

'No, no,' she said, crying harder. 'Not one of the kids. It's Norma, Lou. Norma Crandall. She died this morning. Around eight o'clock, right after breakfast, Jud said. He came over to see if you were here and I told him you'd left half an hour ago. He . . . oh Lou, he just seemed so lost and so dazed . . . so *old* . . . thank God Ellie was gone and Gage is too young to understand . . .'

Louis's brow furrowed, and in spite of this terrible news he found it was Rachel his mind was going out to, seeking, trying to find. Because here it was again. Nothing you could quite put your finger on, because it was so much of an overall attitudinal fix. That death was a secret, a terror, and it was to be kept from the children, above all to be kept from the children, the way that Victorian ladies and gentlemen had believed the nasty, grotty truth about sexual relations was to be kept from the children.

'Jesus,' he said. 'Was it her heart?'

'I don't know,' she said. She was no longer crying, but her voice was choked and hoarse. 'Could you come, Louis? You're his friend, and I think he needs you.'

You're his friend.

Well I am, Louis thought with a small touch of surprise. *I never expected to have an eighty-year-old man for a buddy, but I guess I do.* And then it occurred to him that they had better be friends, considering what was between them. And considering that, he supposed that Jud had known they were friends long before Louis had. Jud had stood by him on that one, and in spite of what had happened since, in spite of the mice, in spite of the birds, Louis felt that Jud's decision had probably been the right one . . . or, if not the right one, at least the compassionate one. He would do what he could for Jud now, and if it meant being best man at the death of his wife, he would be that.

'On my way,' he said, and hung up.

CHAPTER THIRTY-TWO

It had not been a heart attack. It had been a brain embolism, sudden, and probably painless. When Louis called Steve Masterton that afternoon and told him what was going on, Steve said that he wouldn't mind going out just that way.

'Sometimes God dillies and dallies,' Steve said, 'and sometimes he just points at you and tells you to hang up your jock.'

Rachel did not want to talk about it at all, and would not allow Louis to talk to her of it.

Ellie was not so much upset as she was shocked and interested – it was what Louis thought a thoroughly healthy five-year-old reaction should be. She wanted to know if Mrs Crandall had died with her eyes shut or open. Louis said he didn't know.

Jud took hold as well as could have been expected, considering the fact that the lady had been sharing bed and board with him for almost sixty years. Louis found the old man – and on this day he looked very much like an old man of eighty-four – sitting alone at the kitchen table, smoking a Chesterfield, drinking a bottle of beer, and staring blankly into the living room.

He looked up when Louis came in and said, 'Well, she's gone, Louis.' He said this in such a clear and matter-of-fact way that Louis thought it must not have really cleared through all the circuits yet – hadn't hit him yet where he lived. Then Jud's mouth began to work and he covered his eyes with one arm. Louis went to him and put an arm around him, and Jud gave in and wept. It had cleared the circuits, all right. Jud understood perfectly the fact that his wife had died.

'That's good,' Louis said. 'That's good, Jud, she would want

215

you to cry a little, I think. Probably be pissed off if you didn't.'
He had started to cry a little himself. Jud hugged him tightly
and Louis hugged him back.

Jud cried for ten minutes or so, and then the storm passed.
Louis listened to the things Jud said then with great care – he
listened as a doctor as well as a friend. He listened for any
circularity in Jud's conversation; he listened to see if Jud's grasp
of *when* was clear (no need to check him on *where*; that would
prove nothing, because for Jud Crandall the *where* had always
been Ludlow, Maine); he listened most of all for any use of
Norma's name in the present tense. He found little or no sign
that Jud was losing his grip. Louis was aware that it was not
uncommon for two old married people to go almost hand-in-
hand, a month, a week, even a day apart. The shock, he
supposed, or maybe even some deep inner urge to catch up
with the one gone (that was a thought he would not have
had before Church; he found that many of his thoughts concerning the spiritual and the supernatural had undergone a
quiet but nonetheless deep change). His conclusion was that
Jud was grieving hard but that he was – at least for the time
being – still all there. He sensed none of that transparent frailty
that had seemed to surround Norma on New Year's Eve,
when the four of them had sat in the Creed living room,
drinking eggnog.

Jud brought him a beer from the fridge, his face still red
and blotchy from crying.

'A bit early in the day,' he said, 'but sun's over the yardarm
somewhere in the world and under the circumstances . . .'

'Say no more,' Louis told him, and opened the beer. He
looked at Jud. 'Shall we drink to her?'

'I guess we better,' Jud said. 'You should have seen her
when she was sixteen, Louis, coming back from church with
her jacket unbuttoned and her shirtwaist just as clean and white
. . . your eyes would have popped. She could have made the
devil swear off drinking. Thank Christ she never asked me to
do it.'

Louis nodded, raised his beer a little. 'To Norma,' he said. Jud clinked his bottle against Louis's. He was crying again but he was also smiling a little. He nodded. 'May she have peace and let there be no frigging arthritis wherever she is.'

'Amen,' Louis said, and they drank.

It was the only time Louis saw Jud progress beyond a mild tipsiness, and even so, he did not become drunk or in any way incapacitated. He reminisced; a constant stream of warm memories and anecdotes, colorful and clear and sometimes arresting, flowed from him. Yet between the stories of the past, Jud dealt with the present in a way Louis could only admire; if it had been Rachel who had simply dropped dead after her grapefruit and morning cereal, he wondered if he could have done half so well.

Jud called the Brookings–Smith Funeral Home in Bangor and made as many of the arrangements as he could by telephone; he made an appointment to come in the following day and make the rest. Yes, he would have her embalmed; he wanted her in a dress, which he would provide; yes, he would pick out underwear; no, he did not want the mortuary to supply the special shoes which laced up the back. Would they have someone wash her hair? he asked. She washed it last on Monday night, and so it had been dirty when she died. He listened, and Louis, whose uncle had been in what those in the business called 'the quiet trade', knew the undertaker was telling Jud that a final wash and set was part of the service rendered. Jud nodded and thanked the man he was talking to, then listened again. Yes, he said, he would have her cosmeticized, but it was to be a lightly applied layer. 'She's dead and people know it,' he said, lighting a Chesterfield. 'No need to tart her up.' The coffin would be closed during the funeral, he told the director with calm authority, open during the visiting hours the day before. She was to be buried in Mount Hope Cemetery, where they had bought plots in 1951. He had the papers in hand and gave the mortician the plot-number so that preparations could begin out there: H-101. He himself had H-102, he told Louis later on.

He hung up, looked at Louis, and said: 'Prettiest cemetery in the world is right there in Bangor, as far as I'm concerned. Crack yourself another beer, if you want, Louis. All of this is going to take a while.'

Louis was about to refuse – he was feeling a little tiddly – when a grotesque image arose unbidden behind his eyes; Jud pulling Norma's corpse on a pagan litter through the woods. Toward the Micmac burying ground beyond the Pet Sematary.

It had the effect of a slap on him. Without a word, he got up and got another beer out of the fridge. Jud nodded at him and dialed the telephone again. By three that afternoon, when Louis went home for a sandwich and a bowl of soup, Jud had progressed a long way toward organizing his wife's final rites; he moved from one thing to the next like a man planning a dinner party of some importance. He called the North Ludlow Methodist Church, where the actual funeral would take place, and the Cemetery Administration Office at Mount Hope; these were both calls the undertaker at Brookings-Smith would be making, but Jud called first, as a courtesy. It was a step few bereaved ever thought of . . . or, if they thought of it, one they could rarely bring themselves to take. Louis admired Jud all the more for it. Later, he called Norma's few surviving relatives and his own, paging through an old and tattered address book with a leather cover to find the numbers. And between calls, he drank beer and remembered the past.

Louis felt great admiration for him . . . and love?

Yes, his heart confirmed; and love.

When Ellie came down that night in her pajamas to be kissed, she asked Louis if Mrs Crandall would go to heaven. She almost whispered the question to Louis, as if she understood it would be better if they were not overheard. Rachel was in the kitchen making a chicken pie, which she intended to take over to Jud the next day.

Across the street, all the lights were on in the Crandall house. Cars were parked in Jud's driveway and up and down the shoulder of the highway on that side for a hundred feet in either direction. The official viewing hours would be tomorrow, at the mortuary, but tonight people had come to comfort Jud as well as they could, and to help him remember, and to celebrate Norma's passing – what Jud had referred to once that afternoon as 'the foregoing'. Between that house and this, a frigid February wind blew. The road was patched with black ice. The coldest part of the Maine winter was now upon them.

'Well, I don't really know, honey,' Louis said, taking Ellie on his lap. On the TV, a running gunfight was in progress. A man spun and dropped, unremarked upon by either of them. Louis was aware – uncomfortably so – that Ellie probably knew a hell of a lot more about Ronald McDonald and Spiderman and The Burger King than she did Moses, Jesus, and St Paul. She was the daughter of a woman who was a nonpracticing Jew and a man who was a lapsed Methodist, and he supposed her ideas about the whole *spiritus mundi* were of the vaguest sort; not myths, not dreams, but dreams of dreams. *It's late for that*, he thought randomly. *She's only five, but it's late for that. Jesus Christ, it gets late so fast.*

But she was looking at him, and he ought to say something.

'People believe all sorts of things about what happens to us when we die,' he said. 'Some people think we go to heaven or hell. Some people believe we're born again as little children —'

'Sure, Carnation. Like what happened to Audrey Rose in that movie on TV.'

'You never saw that!' Rachel, he thought, would have her own brain embolism if she thought Ellie had seen *Audrey Rose*.

'Marie told me at school,' Ellie said. Marie was Ellie's self-proclaimed best friend, a malnourished, dirty little girl who always looked as if she might be on the edge of impetigo, or ringworm or perhaps even scurvy. Both Louis and Rachel encouraged the friendship as well as they could, but Rachel had once confessed to Louis that after Marie left, she always felt an urge to check Ellie's head for nits and head-lice. Louis had laughed and nodded.

'Marie's mommy lets her watch *all* the shows.' There was an implied criticism in this that Louis chose to ignore.

'Well, it's *re*incarnation, but I guess you've got the idea. The Catholics believe in heaven and hell, but they also believe there's a place called limbo and one called purgatory. And the Buddhists believe in Nirvana—'

There was a shadow on the dining-room wall. Rachel. Listening.

Louis went on more slowly.

'There are probably lots more, too. But what it comes down to, Ellie, is this: no one knows. People *say* they know, but when they say that what they mean is that they believe because of faith. Do you know what faith is?'

'Well . . .'

'Here we are, sitting in my chair,' Louis said. 'Do you think my chair will still be here tomorrow?'

'Yeah, sure.'

'Then you have faith it will be here. As it so happens, I do, too. Faith is believing a thing will be. Get it?'

'Yes.' Ellie nodded positively.

'But we don't *know* it'll be here. After all, some crazed chair-burglar might break in and take it, right?'

Ellie giggled. Louis smiled.

'We just have faith that won't happen. Faith is a great thing, and really religious people would like us to believe that faith and knowing are the same thing, but I don't believe that, myself. Because there are too many different ideas on the subject. What we *know* is this: when we die, one of two things happens. Either our souls and thoughts somehow survive the experience of dying, or they don't. If they do, that opens up every possibility you could think of. If we don't, it's just blotto. The end.'

'Like going to sleep?'

He considered this and then said, 'More like having ether, I think.'

'Which do you have faith in, Daddy?'

The shadow on the wall moved and came to rest again.

For most of his adult life – since college days, he supposed – he had believed that death was the end. He had been present at many deathbeds and had never felt a soul bullet past him on its way to . . . wherever; hadn't this very thought occurred to him upon the death of Victor Pascow? He had agreed with his Psychology I teacher that the life-after-life experiences reported in scholarly journals and then vulgarized in the popular press probably indicated a last-ditch mental stand against the onrush of death; the endlessly inventive human mind, staving off insanity to the very end by constructing a hallucination of immortality. He had likewise agreed with an acquaintance in the dorm who had said, during an all-night bull-session during Louis's sophomore year at Chicago, that the Bible was suspiciously full of miracles that had ceased almost completely during modern times ('totally ceased' he had said at first, but had been forced backward at least one step by others who claimed with some authority that there were still plenty of weird things going on; little pockets of perplexity in a world that had become, by and large, a clean, well-lighted place – there was, for instance, the Shroud of Turin, which had survived every effort to debunk it). 'So Christ brought Lazarus back from the dead,' this acquaintance – who had gone on to become a highly thought-of o.b. man in Dearborn, Michigan – had said. 'That's fine with me. If I have to swallow it, I will. I mean, I had to buy the concept that the fetus of one twin can sometimes swallow the fetus of the other *in utero*, like some kind of goddam unborn cannibal, and then show up with teeth in his testes or hair in his lungs twenty or thirty years later to prove that he did it, and I suppose if I can buy that I can buy anything. But I wanna see the death certificate, you dig what I'm saying? I'm not questioning that he came out of the tomb. But I wanna see the original death certificate.

221

Me, I like Thomas saying he'd only believe Jesus had risen when he could look through the nail-holes and stick his hands in the guy's side. As far as I'm concerned, *he* was the real physician of the bunch, not Luke.'

No, he had never really believed in survival. At least, not until Church.

'I believe that we go on,' he told his daughter slowly. 'But as to what it's like, I have no opinion. It may be that it's different for different people. It may be that you get what you believed all your life. But I believe we go on, and I believe that Mrs Crandall is probably somewhere where she can be happy.'

'You have faith in that,' Ellie said. It was not a question. She sounded awed.

Louis smiled, a little pleased and a little embarrassed. 'I suppose so. And I have faith in the fact that it's time for you to go to bed. Like ten minutes ago.'

He kissed her twice, once on the lips and once on the nose.

'Do you think animals go on?'

'Yes,' he said, without thinking, and for a moment he almost added: *Especially cats*. The words had actually trembled on his lips for a moment, and his skin felt gray and cold.

'Okay,' she said, and slid down. 'Gotta go kiss Mommy.'

'Right on.'

He watched her go. At the dining-room doorway she turned back and said, 'I was really silly about Church that day, wasn't I? Crying like that.'

'No hon,' he said. 'I don't think you were silly.'

'If he died now, I could take it,' she said, and then seemed to consider the thought she had just spoken aloud, as if mildly startled. The she said, as if agreeing with herself: 'Sure I could.' And went to find Rachel.

Later, in bed, Rachel said: 'I heard what you were talking about with her.'

'And don't approve?' Louis asked. He had decided that

maybe it would be best to have this out, if that was what Rachel wanted.

'No,' Rachel said, with a hesitance that was not much like her. 'No, Louis, it's not like that. I just get . . . scared. And you know me. When I get scared, I get defensive.'

Louis could not remember ever hearing Rachel speak with such effort, and suddenly he felt more cautious than he had with Ellie earlier. He felt that he was in a minefield.

'Scared of what? Dying?'

'Not *myself*,' she said. 'I hardly even think of that . . . any more. But when I was a kid, I thought of it a lot. Lost a lot of sleep. Dreamed of monsters coming to eat me up in my bed, and all of the monsters looked like my sister Zelda.'

Yes, Louis thought. *Here it is; at last, after all the time we've been married, here it is.*

'You don't talk about her much,' he said.

Rachel smiled, and touched his face. 'You're sweet, Louis. I never talk about her. I try never to think about her.'

'I always assumed you had your reasons.'

'I did. I do.'

She paused, thinking.

'I know she died . . . spinal meningitis . . .

'Spinal meningitis,' she repeated, and he saw she was very near to tears. 'There are no pictures of her in the house any more.'

'There's a picture of a young girl in your father's —'

'In his study. Yes. I forgot that one. And my mother carries one in her wallet still, I think. She was two years older than I was. She caught it . . . and she was in the back bedroom . . . she was in the back bedroom like a dirty secret, Louis, she was dying in there, my sister died in the back bedroom and that's what she was, a dirty secret, she was always a dirty secret!'

Rachel suddenly broke down completely, and in the loud, rising quality of her sobs, Louis sensed the onset of hysteria and became alarmed. He reached for her and caught a shoulder, which was pulled away from him as soon as he touched it.

He could feel the whisper of her silk nightdress under his fingertips.

'Rachel – babe – don't —'

Somehow she controlled the sobs. 'Don't tell me don't,' she said. 'Don't stop me, Louis. I've only got the strength to tell this once, and then I don't want to ever talk about it again. I probably won't sleep tonight as it is.'

'Was it that horrible?' he asked, knowing the answer already. It explained so much, and even things he had never connected before or only suspected vaguely suddenly came together in his mind. She had never attended a funeral with him, he realized, not even that of Al Locke, a fellow med-student who had been killed when the car he was riding in had collided with a dump-truck. Al had been a regular visitor at their apartment, and Rachel had always liked him. Yet she had not gone to his funeral.

She was sick that day, Louis remembered suddenly. *Got the flu, or something. Looked serious. But the next day she was okay again.*

After the funeral she was all right again, he corrected himself. He remembered thinking even then that her sickness might just be psychosomatic.

'It was horrible, all right. Worse than you can ever imagine. Louis, we watched her degenerate day by day and there was nothing anyone could do. She was in constant pain. Her body seemed to shrivel . . . pull in on itself . . . her shoulders hunched up and her face pulled down until it was like a mask. Her hands were like birds' feet. I had to feed her sometimes. I hated it, but I did it and never said boo about it. When the pain got bad enough they started giving her drugs, mild ones at first, and then ones that would have left her a junkie if she had lived. But of course everyone knew she wasn't going to live. I guess that's why she's such a . . . secret to all of us. Because we *wanted* her to die, Louis, we *wished* for her to die, and it wasn't just so *she* wouldn't feel any more pain, it was so *we* wouldn't feel any more pain, it was because she was starting to look like a monster, and she was starting to *be* a monster . . . oh Christ I know how awful that must sound . . .'

She put her face in her hands.

Louis touched her gently. 'Rachel, it doesn't sound awful at all.'

'It does!' she cried. 'It *does*!'

'It just sounds true,' he said. 'Victims of long illnesses often become demanding, unpleasant monsters. The idea of the saintlike, long-suffering patient is a big romantic fiction. By the time the first set of bedsores crops up on a bed-bound patient's butt, he – or she – has started to snipe and cut and spread the misery. They can't help it, but that doesn't help the people in the situation.'

She looked at him, amazed . . . almost hopeful. Then distrust stole back into her face. 'You're making that up.'

He smiled grimly. 'Want me to show you the textbooks? How about the suicide statistics? Want to see those? In families where a terminal patient has been nursed at home, the suicide statistics spike right up into the stratosphere in the six months following the patient's death.'

'*Suicide!*'

'They swallow pills, or sniff a pipe, or blow their brains out. Their hate . . . their weariness . . . their disgust . . . their sorrow . . .' He shrugged, and brought his closed fists gently together. 'The survivors start feeling as if they'd committed murder. So they step out.'

A crazy, wounded kind of relief had crept into Rachel's puffy face. 'She was demanding . . . hateful. Sometimes she'd piss in her bed deliberately. My mother would ask her if she wanted help getting to the bathroom . . . and later, when she couldn't get up any more, if she wanted the bedpan . . . and Zelda would say no . . . and then she'd piss the bed so my mother or my mother and I would have to change the sheets . . . and she'd say it was an accident, but you could see the smile in her eyes, Louis. You could *see* it. The room always smelled of piss and her drugs . . . she had bottles of some dope that smelled like Smith Brothers Wild Cherry Cough Drops and that smell was always there . . . some nights I wake up . . . even now I wake up and I think I can smell Wild Cherry Cough Drops . . . and I think . . . if I'm not really awake I think "Is Zelda dead yet? Is she?" . . . I think . . .'

Rachel caught her breath. Louis took her hand and she squeezed it with savage, brilliant tightness.

'When we changed her you could see the way her back was twisting and knotting. Near the end, Louis, near the end it seemed like her . . . like her ass had somehow gotten all the way up to the middle of her back.'

Now Rachel's wet eyes had taken on the glassy, horrified look of a child remembering a recurrent nightmare of terrible power.

'And sometimes she'd touch me with her . . . her hands . . . her birdy hands . . . and sometimes I'd almost scream and ask her not to, and once I spilled some of her soup on my arm when she touched my face and I burned myself and that time I *did* scream . . . and I cried and I could see the smile in her eyes then, too.

'Near the end the drugs stopped working. She was the one who would scream then, and none of us could remember the way she was before, not even my mother. She was just this foul, hateful, screaming *thing* in the back bedroom . . . our dirty secret.'

Rachel swallowed. Her throat clicked.

'My parents were gone when she finally . . . when she . . . you know, when she . . .'

With terrible, wrenching effort, Rachel brought it out.

'When she *died* my parents were gone. They were gone but I was with her. It was Passover Season, and they went out for a while to see some friends. Just for a few minutes. I was reading a magazine in the kitchen. Well, I was looking at it, anyway. I was waiting for it to be time to give her some more medicine, because she was screaming. She'd been screaming ever since my folks left, almost. I couldn't read with her

screaming that way. And then ... see, what happened was
... well ... Zelda stopped screaming. Louis, I was eight ...
bad dreams every night ... I had started to think she hated
me because *my* back was straight, because *I* didn't have the
constant pain, because *I* could walk, because *I* was going to
live ... I started to imagine she wanted to kill me. Only,
even now tonight, Louis, I don't really think it was all my
imagination. I *do* think she hated me. I don't really think she
would have killed me, but if she could have taken over my
body some way ... turned me out of it like in a fairy story
... I think she would have done that. But when she stopped
screaming, I went in to see if everything was all right ... to
see if she had fallen over on her side or slipped off her pillows.
I got in and I looked at her and I thought she must have
swallowed her own tongue and she was choking to death.
Louis—' Rachel's voice rose again, teary and frighteningly
childish, as if she were regressing, reliving the experience.
'Louis, I didn't know what to *do*! I was *eight*!'

'No, of course you didn't,' Louis said. He turned to her
and hugged her, and Rachel gripped him with the panicky
strength of a poor swimmer whose boat has suddenly overturned in the middle of a large lake. 'Did someone actually
give you a hard time about it, babe?'

'No,' she said, 'no one blamed me. But nobody could make
it better, either. No one could change it. No one could make
it an unhappening, Louis. She hadn't swallowed her tongue.
She started making a sound, a kind of, I don't know – *Gaaaaaa*
– like that—'

In her distressed, total recall of that day she did a more than
creditable imitation of the way her sister Zelda must have
sounded, and Louis's mind suddenly flashed to Victor Pascow.
His grip on his wife tightened.

'—and there was spit, spit coming down her chin—'

'Rachel, that's enough,' he said, not quite steadily. 'I am
aware of the symptoms.'

'I'm *explaining*,' she said stubbornly. 'I'm explaining why I can't go to poor Norma's funeral, for one thing, and why we had that stupid fight that day—'

'Shh, that's forgotten.'

'Not by me, it isn't,' she said. 'I remember it well, Louis. I remember it as well as I remember my sister Zelda choking to death in her bed on April 14th, 1963.'

For a long moment there was silence in the room.

'I turned her over on her belly and thumped her back,' Rachel went on at last. 'It's all I knew to do. Her feet were beating up and down . . . and her twisted legs . . . and I remember there was a sound like farting . . . I thought she was farting or I was, but it wasn't farts, it was the seams under both arms of my blouse ripping out when I turned her over. She started to . . . to convulse . . . and I saw that her face was turned sideways, turned into the pillows and I thought, oh, she's choking, Zelda's choking and they'll come home and say I murdered her by choking, they'll say *you hated her, Rachel*, and that was true, and they'll say *you wanted her to be dead*, and that was true, too. Because, Louis, see, the first thought that went through my mind when she started to go up and down in the bed like that, I remember it, my first thought was *Oh good, finally, Zelda's choking and this is going to be over.* So I turned her over again and her face had gone *black*, Louis, and her eyes were bulging and her neck was swelled up. Then she died. I backed across the room. I guess I wanted to back out of the door but I hit the wall and a picture fell down, it was a picture from one of the Oz books that Zelda liked before she got sick with the meningitis, when she was well, it was a picture of Oz the Great and Terrible, only Zelda always called him Oz the Gweat and Tewwible, because she couldn't make that sound and so she sounded like Elmer Fudd. My mother got that picture framed because . . . because Zelda liked it most of all . . . Oz the Gweat and Tewwible . . . and it fell down and hit the floor and the glass in the frame shattered and I started to scream because I knew she was dead and I thought . . . I guess I thought it was her ghost, coming back to get me, and I knew that her ghost would hate me like she did, but her ghost wouldn't be stuck in bed, so I screamed ... I screamed and I ran out of the house screaming "*Zelda's dead! Zelda's dead! Zelda's dead!*" And the neighbors ... they came and they looked ... they saw me running down the street with my blouse all ripped out under the arms ... I was yelling "*Zelda's dead!*" Louis, and I guess maybe they thought I was crying but I think ... I think maybe I was laughing, Louis. I think maybe that's what I was doing.'

'If you were, I salute you for it,' Louis said.

'You don't mean that, though,' Rachel said with the utter certainty of one who has been over a point and over it and over it. He let it go. He thought she might eventually get rid of this awful, rancid memory that had haunted her for so long – most of it, anyway – but never this part. Never completely. Louis Creed was no psychiatrist, but he knew that there are half-buried things in the terrain of any life, and that human beings seem compelled to go back to these things and pull at them, even though they cut. Tonight Rachel had pulled almost all of it out, like some grotesque and stinking rotted tooth, its crown black, its nerves infected, its roots fetid. It was out. Let that last noxious cell remain; if God was good it would remain dormant, except in her deepest dreams. That she had been able to remove as much as she had was well nigh incredible – it did not just speak of her courage; it clarioned it. Louis was in awe of her. He felt like cheering.

He sat up now and turned on the light. 'Yes,' he said. 'I salute you for it. And if I needed another reason to ... to really dislike your mother and father, I've got it now. You never should have been left alone with her, Rachel. *Never.*'

Like a child – the child of eight she had been when this dirty, incredible thing had happened – she reprimanded him: 'Lou, it was Passover Season—'

'I don't care if it was Judgment Trump,' Louis said with a sudden low and hoarse savagery that caused her to pull back a little. He was remembering the student nurses, those two

candy-stripers whose evil luck it had been to be in attendance
on the morning Pascow had been brought in dying. One of
them – a tough little lady named Carla Shavers, had returned
the next day and had worked out so well that even Charlton
was impressed. The other they had never seen again. Louis
was not surprised and did not blame her.

*Where was the nurse? There should have been an RN in attendance
. . . they went out, they actually went out and left an eight-year-old
kid alone with her dying sister who was probably clinically insane by
then. Why? Because it was Passover Season. And because elegant
Dory Goldman couldn't stand the stink that particular morning and
had to get away from it for just a little while. So Rachel got the duty.
Right, friends and neighbors? Rachel got the duty. Eight years old,
pigtails, middy blouse. Rachel got the mother-fucking duty. Rachel
could stay and put up with the stink. What did they send her to
Camp Sunset in Vermont for six weeks every year, if not to put up
with the stink of her dying, insane sister? Ten new shirt-and-jumper
combinations for Gage and six new dresses for Ellie and I'll pay your
way through medical school if you'll stay away from my daughter
. . . but where was the overflowing checkbook when your daughter
was dying of spinal meningitis and your other daughter was alone
with her, you cheap bastard? Where was the R-FUCKING-N?*

Louis sat up, got out of bed.

'Where are you going?' Rachel asked, alarmed.

'To get you a Valium.'

'You know I don't—'

'Tonight you do,' he said.

She took the pill and then told him the rest. Her voice
remained calm throughout. The tranquilizer was doing its job.

The next-door neighbor had retrieved eight-year-old
Rachel from behind a tree where she was crouching and
screaming 'Zelda's dead!' over and over. Rachel's nose had
been bleeding. She had blood all over her. The same neighbor
had called the ambulance and then her parents; after getting
Rachel's nosebleed stopped and calming her with a cup of hot

230

tea and two aspirins, she was able to get the location of her parents out of her – they were visiting Mr and Mrs Cabron across town; Peter Cabron was an accountant in her father's business.

By that evening, great changes had taken place in the Goldman household. Zelda was gone. Her room had been cleaned and fumigated. All of the furniture was gone. The room was a bare box. Later – much later – it had become Dory Goldman's sewing room.

The first of the nightmares had come to Rachel that night, and when Rachel woke up at two o'clock in the morning, screaming for her mother, she had been horrified to discover she could barely get out of bed. Her back was in agony. She had strained it moving Zelda. In her spurt of adrenalin-powered strength, she had lifted her with enough force to pull her blouse apart.

That she had strained herself trying to keep Zelda from choking was simple, obvious, elementary-my-dear-Watson. To everyone, that was, except Rachel herself. Rachel had been sure that this was Zelda's revenge from beyond the grave. Zelda knew that Rachel was glad she was dead; Zelda knew that when Rachel burst from the house screaming *Zelda's dead, Zelda's dead*, she had been laughing, not screaming; Zelda knew she had been murdered and she had given Rachel spinal meningitis, and soon her back would start to twist and change and she would have to lie in bed, slowly but surely turning into a monster, her hands hooking into claws.

After a while she would begin screaming with the pain, as Zelda had done, and then she would start wetting the bed, and finally she would choke to death on her own tongue. It was Zelda's revenge.

No one could talk Rachel out of this belief; not her mother, her father, or Dr Murray, who diagnosed a mild back-sprain and then told Rachel brusquely (cruelly, some – Louis, for instance – would have said) to stop behaving so badly. She ought to remember that her sister had just died, Dr Murray told her; her parents were prostrate with grief and this was not the time for Rachel to make a childish play for attention. Only the slowly abating pain had been able to convince her that she was neither the victim of Zelda's supernatural vengeance nor God's just punishment of the wicked. For months (or so she told Louis; it had actually been years, eight of them) afterward she would awaken from nightmares in which her sister died over and over again, and in the dark Rachel's hands would fly to her back to make sure it was all right. In the frightful aftermath of these dreams she often thought that the closet door would bang open and Zelda would lurch out, blue and twisted, her eyes rolled up to shiny whites, her black tongue puffing out through her lips, her hands hooked into claws to murder the murderer cowering in her bed with her hands jammed into the small of her back . . .

She had not attended Zelda's funeral, nor any funeral since.

'If you'd told me this before,' Louis said, 'it would have explained a hell of a lot.'

'Lou, I couldn't,' she said simply. She sounded very sleepy now. 'Since then I've been . . . I guess a little phobic on the subject.'

Just a little phobic, Louis thought. *Yeah, right.*

'I can't . . . seem to help it. In my mind I know you're right, that death is perfectly natural, good, even – but what my mind knows and what happens . . . inside me . . .'

'Yeah,' he said.

'That day I blew up at you,' she said, 'I knew that Ellie was just crying over the idea . . . a way of getting used to it . . . but I couldn't help it. I'm sorry, Louis.'

'No apology needed,' he said, stroking her hair. 'But what the hell, I accept it anyway, if it'll make you feel better.'

She smiled. 'It does, you know. And I feel better. I feel as if I just sicked up something that's poisoned part of me for years.'

'Maybe you have.'

Rachel's eyes slipped closed and then opened again . . .

slowly. 'And don't blame it all on my father, Louis. Please. That was a terrible time for them. The bills — Zelda's bills — were sky-high. My dad had missed his chance to expand into the suburbs, and the sales in the downtown store were off. On top of that, my mother was half-crazy herself.

'Well, it all worked out. It was as if Zelda's death was the signal for good times to come around again. There had been a recession, but then the money loosened up and Daddy got his loan and since then he's never looked back. But that's why they've always been possessive of me, I think. It's not just because I'm the only one left—'

'It's guilt,' Louis said.

'Yes, I suppose. And you won't be mad at me if I'm sick on the day they bury Norma?'

'No, honey, I won't be mad.' He paused, and then took her hand. 'May I take Ellie?'

Her hand tightened in his. 'Oh, Louis, I don't know,' she said, and the fear was back in her voice. 'She's so young—'

'She's known where babies come from for a year or more,' he reminded her again.

She was quiet for a long time, looking up at the ceiling and biting her lips. 'If you think it's best,' she said finally. 'If you think it won't . . . won't hurt her.'

'Come over here, Rachel,' he said, and that night they slept back-to-stomach in Louis's bed, and when she woke up trembling in the middle of the night, the Valium worn off, he soothed her with his hands and whispered in her ear that everything was okay and she slept again.

CHAPTER THIRTY-THREE

'*For man — and woman — is like the flowers in the valley, which bloom today and are tomorrow cast into the oven: the time of man is but a season; it cometh, and so it passeth away. Let us pray.*'

Ellie, resplendent in a navy-blue dress bought especially for the occasion, dropped her head so abruptly that Louis, sitting next to her in the pew, heard her neck creak. Ellie had been in few churches, and of course it was her first funeral; the combination had awed her to silence.

For Louis, it had been a rare occasion with his daughter. Mostly blinded by his love for her, as he was by his love for Gage, he rarely observed her in a detached way; but today he thought he was seeing what was almost a textbook case of the child nearing the end of life's first great developmental stage, an organism of almost pure curiosity, storing up information madly in almost endless circuits. Ellie had been unusually quiet, even when Jud, looking strange but elegant in his black suit and lace-up shoes (Louis believed it was the first time he had ever seen him in anything but loafers or green rubber boots), had bent over, kissed her, and said: 'Glad you could come, honey. And I bet Norma is, too.'

Ellie had gazed at him, wide-eyed, at a loss for words. It was not a common occurrence with her.

Now the Methodist minister, Reverend Laughlin, was pronouncing the benediction, asking God to lift up his countenance upon them and give them peace.

'Will the pallbearers come forward?' he asked.

Louis started to rise, and Ellie halted him, tugging his arm frantically. She looked scared. '*Daddy!*' she stage-whispered. 'Where are you going?'

'I'm one of the pallbearers, honey,' Louis said, sitting down beside her again for a moment and putting an arm around her shoulders. 'That means I'm going to help carry Norma out. There are four of us that are going to do it – me and two of Jud's nephews and his brother-in-law.'

'Where will I find you?' Ellie's face was still tense and set and fearful.

Louis glanced down front. The other three pallbearers had assembled there, along with Jud. The rest of the congregation was filing out, some of them weeping. He saw Missy Dandridge, not actually crying but red-eyed, and she raised a hand to him, in a flick of a salute.

'If you just go out on the steps, I'll meet you there,' he said. 'All right, Ellie?'

'Yes,' she said. 'Just don't forget me.'

'No, I won't.'

He got up again, and she tugged his hand again.

'Daddy?'

'What, babe?'

'Don't drop her,' Ellie whispered.

Louis joined the others, and Jud introduced him to the nephews, who were really second or third cousins . . . descendants of Jud's father's brother. They were big fellows in their twenties with a strong facial resemblance. Norma's brother was somewhere in his late fifties, Louis guessed, and while the strain of a death in the family was on his face, he seemed to be bearing up well.

'Pleased to meet you all,' Louis said. He felt a trifle uncomfortable – an outsider in the family circle.

They nodded at him.

'Ellie okay?' Jud asked, and nodded to her. She was lingering in the vestibule, watching.

Sure – she just wants to make sure I don't go up in a puff of smoke, Louis thought, and almost smiled. But then that thought called up another one: *Oz the Gweat and Tewwible*. And the smile died.

'Yes, I think so,' Louis said, and raised a hand to her. She raised hers in return and went outside then in a swirl of navy-blue dress. For a moment Louis was uneasily struck by how adult she looked. It was the sort of illusion, no matter how fleeting, that could give a man pause.

'You guys ready?' one of the nephews asked.

Louis nodded; so did Norma's younger brother.

'Take it easy with her,' Jud said. His voice had roughened. Then he turned away and walked slowly up the aisle with his head down.

Louis moved to the back left corner of the steel-gray American Eternal coffin Jud had chosen for his wife. He laid hold of his runner and the four of them slowly carried Norma's coffin out into the bright still cold of February. Someone – the church custodian, he supposed – had laid down a good bed of cinders over the slippery path of tamped snow. At the curb, a big Cadillac hearse idled white exhaust into the winter air. The funeral director and his husky son stood beside it, watching them, ready to lend a hand if anyone (her brother, perhaps) should slip or flag.

Jud stood beside him and watched as they slid the coffin inside.

'Goodbye, Norma,' he said, and lit a cigarette. 'I'll see you in a while, old girl.'

Louis slipped an arm around Jud's shoulders and Norma's brother stood close by on his other side, crowding the mortician and his son into the background. The burly nephews (or second cousins, or whatever they were) had already done a fade, the simple job of lifting and carrying done. They had grown distant from this part of the family; they had known the woman's face from photographs and a few duty visits, perhaps – long afternoons spent in the parlor eating Norma's cookies and drinking Jud's beer, perhaps not really minding the old stories of times they had not lived through and people they had not known, but aware of things they could have been doing all the same (a car that could have been washed and Turtle-waxed, a league bowling practice, maybe just sitting around the TV and watching a boxing match with some friends), and glad to be away when the duty was done.

Jud's part of the family was in the past now, as far as they were concerned; it was like an eroded planetoid drifting away from the main mass, dwindling, little more than a speck. The past. Pictures in an album. Old stories told in rooms that perhaps seemed too hot to them – *they* were not old, there was no arthritis in *their* joints, *their* blood had not thinned. The past was runners to be gripped and hefted and later let go. After all, if the human body was an envelope to hold the human soul – God's letters to the universe – as most churches taught, then the American Eternal coffin was an envelope to hold the human body, and to these husky young cousins or nephews or whatever they were, the past was just a dead letter to be filed away.

God save the past, Louis thought, and shivered for no good reason – other than that the day would come when he would be every bit as unfamiliar to his own blood, the spawn of his brother's children, his own grandchildren if Ellie or Gage produced kids and he lived to see them. The focus shifted. Family lines degenerated. Young faces looking out of old photographs.

God save the past, he thought again, and tightened his grip around the old man's shoulders.

The ushers put the flowers into the back of the hearse. The hearse's electric rear window rose and thumped home in its socket. Louis went back to where his daughter was and they walked to the Civic together, Louis holding Ellie's arm so she wouldn't slip in her good shoes with the leather soles. Car engines were starting up.

'Why are they putting on their lights, daddy?' Ellie asked

with mild wonder. 'Why are they putting on their lights in the middle of the day?'

'They do it,' Louis began, and heard the thickness in his own voice, 'to honor the dead, Ellie.' He pulled out the knob that turned on the Civic's headlights. 'Come on.'

They were going home at last, the graveside ceremony over (actually held at the small Mount Hope Chapel; no grave would be dug for Norma until spring), when Ellie suddenly burst into tears.

Louis glanced at her, surprised but not particularly alarmed. 'Ellie, what is it?'

'No more cookies,' Ellie sobbed. 'She made the best oatmeal cookies I ever ate. But she won't make them any more because she's *dead*. Daddy, why do people have to be dead?'

'I don't really know,' Louis said. 'To make room for all the new people, I guess. Little people like you and your brother Gage.'

'I'm never going to get married or do sex and have babies!' Ellie declared, crying harder than ever. 'Then maybe it'll never happen to me! It's *awful*! It's *m-m-mean*!'

'But it's an end to suffering,' Louis said quietly. 'And as a doctor I see a lot of suffering. One of the reasons I wanted the job at the University was because I got sick of looking at it day in and day out. Young people quite often have pain . . . bad pain, even . . . but that's not quite the same as suffering.'

He paused.

'Believe it or not, honey, when people get very old, death doesn't always look so bad, or so scary as it seems to you. And you have years and years and years ahead of you.'

Ellie cried, and then she sniffed, and then she stopped. Before they got home she asked if she could play the radio. Louis said yes, and she found Shakin' Stevens singing 'This Old House' on WACZ. Soon she was singing along. When they got home she went to her mother and prattled about the funeral; to Rachel's credit, she listened quietly, sympathetically, and supportively . . . although Louis thought she looked pale and thoughtful.

Then Ellie asked her if she knew how to make oatmeal cookies, and Rachel put away the piece of knitting she'd been doing and rose at once, as if she had been waiting for this, or something like it. 'Yes,' she said. 'Want to make a batch?'

'Yay!' Ellie shouted. 'Can we really, Mom?'

'We can if your father will watch Gage for an hour.'

'I'll watch him,' Louis said. 'With pleasure.'

Louis spent the evening reading and making notes on a long article in *The Duquesne Medical Digest*; the old controversy concerning dissolving sutures had begun again. In the small world of those relatively few humans on earth concerned with stitching minor wounds, it appeared to be as endless as that old psychological squabbling-point, nature versus nurture.

He intended writing a dissenting letter this very night, proving that the writer's main contentions were specious, his case examples self-serving, his research almost criminally sloppy. In short, Louis was looking forward – with high good humor – to blowing the stupid fuck right off the map. He was hunting around in the study bookcase for his copy of Troutman's *Treatment of Wounds* when Rachel came halfway down the stairs.

'Coming up, Lou?'

'I'll be a while.' He glanced up at her. 'Everything all right?'

'They're deep asleep, both of them.'

Louis looked at her closely. 'Them, yeah. You're not.'

'I'm fine. Been reading.'

'You're okay? Really?'

'Yes,' she said, and smiled. 'I love you, Louis.'

'Love you too, babe.' He glanced at the bookcase and there was Troutman, right where he had been all along. Louis put his hand on the textbook.

'Church brought a rat into the house while you and Ellie

were gone,' she said, and tried to smile. 'Yuck, what a mess.'

'Jeez, Rachel, I'm sorry.' He hoped he did not sound as guilty as, at that moment, he felt. 'It was bad?'

Rachel sat down on the stairs. In her pink flannel night-gown, her face cleaned of make-up and her forehead shining, her hair tied back into a short ponytail with a rubber band, she looked like a child. 'I took care of it,' she said, 'but do you know, I had to beat that dumb cat out the door with the vacuum-cleaner attachment before it would stop guarding the . . . the corpse? It *growled* at me. Church never growled at me before in his life. He seems different lately. Do you think he might have distemper or something, Louis?'

'No,' Louis said slowly, 'but I'll take him to the vet, if you want.'

'I guess it's all right,' she said, and then looked at him nakedly. 'But would you come up? I just . . . I know you're working, but . . .'

'Of course,' he said, getting up as though it were nothing important at all. And, really, it wasn't – except he knew that now the letter would never be written, because the parade has a way of moving on and tomorrow would bring something new. But he had bought that rat, hadn't he? The rat that Church had brought in, surely clawed to bloody ribbons, its intestines dragging, its head perhaps gone. Yes. He had bought it. It was his rat.

'Let's go to bed,' he said, turning off the lights. He and Rachel went up the stairs together. Louis put his arm around her waist and loved her the best he could . . . but even as he entered into her, hard and erect, he was listening to the winter whine outside the frost-traced windows, wondering where Church, the cat that used to belong to his daughter and which now belonged to him, wondering where he was and what he was stalking or killing. *The soil of a man's heart is stonier*, he thought, and the wind sang its bitter black song, and not so many miles distant, Norma Crandall, who had once knitted his daughter and son matching caps, lay in her gray steel American

Eternal coffin on a stone slab in a Mount Hope crypt; by now the white cotton the mortician would have used to stuff her cheeks would be turning black.

CHAPTER THIRTY-FOUR

Ellie turned six. She came home from kindergarten on her birthday with a paper hat askew on her head, several pictures friends had drawn of her (in the best of them, Ellie looked like a friendly scarecrow), and baleful stories about spankings in the schoolyard during recess. The flu epidemic passed. They had to send two students to the EMMC in Bangor, and Surrendra Hardu probably saved the life of one woefully sick freshman boy with the terrible name of Peter Humperton. Mr Humperton puked while lying on his back in his infirmary bed and very nearly strangled. Rachel developed a mild infatuation with the blonde bag-boy at the A&P in Brewer and rhapsodized to Louis at night about how packed his jeans looked. 'It's probably just toilet paper,' she added. 'Squeeze it sometime,' Louis suggested. 'If he screams, it's probably not.' Rachel had laughed until she cried. The blue, still, subzero mini-season of February passed, and brought on the alternating rains and freezes of March, and potholes, and those orange roadside signs which pay homage to the Great God BUMP. The immediate, personal, and most agonizing grief of Jud Crandall passed, that grief which the psychologists say begins about three days after the death of a loved one and holds hard from four to six weeks in most cases – like that period of time New Englanders sometimes call 'deep winter'. But time passes, and time welds one state of human feeling into another until they become something like a rainbow. Strong grief becomes a softer, more mellow grief; mellow grief becomes mourning; mourning at last becomes remembrance – a process that may take from six months to three years and still be considered normal. The day of Gage's first haircut came and passed, and when Louis saw his son's hair growing in darker, he joked about it and did his own mourning – but only in his heart.

Spring came, and it stayed a while.

CHAPTER THIRTY-FIVE

Louis Creed came to believe that the last really happy day of his life was March 24th, 1984. The things that were to come, poised above them like a killing sashweight, were still over six weeks in the future, but looking over those six weeks he found nothing which stood out with the same color, the same impact. He supposed that, even if none of those terrible things had happened, he would have remembered the day for ever. Days which seem genuinely good — good all the way through — are rare enough, anyway, he thought. It might be that there was less than a month of really good ones in any natural man's life in the best of circumstances. It came to seem to Louis that God, in His infinite wisdom, appeared much more generous when it came to doling out pain.

That day was a Saturday, and he was home minding Gage in the afternoon while Rachel and Ellie went after groceries. They had gone with Jud in his old and rattling '59 IH pickup not because the Civic wasn't running but because the old man genuinely liked their company. Rachel asked Louis if he would be okay with Gage, and he told her that of course he would. He was glad to see her get out; after a winter in Maine, most of it in Ludlow, he thought that she needed all the out she could get. She had been an unremittingly good sport about it, but she did seem to him to be getting a little stir-crazy.

Gage got up from his nap around two o'clock, scratchy and out-of-sorts. He had discovered the Terrible Twos and made them his own. Louis had tried several ineffectual gambits to amuse the kid and Gage turned them all down. To make matters worse, the rotten kid had an enormous bowel movement, the artistic quality of which was not improved for Louis when he saw a blue marble sitting in the middle of it. It was one of Ellie's marbles. The kid could have choked. He decided the marbles were going to go – everything Gage got hold of went right to his mouth – but that decision, while undoubtedly laudable, didn't do a goddam thing about keeping the kid amused until his mother got back.

Louis listened to the early spring wind gust around the house, sending big blinkers of light and shadow across Mrs Vinton's field next door, and he suddenly thought of the Vulture he had bought on a whim five or six weeks before, while on his way home from the University. Had he bought twine as well? He had, by God!

'Gage!' he said. Gage had found a green Crayola exactly the color of fresh snot under the couch and was currently scribbling in one of Ellie's favorite books – something else to feed the fires of sibling rivalry, Louis thought, and grinned. If Ellie got really pissy about the scribbles Gage had managed to put in *Where the Wild Things Are* before Louis could get it away from him, Louis would simply mention the unique treasure he had uncovered in Gage's Pampers.

'What!' Gage responded smartly. He was talking pretty well now; Louis had decided the kid might actually be half-bright.

'You wanna go out?'

'Wanna go out!' Gage agreed excitedly. 'Wanna go out. Where my neeks, Daddy?'

This sentence, if reproduced phonetically in its entirety, would have looked something like this: *Weh ma neeks, Dah-dee?* The translation was *Where are my sneakers, Father?* Louis was often struck by Gage's speech, not because it was cute, but because he thought that small children all sounded like immigrants learning a foreign language in some helter-skelter but fairly amiable way. He knew that babies make *all* the sounds the human voice-box is capable of . . . the liquid trill that proves so difficult for first-year French students, the glottal grunts and clicks of the Australian bush people, the thickened, abrupt consonants of German. They lose the capability as they learn English, and Louis wondered now (and not for the first time) if childhood was not more a period of forgetting than of learning.

Gage's neeks were finally found . . . they were also under the couch. One of Louis's other beliefs was that, in families with small children, the area under living-room couches began after a while to develop a strong and mysterious electromagnetic force that eventually sucked in all sorts of litter – everything from bottles and diaper pins to snot-colored Crayolas and old issues of *Sesame Street* magazines with food mouldering between the pages.

Gage's jacket, however, wasn't under the couch – it was halfway down the stairs. His Red Sox cap, without which Gage refused to leave the house, was the most difficult of all to find, because it was where it belonged – in the closet. That was, naturally, the last place they looked.

'Where goin', Daddy?' Gage asked companionably, giving his father his hand.

'Going over in Mrs Vinton's field,' he said. 'Gonna go fly a kite, my man.'

'Kiiiyte?' Gage said doubtfully.

'You'll like it,' Louis said. 'Wait a minute, kiddo.'

They were in the garage now. Louis found his keyring, unlocked the little storage closet and turned on the light. He rummaged through it and found the Vulture, still in its store bag with the sales slip stapled to it. He had bought it in the depths of mid-February, when his soul had cried out for some sort of hope.

'Dat?' Gage asked. This was Gage-ese for *Whatever in the world might you have there, Father?*

'It's the kite,' Louis said, and pulled it out of the bag. Gage watched, interested, as Louis unfurled the Vulture, which spread its wings over perhaps five feet of tough plastic. Its bulgy, bloodshot eyes stared out at them from its small head atop its scrawny, pinkly naked neck.

'Birt!' Gage yelled. 'Birt, Daddy! Got a birt!'

'Yeah, it's a bird,' Louis agreed, slipping the sticks into their pockets at the back of the kite and rummaging again for the five hundred feet of kite-twine that he had bought the same day. He looked back over his shoulder and repeated to Gage: 'You're gonna like it, big guy.'

Gage liked it.

They took the kite over into Mrs Vinton's field and Louis got it up into the blowy late-March sky first shot, although he had not flown a kite since he was ... what? Twelve? Twenty-three years ago? God, that was horrible.

Mrs Vinton was a woman of almost Jud's age, but immeasurably more frail. She lived in a brick house at the head of her field (what had been called Vinton's Field since time out of mind, Jud had once told Louis), but now she came out only rarely. Behind the house, the field ended and the woods began – the woods that led first to the Pet Sematary and then to the Micmac burying ground beyond it.

'Kite's flyne, Daddy!' Gage screamed.

'Yeah, look at it go!' Louis bellowed back, laughing and excited. He paid out kite-twine so fast that the string grew hot and branded thin fire across his palm. 'Look at that Vulture, Gage! She's goin' to beat shit!'

'*Beat-shit!*' Gage cried, and laughed, high and joyously. The sun sailed out from behind a fat gray spring cloud and the temperature seemed to go up five degrees almost at once. They stood in the bright, unreliable warmth of March-straining-to-be-April in the high dead grass of Mrs Vinton's field; above them the Vulture soared up toward the blue, higher, its plastic wings spread taut against that steady current of air, higher, and as he had done as a child, Louis felt himself going up to it, going into it, staring down as the world took on its actual shape, the one cartographers must see in their dreams; Mrs Vinton's field, as white and still as cobwebs following the retreat of the snow, not just a field now but a large parallelogram bounded by rock walls on two of its sides, and then the road at the bottom, a straight black seam, and the river valley – the Vulture saw it all with its soaring, bloodshot eyes. It saw the river like a cool gray band of steel, chunks of ice still floating in it; on the other side it saw Hampden, Newburgh, Winterport, with a ship at dock; perhaps it saw the St Regis Mill at Bucksport below its steaming fume of cloud, or even land's end itself, where the Atlantic pounded the naked rock.

'Look at her go, Gage!' Louis yelled, laughing.

Gage was leaning so far back he was in danger of toppling over. A huge grin covered his face. He was waving to the kite.

Louis got some slack and told Gage to hold out one of his hands. Gage did, not even looking around. He couldn't take his eyes from the kite, which swung and danced in the wind and raced its shadow back and forth across the field.

Louis wound kite-string twice around Gage's hand and now he did look down, comically amazed at the strong tug and pull.

'What!' he said.

'You're flying it,' Louis said. 'You got the hammer, my man. It's your kite.'

'Gage flyne it?' Gage said, as if asking not his father but himself for confirmation. He pulled the string experimentally; the kite nodded in the windy sky. Gage pulled the string harder; the kite swooped. Louis and his son laughed together. Gage reached out his free hand, groping, and Louis took it in his own. They stood together that way in the middle of Mrs Vinton's field, looking up at the Vulture.

It was a moment with his son that Louis never forgot. As he had gone up and into the kite as a child himself, he now found himself going into Gage, his son. He felt himself shrink until he was within Gage's tiny house, looking out of the windows that were his eyes – looking out at a world that was so huge and bright, a world where Mrs Vinton's field was nearly as big as the Bonneville Salt Flats, where the kite soared miles above him, the string drumming in his fist like a live thing as the wind blew around him, tumbling his hair.

'Kite flyne!' Gage cried out to his father, and Louis put his arm around Gage's shoulders and kissed the boy's cheek, in which the wind had bloomed a wild rose.

'I love you, Gage,' he said – it was between the two of them, and that was all right.

And Gage, who now had less than two months to live, laughed shrilly and joyously. '*Kite flyne! Kite flyne, Daddy!*'

They were still flying the kite when Rachel and Ellie came home. They had gotten it so high that they had nearly run out the string and the face of the Vulture had been lost; it was only a small black silhouette in the sky.

Louis was glad to see the two of them, and he roared with laughter when Ellie dropped the string momentarily and chased it through the grass, catching it just before the tumbling, unravelling core-tube gave up the last of its twine. But having them around also changed things a little, and he was not terribly sorry to go in when, twenty minutes later, Rachel said she believed Gage had had enough of the wind. She was afraid he would get a chill.

So the kite was pulled back in, fighting for the sky at every turn of the twine, at last surrendering. Louis tucked it, black wings, buggy bloodshot eyes and all, under his arm and imprisoned it in the storage closet again. That night Gage ate an enormous supper of hot dogs and beans, and while Rachel was dressing him in his Dr Dentons for bed, Louis took Ellie aside and had a heart-to-heart talk with her about leaving her marbles around. Under other circumstances he might have ended up shouting at her, because Ellie could turn quite haughty – insulting, even – when accused of some mistake. It was only her way of dealing with criticism, but that did not keep it from infuriating Louis when she laid it on too thick or when he was particularly tired. But this night the kite-flying had left him in a fine mood, and Ellie was inclined to be reasonable. She agreed to be more careful and then went downstairs to watch TV until 8.30, a Saturday indulgence she treasured. *Okay, that's out of the way, and it might even do some good*, Louis thought, not knowing that marbles were really not the problem, and chills were not really the problem, that a large Orinco truck was going to be the problem, that the road was going to be the problem . . . as Jud Crandall had warned them it might be on their first day here last August.

He went upstairs that night about fifteen minutes after Gage had been put to bed. He found his son quiet but still awake, drinking the last of a bottle of milk and looking contemplatively up at the ceiling.

Louis took one of Gage's feet in one hand and raised it up. He kissed it, lowered it. 'Goodnight, Gage,' he said.

'Kite flyne, Daddy,' Gage said.

'It really did fly, didn't it?' Louis said, and for no reason at all he felt tears behind his eyes. 'Right up to the sky, my man.'

'Kite flyne,' Gage said. 'Up to the kye.'

He rolled over on his side, closed his eyes, and slept. Just like that.

Louis was stepping into the hall when he glanced back and saw green, disembodied eyes staring out at him from Gage's closet. The closet door was open . . . just a crack. His heart took a lurch into his throat, and his mouth pulled back and down in a grimace.

He opened the closet door, thinking

(*Zelda it's Zelda in the closet her black tongue puffing out between her lips*)

he wasn't sure what, but of course it was only Church, the

cat was in the closet, and when it saw Louis it arched its back like a cat on a Halloween card. It hissed at him, its mouth partly open, revealing its needle-sharp teeth.

'Get out of there,' Louis muttered.

Church hissed again. It did not move.

'Get *out*, I said.' He picked up the first thing that came to hand in the litter of Gage's toys, a bright plastic Chuggy-Chuggy-Choo-Choo which in this dim light was the maroon color of dried blood. He brandished it at Church, who not only stood his ground but hissed again.

And suddenly, without even thinking, Louis threw the toy at the cat, not playing, not goofing around; he *pegged* the toy at the cat as hard as he could, furious at it, and scared of it, too, that it should hide here in the darkened closet of his son's room and refuse to leave, as if it had a right to be there.

The toy locomotive struck the cat dead center. Church uttered a squawk and fled, displaying its usual grace by slamming into the door and almost falling over on its way out.

Gage stirred, muttered something, shifted position, and was still again. Louis felt a little sick. There was sweat standing out in beads on his forehead.

'Louis?' Rachel, from downstairs, sounding alarmed. 'Did Gage fall out of his crib?'

'He's fine, honey. Church knocked over a couple of his toys.'

'Oh, all right.'

He felt – irrationally or otherwise – the way he might have felt if he had looked in on his son and found a snake crawling over him or a big rat perched on the bookshelf over Gage's crib. Of *course* it was irrational. But when it had hissed at him from the closet like that . . .

(Zelda did you think it was Zelda did you think it was Oz the Gweat and Tewwible)

He closed Gage's closet door, sweeping a number of toys back in with its moving foot. He listened to the tiny click of the latch. After a moment's further hesitation, he turned the closet's thumb-bolt.

He went back to Gage's crib. In shifting around, the kid had kicked his two blankets down around his knees. Louis disentangled him, pulled the blankets up, and then merely stood there, watching his son, for a long time.

PART TWO

THE MICMAC BURYING GROUND

When Jesus came to Bethany, he found that Lazarus had lain in the grave four days already. When Martha heard that Jesus was coming, she hurried to meet him.

'Lord,' she said, 'if you had been here, my brother would not have died. But now you are here, and I know that whatever you ask of God, God will grant.'

Jesus answered her: 'Your brother shall rise again.'

– John's Gospel (paraphrase)

CHAPTER THIRTY-SIX

It's probably wrong to believe there can be any limit to the horror which the human mind can experience. On the contrary, it seems that some exponential effect begins to obtain as deeper and deeper darkness falls – as little as we may like to admit it, human experience tends, in a good many ways, to support the idea that when the nightmare grows black enough, horror spawns horror, that one coincidental evil begets other, often more deliberate, evils, until finally blackness seems to cover everything. And the most terrifying question of all may be just how much horror the human mind can stand and still maintain a wakeful, staring, unrelenting sanity. That such events have their own Rube Goldberg absurdity goes almost without saying. At some point, it all starts to become rather funny. That may be the point at which sanity begins to either save itself or to buckle and break down; that point when one's sense of humor begins to resurface.

Louis Creed might have harbored such thoughts if he had been thinking rationally following the funeral of his son, Gage William Creed, on May 17th, but any rational thought – or attempt at it – ceased at the funeral parlor, where a fistfight with his father-in-law (bad enough) resulted in an event even more terrible, a final bit of gothic melodrama outrageous enough to shatter whatever remained of Rachel's fragile self-control. That day's penny-dreadful events were only complete when she was pulled, screaming, from the East Room of the Brookings-Smith Funeral Home, where Gage lay in his closed coffin. She was sedated in the foyer by Surrendra Hardu.

The irony of it was that she would not have experienced that final episode at all, that comic-book *extravagance* of horror, one might say, if the fistfight between Louis Creed and Mr Irwin Goldman of Dearborn had taken place at the morning visiting hours (10 a.m. to 11.30) instead of at the afternoon visiting hours (2 p.m to 3.30). Rachel had not been in attendance at the morning visiting hours; she simply had not been able to come. She sat at home with Jud Crandall and Steve Masterton. Louis had no idea how he ever could have gotten through the previous forty-eight hours or so without Jud and Steve.

It was well for Louis – well for all three of the remaining family members – that Steve had shown up as promptly as he had, because Louis was at least temporarily unable to make any kind of decision, even one so minor as giving his wife a shot to mute her deep grief. Louis hadn't even noticed that Rachel had apparently meant to go to the morning viewing in her housecoat, which she had misbuttoned. Her hair was uncombed, unwashed, tangled. Her eyes, blank brown orbits, bulged from sockets so sunken that they had almost become the eyes of a living skull. Her flesh was doughy. It hung from her face. She sat at the breakfast table that morning, munching unbuttered toast and talking in disjointed phrases that made no sense at all. At one point she had said abruptly, 'About that Winnebago you want to buy, Lou —' Louis had last spoken about buying a Winnebago in 1981.

Louis only nodded and went on eating his own breakfast. He was having a bowl of Cocoa Bears. Cocoa Bears had been one of Gage's favorite cereals, and this morning Louis wanted them. The taste of them was appalling, but he still wanted them. He was neatly turned out in his best suit – not black, he didn't have a black suit, but it was at least a deep charcoal gray. He had shaved, showered and combed his hair. He looked fine, although he was lost in shock.

Ellie was dressed in blue jeans and a yellow blouse. She had brought a picture to the breakfast table with her. She would not be parted from it. This picture, an enlargement of a Polaroid Rachel had taken with the SX-70 Louis and the kids had given her for her last birthday, showed Gage, grinning from the depths of his Sears ski parka, sitting on her Speedaway sled as Ellie pulled him. Rachel had caught Ellie looking back over her shoulder and smiling at Gage. Gage was grinning back at her.

Ellie carried the picture, but she didn't talk much. It was as if the death of her brother in the road in front of the house had shocked away most of her vocabulary.

Louis was unable to see the condition of either his wife or his daughter; he ate his breakfast and his mind replayed the accident over and over and over, except in this mind-movie the conclusion was different. In the mind-movie he was quicker and all that happened was that Gage got a spanking for not stopping when they yelled.

It was Steve who really saw how it was going with Rachel, and with Ellie as well. He forbade Rachel to go to the morning viewing (although viewing was really a misnomer because of the closed coffin; if it was open, Louis thought, they'd all run screaming from the room, me included) and forbade Ellie to go at all. Rachel protested. Ellie only sat, silent and grave, with the picture of her and Gage in one hand.

It was Steve who gave Rachel the shot she needed, and who gave Ellie a teaspoon of a colorless liquid to drink. Ellie usually whined and protested about taking medicine – any kind of medicine – but she drank this silently and without a grimace. By ten o'clock that morning she was asleep in her bed (the picture of her and Gage still held in her hand) and Rachel was sitting in front of the television set, watching *Wheel of Fortune*. Her responses to Steve's questions were slow and considered and calm. She was stoned – but her face had lost that thoughtful look of madness which had so worried – and frightened – the PA when he came in that morning at quarter past eight.

Jud, of course, had made all the arrangements. He made them with the same calm efficiency that he had made them for his wife three months before. But it was Steve Masterton who took Louis aside just before Louis left for the funeral home.

'I'll see that she's there this afternoon, if she seems capable of handling it,' he told Louis.

'Okay.'

'The shot will have worn off by then. Your friend Mr Crandall says he'll stay with Ellie during the afternoon viewing hours—'

'Right.'

'—and play Monopoly or something with her—'

'Uh-huh.'

'But—'

'Right.'

Steve stopped. They were standing in the garage, Church's stomping ground, the place where he brought his dead birds and dead rats. The ones that Louis owned. Outside was May sunshine, and a robin bopped across the head of the driveway, as if it had important business somewhere.

'Louis,' Steve said, 'you've got to get hold of yourself.'

Louis looked at Steve, politely questioning. Not much of what Steve had said had gotten through – he had been thinking that if he had been a little quicker he could have possibly saved his son's life – but a little of this last had registered.

'I don't think you've noticed,' Steve said, 'but Ellie isn't vocalizing. Not at all. And Rachel has had such a bad shock that her very conception of time seems to have been twisted out of shape.'

'Right!' Louis said. More force in reply seemed to be indicated here. He wasn't sure why.

Steve put a hand on Louis's shoulder. 'Lou,' he said, 'they need you more now than they ever have in their life. Please, man ... I can give your wife a shot, but ... you ... see, Louis, you gotta ... oh, *Christ*, Louis, what a cock-knocking, motherfucking mess this is!'

Louis saw with something like alarm that Steve was starting

to cry. 'Sure,' he said, and in his mind he saw Gage running across the lawn toward the road, and they were yelling at him to come back, but Gage wouldn't. Lately the game was run away from Mommy-Daddy, and then they were chasing him, Louis quickly outdistancing Rachel, but Gage had a big lead, Gage was laughing, Gage was running away from Daddy, that was the game, and Louis was closing the distance but too slowly, Gage was running down the mild slope of the lawn now to the verge of Route 15, and Louis prayed to God that Gage would fall down, when little kids run fast they almost *always* fall down because a person's control over his legs didn't get really cool until he was maybe seven or eight. Louis prayed to God Gage would fall down, fall down, yes, fall down bloody his nose crack his skull need stitches whatever, because now he could hear the drone of a truck coming toward them, one of those big ten-wheelers that went back and forth endlessly between Bangor and the Orinco plant in Bucksport, and he had screamed Gage's name then, and he believed that Gage had heard him and tried to stop. Gage seemed to realize that the game was over, that your parents didn't *scream* at you when it was just a game, and he had tried to put on the brakes, and by then the sound of the truck was *very* loud, the sound of it filled the world. It was thundering. Louis had thrown himself forward in a long flying tackle, his shadow tracking the ground beneath him as the shadow of the Vulture had tracked the white late-winter grass of Mrs Vinton's field that day in March, and he believed (but was not sure) that the tips of his fingers had actually brushed the back of the light jacket Gage had been wearing, and then Gage's forward motion had carried him out into the road, and the truck had been thunder, the truck had been sunlight on high chrome, the truck had been the deep-throated, shrieking bellow of an air-horn, and that had been Saturday, that had been three days ago.

'I'm okay,' he said to Steve. 'I ought to go now.'

'If you can get yourself together and help them,' Steve said, swiping at his eyes with the arm of his jacket, 'you'll be helping yourself, too. The three of you have got to get through it together, Louis. That's the only way. That's all anybody knows.'

'That's right,' Louis agreed, and in his mind it all started to happen again, only this time he leaped two feet further right at the end, and snagged the back of Gage's jacket, and jerked him back, and none of this was happening.

Ellie missed the scene in the East Room of the Brookings-Smith Funeral Home, but Rachel did not. At the time it happened, Ellie was pushing her Monopoly marker aimlessly – and silently – around the board with Jud Crandall. She shook her dice with one hand and clutched the Polaroid of her pulling Gage on her Speedaway sled with the other.

Steve Masterton had decided it would be all right for Rachel to attend the afternoon viewing – in the light of later developments, it was a decision he came to deeply regret.

The Goldmans had flown into Bangor from Chicago that morning and were staying at the Holiday Inn on Odlin Road. Her father had called four times by noon, and Steve had to be increasingly firm – almost threatening, by call four – with the old man. Irwin Goldman wanted to come out and not all the dogs of hell could keep him from his daughter in her time of need, he said. Steve responded that Rachel needed this time before going to the funeral parlor to get over as much of her initial shock as she could. He didn't know about all the dogs of hell, he said, but he knew one Swedish-American physician's assistant who had no intention of allowing anyone into the Creed home until Rachel had appeared in public, of her own volition. After the viewing in the afternoon, Steve said, he would be more than happy to let the relatives' support system take over. Until then, he wanted her left alone.

The old man swore at him in Yiddish and banged the phone down at his end, breaking the connection. Steve waited to see if Goldman would indeed show up, but Goldman had apparently decided to wait. By noon, Rachel did seem a little better. She was at least aware of the time-frame she was in, and she had gone out to the kitchen to see if there were sandwich-makings or anything for after. People would probably want to come back to the house after, wouldn't they? she asked Steve.

Steve nodded.

There was no bologna or cold roast beef, but there was a Butterball turkey in the freezer, and she put it on the drainboard to thaw. Steve looked into the kitchen a few minutes later and saw her standing by the sink, looking fixedly at the turkey on the drainboard, and weeping.

'Rachel?'

She looked toward Steve. 'Gage really liked these. He especially liked the white meat.' She smiled a wan, terrible smile. 'It was just occurring to me that he was never going to eat another Butterball turkey.'

Steve sent her upstairs to dress – the final test of her ability to cope, really – and when she came down wearing a simple black dress belted at the waist and carrying a small black clutch-bag (an evening bag, really), Steve decided she was all right, and Jud concurred.

Steve drove her into town. He stood with Surrendra Hardu in the lobby of the East Room and watched Rachel drift down the aisle toward the flower-buried coffin like a wraith.

'How is it going, Steve?' Surrendra asked quietly.

'Going fucking terrible,' Steve said in a low, harsh voice. 'How did you think it was going?'

'I thought it was probably going fucking terrible,' Surrendra said, and sighed.

The trouble really began at the morning viewing when Irwin Goldman refused to shake hands with his son-in-law.

The sight of so many friends and relatives had actually forced Louis out of the web of shock a little; had forced him to notice what was going on and be outward. He had reached that stage of malleable grief that funeral directors are so used to handling and turning to its best advantage. Louis was moved around like a pawn.

Outside the East Room was a small foyer where people could smoke and sit in overstuffed easy chairs. The chairs looked as if they might have come directly from a Distress Sale at some old Englishmen's club that had gone broke. Beside the door leading into the viewing room was a small easel, black metal chased with gold, and on this easel was a small sign which said simply GAGE WILLIAM CREED. If you went across this spacious white building that looked misleadingly like a comfortable old house, you came to an identical foyer, this one outside the West Room, where the sign on the easel read ALBERTA BURNHAM NEDEAU. At the back of the house was the River-Front Room. The easel to the left of the door between the foyer and this room was blank; it was not in use on this Tuesday morning. Downstairs was the coffin showroom, each model lit by a baby spotlight mounted on the ceiling. If you looked up – Louis had and the funeral director had frowned severely at him – it looked as though there were a lot of strange animals roosting up there.

Jud had come with him on Sunday, the day after Gage had died, to pick out a coffin. They had gone downstairs, and instead of immediately turning right into the coffin showroom, Louis, dazed, had continued straight on down the hallway toward a plain white swinging door, the sort you see communicating between restaurant dining rooms and the kitchen. Both Jud and the funeral director had said quickly and simultaneously, 'Not that way,' and Louis had followed them away from that swinging door obediently. He knew what was behind that door, though. His uncle had been an undertaker.

The East Room was furnished with neat rows of folding chairs – the expensive ones with plushy seats and backs. At the front, in an area that seemed a combination of nave and bower, was Gage's coffin. Louis had picked the American Casket Company's rosewood model – Eternal Rest, it was called. It was lined with plushy pink silk. The mortician agreed that it was really a beautiful coffin, and apologized that he did not have one with a blue lining. Louis responded that he and Rachel had never made such distinctions. The mortician had nodded. The mortician asked Louis if he had thought about how he would defray the expenses of Gage's funeral. If not, he said, he could take Louis into his office and go quickly over three of their more popular plans—

In Louis's mind, an announcer suddenly spoke up cheerfully: *I got my kid's coffin free, for Raleigh coupons!*

Feeling like a creature in a dream, he said: 'I'm going to pay for everything with my MasterCharge.'

'Fine,' the mortician said.

The coffin was no more than four feet long – a dwarf coffin. Nonetheless, its price was slightly over six hundred dollars. Louis supposed it rested on trestles, but all the flowers made it difficult to see, and he hadn't wanted to go too close. The smell of all those flowers made him want to gag.

At the back of the aisle, just inside the door giving on the foyer-lounge, was a book on a stand. Chained to the stand was a ballpoint pen. It was here that the funeral director positioned Louis, so he could 'greet his friends and relatives'.

The friends and relatives were supposed to sign the book with their names and addresses. Louis had never had the slightest idea what the purpose of this mad custom might be, and he did not ask. He supposed when the funeral was over he and Rachel would get to keep the book. That seemed the maddest thing of all. Somewhere he had a high school yearbook and a college yearbook and a med school yearbook; there was also a wedding book, MY WEDDING DAY stamped on the imitation leather in imitation gold leaf, beginning with a photo of Rachel trying on her bridal veil before the mirror that morning with her mother's help and ending with a photo of two pairs of shoes outside a closed hotel door. There was also a baby book for Ellie – they had tired of adding to it rather quickly, though; that one, with its spaces for FROM MY FIRST HAIRCUT (add a lock of baby's hair) and

WHOOPS! (add a picture of baby falling on her ass), had been just too relentlessly cute.

Now, added to all the others, this one. What do we call it? Louis wondered as he stood numbly beside the stand waiting for the party to begin. MY DEATHBOOK? FUNERAL AUTOGRAPHS? THE DAY WE PLANTED GAGE? Or maybe something more dignified, like A DEATH IN THE FAMILY?

He turned the book back to its cover, which, like the cover to the MY WEDDING DAY book, was imitation leather.

The cover was blank.

Almost predictably, Missy Dandridge had been the first to arrive that morning, good-hearted Missy who had sat with Ellie and Gage on dozens of occasions. Abruptly Louis found himself remembering it had been Missy who had taken the kids on the evening of the day Victor Pascow had died. She had taken the kids and Rachel had made love to him, first in the tub, then in bed.

Missy had been crying, crying hard, and at the sight of Louis's calm, still face, she burst into fresh tears and reached for him – seemed to grope for him. Louis embraced her, realizing that this was the way it worked, or was supposed to work, anyway – some kind of human charge that went back and forth, loosening up the hard earth of loss, venting it, breaking up the rocky pack of shock with the heat of sorrow.

I'm so sorry, Missy was saying, brushing her dark blonde hair back from her pallid face. Such a dear, sweet little boy. I loved him so much, Louis, I'm so sorry, it's an *awful* road, I hope they put that truck-driver in jail for ever, he was going much too fast, he was so sweet, so dear, so bright, why would God take Gage, I don't know, we can't understand, can we, but I'm sorry, sorry, so sorry.

Louis comforted her, held her and comforted her. He felt her tears on his collar. The press of her breasts against him. She wanted to know where Rachel was and Louis told her that Rachel was resting. Missy promised to go see her, and that she would sit with Ellie any time, for as long as they needed her. Louis thanked her.

She had started away, still sniffing, her eyes redder than ever above her black handkerchief. She was moving toward the coffin when Louis called her back. The funeral director, whose name Louis could not even remember, had told him to have them sign the book, and damned if he wasn't going to have them do it.

Mystery guest, sign in please, he thought, and came very close to going off into cackles of bright, hysterical laughter.

It was Missy's woeful, heartbroken eyes that drove the laughter away.

'Missy, would you sign the book?' he asked her, and because something else seemed to be needed, he added: 'For Rachel.'

'Of course,' she said. 'Poor Louis, and poor Rachel.' And suddenly Louis knew what she was going to say next, and for some reason he dreaded it; yet it was coming, unavoidable, like a black bullet of large caliber from a killer's gun, and he knew that he would be struck over and over by this bullet in the next interminable ninety minutes, and then again in the afternoon, while the wounds of the morning were still trickling blood:

'Thank God he didn't suffer, Louis. At least it was quick.'

Yes, it was quick, all right, he thought about saying to her – ah; how that would shatter her face all over again, and he felt a vicious urge to do it, to simply spray the words into her face. *It was quick, no doubt about that, that's why the coffin's closed, nothing could have been done about Gage even if Rachel and I approved of dressing up dead relatives in their best like department store mannequins and rouging and powdering and painting their faces. It was quick, Missy-my-dear, one minute he was there in the road and the next minute he was lying in it, but way down by the Ringers' house. It hit him and killed him and then it dragged him and you better believe it was quick. A hundred yards or more all told, the length of a football field. I ran after him, Missy, I was screaming his name over and over again, almost as if I expected he would still be alive, me, a doctor. I ran ten yards and there was his baseball cap and I ran twenty yards and there was one of his Star Wars sneakers, I ran forty yards and by then the truck had run off the road and the box had jackknifed in that field beyond the Ringers' barn. People were coming out of their houses and I went on screaming his name, Missy, and at the fifty-yard-line there was his jumper, it was turned inside-out, and on the seventy-yard-line there was the other sneaker, and then there was Gage.*

Abruptly the world went dove-gray. Everything passed out of his view. Dimly, he could feel the corner of the stand which held the book digging into his palm, but that was all.

'Louis?' Missy's voice. Distant. The mystery-sound of pigeons in his ears.

'Louis?' Closer now. Alarmed.

The world swam back into focus.

'You all right?'

He smiled. 'Fine,' he said. 'I'm okay, Missy.'

She signed for herself and her husband – Mr and Mrs David Dandridge – in round Palmer-method script; to this she added their address, Rural Box 67, Old Bucksport Road, and then raised her eyes to Louis's and quickly dropped them, as if her very address on the road where Gage had died constituted a crime.

'Be well, Louis,' she whispered.

David Dandridge shook his hand and muttered something inarticulate, his prominent, arrowhead-shaped adam's apple bobbing up and down. Then he followed his wife hurriedly down the aisle for the ritual examination of a coffin which had been made in Storyville, Ohio, a place where Gage had never been and where he was not known.

Following the Dandridges they all came, moving in a shuffling line, and Louis received them, their handshakes, their hugs, their tears. His collar and the upper sleeve of his dark-gray suitcoat soon became quite damp. The smell of the flowers began to reach even the back of the room and to permeate the place with the smell of funeral. It was a smell he remembered from his childhood – that mortuary smell of flowers. Louis was told how merciful it was that Gage hadn't suffered thirty-two times by his own inner count. He was told that God works in mysterious ways his wonders to perform twenty-five times. Bringing up the rear was *he's with the angels now*: a total of twelve times.

It began to get to him. Instead of losing what marginal sense these little aphorisms had (the way your own name will lose its sense and identity if you repeat it over and over again), they seemed to punch deeper each time, angling in toward the vitals. By the time his mother- and father-in-law put in their inevitable appearance, he had begun to feel like a hard-tagged fighter.

His first thought was that Rachel had been right, and how Irwin Goldman had indeed aged. He was – what? fifty-eight? fifty-nine? – today he looked a graven and composed seventy. He looked almost absurdly like Israel's prime minister Mena-chem Begin with his bald head and Coke-bottle glasses. Rachel had told him he had aged when she came back from her Thanksgiving trip, but Louis had not expected this. Of course, he thought, maybe it hadn't been this bad at Thanksgiving. The old man hadn't lost one of his two grandchildren at Thanksgiving.

Dory walked beside him, her face all but invisible under two – possibly three – layers of heavy black netting. Her hair was fashionably blue, the color favored by elderly ladies of an upper-class American persuasion. She held her husband's arm. All Louis could really see behind the veil was the glitter of her tears.

Suddenly he decided it was time to let bygones be bygones. He could not hold the old grudge any longer. Suddenly it was too heavy. Perhaps it was the cumulative weight of all those platitudes.

'Irwin. Dory,' he murmured. 'Thank you for coming.'

He made a gesture with his arms, as if to shake hands with Rachel's father and hug her mother simultaneously, or perhaps even to hug them both. Either way, he felt his own tears start for the first time, and for an instant he had the crazy idea that they could mend all of their fences, that Gage would do that much for them in his dying, as if this were some romantic ladies' novel he had stepped into where the wages of death were reconciliation, where it could cause something more constructive than this endless, stupid, grinding ache which just went on and on and on.

Dory started toward him, making a gesture, beginning, perhaps, to hold out her own arms. She said something – 'Oh, Louis—' and something else that was garbled – and then Goldman pulled his wife back. For a moment the three of them stood in a tableau that no one noticed except themselves (unless perhaps the funeral director, standing unobtrusively in the far corner of the East Room, saw – Louis supposed that Uncle Carl would have seen), Louis with his arms partly out-stretched, Irwin and Dory Goldman standing as stiff and straight as a couple on a wedding cake.

Louis saw then that there were no tears in his father-in-law's eyes; they were bright and clear with hate. (*Does he think I killed Gage to spite him?* Louis wondered.) Those eyes seemed to measure Louis, to find him the same small and pointless man who had kidnapped his daughter and brought her to this sorrow . . . and then to dismiss him. His eyes shifted to Louis's left – to Gage's coffin, in fact – and only then did they soften.

Still, Louis made a final effort, 'Irwin,' he said. 'Dory. Please. We have to get together on this.'

'Louis,' Dory said again, kindly, he thought, and then they were past him, Irwin Goldman perhaps pulling his wife along, not looking to the left or the right, certainly not looking at Louis Creed. They approached the coffin, and Goldman fumbled a small black skullcap out of his suitcoat pocket.

You didn't sign the book, Louis thought, and then a silent belch of such malignantly acidic content rose through his digestive works that his face clenched in pain.

The morning viewing ended at last. Louis called home. Jud answered and asked him how it had gone. All right, Louis said. He asked Jud if he could talk to Steve.

'If she can dress herself, I'm going to let her come this afternoon,' Steve said. 'Okay by you?'

'Yes.' Louis said.

'How are you, Lou? No bullshit and straight on – how are you?'

'All right,' Louis said briefly. 'Coping.' *I had all of them sign the book. All of them except Dory and Irwin, and they wouldn't.*

'All right,' Steve said. 'Look, shall we meet you for lunch?'

Lunch. Meeting for lunch. This seemed such an alien idea that Louis thought of the science-fiction novels he had read as a teenager – novels by Robert Heinlein, Murray Leinster, Gordon Dickson. *The natives here on Planet Quark have an odd custom when one of their children dies, Lieutenant Abelson: they 'meet for lunch'. I know how grotesque and barbaric that sounds, but remember, this planet has not been terraformed yet.*

'Sure,' Louis said. 'What's a good restaurant for half-time between funeral viewings, Steve?'

'Take it easy, Lou,' Steve said, but he didn't seem entirely displeased. In this state of crazy calm, Louis felt better able to see into people than ever before in his life. Perhaps it was an illusion, but right now he suspected Steve was thinking that even a sudden spate of sarcasm, squirted out like an abrupt mouthful of bile, was preferable to his earlier state of disconnection.

'Don't worry,' he said to Steve now. 'What about Benjamin's?'

'Sure,' Steve said. 'Benjamin's would be fine.'

He had made the call from the office of the funeral director. Now, as Louis passed the East Room on his way out, he saw that the room was almost empty, but Irwin and Dory Goldman

269

sat down in the front row, heads bowed. They looked to Louis as if they might sit there for ever.

Benjamin's was the right choice. Bangor was an early-lunch town, and around one o'clock it was nearly deserted. Jud had come along with Steve and Rachel, and the four of them ate fried chicken. At one point Rachel went to the ladies' room and remained in there so long that Steve became nervous. He was on the verge of asking a waitress to check on her when she came back to the table, her eyes red.

Louis picked at his chicken and drank a lot of Schlitz beer. Jud matched him bottle for bottle, not talking much.

Their four meals went back almost uneaten, and with his preternatural insight, Louis saw the waitress, a fat girl with a pretty face, debating with herself about whether or not to ask them if their meals had been all right, finally taking another look at Rachel's red-rimmed eyes, and deciding it would be the wrong question. Over coffee Rachel said something so suddenly and so baldly that it rather shocked them all – particularly Louis, who at last was becoming sleepy with the beer. 'I'm going to give his clothes to the Salvation Army.'

'Are you?' Steve said after a moment.

'Yes,' Rachel said. 'There's a lot of wear in them yet. All his jumpers . . . his corduroy pants . . . his shirts. Someone will be glad to get them. They're all very serviceable. Except for the ones he was wearing, of course. They're . . . ruined.'

The last word became a miserable choke. She tried to drink coffee, but that was no good. A moment later she was sobbing into her hands.

There was a queer moment then. There were crossing lines of tension then, and they all seemed to focus on Louis. He felt this with the same preternatural insight he'd had all this day, and of them all, this was the clearest and surest. Even the waitress felt those converging lines of awareness. He saw her pause at a table near the back where she was laying placemats and silver. For a moment Louis was puzzled, and then he understood: they were waiting for him to comfort his wife.

He couldn't do it. He wanted to do it. He understood it was his responsibility to do it. All the same, he couldn't. It was the cat that got in his way. Suddenly, and with no rhyme or reason. The cat. The fucking cat. Church with his ripped mice and the birds he had grounded for ever. When he found them, Louis cleaned up the messes promptly, with no complaint or comment; certainly without protest. He had, after all, bought them. But had he bought this?

He saw his fingers. Louis saw his fingers. He saw his fingers lightly skating over the back of Gage's jacket. Then Gage's jacket had been gone. Then Gage had been gone.

He looked into his coffee cup and let his wife cry beside him, uncomforted.

After a moment – in terms of clock-time probably quite short, but both then and in retrospect it seemed long – Steve put an arm around her and hugged her gently. His eyes on Louis's were reproachful and angry. Louis turned from them toward Jud, but Jud was looking down, as if in shame. There was no help there.

CHAPTER THIRTY-SEVEN

'I knew something like this would happen,' Irwin Goldman said. That was how the trouble started. 'I knew it when she married you. "You'll have all the grief you can stand, and more," I said. And look at this. Look at this . . . this *mess*.'

Louis looked slowly around at his father-in-law, who had appeared before him like some malign jack-in-the-box in a skullcap, and then, instinctively, he looked around at where Rachel had been, by the book on the stand – the afternoon shift was hers by default – but Rachel was gone.

The afternoon viewing had been less crowded, and after half an hour or so, Louis had gone down to the front row of seats and sat there on the aisle, aware of very little (only peripherally aware of the cloying stink of the flowers) except the fact that he was very tired and sleepy. It was only partly the beer, he supposed. His mind was finally ready to shut down. Probably a good thing. Perhaps, after twelve or sixteen hours of sleep, he would be able to comfort Rachel a little.

After a while his head had sunk until he was looking at his hands, loosely linked between his knees. The hum of voices near the back was soothing. He had been relieved to see that Irwin and Dory weren't here when the four of them returned from lunch, but he should have known their continued absence was too good to be true.

'Where's Rachel?' Louis asked now.

'With her mother. Where she should be.' Goldman spoke with the studied triumph of a man who has closed a big deal. There was Scotch on his breath. A lot of it. He stood before Louis like a banty little district attorney before a man in the bar of justice, a man who is patently guilty. He was unsteady on his feet.

'What did you say to her?' Louis said, feeling the beginnings of anger now. He knew Goldman had said something. It was in the man's face.

'Nothing but the truth. I told her this is what it gets you, marrying against your parents' wishes. I told her —'

'Did you say that?' Louis asked incredulously. 'You didn't really say that, did you?'

'That and more,' Irwin Goldman said. He spoke with the smugness of a man who has discovered where the blame goes. 'I always knew it would come to this – this or something like it. I knew what kind of a man you were the first time I saw you.' He leaned forward, exhaling Scotch fumes. He now spoke with the air of a man imparting a great secret. 'I saw through you, you prancing little fraud of a doctor. You enticed my daughter into a stupid, feckless marriage and then you turned her into a scullery-maid and then you let her son be run down in the highway like a . . . a chipmunk.'

Most of this went over Louis's head. He was still groping with the idea that this stupid little man could have—

'You *said* that to her?' he repeated. 'You *said* it?'

'I hope you rot in hell!' Goldman said, and heads turned sharply toward the sound of his voice. Tears began to squeeze out of Irwin Goldman's bloodshot brown eyes. His bald head glowed under the muted fluorescent lights. 'You made my wonderful daughter into a scullery-maid . . . destroyed her future . . . took her away . . . and let my grandson die a dirty death in a country road.'

His voice rose to a hectoring scream.

'*Where were you? Sitting on your ass while he was playing in the road? Thinking about your stupid medical articles? What were you doing, you shit? You stinking shit! Killer of children! Ki—*'

There they were. There they were at the front of the East Room. There they were and Louis saw his arm go out. He saw the sleeve of his suitcoat pull back from the cuff of his white shirt. He saw the mellow gleam of one cufflink – Rachel had given him the set for their third wedding anniversary, never knowing that her husband would someday wear these cufflinks to the funeral ceremonies of their then-unborn son. His fist was just something tied to the end of his arm. It connected with Goldman's mouth, and he felt the old man's lips squash and splay back. It was a sickening feeling, really; squashing a slug with your fist might feel something like that. There was no satisfaction in it. Beneath the flesh of his father-in-law's lips he could feel the stern, unyielding regularity of his dentures.

Goldman went stumbling backward. His arm came down against Gage's coffin, knocking it aslant. One of the vases, top heavy with flowers, fell over with a crash. Someone screamed.

It was Rachel, struggling with her mother, who was trying to hold her back. The people who were there – ten or fifteen in all – seemed frozen between fright and embarrassment. Steve had taken Jud back to Ludlow, and Louis was dimly grateful for that. This was not a scene he would have wished Jud to witness. It was unseemly.

'Don't hurt him!' Rachel screamed. 'Louis, don't hurt my father!'

'You like to hit old men, do you?' Irwin Goldman of the overflowing checkbook cried out shrilly. He was grinning through a mouthful of blood the color of rubies. 'You like to hit old men? I am not surprised, you stinking bastard. That does not surprise me at all.'

Louis turned toward him and Goldman struck him in the neck. It was a clumsy, side-handed, chopping blow, but Louis was unprepared for it. A paralyzing pain that would make it hard for him to swallow for the next two hours exploded in his throat. His head rocked back and he fell to one knee in the aisle.

First the flowers, now me, he thought. *What is it the Ramones say? Hey-ho, let's go!* He thought he wanted to laugh, but there

was no laugh in him. What came out of his hurt throat was
a little groan.

Rachel screamed again.

Irwin Goldman, his mouth dripping blood, kicked Louis
in the kidneys. The pain was a bright flare of agony. He put
his hands down on the rug-runner to keep from going flop
on his belly.

'You don't do so good even against old men, sonny!'
Goldman cried with cracked excitement. He kicked out
at Louis again, missing the kidney this time, getting Louis
on the high part of the left buttock with one black old man's
shoe. Louis grunted in pain and this time he did go down
on the carpet. His chin hit with an audible crack. He bit his
tongue.

'There!' Goldman cried. 'There's the kick in the ass I should
have given you the first time you came sucking around, you
bastard. There!' He kicked Louis in the ass again, this time
connecting with the other buttock. He was weeping and grinning. Louis saw for the first time that Goldman was unshaven
– a sign of mourning. The funeral director raced toward them.
Rachel had broken Mrs Goldman's hold and was also racing
toward them, screaming.

Louis rolled clumsily over on his side and sat up. His father-
in-law kicked out at him again and Louis caught his shoe
in both hands – it thwapped solidly into his palms like a
well-caught football – and shoved backwards, as hard as he
could.

Bellowing, Goldman flew backwards at an angle, pin-
wheeling his arms for balance. He fell on Gage's Eternal Rest
casket, which had been manufactured in the town of Storyville,
Ohio, and which had not come cheap.

*Oz the Gweat and Tewwible has just fallen on top of my son's
coffin*, Louis thought dazedly. The casket fell from the trestle
with a huge crash. The left end fell first, then the right. The
latch snapped. Even over the screams and the crying, even
over the bellows of Goldman, who after all was only an old

child playing a children's party-game of Pin the Blame on the Donkey, Louis heard the lock snap.

The coffin did not actually open and spill Gage's sad, hurt remains out on to the floor for all of them to gawp at, but Louis was sickly aware that they had only been spared that by the way the coffin had fallen – on its bottom instead of its side. It easily could have fallen that other way. Nonetheless, in that split instant before the lid slammed shut on its broken latch again, he saw a flash of gray – the suit they had bought to put in the ground around Gage's body – and a bit of pink. Gage's hand.

Sitting there on the floor, Louis put his face in his hands and began to weep. He had lost all interest in his father-in-law, in the MX missile, in permanent versus dissolving sutures, in the heat-death of the universe. At that moment, Louis Creed wished he were dead. And suddenly, weirdly, an image rose in his mind: Gage in Mickey Mouse ears, Gage laughing and shaking hands with a great big Goofy on Main Street, in Disney World. He saw this with utter clarity.

One of the trestle supports had fallen over; the other leaned with drunken casualness against the low dais where a minister might stand to offer a eulogy. Sprawled in the flowers was Goldman, also weeping. Water from the overturned vases trickled. The flowers, some of them crushed and mangled, gave off their turgid scent even more strongly.

Rachel was screaming and screaming.

Louis could not respond to her screams. The image of Gage in Mickey Mouse ears was fading, but not before he heard a voice announcing there would be fireworks later that evening. He sat with his face in his hands, not wanting them to see him any more, his tear-stained face, his loss, his guilt, his pain, his shame, most of all his cowardly wish to be dead and out of this blackness.

The funeral director and Dory Goldman led Rachel out. She was still screaming. Later on, in another room (one Louis assumed was reserved especially for those overcome with grief

– the Hysterics' Parlor, perhaps) she became very silent. Louis himself, dazed but sane and in control, sedated her this time, after insisting that the two of them be left alone.

At home, he led her up to bed and gave her another shot. Then he pulled the covers up to her chin and regarded her waxy, pallid face.

'Rachel, I'm sorry,' he said. 'I'd give anything in the world to take that back.'

'It's all right,' she said in a strange, flat voice, and then rolled over on her side, turning away from him.

He heard the tired old question *Are you all right?* rising to his lips and pushed it back. It wasn't a true question; it wasn't what he really wanted to know.

'How bad are you?' he asked finally.

'Pretty bad, Louis,' she said, and then uttered a sound that could have been a laugh. 'I am fucking terrible, in fact.'

Something more seemed required, but Louis could not supply it. He felt suddenly resentful of her, of Steve Masterton, of Missy Dandridge and her husband with his arrowhead-shaped adam's apple, of the whole damned crew. Why should he have to be the eternal supplier? What sort of shit was that?

He turned off the light and left. He found that he could not give much more to his daughter.

For one wild moment, regarding her in her shadowy room, he thought she was Gage – the thought that the whole thing had been a hideous nightmare, like his dream of Pascow leading him into the woods, came to him, and for a moment his tired mind grasped at it. The shadows helped – there was only the shifting light of the portable TV that Jud had taken up for her to pass the hours. The long, long hours.

But it wasn't Gage, of course; it was Ellie, who was now not only grasping the picture in which she was pulling Gage on the sled, but sitting in Gage's chair. She had taken it out of his room and brought it into hers. It was a small director's chair with a canvas seat and a canvas strip across the back.

Stencilled across that strip was GAGE. Rachel had mail-ordered four of these chairs. Each member of the family had one with his or her name stencilled on the back.

Ellie was too big for Gage's chair. She was crammed into it, and the canvas bottom bulged downward dangerously. She held the Polaroid picture to her chest and stared at the TV, where some movie was showing.

'Ellie,' he said, snapping off the TV, 'bedtime.'

She worked her way out of the chair, then folded it up. She apparently meant to take the chair into bed with her.

Louis hesitated, wanting to say something about the chair, and finally settled for, 'Do you want me to tuck you in?'

'Yes, please,' she said.

'Do you ... would you want to sleep with Mommy tonight?'

'No, thanks.'

'You sure?'

She smiled a little. 'Yes. She steals the covers.'

Louis smiled back. 'Come on, then.'

Instead of trying to put the chair in bed with her, Ellie unfolded it by the head of the bed, and an absurd image came to Louis – here was the consulting room of the world's smallest psychiatrist.

She undressed, putting the picture of her and Gage on her pillow to do it, put on her baby-doll pajamas, picked up the picture, went into the bathroom, put it down to wash up, brush, floss, and to take her fluoride tablet. Then she picked it up again and got into bed with it.

Louis sat down beside her and said, 'I want you to know, Ellie, that if we keep on loving each other, we can get through this.'

Each word was like moving a handcar loaded with wet bales, and the total effort left Louis feeling exhausted.

'I'm going to wish really hard,' Ellie said calmly, 'and pray to God for Gage to come back.'

'Ellie—'

'God can take it back if he wants to,' Ellie said. 'He can do anything He wants to.'

'Ellie, God doesn't do things like that,' Louis said uneasily, and in his mind's eye he saw Church squatting on the closed lid of the toilet, staring at him with those muddy eyes as Louis lay in the tub.

'He does so,' she said. 'In Sunday School the teacher told us about this guy Lazarus. He was dead and Jesus brought him back to life. He said, "Lazarus, come forth," and the teacher said if he'd just said "Come forth," probably everybody in that graveyard would have come out, and Jesus only wanted Lazarus.'

An absurdity popped out of his mouth (but the day had sung and gibbered with absurdity): 'That was a long time ago, Ellie.'

'I'm going to keep things ready for him,' she said. 'I've got his picture and I'm going to sit in his chair—'

'Ellie, you're too big for Gage's chair,' Louis said, taking her hot, feverish hand. 'You'll break it.'

'God will help it not to break,' Ellie said. Her voice was serene, but Louis observed the brown half-moons under her eyes. Looking at her made his heart ache so badly that he turned away from her. Maybe when Gage's chair broke, she would begin to understand what had happened a little better.

'I'm going to carry the picture and sit in his chair,' she said. 'I'm going to eat his breakfast, too.' Gage and Ellie had each had their own breakfast cereals; Gage's, Ellie had once claimed, tasted like dead boogers. If Cocoa Bears was the only cereal in the house, Ellie would sometimes eat a boiled egg . . . or nothing at all. 'I'll eat lima beans even though I hate them, and I'll read all of Gage's picture books and I'll . . . I'll . . . you know . . . get things ready . . . in case . . .'

She was crying now. Louis did not try to comfort her, but only brushed her hair back from her forehead. What she was talking about made a certain crazed sense. Keeping the lines open. Keeping things current. Keeping Gage in the present, in the Hot One Hundred, refusing to let him recede; remember when Gage did this . . . or that . . . Yeah, that was great . . . good old Gage, wotta kid. When it started not to hurt, it started not to matter. She understood, perhaps, Louis thought, how easy it would be to let Gage become dead.

'Ellie, don't cry any more,' he said, 'this isn't for ever.'

She *cried* for ever . . . for fifteen minutes. She actually fell asleep before her tears stopped. But eventually she slept, and downstairs the clock struck ten in the quiet house.

Keep him alive, Ellie, if that's what you want, he thought, and kissed her. *The shrinks would probably say it's as unhealthy as hell, but I'm for it. Because I know the day will come — maybe as soon as this Friday — when you forget to carry the picture and I'll see it lying on your bed in this empty room while you ride your bike around the driveway or walk in the field behind the house or go over to Kathy McGown's house to make clothes with her Sew Perfect. Gage won't be with you, and that's when Gage drops off whatever Hot One Hundred there is that exists in little girls' hearts and starts to become Something That Happened In 1984. A blast from the past.*

Louis left the room and stood for a moment at the head of the stairs, thinking — not seriously — about going to bed.

He knew what he needed. He went downstairs to get it.

Louis Albert Creed methodically set about getting drunk. Downstairs in the cellar were five cases of Schlitz Light beer. Louis drank beer, Jud drank it, Steve Masterton drank it, Missy Dandridge would occasionally have a beer or two while watching the kids (*kid*, Louis reminded himself, going down the cellar stairs). Even Charlton, on the few occasions she had come over to the house, preferred a beer — as long as it was a light beer — to a glass of wine. So one day last winter Rachel had gone out and bought a staggering ten cases when Schlitz Light went on sale at the Brewer A&P. *Stop you running down to Julio's in Orrington every time somebody drops in*, she had said. *And you're always quoting Robert Parker to me, love — any beer that's in the refrigerator after the stores close is good beer, right? So drink this and think about the dough you're saving.* Last winter. When things had been okay. *When things had been okay.* It was funny, how quickly and easily your mind made that crucial division.

Louis brought up a case of beer and shoved the cans into the fridge. Then he took one can, closed the fridge door, and opened it. Church came oiling slowly and rustily out of the pantry at the sound of the refrigerator door and stared inquiringly up at Louis. He did not come too close; Louis had perhaps kicked him too many times.

'Nothing for you,' he told the cat. 'You had your can of Calo today. If you want something else, go kill a bird.'

Church stood there, looking up at him. Louis drank off half the can of beer and felt it go to his head almost at once.

'You don't even eat them, do you?' he asked. 'Just killing them is enough for you.'

Church strolled into the living room, apparently deciding there was going to be no food, and after a moment, Louis followed him.

He thought again, randomly: *Hey-ho, let's go.*

Louis sat down in his chair and looked at Church again. The cat was reclining on the rug by the TV stand, watching Louis carefully, probably ready to run if Louis should suddenly become aggressive and decide to put his kicking-foot in gear.

Instead, Louis raised his beer. 'To Gage,' he said. 'To my son, who might have been an artist or an Olympic swimmer or the mother-fucking President of the United States. What do you say, asshole?'

Church regarded him with those dull, strange eyes.

Louis drank off the rest of his beer in big gulps that hurt his tender throat, arose, went to the fridge, and got a second one.

By the time Louis had finished three beers, he felt that he had some sort of equilibrium for the first time that day. By the time he had gotten through the first six-pack, he felt that sleep might actually be possible in another hour or so. He came back from the fridge with his eighth or ninth (he had really lost count by then, and was walking on a slant), and his eyes fell on Church, who was dozing – or pretending to – on the rug now. The thought came so naturally that it surely must have been there all along, simply waiting its time to come forward from the back of his mind:

When are you going to do it? When are you going to bury Gage in the Pet Sematary?

And on the heels of that:

Lazarus, come forth.

Ellie's sleepy, dazed voice:

The teacher said if he'd just said 'Come forth,' probably everybody in that graveyard would have come out.

A chill of such elemental force struck him that Louis clutched himself as the shudder twisted through his body. He suddenly found himself remembering Ellie's first day of school, how Gage had gone to sleep on his lap while he and Rachel were listening to Ellie prattle on about *Old MacDonald* and Mrs Berryman; he had said *Just let me put the baby to bed* and when he took Gage upstairs a horrible premonition had struck him, and now he understood: back in September, part of him had known Gage was going to die soon. Part of him had known that Oz the Gweat and Tewwible was at hand. It was nonsense, it was rot, it was superstitious bullshit of the purest ray serene . . . and it was true. He had *known*. Louis spilled some of his beer on his shirt and Church looked up warily to see if this was a signal that the evening's cat-kicking festivities were about to commence.

Louis suddenly remembered the question he had asked Jud; he remembered the way Jud's arm had jerked, knocking two empty beer-bottles off the table. One of them had shattered. *You don't even want to talk about such things, Louis!*

But he *did* want to talk about them – or at least think about them. The Pet Sematary. What was beyond the Pet Sematary. The idea had a deadly attraction. It made a balance of logic which was impossible to deny. Church had been killed in the road; Gage had been killed in the road. Here was Church – changed, of course, distasteful in some ways – but here. Ellie, Gage and Rachel all had a working relationship with him. He killed birds, true, and had turned a few mice inside out, but killing small animals was a cat thing to do. Church had by no means turned into Frankencat. He was, in many ways, as good as ever.

You're rationalizing, a voice whispered. *He's* not *as good as ever. He's spooky. The crow, Louis . . . remember the crow?*

'Good God,' Louis said aloud in a shaky, distracted voice he was barely able to recognize as his own.

God, oh yes, fine, sure. If there had ever been a time to invoke the name of God outside of a spook novel about ghosts or vampires, this was it. So: just what – what in the name of God – was he thinking about? He was thinking about a dark blasphemy which he was even now not wholly able to credit. Worse, he was telling himself lies. Not just rationalizing; outright *lying*.

So what's the truth? You want the truth so fucking bad, what's the truth?

That Church wasn't really a cat any more at all, start with that. He *looked* like a cat, and he *acted* like a cat, but he was really only a poor imitation. People couldn't actually see through that imitation, but they could *feel* through it. He remembered a night when Charlton had been at the house. The occasion had been a small pre-Christmas dinner party. They'd been sitting in here, talking after the meal, and Church had jumped up in her lap. Charlton had pushed the cat off immediately, a quick and instinctive *moue* of distaste puckering her mouth.

It had been no big deal. No one had even commented on it. But . . . it was there. Charlton had felt what the cat *wasn't*. Louis killed his beer and went back for another. If Gage came back changed in such a way, that would be an obscenity.

He popped the top and drank deeply. He was drunk now,

drunk for fair, and there would be a big head for him to deal with tomorrow. How I Went to My Son's Funeral with a Hangover, by Louis Creed. Author of How I Just Missed Him at the Crucial Moment and numerous other works.

Drunk. Sure. And he suspected now that the reason he had gotten drunk was so he could consider this crazy idea soberly.

In spite of everything, the idea had that deadly attraction, that sick luster, that *glamor*. Yes, that above all else – it had *glamor*.

Jud was back, speaking in his mind.

You do it because it gets hold of you. You do it because that burial place is a secret place and you want to share the secret . . . you make up reasons . . . they seem like good reasons . . . but mostly you do it because you want to. Or because you have to.

Jud's voice, low and drawling with Yankee intonation, Jud's voice chilling his flesh, bringing out the goosebumps, making the hackles on the back of his neck rise.

These are secret things, Louis . . . the soil of a man's heart is stonier . . . like the soil up in the old Micmac burying ground. A man grows what he can . . . and he tends it.

Louis began to go over the other things Jud had told him about the Micmac burying ground. He began to collate the data, to sort through it, to compress it – he proceeded in exactly the same way he had once readied himself for big exams.

The dog. Spot.

I could see all the places where the barbed wire had hooked him – there was no fur in any of those places, and the flesh looked dimpled in.

The bull. Another file turned over in Louis's mind.

Lester Morgan buried his prize bull up there. Black Angus bull, named Hanratty . . . Lester dragged him all the way up there on a sledge . . . shot him dead two weeks later. That bull turned mean, really mean. But he's the only animal I ever heard of that did.

He turned mean.

The soil of a man's heart is stonier.

He turned really mean.

He's the only animal I heard of that did.

Mostly you do it because once you've been up there, it's your place.

The flesh looked dimpled in.

Hanratty, ain't that a silly name for a bull?

A man grows what he can . . . and tends it.

They're my rats. And my birds. I bought the fuckers.

It's your place, a secret place, and it belongs to you, and you belong to it.

He turned mean, but he's the only animal I heard of that did.

What do you want to buy next, Louis, when the wind blows hard at night and the moon lays a white path through the woods to that place? Want to climb those stairs again? When they're watching a horror movie, everyone in the audience knows the hero or the heroine is stupid to go up those stairs, but in real life they always do – they smoke, they don't wear seat-belts, they move their family in beside a busy highway where the big rigs drone back and forth all day and all night. So, Louis, what do you say? Want to climb the stairs? Would you like to keep your dead son or go for what's behind Door Number One, Door Number Two, or Door Number Three?

Hey-ho, let's go.

Turned mean . . . only animal . . . the flesh looked . . . a man . . . yours . . . his . . .

Louis dumped the rest of the beer down the sink, feeling suddenly that he was going to vomit. The room was moving around in great swinging motions.

There was a knock at the door.

For a long time – it seemed like a long time, anyway – he believed it was only in his head, a hallucination. But the knocking just went on and on, patient, implacable. And suddenly Louis found himself thinking of the story of the monkey's paw, and a cold terror slipped into him. He seemed to feel it with total physical reality – it was like a dead hand that had been kept in a refrigerator, a dead hand which had suddenly taken on its own disembodied life and slipped inside his shirt to clutch the flesh over his heart. It was a silly image, fulsome and silly, but oh, it didn't *feel* silly. No.

Louis went to the door on feet he could not feel and lifted the latch with nerveless fingers. And as he swung it open he thought: *It'll be Pascow. Like they said about Jim Morrison, back from the dead and bigger than ever. Pascow standing there in his jogging shorts, big as life and as mouldy as month-old bread, Pascow with his horribly ruined head, Pascow bringing the warning again: Don't go up there. What was that old song by The Animals? Baby, please don't go, baby PLEASE don't go, you know I love you so, baby please don't go . . .*

The door swung open and standing there on his front step in the blowing dark of this midnight, between the day of the funeral parlor visitation and the day of his son's burial, was Jud Crandall. His thin white hair blew randomly in the chilly dark.

'Think of the devil, and he stands on your doorstep,' Louis said thickly. He tried to laugh. Time seemed to have turned cleverly back on itself. It was Thanksgiving again. Soon they would put the stiff, unnaturally thickened body of Ellie's cat Winston Churchill into a plastic garbage bag, and start off. *Oh do not ask what is it, let us go and make our visit.*

'Can I come in, Louis?' Jud asked. He took a pack of Chesterfields from his shirt pocket and poked one into his mouth.

'Tell you what,' Louis said. 'It's late and I've been drinking a pile of beer.'

'Ayuh, I could smell it,' Jud said. He struck a match. The wind snuffed it. He struck another around cupped hands, but the hands trembled and betrayed the match to the wind again. He got a third match, prepared to strike it, then looked up at

Louis standing in the doorway. 'I can't get this thing lit,' Jud said. 'Gonna let me in or not, Louis?'

Louis stepped aside and let Jud walk in.

CHAPTER THIRTY-EIGHT

They sat at the kitchen table over beers – *first time we've ever tipped one in our kitchen*, Louis thought, a little surprised. Halfway across the living room, Ellie had cried out in her sleep, and both of them had frozen like statues in a children's game. The cry had not been repeated.

'Okay,' Louis said. 'What are you doing over here at quarter past twelve on the morning my son gets buried? You're a friend, Jud, but this is stretching it.'

Jud drank, wiped his mouth with the heel of his hand, and looked directly at Louis. There was something clear and positive in his eyes, and Louis at last looked down from it.

'You know why I'm here,' Jud said. 'You're thinking about things that are not to be thought of, Louis. Worse still, I fear you're considering them.'

'I wasn't thinking about anything but going up to bed,' Louis said. 'I have a burying to go to tomorrow.'

'I'm responsible for more pain in your heart than you should have tonight,' Jud said softly. 'For all I know, I may even have been responsible for the death of your son.'

Louis looked up, startled. 'What—? Jud, don't talk crazy!'

'You are thinking of trying to put him up there,' Jud said. 'Don't you deny the thought has crossed your mind, Louis.'

Louis did not reply.

'How far does its influence extend?' Jud said. 'Can you tell me that? No. I can't answer that question myself, and I've lived my whole life in this patch of the world. I know about the Micmacs, and that place was always considered to be a kind of holy place to them . . . but not in a good way. Stanny B. told me that. My father told me, too – later on. After Spot died the second time. Now the Micmacs, the State of Maine, and the government of the United States are arguing in court about who owns that land. Who does own it? No one really knows, Louis. Not any more. Different people laid claim to it at one time or another, but no claim ever stuck. Anson Ludlow, the great-grandson of this town's founding father, for one. His claim was maybe the best for a white man, since Joseph Ludlow the Elder had the whole shebang as a grant from Good King Georgie back when Maine was just a big province of the Massachusetts Bay Colony. But even then he would have been in a hell of a court fight, because there was cross-claims to the land by other Ludlows, and by a fellow named Peter Dimmart who claimed he could prove pretty convincingly that he was a Ludlow on the other side of the sheets. And Joseph Ludlow the Elder was money-poor but land-rich towards the end of his life, and every now and then he'd just gift somebody with two or four hundred acres when he got into his cups.'

'Were none of those deeds recorded?' Louis asked, fascinated in spite of himself.

'Oh, they was regular bears for recording deeds, were our grandfathers,' Jud said, lighting a new cigarette from the butt of the old one. 'The original grant on your land goes like this.' Jud closed his eyes and quoted: ' "From the great old maple which stands atop Quinceberry Ridge to the verge of Orrington Stream; thus runneth the tract from north until south." ' Jud grinned without much humor. 'But the great old maple fell down in 1882, let's say, and was rotted to moss by the year 1900, and Orrington Stream silted up and turned to marsh in the ten years between the end of the Great War and the crash of the stock market. A nice mess it made in the end. It ended up not mattering to old Anson, anyways. He was struck and killed by lightning in 1921, right up around where that burying ground is.'

Louis stared at Jud. Jud sipped his beer.

'It don't matter. There's lots of places where the history of ownership is so tangled it never gets unravelled and only the lawyers end up makin' money. Hell, Dickens knew that. I suppose the Indians will get it back in the end, and I think that's the way it should be. But that don't really matter, Louis. I came over here tonight to tell you about Timmy Baterman and his dad.'

'Who's Timmy Baterman?'

'Timmy Baterman was one of the twenty or so boys from Ludlow that went overseas to fight Hitler. He left in 1942. He come back in a box with a flag on the top of it in 1943. He died in Italy. His daddy, Bill Baterman, lived his whole life in this town. He about went crazy when he got the telegram . . . and then he quieted right down. He knew about the Micmac burying ground, you see. And he'd decided what he wanted to do.'

The chill was back. Louis stared at Jud for a long time, trying to read the lie in the old man's eyes. It was not there. But the fact of this story surfacing just now was damned convenient.

'Why didn't you tell me this the other night?' he said finally. 'After we . . . after we did the cat? When I asked you if anyone had ever buried a person up there, you said no one ever had.'

'Because you didn't need to know,' Jud said. 'Now you do.'

Louis was silent for a long time. 'Was he the only one?'

'The only one I know of personally,' Jud said gravely. 'The only one to *ever* try it? I doubt that, Louis. I doubt it very much. I'm kind of like the Preacher in 'Clessiastes − I don't believe that there's anything new under the sun. Oh, sometimes the glitter they sprinkle over the top of a thing changes, but that's all. What's been tried once has been tried once before . . . and before . . . and before.'

He looked down at his liver-spotted hands. In the living room, the clock softly chimed twelve-thirty.

'I decided that a man in your profession is used to looking at symptoms and seeing the diseases underneath . . . and I decided I had to talk straight to you when Mortonson down at the funeral home told me you'd ordered a grave-liner instead of a sealing vault.'

Louis looked at Jud for a long time, saying nothing. Jud flushed deeply but didn't look away.

Finally, Louis said: 'Sounds like maybe you did a little snooping on me, Jud. I am sorry because of it.'

'I didn't ask him which you bought.'

'Not right out, maybe.'

But Jud did not reply, and although his blush had deepened even more – his complexion was approaching a plum color now – his eyes still didn't waver.

At last, Louis sighed. He felt unutterably tired. 'Oh, fuck it. I don't care. Maybe you're even right. Maybe it was on my mind. If it was, it was on the downside of it. I didn't think much about what I was ordering. I was thinking about Gage.'

'I know you were thinking about Gage. But you knew the difference. Your uncle was an undertaker.'

Yes, he had known the difference. A sealing vault was a piece of construction work, something which was meant to last a long, long time. Concrete was poured into a rectangular mould reinforced with steel rods, and then, after the graveside services were over, a crane lowered a slightly curved concrete top into place. The lid was sealed with a substance like the hot-patch highway departments used to fill potholes. Uncle Carl had told Louis that sealant – trade-named Ever-Lock – got itself a fearsome grip after all that weight had been on it for a while.

Uncle Carl, who liked to yarn as much as anyone (at least when he was with his own kind, and Louis, who had worked with him summers for a while, qualified as a sort of apprentice undertaker), told his nephew of an exhumation order he'd gotten once from the Cook County DA's office. Uncle Carl went out to Groveland to oversee the exhumation. They could be tricky things, he said – people whose only ideas concerning disinterral came from those horror movies starring Boris Karloff as Dr Frankenstein and Dwight Frye as Igor had an entirely wrong impression. Opening a sealing vault was no job for two men with picks and shovels – not unless they had about six weeks to spend on the job. This one went all right . . . at first. The grave was opened and the crane grappled on to the top of the vault. Only the top didn't just pull off, as it was supposed to do. The whole vault, its concrete sides already a little wet and discolored, started to rise out of the ground instead. Uncle Carl screamed for the crane operator to back off. Uncle Carl wanted to go back to the mortuary and get some stuff that would weaken the sealant's grip a bit.

The crane operator either didn't hear or wanted to go for the whole thing, like a little kid playing with a toy crane and junk prizes in a penny arcade. Uncle Carl said that the damned fool almost got it, too. The vault was three quarters of the way out and he and his assistant could hear water pattering from the underside of the vault on to the floor of the grave – it had been a wet week in Chicagoland – when the crane just tipped over and went kerplunk into the grave. The crane operator crashed into the windshield and broke his nose. That day's festivities cost Cook County roughly $3,000–$2,100 over the usual price of such gay goings-ons. The real point of the story for Uncle Carl was that the crane operator had been elected President of the Chicago local Teamsters six years later.

Grave-liners were simpler matters. Such a liner was no more than a humble concrete box, open at the top. It was set into the grave on the morning of a funeral. Following the services, the coffin was lowered into it. The sextons then brought on the top, which was in either two or three segments. These segments were lowered vertically into the ends of the grave, where they stood up like queer bookends. Iron rings were embedded into the concrete at the ends of each segment. The sextons would run lengths of chain through them and lower them gently onto the top of the grave-liner. Each section would weigh sixty, perhaps seventy pounds – eighty, tops. And no sealer was used.

Easy enough for a man to open a grave-liner, that's what Jud was implying.

Easy enough for a man to disinter the body of his son and bury it someplace else.

Shhhhh . . . shhhh. We will not speak of such things. These are secret things.

'Yes, I guess I knew the difference between a sealing vault and a grave-liner,' Louis said. 'But I wasn't thinking about . . . about what you think I was thinking about.'

'Louis—'

'It's late,' Louis said. 'It's late, I'm drunk, and my heart aches. If you feel like you have to tell me this story, then tell me and let's get it over with.' *Maybe I should have started with martinis,* he thought. *Then I could have been safely passed out when he came knocking.*

'All right, Louis. Thank you.'

'Just go on.'

Jud paused a moment, thinking, then began to speak.

CHAPTER THIRTY-NINE

'In those days – back during the war, I mean – the train still stopped in Orrington, and Bill Baterman had a funeral hack there at the loading depot to meet the freight carrying the body of his son Timmy. The coffin was unloaded by four railroad men. I was one of them. There was an army fellow on board from Graves and Registration – they was the Army's wartime version of undertakers, Louis – but he never got off the train. He was sitting drunk in a boxcar that still had twelve coffins in it.

'We put Timmy into the back of a mortuary Cadillac – in those days it still wasn't uncommon to hear such things called "hurry-up wagons", because in the old days the major concern, Louis, was to get them into the ground before they rotted. Bill Baterman stood by, his face stony and kinda . . . I dunno . . . kinda dry, I guess you'd say. He wept no tears. Huey Garber was driving the train that day, and he said that Army fella had really had a tour for himself. Huey said they'd flown in a whole shitload of those coffins to Limestone in Presque Isle, at which point both the coffins and their keeper entrained for points south.

'The Army fella comes walking up to Huey, and he takes a fifth of rye whiskey out of his uniform blouse, and he says in this soft, drawly Dixie voice, "Well, Mr Engineer, you're driving a mystery train today, did you know that?"

'Huey shakes his head.

'"Well, you are. At least, that's what they call a funeral train down in Alabama, which is where I hail from." Huey says the fella took a list out of his pocket and squinted at it. "We're going to start by dropping two of those coffins off in

Houlton, and then I've got one for Passadumkeag, two for Bangor, one for Derry, one for Ludlow, and so on. I feel like a fugging milkman. You want a drink?"

'Well, Huey declines the drink on the grounds that the Bangor and Aroostook is pretty fussy on the subject of train-drivers with rye on their breaths, and the fella from Graves and Registration don't hold it against Huey any more than Huey holds the fact of the Army fella's drunkenness against him. They even shook on her, Huey said.

'So off they go, dropping those flag-covered coffins every other stop or two. Eighteen or twenty of 'em in all. Huey said it went on all the way to Boston, and there was weeping and wailing relatives at every stop except Ludlow . . . and at Ludlow he was treated to the sight of Bill Baterman, who, he said, looked like he was dead inside and just waiting for his soul to stink. When he got off that train he said he woke up that Army fellow and they hit some spots — fifteen or twenty — and Huey got drunker than he had ever been, and went to a whore, which he'd never done in his whole life, and woke up with a set of crabs so big and mean they gave him the shivers, and he said that if that was what they called a mystery train, he never wanted to drive no mystery train again.

'Timmy's body was taken up to the Greenspan Funeral Home on Fern Street — it used to be across from where the New Franklin Laundry stands now — and two days later he was buried in Pleasantview Cemetery with full military honors.

'Well, I tell you, Louis: Missus Baterman was dead ten years then, along with the second child she tried to bring into the world, and that had a lot to do with what happened. A second child might have helped to ease the pain, don't you think? A second child might have reminded old Bill that there's others that feel the pain and have to be helped through. I guess in that way, you're luckier — having another child and all, I mean. A child and a wife who are both alive and well.

'According to the letter Bill got from the lieutenant in charge of his boy's platoon, Timmy was shot down on the road to Rome on July 15th, 1943. His body was shipped home two days later, and it got to Limestone on the 19th. It was put aboard Huey Garber's mystery train the very next day. Most of the GIs who got killed in Europe were buried in Europe, but all of the boys who went home on that train were special – Timmy had died charging a machine-gun nest, and he had won the Silver Star posthumously.

'Timmy was buried – don't hold me to this, but I think it was July 22nd. It was four or five days later that Marjorie Washburn, who was the mailwoman in those days, saw Timmy walking up the road toward York's Livery Stable. Well, Margie damn near drove right off the road, and you can understand why. She went back to the post office, tossed her leather bag with all her undelivered mail still in it on George Anderson's desk, and told him she was going home and to bed right then.

'"Margie, are you sick?" George asks. "You are just as white as a gull's wing."

'"I've had the fright of my life, and I don't want to talk to you about it," Margie Washburn says. "I ain't going to talk to Brian about it, or my mom, or anybody. When I get up to heaven, if Jesus asks me to talk to Him about it, maybe I will. But I don't believe it." And out she goes.

'Everybody knew Timmy was dead, there was his 'bituary in the Bangor *Daily News* and the Ellsworth *American* just the week before, picture and all, and half the town turned out for his funeral up to the city. And here Margie sees him, walking up the road – *lurching* up the road, she finally told old George Anderson – only this was twenty years later, and she was dying, and George told me it seemed to him like she wanted to tell somebody what she'd seen. George said it seemed to him like it preyed on her mind, you know.

'Pale, he was, she said, and dressed in an old pair of chino pants and a faded flannel hunting shirt, although it must have been ninety degrees in the shade that day. Margie said all his hair was sticking up in the back like he hadn't put a comb to it in a month or more. "His eyes were like raisins stuck in bread-dough. I saw a ghost that day, George. That's what scared me so. I never thought I'd see such a thing, but there it was."

'Well, word got around. Pretty soon some other people saw Timmy, too. Missus Stratton – well, we called her "Missus," but so far as anyone knew she could have been single or divorced or grass-widowed; she had a little two-room house down where the Pedersen Road joins the Hancock Road, and she had a lot of jazz records and sometimes she'd be willing to throw you a little party if you had a ten-dollar bill that wasn't working too hard. Well, she saw him from her porch, and she said he walked right up to the edge of the road and stopped there.

'He just stood there, she said, his hands dangling at his sides and his head pushed forward a little bit, so he was leadin' with his chin like a boxer who's ready to eat him some canvas. And she said she stood there on her porch, heart goin' like sixty, too scared to move. Then she said he turned around and it was like watching a drunk man try to do an about-face. One leg went way out and the other foot turned and he just about fell over. She said he looked right at her and all the strength just run out of her hands and she dropped the basket of washing she had, and the clothes fell out and got smutty all over again.

'She said his eyes . . . she said they looked as dead and dusty as marbles, Louis. But he saw her . . . and he grinned . . . and she said he talked to her. Asked her if she still had those records, because he wouldn't mind cutting a rug with her. Maybe that very night. And Missus Stratton went back inside, and she wouldn't come out for most of a week, and by then it was over, anyway.

'Lot of people saw Timmy Baterman. Many of them are dead now – Missus Stratton is, for one, and others have moved on, but there are a few old crocks like me left around who'll tell you . . . if you ask 'em right.

'They saw him, I tell you, walking back and forth along the Pedersen Road, a mile east of his daddy's house, and a mile west. Back and forth he went, back and forth all day, and for all anyone knew, all night. Shirt untucked, pale face, hair all stuck up in spikes, fly unzipped sometimes, and this look on his face . . . this *look* . . .'

Jud paused to light a cigarette, and Louis spoke for the first time.

'Did you ever see him?'

Jud shook the match out and looked at Louis through the haze of drifting blue smoke. And although the story was, of course, utterly mad, there was no lie in Jud's eyes.

'Yeah, I saw him. You know, they have these stories and these movies − I don't know if they're true − about zombies down in Haiti. In the movies they just sort of shamble along, with their dead eyes starin' straight ahead, real slow and sort of clumsy. Timmy Baterman was like that, Louis, like a zombie in a movie, but he *wasn't*. There was somethin' *more*. There was somethin' goin' on behind his eyes, and sometimes you could see it and sometimes you couldn't see it. *Somethin' behind his eyes, Louis.* I don't think that thinkin' is what I want to call it. I don't know what in the hell I want to call it.

'It was sly, that was one thing. Like him tellin' Missus Stratton he wanted to cut a rug with her. There was somethin' *goin' on* in there, Louis, but I don't think it was thinkin' and I don't think it had much − maybe nothing at all − to do with Timmy Baterman. It was more like a . . . a radio signal that was comin' from somewhere else. You looked at him and you thought, 'If he touches me, I'm gonna scream.' Like that.

'Back and forth he went, up and down the road, and one day after I got home from work − this must have been, oh, I'm going to say it was July 30th or so − here is George Anderson, the postmaster, don't you know, sitting on my back porch, drinking iced tea with Hannibal Benson, who was then our second selectman, and Alan Purinton, who was fire-chief. Norma sat there too, but never said a thing.

'George kept rubbing the stump at the top of his right leg. Lost most of that leg working on the railroad, he did, and the stump used to bother him something fierce on those hot and muggy days. But here he was, misery or not.

' "This has gone far enough," George says to me. "I got a mailwoman who won't deliver out on the Pedersen Road, that's one thing. It's starting to raise Cain with the government, and that's something else."

' "What do you mean, it's raising Cain with the government?" I asked.

'Hannibal said he'd had a call from the War Department. Some lieutenant named Kinsman whose job it was to sort out malicious mischief from plain old tomfoolery. "Four or five people have written anonymous letters to the War Department," Hannibal says, "and this Lieutenant Kinsman is starting to get a little bit concerned. If it was just one fellow who had written one letter, they'd laugh it off. If it was just one fellow writing a whole bunch of letters, Kinsman says he'd call the State Police up in Derry Barracks and tell 'em they might have a psychopath with a hate on against the Baterman family in Ludlow. But these letters all came from different people. He said you could tell that by the handwriting, name or no name, and they all say the same crazy thing – that if Timothy Baterman is dead, he makes one hell of a lively corpse walking up and down the Pedersen Road with his bare face hanging out.

' "This Kinsman is going to send a fellow out or come himself if this don't settle down," Hannibal finishes up. "They want to know if Timmy's dead, or AWOL, or what, because they don't like to think their records are all at sixes and sevens. Also, they're gonna want to know who was buried in Timmy Baterman's box, if he wasn't."

'And Hannibal mopped his brow with his bandanna.

'Well, you can see what kind of a mess it was, Louis. We sat there most of an hour, drinking iced tea and talking it over. Norma asked us if we wanted sandwidges, but no one did. Christ, that business with Timmy Baterman was like finding a woman with three tits . . . you know it ain't right, but what the hell do you do about it?

'We talked it around and talked it around, and finally we decided we had to go out there, to the Baterman place. I'll never forget that night, not if I live to be twice as old's I am now. It was hot, hotter than the hinges of hell, with the sun going down like a bucket of guts behind the clouds. There was none of us wanted to go, but we had to. Norma knew it before any of us. She got me inside on some pretext or other and said, "Don't you let them dither around and put this off, Judson. You got to get this taken care of. It's an abomination."'

Jud measured Louis evenly with his eyes.

'That was what she called it, Louis. It was her word. Abomination. And she kind of whispers in my ear, "If anything happens, Jud, you just run. Never mind these others; they'll have to look out for themselves. You remember me and bust your hump right out of there if anything happens."'

'We drove over in Hannibal Benson's car — that son of a bitch got all the A-coupons he wanted, I don't know how. Nobody said much, but all four of us was smokin' like chimblies. We was scared, Louis, just as scared as we could be. But the only one who really said anything was Alan Purinton. He says to George, "Bill Baterman has been up to dickens in that woods north of Route 15, and I'll put my warrant to that." Nobody answered, but I remember George noddin' his head.

'Well, we got there, and Alan knocked, but nobody answered, so we went around to the back and there the two of them were. Bill Baterman was sitting there on his back stoop with a pitcher of beer and Timmy was at the back of the yard, just staring up at that red, bloody sun as it went down. His whole face was orange with it, like he'd been flayed alive. And Bill . . . he looked like the devil had gotten him after his seven years of highfalutin'. He was floatin' in his clothes, and I judged he'd lost forty pounds. His eyes had gone back in their sockets until they were like little animals in a pair of caves . . . and his mouth kep' goin' tick-tick-tick on the left side. He looked like someone who has a cancer that is doing right well someplace inside him.'

Jud paused, seemed to consider, and then nodded imperceptibly. 'Louis, he looked *damned*. Timmy looked around at us and grinned. Just seeing him grin made you want to scream. Then he turned and went back to looking at the sun go down. Bill says, "I didn't hear you boys knock," which was a bald-faced lie, of course, since Alan laid on that door loud enough to wake the . . . to wake up a deaf man.

'No one seemed like they was going to say anything, so I says, "Bill, I heard your boy was killed over in Italy."

' "That was a mistake," he says, looking right at me.

' "Was it?" I says.

' "You see him standin' right there, don't you?" he says.

' "So who do you reckon was in that coffin you had buried out at Pleasantview?" Alan Purinton asks him.

' "Be damned if I know," Bill says, "and be damned if I care." He goes to get a cigarette and spills them all over the back porch, then breaks two or three trying to pick them up.

' "Probably have to be an exhumation," Hannibal says. "You know that, don't you? I had a call from the goddam War Department, Bill. They are going to want to know if they buried some other mother's son under Timmy's name."

' "Well, what in the hell of it?" Bill says in a loud voice. "That's nothing to me, is it? I got my boy. Timmy come home the other day. He's been shell-shocked or something. He's a little strange now, but he'll come around."

' "Let's quit this, Bill," I says, and all at once I was pretty mad at him. "If and when they dig up that Army coffin, they're gonna find it dead empty, unless you went to the trouble of filling it up with rocks after you took your boy out of it, and I don't think you did. I know what happened, Hannibal and George and Alan here know what happened, and you know what happened, too. You been foolin' around up in the woods, Bill, and you have caused yourself and this town a lot of trouble."

' "You fellas know your way out, I guess," he says. "I don't have to explain myself to you, or justify myself to you, or nothing. When I got that telegram, the life ran right out of me. I felt her go, just like piss down the inside of my leg. Well, I got my boy back. They had no right to take my boy. He was only seventeen. He was all I had left of his dear mother and it was ill-fuckin'-legal. So fuck the Army, and fuck the War Department, and fuck the United States of America, and fuck you boys, too. I got him back. He'll come around. And that's all I got to say. Now you all just march your boots back where you came from."

'And his mouth is tick-tick-tickin', and there's sweat all over his forehead in big drops, and that was when I saw he was crazy. It would have driven me crazy, too. Living with that . . . that thing.'

Louis was feeling sick to his stomach. He had drunk too much beer too fast. Pretty soon it was all going to come up on him. The heavy, loaded feeling in his stomach told him it would be coming up soon.

'Well, there wasn't much else we could do. We got ready to go. Hannibal says, "Bill, God help you."

'Bill says, "God never helped me. I helped myself."

'That was when Timmy walked over to us. He even *walked* wrong, Louis. He walked like an old, old man. He'd put one foot high up and then bring it down and then kind of shuffle and then lift the other one. It was like watchin' a crab walk. His hands dangled down by his legs. And when he got close enough you could see red marks across his face on the slant, like pimples or little burns. I reckon that's where the Kraut machine-gun got him. Must have damn near blowed his head off.

'And he stank of the grave. It was a black smell, like everything inside him was just lying there, black and festering and spoilt. I saw Alan Purinton put a hand up to cover his nose and mouth. The stench was just awful. You almost expected to see grave-maggots squirming around in his hair—'

'Stop,' Louis said hoarsely. 'I've heard enough.'

'You ain't,' Jud said. He spoke with haggard earnestness. 'That's it, you *ain't*. And I can't even make it as bad as it was. Nobody could understand how bad it was unless they was there. He was *dead*, Louis. But he was alive, too. And he . . . he . . . he knew things.'

'Knew things?'

'Ayuh. He looked at Alan for a long time, kind of grinning – you could see his teeth, anyway – and then he spoke in this low voice, you felt like you had to strain forward to hear it. It sounded like he had gravel down in his tubes. 'Your wife is fucking that man she works with down at the drugstore, Purinton. What do you think of that? She screams when she comes. What do you think of that?'

'Alan, he kind of gasped, and you could see it had hit him. Alan's in a nursing home up in Gardener now, or was the last I heard – he must be pushing ninety. Back when all this happened he was fifty or so, and there had been some talk around about his second wife. She was his second cousin, and she had come to live with Alan and Alan's first wife, Lucy, just before the war. Well, Lucy died, and a year and a half later Alan up and married this girl. Laurine, her name was. She was no more than twenty-four when they married. And there *had* been some talk about her, you know. If you were a man, you might have called her ways sort of free and easy and let it go at that. But the women thought she might be loose. And maybe Alan had had a few thoughts in that direction, too, because, he says: "Shut up! Shut up or I'll knock you down, whatever you are!"

' "Shush now, Timmy," Bill says, and he looks worse than ever, you know, like maybe he's going to puke or faint dead away, or do both. "You shush, Timmy."

'But Timmy didn't take no notice. He looks around at George Anderson and he says. "That grandson you set such a store by is just waiting for you to die, old man. The money is all he wants, the money he thinks you got socked away in your lockbox at the Bangor Eastern Bank. That's why he makes up to you, but behind your back he makes fun of you, him and his sister. Old wooden-leg, that's what they call you," Timmy says, and Louis, his voice – it *changed*. It got mean. It sounded like the way that grandson of George's would have sounded if . . . you know, if the things Timmy was saying was true.

' "Old wooden-leg," ' Timmy says, "and won't they shit when they find out you're poor as a church-mouse because you lost it all in 1938? Won't they shit, George? Won't they just *shit*?"

'George, he backed away then, and his wooden leg buckled under him and he fell back on Bill's porch and upset his pitcher of beer, and he was as white as your undershirt, Louis.

'Bill, he gets back on his feet somehow, and he's roarin' at his boy, "Timmy, you stop it! You stop it!" But Timmy wouldn't. He said somethin' bad about Hannibal, and then he said something bad about me, too, and by then he was . . . ravin', I'd say. Yeah, he was ravin', all right. Screamin'. And we started to back away, and then we started to run, draggin' George along the best we could by the arms because he'd gotten the straps and harnesses on that fake leg twisted somehow, and it was all off to one side with the shoe turned around backwards and draggin' on the grass.

'The last I seen of Timmy Baterman, he was on the back lawn by the clothesline, his face all red in the settin' sun, those marks standin' out on his face, his hair all crazy and dusty somehow . . . and he was laughin' and screechin' over and over again "Old wooden-leg! Old wooden-leg! And the cuckold! And the whoremaster! Goodbye, gentlemen! Goodbye! Goodbye!' And then he laughed, but it was screaming, really . . . something inside him . . . screaming . . . and screaming . . . and screaming.'

Jud stopped. His chest moved up and down rapidly.

'Jud,' Louis said. 'The thing this Timmy Baterman told you . . . was it true?'

'It was true,' Jud muttered. 'Christ! It was true. I used to go to a whorehouse in Bangor betimes. Nothing many a man hasn't done, although I s'pose there are plenty that walk the straight and narrow. I just would get the urge – the compulsion, maybe – to sink it into strange flesh now and then. Or pay some woman to do the things a man can't bring himself to ask his wife to do. Men keep their gardens too, Louis. It wasn't a terrible thing, what I done, and all of that has been behind me for the last eight or nine years, and Norma would not have left me if she had known. But something in her would have died for ever. Something dear and sweet.'

Jud's eyes were red and swollen and bleary; the tears of the old are singularly unlovely, Louis thought. But when he groped across the table for Louis's hand, Louis took it firmly.

'He told us only the bad,' he said after a moment. 'Only the bad. God knows there is enough of that in any human being's life, isn't there? Two or three days later, Alan Purinton's wife left Ludlow for good, and folks in town who saw her before she got on the train said she was sporting two shiners and had cotton stuffed up her nose. Alan, he would never talk about it. George died in 1950, and if he left anything to that grandson and granddaughter of his, I never heard about it. Hannibal got kicked out of office because of something that was just like what Timmy Baterman accused him of – I won't tell you exactly what it was, you don't need to know, but misappropriation of town funds for his own use comes close enough to cover it, I reckon. There was even talk of trying him on embezzlement charges, but it never came to much. Losing the post was enough punishment for him, anyway; his whole life was playing the big cheese.

'But there was good in those men, too. That's what I mean; that's what folks always find it so hard to remember. It was Hannibal got the fund started for the Eastern General Hospital, right before the war. Alan Purinton was one of the most generous, open-handed men I ever knew. And old George

Anderson only wanted to go on running the post office for ever.

'It was only the bad *it* wanted to talk about, though. It was only the bad *it* wanted us to remember, because *it* was bad . . . and because *it* knew we meant danger for it. The Timmy Baterman that went off to fight the war was a nice, ordinary kid, Louis, maybe a little dull, but goodhearted. The thing we saw that night, lookin' up into that red sun . . . that was a monster. Maybe it was a zombie, or a *dybbuk*, or a demon. Maybe there's no name for such a thing as that, but the Micmacs would have known what it was, name or no.'

'What?' Louis said numbly.

'Something that had been touched by the Wendigo,' Jud said evenly. He took a deep breath, held it for a moment, let it out, and looked at his watch.

'Welladay. The hour's late, Louis. I've talked nine times as much as I meant to.'

'I doubt that,' Louis said. 'You've been very eloquent. Tell me how it came out.'

'There was a fire at the Baterman place two nights later,' Jud said. 'It burned flat. Alan Purinton said there was no doubt about the fire being set. Range-oil had been splashed from one end of that little house to the other. You could smell the reek of it for three days after the fire was out.'

'So they both burned up.'

'Oh, ayuh, they burned. But they was dead beforehand. Timmy was shot twice in the chest with a pistol Bill Baterman kept handy, an old Colt. They found it in Bill's hand. What he'd done, or so it looked like, was to kill his boy, lay him on the bed, and then spill out that range-oil. Then he sat down in his easy chair by the radio, flicked a match, and ate the barrel of that Colt .45.'

'Jesus,' Louis said.

'They were pretty well charred, but the county medical examiner said it looked to him like Timmy Baterman had been dead two or three weeks.'

Silence, ticking out.

Jud got up. 'I wasn't exaggerating when I said I might have killed your boy, Louis, or had a hand in it. The Micmacs knew that place, but that doesn't necessarily mean they made it what it was. The Micmacs weren't always here. They came maybe from Canada, maybe from Russia, maybe from Asia way back in the beginning. They stayed here in Maine for a thousand years, or maybe it was two thousand – it's hard to tell, because they did not leave their mark deep on the land. And now they are gone again . . . same way we'll be gone, someday, although I guess our mark will go deeper, for better or worse. But the place will stay no matter who's here, Louis. It isn't as though someone owned it, and could take its secret when they moved on. It's an evil, curdled place, and I had no business taking you up there to bury that cat. I know that now. It has a power you'll beware of if you know what's good for your family and what's good for you. I wasn't strong enough to fight it. You saved Norma's life, and I wanted to do something for you and that place turned my good wish to its own evil purpose. It has a power . . . and I think that power goes through phases, same as the moon. It's been full of power before, and I'm scared it's coming around to full again. I'm scared it used me to get at you through your son. Do you see, Louis, what I'm getting at?' His eyes pleaded with Louis.

'You're saying the place knew Gage was going to die, I think,' Louis said.

'No, I am saying the place might have *made* Gage die because I introduced you to the power in the place. I am saying I may have murdered your son with good intentions, Louis.'

'I don't believe it,' Louis said at last, shakily. Didn't; wouldn't. *Couldn't.*

He held Jud's hand tightly. 'We're burying Gage tomorrow. In Bangor. And in Bangor he will stay. I don't plan to go up there to the Pet Sematary or beyond it ever again.'

'Promise me!' Jud said harshly. 'Promise.'

'I promise,' Louis said.

But in the back of his mind, contemplation remained; a dancing flicker of promise that would not quite go away.

CHAPTER FORTY

But none of those things happened.

All of them – the droning Orinco truck, the fingers that just touched the back of Gage's jumper and then slid off, Rachel preparing to go to the viewing in her housecoat, Ellie carrying Gage's picture and putting his chair next to her bed, Steve Masterton's tears, the fight with Irwin Goldman, Jud Crandall's terrible story of Timmy Baterman – all of them existed only in Louis Creed's mind during the few seconds that passed while he raced his laughing son to the road. Behind him, Rachel screamed again – *Gage, come back, don't RUN!* – but Louis did not waste his breath. It was going to be close, very close, and yes, *one* of those things really happened: from somewhere up the road he could hear the drone of the oncoming truck and somewhere inside a memory circuit opened and he could hear Jud Crandall speaking to Rachel on that very first day in Ludlow: *You want to watch 'em around the road, Missus Creed. It's a bad road for kids and pets.*

Now Gage was running down the gentle slope of lawn that merged with the soft shoulder of Route 15, his husky little legs pumping, and by all the rights of the world he should have fallen over sprawling but he just kept going and now the sound of the truck was very loud indeed, it was that low, snoring sound that Louis sometimes heard from his bed as he floated just beyond the rim of sleep. Then it seemed a comforting sound, but now it terrified him.

Oh my dear God, oh my dear Jesus, let me catch him, don't let him get into the road!

Louis put on a final burst of speed and leaped, throwing himself out straight and parallel to the ground like a football player about to make a tackle; he could see his shadow tracking along on the grass below him in the lowest periphery of his vision and he thought of the kite, the Vulture, printing its shadow all the way across Mrs Vinton's field, and just as Gage's forward motion carried him into the road, Louis's fingers brushed the back of his jacket . . . and then snagged it.

He yanked Gage backward and landed on the ground at the same instant, crashing his face into the rough gravel of the shoulder, giving himself a bloody nose. His balls signalled a much more serious flash of pain – *Ohhh, if I'd'a known I was gonna be playing football, I woulda worn my jock* – but both the pain in his nose and the driving agony in his testes was lost in the swelling relief of hearing Gage's wail of pain and outrage as his bottom landed on the shoulder and he fell over backwards on to the edge of the lawn, thumping his head. A moment later his wails were drowned by the roar of the passing truck and the almost regal blat of its airhorn.

Louis managed to get up in spite of the lead ball sitting in his lower stomach, and cradled his son in his arms. A moment later Rachel joined them, also weeping, crying out to Gage, 'Never run in the road, Gage! Never, never, never! The road is bad! *Bad!*' And Gage was so astonished at this tearful lecture that he left off crying and goggled up at his mother, astonished.

'Louis, your nose is bleeding,' she said, and then hugged him so suddenly and strongly that for a moment he could barely breathe.

'That isn't the worst of it,' he said. 'I think I'm sterile, Rachel. Oh boy, the pain.'

And she laughed so hysterically that for a few moments he was frightened for her, and the thought crossed his mind: *If Gage really had been killed, I believe it would have driven her crazy.*

But Gage was not killed, all of that had only been a hellishly detailed moment of imagination as Louis outraced his son's death across a green lawn on a sunshiny May afternoon.

Gage went to grammar school, and at the age of seven he began going to camp, where he showed a wonderful and surprising aptitude for swimming. He also gave his parents a rather glum surprise by proving himself able to handle a month's separation with no noticeable psychic trauma. By the time he was ten, he was spending the entire summer away at Camp Agawam in Raymond, and at eleven he won two blue ribbons and a red at the Four Camps Swimathon that ended the summer's activities. He grew tall, and yet through it all he was the same Gage, sweet and rather surprised at the things the world held out ... and for Gage, the fruit was somehow never bitter or rotten.

He was an honors student in high school and a member of the swim-team at John Baptist, the parochial school he had insisted on attending because of its swimming facilities. Rachel was upset, Louis not particularly surprised when, at seventeen, Gage announced his intention to convert to Catholicism. Rachel believed that all of it was because of the girl Gage was going out with; she saw marriage in his immediate future ('if that little slut with the St Christopher's medal isn't balling him, I'll eat your shorts, Louis,' she said), the wreckage of his college plans and his Olympic hopes, and nine or ten little Catholics running around by the time Gage was forty. By then he would be (according to Rachel, anyway) a cigar-smoking truck-driver with a beer belly, Our-Fathering and Hail-Marying his way into oblivion.

Louis suspected his son's motives were rather more pure, and although Gage converted (and on the day he actually did the deed, Louis sent an unabashedly nasty postcard to Irwin Goldman; it read, *Perhaps you'll have a Jesuit grandson yet. Your goy son-in-law, Louis*), he did not marry the rather nice (and decidedly un-slutty) girl he had dated through most of his senior year.

He went on to Johns Hopkins, made the Olympic swimming team, and on one long, dazzling, and incredibly proud afternoon sixteen years after Louis had raced an Orinco truck for his son's life, he and Rachel – who had now gone almost entirely gray, although she covered it with a rinse – watched their son win a gold medal for the USA. When the NBC cameras moved in for a close-up of him, standing with his dripping, seal-sleek head back, his eyes open and calm and fixed on the flag as the National Anthem played, the ribbon around his neck and the gold lying against the smooth skin of his chest, Louis wept. He and Rachel both wept.

'I guess this caps everything,' he said huskily, and turned to embrace his wife. But she was looking at him with dawning horror, her face seeming to age before his eyes as if whipped by days and months and years of evil time; the sound of the National Anthem faded and when Louis looked back at the TV he saw a different boy there, a black boy with a head of tight curls in which gems of water still gleamed.

This caps everything.

His cap.

His cap is . . .

. . . oh dear God, his cap is full of blood.

Louis woke up in the cold dead light of a rainy seven o'clock, clutching his pillow in his arms. His head thumped monstrously with his heartbeat; the ache swelled and faded, swelled and faded. He burped acid that tasted like old beer, and his stomach heaved miserably. He had been weeping; the pillow was wet with his tears, as if he had somehow stumbled in and then out of one of those hokey country-and-western laments in his sleep. Even in the dream, he thought, some part of him had known the truth, and had cried for it.

He got up and stumbled to the bathroom, heart racing threadily in his chest, consciousness itself fragmented by the fierceness of his hangover. He reached the toilet bowl barely in time, and threw up a glut of last night's beer.

He knelt on the floor, eyes closed, until he felt capable of actually making it to his feet. He groped for the handle and flushed the john. Then he went to the mirror to see how badly bloodshot his eyes were, but the glass had been covered with a square of sheeting. Then he recalled. Drawing almost randomly on a past she professed to barely remember, Rachel had covered all the mirrors in the house, and took off her shoes before entering through the door.

No Olympic swimming team, Louis thought dully as he walked back to his bed and sat down on it. The sour taste of beer coated his mouth and throat, and he swore to himself (not for the first time, or the last) that he would never touch that poison again. No Olympic swimming team, no 3.0 in college, no little Catholic girlfriend or conversion, no Camp Agawam, no nothing. His sneakers had been torn off, his jumper turned inside out, his sweet little boy's body, so tough and sturdy, nearly dismembered. His cap had been full of blood.

Now, sitting on his bed in the grip of this numbing hangover, rainwater spilling its lazy courses down the window beside him, his grief came for him fully, like some gray matron from Ward Nine in purgatory. It came and dissolved him, unmanned him, took away whatever defenses remained, and he put his face in his hands and cried, rocking back and forth on his bed, thinking he would do anything to have a second chance, anything at all.

CHAPTER FORTY-ONE

Gage was buried at two o'clock that afternoon. By then the rain had stopped. Tattered clouds still moved overhead, and most of the mourners arrived carrying black umbrellas provided by the undertaker.

At Rachel's request, the funeral director, who officiated at the short, non-sectarian graveside service, read the passage from Matthew which begins 'Suffer the little children to come unto Me'. Louis, standing on one side of the grave, looked across at his father-in-law. For a moment Goldman looked back at him, and then he dropped his eyes. There was no fight left in him today. The pouches under his eyes now resembled mailbags, and around his black silk skullcap, hair as fine and white as tattered spiderwebs flew randomly in the breeze. With grayish-black beard scragging his cheeks, he looked more like a wino than ever. He gave Louis the impression of a man who did not really know where he was. Louis tried, but found he could still find no pity in his heart for him.

Gage's small white coffin, its latch presumably repaired, sat on a pair of chromed runners over the grave-liner. The verges of the grave had been carpeted with Astroturf so violently green it hurt Louis's eyes. Several baskets of flowers had been set on top of this artificial and strangely gay surface. Louis's eyes looked over the funeral director's shoulder. Here was a low hill, covered with graves, family plots, one Romanesque monument with the name PHIPPS engraved on it. Just above the sloping roof of the PHIPPS monument, he could see a sliver of yellow. Louis looked at this, pondering it. He continued to look at it even after the funeral director said, 'Let us bow our heads for a moment of silent prayer.' It took Louis a few minutes, but he got it. It was a payloader. A payloader parked over the hill where the mourners wouldn't have to look at it. And, when the funeral was over, Oz would crush his cigarette on the heel of his tewwible workboot, put it in whatever container he carried around with him (in a cemetery, sextons caught depositing their butts on the ground were almost always summarily fired – it looked bad, and too many of the clientele had died of lung cancer), jump in the payloader, fire that sucker up, and cut his son off from the sun for ever . . . or at least until the day of the Resurrection.

Resurrection . . . ah, there's a word—

(*that you should put right the fuck out of your mind and you know it*)

When the funeral director said 'Amen', Louis took Rachel's arm and guided her away. Rachel murmured some protest – she wanted to stay a bit longer, please, Louis – but Louis was firm. They approached the cars. He saw the funeral director taking umbrellas with the home's name discreetly printed on the handles from the mourners who passed and handing them to an assistant. The assistant put them in an umbrella stand which looked weird and surreal, standing there on the dewy turf. He held Rachel's arm with his right hand and Ellie's white-gloved hand with his left. Ellie was wearing the same dress she had worn to Norma Crandall's funeral.

Jud came over as Louis handed his ladies into the car. Jud also looked as if he'd had a hard night.

'You okay, Louis?'

Louis nodded.

Jud bent to look into the car. 'How are you, Rachel?' He asked.

'I'm all right, Jud,' she whispered.

Jud touched her shoulder gently and then looked at Ellie. 'How about you, dear one?'

'I'm fine,' Ellie said, and produced a hideous smile of shark-like proportions to show him how fine she was.

'What's that picture you got there?'

For a moment Louis thought she would hold it, refuse to show him, and then with a painful shyness she passed it to Jud. He held it in his big fingers, fingers that were so splayed and somehow clumsy-looking, fingers that looked fit mostly for grappling with the transmissions of big road machines or making couplings on the B&M Line – but they were also the fingers that had pulled a bee-stinger from Gage's neck with all the offhand skill of a magician . . . or a surgeon.

'Why, that's real nice,' Jud said. 'You pullin' him on a sled. Bet he liked that, didn't he, Ellie?'

Beginning to weep, Ellie nodded.

Rachel began to say something, but Louis squeezed her arm – *be still a while.*

'I used to pull 'im a lot,' Ellie said, weeping, 'and he'd laugh and laugh. Then we'd go in and Mommy would fix us cocoa and say, "Put your boots away," and Gage would grab them all up and scream "Boots! Boots!" so loud it hurt your ears. Remember that, Mom?'

Rachel nodded.

'Yeah, I bet that was a good time, all right,' Jud said, handing the picture back. 'And he may be dead now, Ellie, but you can keep your memories of him.'

'I'm going to,' she said, wiping at her face. 'I loved Gage, Mr Crandall.'

'I know you did, dear.' He leaned in and kissed her, and when he withdrew, his eyes swept Louis and Rachel stonily. Rachel met his gaze, puzzled and a little hurt, not understanding. But Louis understood well enough: *What are you doing for her?* Jud's eyes asked. *Your son is dead, but your daughter is not. What are you doing for her?*

Louis looked away. There was nothing he could do for her, not yet. She would have to swim in her grief as best she could. His thoughts were too full of his son.

CHAPTER FORTY-TWO

By evening a fresh rack of clouds had come in and a strong west wind had begun to blow. Louis put on his light jacket, zipped it up, and took the Civic keys from the peg on the wall.

'Where you going, Lou?' Rachel asked. She spoke without much interest. After supper she had begun crying again, and although her weeping was gentle, she had seemed incapable of stopping. Louis had forced her to take a Valium. Now she sat with the paper folded open to the barely started crossword puzzle. In the other room, Ellie sat silently watching *Little House on the Prairie* with Gage's picture on her lap.

'I thought I'd pick up a pizza.'

'Didn't you get enough to eat earlier?'

'I just didn't seem hungry then,' he said, telling the truth and then adding a lie: 'I am now.'

That afternoon, between three and six, the final rite of Gage's funeral had taken place at the Ludlow house. This was the rite of food. Steve Masterton and his wife had come with a hamburger and noodle casserole. Charlton had appeared with a quiche ('It will keep until you want it, if it doesn't all get eaten,' she told Rachel. 'Quiche is easy to warm up.') The Dannikers from up the road brought a baked ham. The Goldmans appeared – neither of them would speak to Louis, or even come close to him, for which he was not sorry – with a variety of cold cuts and cheeses. Jud also brought cheese – a large wheel of his old favorite, Mr Rat. Missy Dandridge brought a key lime pie. And Surrendra Hardu brought apples. The rite of food apparently transcended religious differences.

This was the funeral party, and while it was quiet, it was

not quite subdued. There was rather less drinking than at an ordinary party, but there was some. After a few beers (only the night before he had sworn he would never touch the stuff again, but in the cold afternoon light the previous evening had seemed impossibly long ago), Louis thought to pass on a few little funerary anecdotes his Uncle Carl had told him – that at Sicilian funerals unmarried women sometimes snipped a piece of the deceased's shroud and slept with it under their pillows, believing it would bring them luck in love, that at Irish funerals mock weddings were sometimes performed, and the toes of the dead were tied together because of an ancient Celtic belief that it kept the deceased's ghost from walking. Uncle Carl said that the custom of tying DOA tags to the great toes of corpses had begun in New York, and since all of the early morgue-keepers had been Irish, he believed this to be a survival of that old superstition. Then, looking at their faces, he had decided such tales would be taken wrong.

Rachel had broken down only once, and her mother was there to comfort her. Rachel clung to Dory Goldman and sobbed against her shoulder in an open, let-it-all-go way that had been so far impossible for her with Louis, perhaps because she saw them both as culpable in Gage's death, or perhaps because Louis, lost in the peculiar half-world of his own fancies, had not encouraged her grief. Either way, she had turned to her mother for comfort, and Dory was there to give it, mingling her tears with her daughter's. Irwin Goldman stood behind them, his hand on Rachel's shoulder, and looked with sickly triumph across the room at Louis.

Ellie circulated with a silver tray loaded with canapés, little rolls with a feathered toothpick poked through each one. Her picture of Gage was tucked firmly under her arm.

Louis received condolences. He nodded and thanked the condolers. And if his eyes seemed distant, his manner a little cold, people supposed he was thinking of the past, of the accident, of the Gageless life ahead; none (perhaps not even Jud) would have suspected that Louis had begun to think about the strategies of grave-robbing . . . only in an academic way, of course; it was not that he intended to *do* anything. It was only a way to keep his mind occupied.

It was not as if he intended to *do* anything.

Louis stopped at the Orrington Corner Store, bought two six-packs of cold beer, and called ahead to Napoli's for a pepperoni and mushroom pizza.

'Want to give me a name on that, sir?'

Oz the Gweat and Tewwible, Louis thought.

'Lou Creed.'

'Okay, Lou, we're real busy so that'll be maybe forty-five minutes — that okay for you?'

'Sure,' Louis said, and hung up. As he got back into the Civic and keyed the engine, it occurred to him that although there were maybe twenty pizza joints in the Bangor area, he had picked the one closest to Pleasantview, where Gage was buried. *Well, what the hell?* he thought uneasily. *They make good pizza. No frozen dough. Throw it up and catch it on their fists, right there where you can watch, and Gage used to laugh—*

He cut that thought off.

He drove past Napoli's to Pleasantview. He supposed he had known that he would do that, but what harm? None.

He parked across the street and crossed the road to the wrought-iron gates, which glimmered in the final light of day. Above them, in a semi-circle, were wrought-iron letters spelling PLEASANTVIEW. The view was, in Louis's mind, neither pleasant nor unpleasant. The cemetery was nicely landscaped on several rolling hills, there were long aisles of trees (ah, but in these last few minutes of fading daylight, the shadows those trees threw seemed deeply pooled and as blackly unpleasant as still quarry-water), a few isolated weeping willows. It wasn't quiet. The turnpike was near — the drone of traffic came on the steady, chill wind — and the glow in the darkening sky was Bangor International Airport.

He stretched his hand out to the gate, thinking *They'll be locked*, but they were not. Perhaps it was too early to lock them, and if they locked them at all it would only be to protect the place against drunks, vandals, and teenaged neckers. The days of the Dickensian Resurrection Men

(*there's that word again*)

were over. The right-hand gate swung in with a faint, screeing noise, and after a glance over his shoulder to make sure he was unobserved, Louis stepped through. He closed the gate behind him and heard the click of the latch.

He stood in this modest suburb of the dead, looking around. *A fine and private place*, he thought, *but none, I think, do there embrace.* Who? Andrew Marvell? And why did the human mind store up such amazing middens of useless junk, anyway?

Jud's voice spoke up in his mind then, worried and — frightened? Yes. Frightened.

Louis, what are you doing here? You're looking up a road you don't want to travel.

He pushed the voice aside. If he was torturing anyone, it was only himself. No one need know he had been here as the daylight wound down to dark.

He began to walk toward Gage's grave, taking one of the winding paths. In a moment he was in a lane of trees; they rustled their new leaves mysteriously over his head. His heart was thudding too loudly in his chest. The graves and monuments were in rough rows. Somewhere there would be a caretaker's building, and in it would be a map of Pleasantview's twenty or so acres, neatly and sanely divided into quadrants, each quadrant showing the occupied graves and the unsold plots. Real estate for sale. One-room apartments. Sleepers.

Not much like the Pet Sematary, he thought, and this caused him to stop and consider for a moment, surprised. No. It wasn't. The Pet Sematary had given him an impression of order rising almost unknown out of chaos. Those rough, concentric circles, moving inward to the center; rude slates, crosses made out of boards. As if the children who buried their pets there

had created the pattern out of their own collective unconsciousness, as if . . .

For a moment Louis saw the Pet Sematary as a kind of
advertisement . . . a come-on, like the kind they gave you on
freak alley at the carnival. They'd bring out the fire-eater and
you got to watch his show for free because the owners knew
you wouldn't buy the steak unless you saw the sizzle, you
won't cough up the cash if you don't see the flash—

Those graves, those graves in their almost Druidic circles.

The graves in the Pet Sematary mimed the most ancient
religious symbol of all: diminishing circles indicating a spiral
leading down, not to a point, but to infinity; order from chaos
or chaos from order, depending on which way your mind
worked. It was a symbol the Egyptians had chiseled on the
tombs of the pharaohs, a symbol the Phoenicians had drawn
on the barrows of their fallen kings; it was found on cave walls
in ancient Mycenae; the guildkings of Stonehenge had created
it as a clock to time the universe; it appeared in the Christian
Bible as the whirlwind from which God had spoken to Job.

The spiral was the oldest sign of power in the world, man's
oldest symbol of that twisty bridge which may exist between
the world and the Gulf.

Louis reached Gage's grave at last. The payloader was gone.
The Astroturf had been removed, rolled up by some whistling
workman with his mind on an after-work beer at the Fairmount Lounge, stored in an equipment shed somewhere.
Where Gage lay there was a neat rectangle of bare, raked earth,
perhaps five feet by three feet. The headstone had not been
set up yet.

Louis knelt. The wind blew through his hair, tumbling it.
The sky was almost entirely dark, now. It raced with clouds.

*No one has shone a light in my face and asked me what I'm
doing here. No watchdog has barked. The gate was unlocked. The
days of the Resurrection Men are past. If I came up here with a pick
and a shovel—*

He came back to himself with a jerk. He was only playing

a dangerous mind-game with himself if he pretended that Pleasantview stood unwatched during the night hours. Suppose he were discovered belly-deep in his son's new grave by the caretaker or the watchman? It might not get into the papers, but then again it might. He might be charged with a crime. What crime? Grave-robbing? Unlikely. Malicious mischief or vandalism would be more likely. And, in the paper or out of it, the word would get around. People would talk; it was a story too juicy not to be told. Local doctor is discovered digging up his two-year-old son, recently killed in a tragic road accident. He would lose his job. Even if not, Rachel would be chilled by the wind of such tales, and Ellie might be harried by them at school until her life was a misery of chanting children. There might be the humiliation of a sanity test in exchange for dropping charges.

But I could bring Gage back to life! Gage could live again!

Did he really, actually believe that?

The fact was that he did. He had told himself time and time again, both before Gage's death and after it, that Church had not really been dead, only stunned. That Church had dug his way out and come home. A kiddie story with gruesome undertones – Winnie the Poe. Master unwittingly piles a cairn of stones over a living animal. Faithful beast digs itself out and comes home. Fine. Except it was not true. Church had been *dead*. The Micmac burying ground had brought him back to life.

He sat by Gage's grave, trying to place all the known components in an order as rational and logical as this dark magic would allow.

Timmy Baterman, now. First, did he believe the story? And second, did it make a difference?

In spite of its convenience, he believed most of it. It was undeniable that if a place like the Micmac burying ground existed (as it did), and if people knew of it (as a few of the older Ludlow-ites did), then sooner or later, someone would try the experiment. Human nature as Louis understood it made it more difficult to believe that it had stopped at a few pets and valuable breed animals.

All right, then – did he also believe that Timmy Baterman had been transformed into some sort of all-knowing demon? That was a more difficult question, and he was wary of it because he didn't want to believe it, and he had seen the results of that sort of mind-set before.

No, he did not want to believe Timmy Baterman had been a demon, but he would not – absolutely *could* not – allow himself to let what he wanted cloud his judgment.

Louis thought about Hanratty, the bull. Hanratty, Jud said, had turned mean. So, in his way, had Timmy Baterman. Hanratty had later been 'put down' by the same man who had somehow dragged the bull's body up to the Micmac burying ground on a sledge. Timmy Baterman had been 'put down' by his father.

But because Hanratty had gone bad, did that mean that all animals went bad? No. Hanratty the bull did not prove the general case; Hanratty was in fact an *exception* to the general case. Look back at the other animals – Jud's dog Spot, the old woman's parakeet, Church himself. They had all come back changed, and the change had been noticeable in all cases, but in the case of Spot, at least, the change hadn't been so great that Jud had forborne to recommend the process of . . . of . . .

(resurrection)

Yes, of *resurrection* to a friend years later. Of course, further down the line he had tried to justify and hem and haw and had spouted a lot of ominous, confused bullshit that could not even rightly be called philosophy.

How could he refuse to take the chance available to him – this one, unbelievable chance – on the basis of the Timmy Baterman story? One swallow did not a summer make.

You're slanting all the evidence in favor of the conclusion you want to produce, his mind protested. *At least tell yourself the goddamned truth about the change in Church. Even if you want to disqualify the animals — the mice and the birds — what about the way he is? Muddled . . . that's the best word of all, that sums it up. The day we were out with the kite. You remember how Gage was the day we were out with the kite? How vibrant and alive he was, reacting to everything? Wouldn't it be better to remember him that way? Do you want to resurrect a zombie from a grade-B horror picture? Or even something so prosaic as a retarded little boy? A boy who eats with his fingers and stares blankly at images on the TV screen and who will never learn to write his own name? What did Jud say about his dog? 'It was like washing a piece of meat.' Is that what you want? A piece of meat? And even if you're able to be satisfied with that, how do you explain the return of your son from the dead to your wife? To your daughter? To Steve Masterton? To the world? What happens the first time Missy Dandridge pulls into the driveway and sees Gage riding his trike in the yard? Can't you hear her screams, Louis? Can't you see her harrowing her face with her fingernails? What do you say to the reporters? What do you say when a film crew from* Real People *turns up on your doorstep, wanting to shoot film of your resurrected son?*

Did any of this really matter, or was it only the voice of cowardice? Did he believe these things could not be dealt with? That Rachel would greet her dead son with anything but tears of joy?

Yes, he supposed there was a real possibility that Gage might return . . . well . . . diminished. But would that change the quality of his love? Parents loved children who were hydrocephalic, mongoloids, autistic. They loved children who were born blind, children born as Siamese twins, children who were born with guts abysmally rearranged. Parents pled for judicial mercy or executive clemency on behalf of children who had grown up to commit rape and murder and to torture the innocent.

Did he believe it would be impossible for him to love Gage even if Gage had to go on wearing diapers until he was eight? If he did not master the first primer until he was twelve? If he never mastered it at all? Could he simply dismiss his son as a . . . a sort of divine abortion, when there was another recourse?

But, Louis, my God, you don't live in a vacuum! People will say—

He cut that thought off with rude, angry force. Of all the things *not* to consider now, public notice was probably the greatest of them.

Louis glanced down at the raked dirt of Gage's grave and felt a wave of awe and horror course through him. Unknowing, moving by themselves, his fingers had drawn a pattern of concentric circles in the dirt – he had drawn a spiral with circles.

He swept the fingers of both hands though the dirt, rubbing the pattern out. Then he left Pleasantview, hurrying, feeling very much a trespasser now, believing that he would be seen, stopped, questioned at every turn of the path.

He was late collecting his pizza, and although it had been left on top of one of the big ovens, it was semi-cold and greasy and every bit as tasty as cooked clay. Louis ate one piece and then tossed the rest out of the window, box and all, as he headed back to Ludlow. He wasn't a litterbug by nature, but he did not want Rachel to see a mostly uneaten pizza at home in the wastebasket. It might raise a surmise in her mind that a pizza wasn't really what he'd had in mind when he went to Bangor.

Louis now began to think about time and circumstance.

Time. Time might be of extreme, even crucial, importance. Timmy Baterman had been dead a good while before his father could get him up to the Micmac burying ground. *Timmy was shot the 19th . . . Timmy was buried – don't hold me to this, but I think it was July 22nd. It was four or five days later that Marjorie Washburn . . . saw Timmy walking up the road.*

All right, say that Bill Baterman had done it four days after his son's original interment . . . no. If he was going to err, let him err on the side of conservatism. Say three days. For the sake of argument, assume that Timmy Baterman returned from the dead – on July 29th. That made ten days between the boy's death and his return, and that was a conservative estimate. It might have been as long as twelve days. For Gage, it had now been four days. Time had already gotten away from him to a degree, but it was still possible to cut Bill Baterman's time in half. If . . .

If he could bring about circumstances similar to those which had made the resurrection of Church possible. Because Church had died at the best possible time, hadn't he? His family had been away when Church was struck and killed. No one the wiser, except for him and Jud.

His family had been in Chicago.

For Louis, the final piece fell into place with a neat little click.

'You want us to *what?*' Rachel asked, staring at him, astounded.

It was quarter of ten. Ellie had gone to bed. Rachel had taken another Valium after cleaning up the detritus of the funeral party ('funeral party' was another of those horrible phrases full of unstated paradox, like 'visiting hours', but there seemed no other phrase for the way they had spent their afternoon) and had seemed dazed and quiet ever since he returned from Bangor . . . but this had gotten through.

'To go back to Chicago with your mother and father,' Louis repeated patiently. 'They'll be going tomorrow. If you call them now and Delta right after, you may be able to get on the same plane with them.'

'Louis, have you lost your *mind?* After the fight you had with my father—'

Louis found himself speaking with a quick glibness that was totally unlike him. It afforded him a cheesy sort of exhilaration. He felt like a football sub who suddenly gets the ball and makes a seventy-yard touchdown run, cutting and weaving, out-thinking potential tacklers with a delirious one-time-only ease. He had never been a particularly good liar, and he had not planned this encounter in any detail at all, but now a string of plausible lies, half-truths, and inspired justification poured out of him.

'The fight we had is one of the reasons I want you and Ellie to go back with them. It's time we sewed up this wound, Rachel. I knew that . . . felt it . . . at the funeral parlor. When the fight started, I was trying to patch things up.'

'But this trip . . . I don't think it's a good idea at all, Louis. We need you. And you need us.' Her eyes measured him doubtfully. 'At least, I *hope* you need us. And neither of us are in any shape to—'

'—in any kind of shape to stay here,' Louis said forcefully. He felt as if he might be coming down with a fever. 'I'm glad you need me, and I *do* need you and Ellie. But right now this is the worst damn place in the world for you, honey. Gage is everywhere in this house, around every corner. For you and me, sure. But it's even worse for Ellie, I think.'

He saw pain flicker in her eyes and knew he had touched her. Some part of himself felt shame at this cheap victory. All the textbooks he'd read on the subject of death told him that the bereaved's first strong impulse in the aftermath of death-shock is to get away from the place where it happened . . . and that to follow such an impulse may turn out to be the most harmful course of action, because it allows the bereaved the dubious luxury of refusing to come to terms with the new reality. The books said it was best to remain where you were, to battle grief on its home ground until it subsided into remembrance. But Louis simply did not dare make the experiment with his family at home. He had to get rid of them, at least for a while.

'I know,' she said. 'It just . . . hits you all over the place. I moved the couch while you were in Bangor . . . I thought running the vacuum around would take my mind off . . . off things . . . and I found four of his little Matchbox cars under there . . . as if they were waiting for him to come back and . . . you know, play with them . . .' Her voice, already wavering, now broke. Tears spilled down her cheeks. 'And that's when I took the second Valium, because I started crying again, the way I'm crying now ... oh what a fucking soap opera all of this is ... hold me, Lou, will you hold me?'

He did hold her, and he did it well, but he felt like an imposter. His mind spun with ways to turn these tears to his further benefit. *Some nice guy, all right. Hey-ho, let's go.*

'How long does it go on?' she wept. 'Does it ever end? If only we could have him back, Louis, I swear I'd watch him better, it would never happen, and just because that driver was going too fast that doesn't let me – us – off the hook. I didn't know there could ever be hurt like this, and that's the truth. It comes, over and over it comes, and it hurts so *much*, Louis, there's no rest from it even when I go to sleep, when I go to sleep I *dream* it, over and over again I see him running to the road ... and I scream to him ...'

'Shhh,' he said. 'Rachel. Shhhh.'

She lifted her puffy face to him. 'It wasn't even as if he were being *bad*, Louis. It was just a game to him ... the truck came at the wrong time ... and Missy Dandridge called while I was still crying ... and said she read in the Ellsworth *American* that the driver tried to kill himself.'

'What?'

'He tried to hang himself in his garage. He's in shock and deep depression, the paper said ...'

'Too fucking bad he didn't make good on it,' Louis said savagely, but his voice sounded distant to his own ears and he felt a chill spreading through. *The place has a power, Louis ... it's been full of power before, and I'm ascared it's coming round to full again.* 'My boy's dead and he's out on a thousand dollars' bail and he'll go on feeling depressed and suicidal until some judge takes away his licence for ninety days and gives him a slap-on-the-wrist fine.'

'Missy says his wife has taken the kids and left him,' Rachel said dully. 'She didn't get that from the paper, but from somebody who knows somebody down Ellsworth way. He wasn't drunk. He wasn't on drugs. He didn't have any previous speeding violations. He said that when he got to Ludlow, he just felt like putting the pedal to the metal. He said he didn't even know why. So around and around it goes.'

He just felt like putting the pedal to the metal.

The place has a power . . .

Louis thrust these thoughts away. He gripped his wife's forearm gently. 'Call your mother and father. Do it now. There's no need for you and Ellie to be in this house another day. Not another day.'

'Not without you,' she said. 'Louis, I want us . . . I *need* us to stick together.'

'I'll follow you in three days, four at the most.' If things went well, Rachel and Ellie might be back here in forty-eight hours. 'I've got to find someone to fill in for me, on a part-time basis, at least, at the University. I've got sick-time and vacation-time coming, but I don't want to leave Surrendra on the hot-seat. Jud can watch the house while we're gone, but I'll want to cut off the electricity and store what we've got in the deep-freeze somewhere. Dandridges', I guess.'

'Ellie's school . . .'

'The hell with it. It's out in three weeks, anyway. They'll understand, the circumstances being what they are. They'll arrange an early dismissal. It'll all work just—'

'Louis?'

He broke off. 'What?'

'What are you hiding?'

'Hiding?' He looked at her openly, clearly. 'I don't know what you're talking about.'

'Don't you?'

'No. I don't.'

'Never mind. I'll call them right now . . . if that's what you really want.'

'It is,' he said, and the words seemed to echo in his mind with an iron clang.

'It might even be best . . . for Ellie.' She looked at him

329

with her red-rimmed eyes, still slightly glazed from Valium. 'You look feverish, Louis. As if you might be coming down with something.'

She went to the telephone and called the motel where her parents were staying before Louis could reply.

The Goldmans were overjoyed at Rachel's proposal; they were overjoyed. They were not so wild about the idea of Louis joining them in three or four days, but in the end they wouldn't have to worry about it at all, of course. Louis had not the slightest intention of going to Chicago. He had suspected that if there was to be a snag, it would be getting air reservations this late. But luck was with him there, too. There were still available seats on Delta's Bangor-to-Cincinnati run, and a quick check showed two cancellations on a Cincinnati-to-Chicago flight. It meant that Rachel and Ellie would be able to travel with the Goldmans only as far as Cincinnati, but they would get to Chicago less than an hour after.

It's almost like magic, Louis thought, hanging up the telephone, and Jud's voice responded promptly: *It's been full of power before, and I'm ascared . . .*

Oh, get fucked, he told Jud's voice rudely. *I've learned to accept a great many strange things in the last ten months, my good old friend — if you'd told me the half of them, I would have told you my mind would probably snap under the strain. But am I ready to believe that a haunted patch of ground can influence airline ticketing? I don't think so.*

'I'll have to pack,' Rachel said. She was looking at the flight information Louis had jotted down on the pad by the phone.

'Take just the one big suitcase,' Louis said.

She looked at him wide-eyed, mildly startled. 'For both of us? Louis, you're joking.'

'All right, take a couple of tote-bags, too. But don't exhaust yourself packing a different outfit for the next three weeks,' he said, thinking: *Especially since you may be back in Ludlow very soon.* 'Take enough for a week, ten days. You've got the checkbook and the credit cards. Buy what you need.'

'But we can't afford—' she began doubtfully. She seemed doubtful about everything now, malleable, easily confused. He remembered her cold, dangling comment about the Winnebago he had once spoken idly about buying.

'We have the money,' he said.

'Well . . . I suppose we could use Gage's college fund if we needed to, although it would take a day or two to process the savings account and a week to get the treasury bills cashed—'

Her face began to crumple and dissolve again. Louis held her. *She's right. It just keeps right on hitting you, it never lets up.* 'Rachel, don't,' he said. 'Don't cry.'

But of course she did – she had to.

While she was upstairs packing, the phone rang. Louis sprang for it, thinking it would be someone from Delta ticketing, saying a mistake had been made, no flights were available. *I should have known everything was going too smoothly.*

But it wasn't Delta ticketing. It was Irwin Goldman.

'I'll get Rachel,' Louis said.

'No.' For a moment there was nothing else, only silence. *He's probably sitting there and trying to decide which name to call you first.*

When Goldman spoke again, his voice was strained. He seemed to be pushing the words out against some great inner resistance. 'It's you I want to talk to. Dory wanted me to call and apologize for my . . . for my behavior. I guess . . . Louis, I guess I wanted to apologize, too.'

Why, Irwin! How big of you! My God, I think I just wet my pants!

'You don't need to apologize,' Louis said. His voice was dry and mechanical.

'What I did was inexcusable,' Goldman said. Now he did not just seem to be pushing the words out; he seemed to be *coughing* them out. 'You suggesting that Rachel and Eileen come out has made me see what a big man you have been about this . . . and how small I have been.'

There was something very familiar in this rap, something eerily familiar—

Then he got it, and his mouth suddenly pulled together in a tight pucker, as if he had bitten straight through a plump yellow lemon. Rachel's way – she was completely unaware of it, Louis was sure – of saying contritely: *Louis, I'm sorry I was such a bitch* after her bitchiness had gotten her her own way about something she really wanted. Here was that voice, robbed of Rachel's life and merriness, true, but that same voice saying *I'm sorry I was such a bastard, Louis.*

The old man was getting his daughter and granddaughter back; they were running home from Maine to Daddy. Courtesy of Delta and United, they were coming back to where they belonged, back to where Irwin Goldman wanted them. Now he could afford to be magnanimous. As far as old Irwin knew, he had won. *So let's just forget that I took a swing at you over your dead son's body, Louis, or that I kicked you when you were down, or that I knocked his coffin off its bier and snapped the latch so you could see – or think that you saw – that one last flash of your child's hand. Let's forget all of that. Let bygones be bygones.*

Terrible as it may be, Irwin, you old prick, I'd wish for you to drop dead right this second, if it wouldn't screw up my plans.

'That's all right, Mr Goldman,' he said evenly. 'It was . . . well . . . an emotional day for all of us.'

'It was *not* all right,' he persisted, and Louis realized – although he did not want to – that Goldman was not just being political, not just saying that he was sorry he had been such a bastard now that he was getting his own way. The man was nearly weeping, and he was speaking with a slow and trembling urgency. 'It was a *terrible* day for all of us. Thanks to me. Thanks to a stupid, bullheaded old man. I hurt my daughter when she needed my help . . . I hurt you, and maybe you needed my help, too, Louis. That you do this . . . behave this way . . . after I behaved *that* way . . . it makes me feel like garbage, Louis. And I think that is just the way I *should* feel.'

Oh let him stop this, let him stop before I start to scream at him and blow the whole deal.

'Rachel's probably told you, Louis, we had another daughter—'

'Zelda,' Louis said. 'Yes, she told me about Zelda.'

'It was difficult,' Goldman said in that trembling voice. 'Difficult for all of us. Most difficult for Rachel, perhaps, yes, Rachel was there when Zelda died, but difficult for Dory and me, too. Dory almost had a breakdown—'

What do you think Rachel had? Louis wanted to shout. *Do you think a kid can't have a nervous breakdown? Twenty years later she's still jumping at death's shadow. And now this happens. This miserable, awful thing. It's a minor miracle that she isn't in the fucking hospital, being fed through an IV-tube. So don't talk to me about how difficult it was for you and your wife, you bastard.*

'Ever since Zelda died, we have . . . I suppose we have clung to Rachel . . . always wanting to protect her . . . and to make it up to her. Make up for the problems she had with her . . . her back . . . for years afterward. Make up for not being there.'

Yes, the old man was really crying. Why did he have to be crying? It made it harder for Louis to hold on to his clean, pure hate. More difficult, but not impossible. He deliberately called up the image of Goldman reaching into the pocket of his smoking jacket for his overflowing check-book . . . but he suddenly saw Zelda Goldman in the background, an unquiet ghost in a stinking bed, her cheesy face full of spite and agony, her hands pulled into claws. The Goldman ghost. Oz, the Gweat and Tewwible.

'Please,' he said. 'Please, Mr Goldman. Irwin. No more. Let's not make things any worse than they have to be, okay?'

'I believe now that you are a good man and that I misjudged you, Louis. Oh, listen, I know what you think. Am I that stupid? No. Stupid, but not *that* stupid. You think I'm saying all of this because now I can, you're thinking oh yeah, he's getting what he wants and once he tried to buy me off, but . . . but Louis, I swear . . .'

'No more,' Louis said gently. 'I can't . . . I really can't take any more.' Now his voice was trembling as well. 'Okay?'

'All right,' Goldman said, and sighed. Louis thought it was a sigh of relief. 'But let me say again that I apologize. You don't have to accept it. But that is what I called to say, Louis. I apologize.'

'All right,' Louis said. He closed his eyes. His head was thudding. 'Thank you, Irwin. Your apology is accepted.'

'Thank *you*,' Goldman said. 'And thank you . . . for letting them come. Perhaps it is what they both need. And we'll meet them at the airport.'

'Fine,' Louis said, and an idea suddenly occurred to him. It was crazy and attractive in its very sanity. He would let bygones be bygones . . . and he would let Gage lie in his Pleasantview grave. Instead of trying to re-open a door that had swung shut, he would latch it and double-bolt it and throw away the key. He would do just what he had told his wife he was going to do: tidy up their affairs here and catch a plane back to Shytown. They would perhaps spend the entire summer there, he and his wife and his good-hearted daughter. They would go to the zoo and the planetarium and go boating on the lake. He would take Ellie to the top of the Sears Tower and show her the Midwest stretching away like a great flat game-board, rich and dreaming. Then when mid-August came, they would come back to this house which now seemed so sad and so shadowy, and perhaps it would be like starting over again. Perhaps they could begin weaving from fresh thread. What was on the Creed loom right now was ugly, splattered with drying blood.

But would that not be the same as murdering his son? Killing him a second time?

A voice inside tried to argue that this was not so, but he would not listen. He shut the voice up briskly.

'Irwin, I ought to go now. I want to make sure Rachel's got what she needs and then get her to bed.'

'All right. Goodbye, Louis. And once more—'

If he says he's sorry one more time, I'll fucking scream.

'Goodbye, Irwin,' he said, and hung up the phone.

Rachel was deep in a litter of clothes when he came upstairs. Blouses on the beds, bras hung over the backs of chairs, slacks on hangers that had been hung over the doorknob. Shoes were lined up like soldiers under the window. She appeared to be packing slowly but competently. Louis could see it was going to take her at least three suitcases (maybe four), but he could also see no sense in arguing with her about it. Instead, he pitched in and helped.

'Louis,' she said as they closed the last suitcase (he had to sit on it before Rachel could snap the catches), 'are you sure there's nothing you want to tell me?'

'For God's sake, hon, what *is* this?'

'I don't know what it is,' she replied evenly. 'That's why I'm asking.'

'What do you think I'm going to do? Creep off to a bordello? Join the circus? What?'

'I don't know. But this feels wrong. It feels as if you're trying to get rid of us.'

'Rachel, that's *ridiculous*!' He said this with a vehemence that was partly exasperation. Even in such straits as these, he felt a certain pique in being seen through so easily.

She smiled wanly. 'You never were a very good liar, Lou.'

He began to protest again and she cut him off.

'Ellie dreamed you were dead,' she said. 'Last night. She woke up crying, and I went in to her. I slept with her for two or three hours and then came back in with you. She said that in her dream you were sitting at the kitchen table and your eyes were open but she knew you were dead. She said she could hear fire engines, and smell something burning. And she said that she could hear Steve Masterton screaming.'

Louis looked at her, dismayed. 'Rachel,' he said at last, 'her brother just died. It's normal enough for her to dream that other members of her family—'

'Yes, I surmised that much for myself. But the way she told it . . . the elements . . . it seemed to me to have a quality of prophecy.'

She laughed weakly.

'Or maybe you had to be there.'

'Yes, maybe so,' Louis said.

In spite of his rational tone, he could feel gooseflesh crawling all over him. The roots of his hair had gone stiff.

It seemed to me to have a quality of prophecy.

'Come to bed with me,' Rachel said. 'The Valium's all worn off and I don't want to take any more. But I'm afraid. I've been having my own dreams . . .'

'Dreams of what?'

'Of Zelda,' she said simply. 'The last few nights, since Gage died, when I go to sleep, Zelda's there. She says she's coming for me, and this time she'll get me. That both she and Gage will get me. For letting them die.'

'Rachel, that's—'

'I know. Just a dream. Normal enough. But come to bed with me and keep the dreams away if you can, Louis.'

They lay together in the dark.

'Rachel? You still awake?'

'Yes.'

'I want to ask you something.'

'Go ahead.'

He hesitated, not wanting to cause her even more pain, but needing to know.

'Do you remember the scare we had with him, when he was nine months old?' he asked finally.

'Yes. Yes, of course I do. Why?'

By the time Gage was nine months old, Louis had become deeply concerned about his son's cranial size. It was right off

Louis's Berterier Chart, which showed the normal range of infant head-sizes on a per-month basis. At four months, Gage's skull size had begun to drift toward the highest part of the curve, and then it began to go even higher than that. He wasn't having any trouble holding his head up – that would have been a dead giveaway – but Louis had taken him to George Tardiff, who was perhaps the best neurologist in the Midwest, nevertheless. Rachel had wanted to know what was wrong, and Louis had told her the truth: he was worried that Gage might be hydrocephalic. Rachel's face had grown very white, but she had remained calm.

'He seems normal to me,' she said.

Louis nodded. 'He does to me, too. But I don't want to ignore this, babe.'

'No, you mustn't,' she said. '*We* mustn't.'

Tardiff had measured Gage's skull and frowned. Tardiff poked two fingers at Gage's face, Three Stooges style. Gage flinched. Tardiff smiled. Louis's heart thawed out a little. Tardiff gave Gage a ball to hold. Gage held it for a while and then dropped it. Tardiff retrieved the ball and bounced it, watching Gage's eyes. Gage's eyes tracked the ball.

'I'd say there's a fifty-fifty chance he's hydrocephalic,' Tardiff said to Louis in his office later. 'No – odds may actually be a bit higher than that. If so, it's mild. He seems very alert. The new shunt operation should take care of the problem easily . . . if there *is* a problem.'

'A shunt means brain surgery,' Louis said.

'*Minor* brain surgery.'

Louis had studied the process not long after he began to worry about the size of Gage's skull, and the shunt operation, designed to drain excess fluid from the patient's skull, had not looked very minor to *him*. But he kept his mouth shut, telling himself to just be grateful the operation existed at all.

'Of course,' Tardiff went on, 'there's still a large possibility that your kid just has a real big head for a nine-month-old. I think a CAT-scan is the best place to start. Do you agree?'

Louis had agreed.

Gage had spent a night in Our Sisters of Charity Hospital, underwent general anesthesia, and had had his sleeping head stuck into a gadget that looked like a giant clothes-dryer. Rachel and Louis waited downstairs while Ellie spent the day at her grandma and grandda's, watching *Sesame Street* nonstop on grandda's new video recorder. For Louis, those had been long, gray hours in which he found himself totting up sums of varying ugliness and comparing results. Death under g-a; death during a shunt operation; mild retardation as a result of hydrocephalia; cataclysmic retardation as a result of same; epilepsy; blindness . . . oh, there were all sorts of possibilities. *For really complete disaster maps,* Louis remembered thinking, *see your local doctor.*

Tardiff had come into the waiting room around five o'clock. He had three cigars. He plugged one into Louis's mouth; plugged one into Rachel's (she was too flabbergasted to protest), and one into his own.

'The kid is fine. No hydrocephalia.'

'Light this thing,' Rachel had said, weeping and laughing at the same time. 'I'm going to smoke it till I puke.'

Grinning, Tardiff lit their cigars.

God was saving him for Route 15, Dr Tardiff, Louis thought now.

'Rachel, if he *had* been hydrocephalic, and if the shunt hadn't worked . . . could you have still loved him?'

'What a weird question, Louis!'

'*Could* you?'

'Yes, of course. I would have loved Gage no matter what.'

'Even if he was retarded?'

'Yes.'

'Would you have wanted him institutionalized?'

'No, I don't think so,' she said slowly. 'I suppose, with the money you're making now, we could afford that . . . a really good place, I mean . . . but I think I'd want him with us if we could . . . Louis, why do you ask?'

'Why, I suppose I was still thinking of your sister Zelda,' he said. He was still astonished at this eerie glibness. 'Wondering if you could have gone through that again.'

'It wouldn't have been the same,' she said, sounding almost amused. 'Gage was . . . well, Gage was Gage. He was our son. That would have made all the difference. It would have been hard, I guess, but . . . would *you* have wanted him in an institution? A place like Pineland?'

'No.'

'Let's go to sleep.'

'That's a good idea.'

'I feel like I *can* sleep now,' she said. 'I want to put this day behind me.'

'Amen to that,' Louis said.

A long time later she said drowsily: 'You're right, Louis . . . just dreams and vapors . . .'

'Sure,' he said, and kissed her earlobe. 'Now sleep.'

It seemed to me to have the quality of prophecy.

He did not sleep for a long time, and before he did, the curved bone of May's dying moon looked in the window at him.

CHAPTER FORTY-THREE

The following day was overcast but very warm, and Louis was sweating heavily by the time he had checked Rachel's and Elllie's baggage through and gotten their tickets out of the computer. He supposed just being able to keep busy was something of a gift, and he felt only a small, aching comparison to the last time he had put his family on a plane to Chicago, at Thanksgiving. That had been Gage's first and last plane trip.

Ellie seemed distant and a trifle odd. Several times that morning Louis had looked up and had seen an expression of peculiar speculation on her face.

Conspirator's complex working overtime, boyo, he told himself.

She said nothing when told they were all going to Chicago, she and Mommy first, perhaps for the whole summer, only went on eating her breakfast (Cocoa Bears). After breakfast she went silently upstairs and got into the dress and shoes Rachel had laid out for her. She had brought the picture of her pulling Gage on her sled to the airport with her, and she had sat calmly in one of the plastic contour seats in the lower lobby while Louis stood in line for their tickets and the loudspeaker blared intelligence of arriving and departing flights.

Mr and Mrs Goldman showed up forty minutes before flight-time. Irwin Goldman was natty (and apparently sweatless) in a cashmere topcoat in spite of the sixty-degree temperatures; he went over to the Avis desk to check his car in while Dory Goldman sat with Rachel and Ellie.

Louis and Irwin Goldman joined the others at the same time. Louis was a bit afraid that there might be a reprise of the *my-son my-son* playlet, but he was spared. Goldman contented himself with a rather limp handshake and a muttered hello. The quick, embarrassed glance he afforded his son-in-law confirmed the certainty Louis had awakened with this morning: the man must have been drunk.

They went upstairs on the escalator and sat in the boarding lounge, not talking much. Dory Goldman thumbed nervously at her copy of the new Erica Jong novel but did not open it. She kept glancing, a little anxiously, at the picture Ellie was holding.

Louis asked his daughter if she would like to walk over to the bookstore with him and pick out something to read on the plane.

Ellie had been looking at him in that speculative way again. Louis didn't like it. It made him nervous.

'Will you be good at Grandma and Grandda's?' he asked her as they walked over.

'Yes,' she said. 'Daddy, will the truant officer get me? Andy Pasioca says there's a truant officer and he gets school-skippers.'

'Don't you worry about the truant officer,' he said. 'I'll take care of the school, and you can start again in the fall with no trouble.'

'I hope I'll be okay in the fall,' Ellie said. 'I never was in a grade before. Only kindergarten. I don't know what kids do in grades. Homework, probably.'

'You'll be fine.'

'Daddy, are you still pissed off at Grandda?'

He gaped at her. 'Why in the world would you think I was . . . that I didn't like your grandda, Ellie?'

She shrugged as if the topic held no particular interest for her. 'When you talk about him you always look pissed off.'

'Ellie, that's vulgar.'

'Sorry.'

She gave him that strange, fey look and then drifted off to look at the racks of kid-books – Mercer Meyer and Maurice Sendak and Richard Scary and Beatrix Potter and that famous old stand-by, Dr Seuss. *How do they find this stuff out? Or do they just know? How much does Ellie know? How's it affecting her? Ellie, what's behind that pale little face? Pissed off at him, Christ!*

'Can I have these, Daddy?' She was holding out a Dr Seuss and a book Louis hadn't seen since his own childhood – the story of Little Black Sambo and how the tigers had gotten his clothes one fine day.

Christ, I thought they'd made that one an un-book, Louis thought, bemused.

'Yes, fine,' he said, and they stood in a short line at the cash-register. 'Your Grandda and I like each other fine,' he said, and thought again of his mother's story of how, when a woman really wanted a baby, she 'found' one. He remembered his own foolish promises to himself that he would never lie to his own children. Over the last few days he had developed into quite a promising liar, he felt, but he would not let himself think about it now.

'Oh,' she said, and fell silent.

The silence made him uneasy. To say something and break the silence, he said: 'So do you think you'll have a good time in Chicago?'

'No.'

'No? Why not?'

She looked up at him with that fey expression. 'I'm scared.'

He put his hand on her head. 'Scared? Honey, what for? You're not scared of the plane, are you?'

'No,' she said. 'I don't know what I'm scared of. Daddy, I dreamed we were at Gage's funeral and the funeral man opened his coffin and it was empty. Then I dreamed I was home and I looked in Gage's crib and that was empty, too. But there was dirt in it.'

Lazarus, come forth.

Then, for the first time in months, he consciously remembered the dream he had had after Pascow's death – the dream, and then waking up to find his feet dirty and the foot of the bed caked with fir needles and muck.

The hairs at the nape of his neck stirred.

'Just dreams,' he said to Ellie, and his voice sounded, to his ears at least, perfectly normal. 'They'll pass.'

'I wish you were coming with us,' she said, 'or that we were staying here. Can we stay, Daddy? Please? I don't want to go to Grandma and Grandda's . . . I just want to go back to school. Okay?'

'Just for a little while, Ellie,' he said. 'I've got . . .' he swallowed '. . . a few things to do here, and then I'll be with you. We can decide what to do next.'

He expected an argument, perhaps even an Ellie-style tantrum. He might even have welcomed it; a known quantity, as that look was not. But there was only that pallid, disquieting silence which seemed so deep. He could have asked her more, but found he didn't dare; she had already told him more than he perhaps wanted to hear.

Shortly after he and Ellie returned to the boarding lounge, the flight was called. Boarding passes were produced, and the four of them got in line. Louis embraced his wife, kissed her hard. She clung to him for a moment and then let him go so he could pick Ellie up and buss her cheek.

Ellie gazed at him solemnly with sybil's eyes. 'Your lips are so cold,' she said. 'Why is that, Daddy?'

'I don't know,' he said, now more uneasy than ever. He set her down. 'You be good, pun'kin.'

'I don't want to go,' she said again, but so low only Louis could really hear over the shuffle and murmur of the boarding passengers. 'I don't want Mommy to go, either.'

'Ellie, come on,' Louis said. 'You'll be fine.'

'I'll be fine,' she said, 'but what about you? Daddy, what about you?'

The line had begun to move, now. People were walking down the jetway to the 727. Rachel pulled Ellie's hand and for a moment she resisted, holding up the line, her eyes fixed on her father, and Louis found himself remembering her impatience last time, her cries of come on–come on–come on.

'Daddy?'

'Go now, Ellie. Please.'

Rachel looked at Ellie and saw that dark, dreamy look for the first time. 'Ellie?' she said, startled and, Louis thought, a little afraid. 'You're holding up the line, baby.'

Ellie's lips trembled and grew white. Then she allowed herself to be led into the jetway. She looked back at him, and he saw naked terror in her face. He raised his hand to her in false cheeriness.

Ellie did not wave back.

CHAPTER FORTY-FOUR

As Louis left the BIA terminal building, a cold cloak seemed to fall over his mind. He became aware that he meant to go through with this. His mind, which had been sharp enough to get him through med school mostly on scholarship and on what his wife could earn pushing coffee-and-Danish on the five a.m. to eleven a.m. shift six days a week, had taken the problem over and broken it down into components, as if this was just another prelim – the biggest one he had ever taken. And he intended to pass it with an A-plus, one hundred per cent.

He drove to Brewer, the little city across the Penobscot River from Bangor. He found a parking spot across the street from Watson's Hardware.

'Can I help you?' the clerk asked.

'Yes,' Louis said. 'I'd like a heavy flashlight – one of the square ones – and something I can hood it with.'

The clerk was a small slim man with a high forehead and sharp eyes. He smiled now, but his smile was not particularly pleasant. 'Going jacking, good buddy?'

'I beg your pardon?'

'Gonna jacklight a few deer tonight?'

'Not at all,' Louis said, unsmiling. 'I haven't a licence to jack.'

The clerk blinked, then decided to laugh. 'In other words, mind my own business, huh? Well, look – you can't hood one of those big lights, but you can get a piece of felt and poke a hole in the middle of it. Cut the beam down to a penlite.'

'That sounds fine,' Louis said. 'Thanks.'

'Surely. Anything else for you today?'

'Yes indeed,' Louis said. 'I need a pick, a shovel, and a spade. Short-handled shovel, long-handled spade. A stout length of rope, eight feet long. A pair of work-gloves. A canvas tarpaulin, maybe eight by eight.'

'I can do all that,' the clerk said.

'I've got a septic tank to dig up,' Louis said. 'It looks like I'm in violation of the zoning ordinances, and I've got some very nosy neighbors. I don't know if hooding my light will do any good or not, but I thought I might give it a try. I could get a pretty good fine.'

'Oh-oh,' the clerk said. 'Better get a clothespin for your nose while you're at it.'

Louis laughed dutifully. His purchases came to fifty-eight-sixty. He paid cash.

The Civic was a hatchback, and Louis was nervous about going back to Ludlow with the pick, shovel and spade in there. Jud Crandall's eyes were sharp, and there was nothing wrong with his brains, either. He would know what was up.

Then it occurred to him that there was no real reason to go back to Ludlow anyway. Louis re-crossed the Chamberlain Bridge into Bangor, and checked into the Howard Johnson's Motor Lodge on the Odlin Road – once again near the airport, once again near Pleasantview Cemetery, where his son was buried. He checked in under the name Dee Dee Ramone, and paid cash for his room.

He tried to nap, reasoning that he would be glad of the rest before tomorrow morning. In the words of some Victorian novel or other, there was wild work ahead of him tonight – enough wild work to last a lifetime.

But his brain simply would not shut down.

He lay on the anonymous motel bed beneath a nondescript motel picture of picturesque boats at dock beside a picturesque old wharf in a picturesque New England harbor, fully dressed except for his shoes, his wallet and coins and keys on the night-table beside him, his hands behind his head. That feeling of coldness still held; he felt totally unplugged from his people, the places that had become so familiar to him, even his work. This could have been any HoJo's in the world – in San Diego, or Duluth, or Bangkok, or Charlotte Amalie. He was nowhere, and now and then a thought of surpassing oddity struck him: before he saw any of those familiar places and faces again, he would see his son.

His plan kept unreeling in his mind. He looked at it from all angles, poked it, prodded it, looked for holes or soft places. And he felt that, in truth, he was walking along a narrow beam over a gulf of insanity. Madness was all around him, softly fluttering as if with wings of night-hunting owls with great golden eyes: he was heading into madness.

The voice of Tom Rush echoed dreamily in his head: *O death your hands are clammy . . . I feel them on my knees . . . you came and took my mother . . . won't you come back after me?*

Madness. Madness all around, close, hunting him.

He walked the balance-beam of rationality; he studied his plan.

Tonight, around eleven o'clock, he would dig up his son's grave, use the rope to pull up the top of the graveliner, remove his son's body from the coffin in which it lay, wrap Gage in a cut-down piece of the tarpaulin, and put it in the trunk of the Civic. He would replace the coffin and refill the grave. He would drive to Ludlow, take Gage's body from the trunk . . . and take a walk. Yes, he would take a walk.

If Gage returned, the single path forked into two possibilities. Along one, he saw Gage returning as Gage, perhaps stunned, or slow, or even retarded (only in the deepest recesses of his mind did Louis allow himself to hope that Gage would return whole, and just as he had been – but surely even that was possible, wasn't it?), but still his son, Rachel's son, Ellie's brother.

Along the other, he saw some sort of monster emerging

from the woods behind the house. He had accepted so much that he did not balk at the idea of monsters, or even of demons, discorporeal beings of evil from the outerworld which might well take charge of a reanimated body from which the original soul had fled.

Either way, he and his son would be alone. And he would . . .

I will make a diagnosis.

Yes. That is what he would do.

I will make a diagnosis, not only of his body but of his spirit. I will make allowances for the trauma of the accident itself, which he may or may not remember. Keeping the example of Church before me, I will expect retardation, perhaps mild, perhaps profound. I will judge our ability to reintegrate Gage into our family on the basis of what I see over a period of from twenty-four to seventy-two hours. And if the loss is too great – or if he comes back as Timmy Baterman apparently came back, as a thing of evil – I will kill him.

He discovered that he had advanced even further along these two paths.

As a doctor, he felt he could kill Gage, if Gage was only the vessel containing some other being, quite easily. He would not allow himself to be swayed by its pleadings or its wiles. He would kill it as he would kill a rat carrying bubonic plague. There need be no melodrama about it. A pill in solution, perhaps two or three of them. If necessary, a shot. There was morphine in his bag. The following night, he would return the lifeless clay to Pleasantview and reinter it, simply trusting that his luck would hold a second time (*you don't even know if it will hold once,* he reminded himself). He had considered the easier and safer alternative of burying Gage this second time in the Pet Sematary, but he would not have his son up there. There were a lot of reasons. A child burying his pet five years or ten years or even twenty years later might stumble on the remains – that was one reason. But the most compelling one was simpler. The Pet Sematary might be . . . too close.

The reinterment completed, he would fly to Chicago and

join his family. Neither Rachel nor Ellie need ever know about his failed experiment.

Then, looking further along the other path, the path he hoped for blindly with all his love for his son: he and Gage would leave the house when the examination period was over, leave at night. He would take certain papers with him, and plan never to return to Ludlow again. He and Gage would check into a motel – perhaps this very one in which he now lay.

The following morning he would cash every account they had, converting everything into American Express travellers' checks (*don't leave home with your resurrected son without them*, he thought, and a little giggle escaped his lips) and flat cash. He and Gage would fly somewhere – Florida, most likely. From there he would call Rachel, tell her where he was, tell her to take Ellie and catch a plane without telling her mother and father where she was going. Louis believed he could convince her to do this. *Ask no questions, Rachel. Just come. Come now. This minute.*

He would tell her where he (they) were staying. Some motel. She and Ellie would arrive in a rental car. He would bring Gage to the door when they knocked. Perhaps Gage would be wearing a bathing suit.

And then—

Ah, but beyond that he did not dare go; instead he turned back to the plan's beginning and began to go over it again. He supposed that, if things worked out, it would mean accumulating the identification minutiae of whole new lives so that Irwin Goldman could not use his over-flowing checkbook to trace them. Such things could be done.

Vaguely, he remembered arriving at the Ludlow house, tense, tired, and more than a little scared, and having some fantasy about just driving down to Orlando and hiring on as a medic at Disney World. Maybe that wasn't so farfetched after all.

He saw himself, dressed in white, resuscitating a pregnant

woman who had foolishly gone on the Magic Mountain ride and had fainted. *Stand back, stand back, give her some air*, he heard himself saying, and the woman opened her eyes and smiled gratefully at him.

As his mind spun out this not disagreeable fantasy, Louis fell asleep. He slept as his daughter awoke in an airplane somewhere above Niagara Falls, screaming from a nightmare of clutching hands and stupid yet merciless eyes; he slept as the stewardess rushed down the aisle to see what was wrong; he slept as Rachel, totally unnerved, tried to soothe her; he slept as Ellie cried over and over again: *It's Gage! Mommy! It's Gage! It's Gage! Gage is alive! Gage has got the knife from Daddy's bag! Don't let him get me! Don't let him get Daddy!*

He slept as Ellie quieted at last and lay shuddering against her mother's breast, her eyes wide and tearless, and as Dory Goldman thought what an awful thing all of this had been for Ellie, and how much she reminded Dory of Rachel after Zelda had died.

He slept and woke up at quarter past five, with the afternoon light beginning to slant down toward the coming night.

Wild work, he thought stupidly, and got up.

CHAPTER FORTY-FIVE

By the time United Airlines flight 419 touched down at O'Hare Airport and offloaded its passengers at ten minutes past three, central standard time, Ellie Creed was in a state of low hysteria, and Rachel was very frightened. Never since the time she had taken the kids out to McDonalds by herself and Gage had begun to choke on a throatful of french fries had she so much wished Louis was with her.

If you touched Ellie casually on the shoulder, she jumped and stared around at you with big wall-eyes, and her whole body quivered steadily and without let-up. It was as if she were full of electricity. The nightmare on the airplane had been bad enough, but this . . . Rachel simply didn't know how to cope with it.

Going into the terminal, Ellie tripped over her own feet and fell down. She did not get up; merely lay there on the carpet with people passing around her (or looking down at her with that mildly sympathetic but disconnected glance of people who are in transit and cannot be bothered) until Rachel picked her up in her arms.

'Ellie, what's wrong with you?' Rachel asked.

But Ellie would not answer. They moved across the lobby toward the luggage carousels, and Rachel saw her mother and father waiting there for them. She waved at them with her free hand and they came over.

'They told us not to go to the gate and wait for you,' Dory said, 'so we thought . . . Rachel? How's Ellie?'

'Not good.'

'Is there a ladies' room, Mommy? I'm going to throw up.'

'Oh, God,' Rachel said despairingly, and took her by the

hand. There was a ladies' across the lobby, and she led Ellie toward it quickly.

'Rachel, shall I come?' Dory called.

'No, get the luggage, you know what it looks like. We're okay.'

Mercifully the ladies' was deserted. Rachel led Ellie to one of the stalls, fumbling in her purse for a dime, and then she saw – thank God – that the locks on three of them were broken. Over one broken lock, someone had written in grease-pencil: SIR JOHN CRAPPER WAS A SEXIST PIG!

Rachel pulled the door open quickly; Ellie was now moaning and holding her stomach. She retched twice, but there was no vomiting; they were the dry heaves of total nervous exhaustion.

When Ellie told her she felt a little better, Rachel took her over to the basins and washed her daughter's face. Ellie was wretchedly white, and there were circles under her eyes.

'Ellie, what is *wrong*? Can't you tell me?'

'I don't know what's wrong,' she said. 'But I knew *something* was wrong ever since Daddy told me about the trip. Because something was wrong with him.'

Louis, what are you hiding? You were hiding something. I could see it; even Ellie could see it.

It occurred to her that she had also been nervous all day, as though waiting for a blow to fall. She felt the way she did in the two or three days before her period, tense and on edge, ready to laugh or cry or get a headache that would come bulleting through like a fast express, there and then gone three hours later.

'*What?*' she said now to Ellie's reflection in the mirror. 'Honey, what could be wrong with Daddy?'

'I don't know,' Ellie said. 'It was the dream. Something about Gage. Or maybe it was Church. I don't remember. I don't *know*.'

'Ellie, what was your dream?'

'I dreamed I was in the Pet Sematary,' Ellie said. 'Paxcow

took me to the Pet Sematary and said Daddy was going to go there and something terrible was going to happen.'

'Paxcow?' A bolt of terror both sharp and yet undefined struck her. What was that name, and why did it seem familiar? It seemed that she had heard that name — or one like it — but she could not for the life of her remember where. 'You dreamed someone named Paxcow took you to the Pet Sematary?'

'Yes, that's what he said his name was. And—' Her eyes suddenly widened.

'Do you remember something else?'

'He said that he was sent to *warn* but that he couldn't *interfere*. He said that he was . . . I don't know . . . that he was near daddy because they were together when his soul was dis—dis— *I can't remember!*' She wailed.

'Honey,' Rachel said, 'I think you dreamed about the Pet Sematary because you're still thinking about Gage. And I'm sure Daddy is fine. Do you feel any better now?'

'No,' Eileen whispered. 'Mommy, I'm scared. Aren't you scared?'

'Huh-uh,' Rachel said, with a brisk little shake of her head and a smile — but she was, she was scared, and that name, Paxcow, haunted her with its familiarity. She felt she had heard it in some dreadful context months or even years ago, and that nervy feeling would not leave her.

She felt something — something *pregnant*, swollen and waiting to burst. Something terrible that needed to be averted. But what? *What?*

'I'm sure everything is fine,' she told Eileen. 'Want to go back to Grandma and Grandda?'

'I guess so,' Ellie said listlessly.

A Puerto Rican woman led her very young son into the ladies', scolding him. A large wet stain had spread on the crotch of the little boy's natty travelling pants, and Rachel found herself reminded of Gage with a kind of paralyzing poignancy. This fresh sorrow was like Novocaine, smothering her jitters.

'Come on,' she said. 'We'll call Daddy from Grandda's house.'

'He was wearing shorts,' Ellie said suddenly.

'Who was, honey?'

'Paxcow,' Ellie said. 'He was wearing red shorts. In my dream.'

That brought the name momentarily into focus and Rachel felt that knee-weakening fear again . . . then it danced away.

They could not get close to the luggage carousel; Rachel could just see the top of her father's hat, the one with the feather. She turned, saw Dory Goldman holding two seats against the wall for them and waving. Rachel brought Ellie over.

'Are you feeling any better, dear?' Dory asked.

'A little bit,' Ellie said. 'Mommy—'

She turned to Rachel and broke off. Rachel was sitting bolt upright, her hand clapped to her mouth, her face white. She had it. It had suddenly gone through with a terrible thud. Of course she should have known at once, but she had tried to put it out of her mind. Of course.

'*Mommy?*'

Rachel turned slowly to her daughter, and Ellie could hear the tendons in her neck creak. She took her hand away from her mouth.

'Did the man in your dream tell you his first name, Ellie?'

'Mommy, are you all—'

'*Did the man in your dream tell you his first name?*'

Dory was looking at her daughter and granddaughter as if they might have both gone crazy.

'Yes, but I can't remember . . . Mommy, you're *hurrrrting* me—'

Rachel looked down and saw that her free hand was clamped around Ellie's lower forearm like a manacle.

'Was it Victor?'

Ellie drew sharp breath. 'Yes, Victor! He said his name was Victor! Mommy, did you dream him, too?'

'Not Paxcow,' Rachel said. '*Pascow.*'

'That's what I *said*. Paxcow.'

'Rachel, what's wrong?' Dory said. She took Rachel's free hand and winced at its chill. 'And what's wrong with Ellie?'

'It's not Ellie,' Rachel said. 'It's Louis, I think. Something is wrong with Louis. Or something is going to be wrong. Sit with Ellie, Mom. I want to call home.'

She got up and crossed to the telephones, digging in her purse for a quarter. She made the call collect, but there was no one to accept the charges. The phone simply rang.

'Will you try your call later?' the operator asked her.

'Yes,' Rachel said, and hung up.

She stood there, staring at the phone.

He said that he was sent to warn but that he couldn't interfere. He said that he was . . . that he was near Daddy because they were together when his soul was dis— dis— I can't remember!

'Discorporated,' Rachel whispered. Her fingers dug at the fabric of her handbag. 'Oh my God, was that the word?'

She tried to catch at her thoughts, to arrange them. Was something going on here, something beyond their natural upset at Gage's death and this queer cross-country trip that was so much like flight? How much had Ellie known about the young man who had died on Louis's first day at work?

Nothing, her mind answered inexorably. *You kept it from her, the way you tried to keep anything from her that had to do with death – even the possible death of her cat, remember that dumb, stupid argument we had that day in the kitchen? You kept it from her. Because you were scared then and you're scared now. His name was Pascow, Victor Pascow, and how desperate is the situation now, Rachel? How bad is this? What in the name of God is happening?*

Her hands were trembling so badly that it took her two tries to redeposit her quarter. This time she called the infirmary at the University and got Charlton, who accepted the call, a little mystified. No, she hadn't seen Louis, and would have been surprised if he came in today. That said, she offered her sympathies to Rachel again. Rachel accepted them and then asked Charlton to have Louis call her at her folks' house if he did come in. Yes, he had the number, she answered Charlton's question, not wanting to tell the nurse (who probably knew anyway; she had a feeling that Charlton didn't miss much) that her folks' house was half the continent away.

She hung up, feeling hot and trembly.

She heard Pascow's name somewhere else, that's all. My God, you don't raise a kid in a glass box like a . . . a hamster, or something. She heard an item about it on the radio. Or some kid mentioned it to her at school, and her mind stored it away. Even that word she couldn't say — suppose it was a jawbreaker like 'discorporated' or 'discorporeal,' so what? That proves nothing except that the subconscious is exactly the kind of sticky flypaper they say it is.

She remembered a college psych instructor who had asserted that, under the right conditions, your memory could play back the names of every person to whom you had ever been introduced, every meal you had ever eaten, the weather conditions which had obtained on every day of your life. He made a persuasive case for this incredible assertion, telling them that the human mind was a computer with staggering numbers of memory chips — not 16K, or 32K, or 64K, but perhaps as much as *one billion K*: literally, a thousand billions. And how much might each of these organic 'chips' be capable of storing? No one knew. But there were so many of them, he said, that there was no need for any of them to be erasable so they could be re-used. In fact, the conscious mind had to turn down the lights on some of them as a protection against informational insanity. 'You might not be able to remember where you keep your socks,' the psych instructor had said, 'if the entire contents of the *Encyclopedia Britannica* was stored in the adjacent two or three memory cells.'

This had produced dutiful laughter from the class.

But this isn't a psych class under good fluorescent lights with all that comforting jargon written on the board and some smartass assistant prof cheerfully blueskying his way through the last fifteen minutes of the period. Something is dreadfully wrong here and you know it — you feel it. I don't know what it has to do with Pascow, or Gage, or Church, but it has something to do with Louis. What? Is it—

Suddenly a thought as cold as a handful of jelly struck her. She picked up the telephone receiver again and groped in the coin-return for her dime. Was Louis contemplating suicide? Was that why he had gotten rid of them, nearly pushed them out the door? Had Ellie somehow had a ... a ... oh, fuck the psychology! Had she had a psychic flash of some sort?

This time she made the call collect to Jud Crandall. It rang five times ... six ... seven. She was about to hang up, when his voice, breathless, answered. 'H'lo?'

'Jud! Jud, this is—'

'Just a minute, ma'am,' the operator said. 'Will you accept a collect call from Mrs Louis Creed?'

'Ayuh,' Jud said.

'Pardon, sir, is that yes or no?'

'I guess I will,' Jud said.

There was a doubtful pause as the operator translated Yankee into American. Then: 'Thank you. Go ahead, ma'am.'

'Jud, have you seen Louis today?'

'Today? I can't say I have, Rachel. But I was away to Brewer this mornin', gettin' my groceries. Been out in the garden this afternoon, behind the house. Why?'

'Oh, it's probably nothing, but Ellie had a bad dream on the plane and I just thought I'd set her mind at ease if I could.'

'Plane?' Jud's voice seemed to sharpen a trifle. 'Where are you, Rachel?'

'Chicago,' she said. 'Ellie and I came back to spend some time with my parents.'

'Louis didn't go with you?'

'He's going to join us by the end of the week,' Rachel said, and now it was a struggle to keep her voice even. There was something in Jud's voice she didn't like.

'Was it his idea that you should go out there?'

'Well . . . yes. Jud, what's wrong? Something *is* wrong, isn't it? And you know something about it.'

'Maybe you ought to tell me the child's dream,' Jud said after a long pause. 'I wish you would.'

CHAPTER FORTY-SIX

After he and Rachel were done talking, Jud put on his light coat — the day had clouded up and the wind had begun to blow — and crossed the road to Louis's house, pausing on his side of the road to look carefully for trucks before crossing. It was the trucks that had been the cause of all this. The damned trucks.

Except it wasn't.

He could feel the Pet Sematary pulling at him — and something beyond. Where once its voice had been a kind of seductive lullaby, the voice of possible comfort and a dreamy sort of power, it was now lower, and more than ominous — it was threatening and grim. *Stay out of this, you.*

But he would not stay out of it. His responsibility went back too far.

He saw that Louis's Honda Civic was gone from the garage. He tried the back door and found it open.

'Louis?' he called, knowing that Louis was not going to answer, but needing to cut across the heavy silence of this house somehow. Oh, getting old was starting to be a pain in the ass — his limbs felt heavy and clumsy most of the time, his back was a misery to him after a mere two hours in the garden, and it felt like there was a screw-auger planted in his hip.

He began to go through the house methodically, looking for the signs he had to look for — *world's oldest house-breaker*, he thought without much humor, and went right on looking. He found none of the things that would have seriously upset him: boxes of toys held back from the Salvation Army, clothes for a small boy put aside behind a door or in the closet or under a bed . . . perhaps worst of all, the crib carefully set up in Gage's room again. There were absolutely none of the signs he had come looking for, but the house still had an unpleasant blank feel, as if it were waiting to be filled with ... well, something.

P'raps I ought to take a little run out to Pleasantview Cemetery. See if anything's doing out there. Might even run into Louis Creed. I could buy him a dinner, or somethin'.

But it wasn't at Pleasantview Cemetery in Bangor that there was danger; the danger was here, in this house, and beyond it.

Jud left again and crossed the road to his own house. He pulled a six-pack of beer out of the kitchen fridge and took it into the living room. He sat down in front of the bay window that looked out on the Creed house, cracked a beer, and lit a cigarette. The afternoon drew down around him, and as it did so often these last few years, he found his mind turning back and back in a widening gyre, and if he had known the run of Rachel Creed's earlier thoughts he could have told her what her psych teacher had told her was maybe the truth, but when you got older that dimming function of the memory broke down little by little, the same way that everything else in your body broke down, and you found yourself recalling places and faces and events with an eerie surety. Sepia-toned memories grew bright again, the colors trueing up, the voices losing that tinny echo of time and regaining their original resonance. It wasn't informational breakdown at all, Jud could have told him. The name for it is senility.

In his mind Jud again saw Lester Morgan's bull Hanratty, his eyes rimmed with red, charging at everything in sight, everything that moved. Charging at trees when the wind jigged the leaves. Before Lester gave up and called it off, every tree in Hanratty's fenced meadow was gored with his brainless fury and his horns were splintered and his head was bleeding. When Lester put Hanratty down, Lester had been sick with dread — the way Jud himself was right now.

He drank beer and smoked. Daylight faded. He did not

put on the light. Gradually the tip of his cigarette became a small red pip in the darkness. He sat and drank beer and watched Louis Creed's driveway. He believed that when Louis came home from wherever he was, he would go over and have a little talk with him. Make sure Louis wasn't planning to do anything he shouldn't.

And still he felt the soft tug of whatever it was, whatever sick power it was that inhabited that devil's place, reaching down from its bluff of rotted stone where all those cairns had been built.

Stay out of this, you. Stay out of it or you're going to be very, very sorry. That voice was like runners of mist issuing from an open grave.

Ignoring it as best he could, Jud sat and smoked and drank beer. And waited.

CHAPTER FORTY-SEVEN

While Jud Crandall was sitting in the ladderbacked rocker and watching for him out of his bay window and while Rachel and Ellie were headed up the turnpike toward the Goldman home (Rachel was working incessantly at her fingernails, unable to shake her feeling of dread; Ellie sat pale as a stone), Louis was eating a big tasteless dinner in the Howard Johnson's dining room.

The food was plentiful and dull; exactly what his body seemed to want. Outside it had grown dark. The headlights of the passing cars probed like fingers. He shoveled the food in. A steak. A baked potato. A side-dish of beans which were a bright green nature had never intended. A wedge of apple pie with a scoop of ice cream on top of it melting into a soft drool. He ate at a corner table, watching people come and go, wondering if he might not see someone he knew. In a vague way, he rather hoped that would happen. It would lead to questions – *where's Rachel, what are you doing here, how's it going?* – and perhaps the questions would lead to complications, and maybe complications were what he really wanted. A way out.

And as a matter of fact, a couple whom he did know came in just as he was finishing his apple pie and his second cup of coffee. Rob Grinnell, a Bangor doctor, and his pretty wife Barbara. He waited for them to see him, sitting here in the corner at his table for one, but the hostess led them to the booths on the far side of the room and Louis lost sight of them entirely, except for an occasional glimpse of Grinnell's prematurely graying hair.

The waitress brought Louis his check. He signed for it,

jotting his room number under his signature, and left by the side door.

Outside, the wind had risen to near gale force. It was a steady droning presence, making the electrical wires hum oddly. He could see no stars, but had a sense of clouds rushing past overhead at high speed. Louis stood on the walk for a moment, hands in pockets, face tilted into that wind. Then he turned back and went up to his room and turned on the television. It was too early to do anything serious, and that nightwind was too full of possibilities. It made him nervous.

He watched four hours of TV, eight back-to-back half-hour comedy programs. He realized it had been a very long time since he had watched so much TV in a steady, uninterrupted stream. He thought that all the female leads on the sitcoms were what he and his friends had called 'cockteasers' back in high school.

In Chicago, Dory Goldman was wailing, 'Fly *back*? Honey, why do you want to fly *back*? You just *got* here!'

In Ludlow, Jud Crandall sat by his bay window, smoking and drinking beer, motionless, examining the mental scrapbook of his own past and waiting for Louis to come home. Sooner or later Louis would come home, just like Lassie in that old movie. There were other ways up to the Pet Sematary, but Louis didn't know them. If he intended to do it, he would have to begin from his own dooryard.

Unaware of these other happenings, like slow-moving projectiles aimed not at where he was, but rather in the best ballistics tradition at the place where he would be, Louis sat and watched the HoJo color television set. He had never seen any of these programs before, but he had heard vague rumors of them: a black family, a white family, a little kid who was smarter than the rich grown-ups he lived with, a woman who was single, a woman who was married, a woman who was divorced. Then the three girl private eyes who did all their sleuthing in halter tops. He watched it all, sitting in the HoJo chair and glancing out every now and then at the blowy night.

When the eleven o'clock news came on, he turned the television set off and went out to do what he had decided to do perhaps at the very moment he had seen Gage's baseball cap lying in the road, full of blood. The coldness was on him again, stronger than ever; but there was something beneath it – an ember of eagerness, or passion, or perhaps lust. It did not matter. It warmed him against the cold and kept him together in the wind. As he started the Honda's engine, he thought that perhaps Jud was right about the growing power of that place; for surely he felt it around him now, leading (or pushing) him on, and he wondered:

Could I stop? Could I stop even if I wanted to?

Louis pulled out.

CHAPTER FORTY-EIGHT

'You want to what?' Dory asked again. 'Rachel . . . you're upset . . . a night's sleep . . .'

Rachel only shook her head. She could not explain to her mother why she had to go back. The feeling had risen in her the way a wind rises – an early stirring of the grasses, hardly noticed; then the air begins to move faster and harder, and there is no calm left; then the gusts become hard enough to make eerie screaming noises around the eaves; then they are shaking the house and you realize that this is something like a hurricane and if the wind gets much higher, things are going to fall down.

It was six o'clock in Chicago. In Bangor, Louis was just sitting down to his big, tasteless meal. Rachel and Ellie had done no more than pick at their dinners. Rachel kept raising her eyes from her plate to find her daughter's dark glance upon her, asking her what she was going to do about whatever trouble Daddy was in, asking her what she was going to do.

She waited for the telephone to ring, for Jud to call and tell her that Louis had come home, and once it did ring – she jumped, and Ellie almost spilled her glass of milk – but it was only a lady from Dory's bridge-club, wanting to know if she had gotten home all right.

They were having their coffee when Rachel had abruptly tossed down her napkin and said, 'Daddy . . . Mom . . . I'm sorry, but I have to go home. If I can get a plane, I'm going tonight.'

Her mother and father had gaped at her, but Ellie had closed her eyes in an adult expression of relief – it would have been funny if not for the waxy, stretched quality of her skin.

They did not understand, and Rachel could no more explain than she could have explained how those tiny puffs of wind, so faint they can barely stir the tips of short grass, can gradually grow in power until they can knock a steel building flat. She did not believe that Ellie had heard a news item about the death of Victor Pascow and filed it away in her subconscious.

'Rachel. Honey.' Her father spoke slowly, kindly, the way one might speak to someone in the grip of a transitory but dangerous hysteria. 'This is all just a reaction to your son's death. You and Ellie are both reacting strongly to that, and who could blame you? But you'll just collapse if you try to—'

Rachel did not answer him. She went to the telephone in the hall, found AIRLINES in the Yellow Pages and dialed Delta's number while Dory stood close by, telling her they ought to just think about this, didn't she think, they ought to talk about it, perhaps make a list ... and beyond her Ellie stood, her face still dark — but now it was lit by enough hope to give Rachel some courage.

'Delta Airlines,' the voice on the other end said brightly. 'This is Kim, may I help you?'

'I hope so,' Rachel said. 'It's extremely important that I get from Chicago to Bangor tonight. It's ... it's a bit of an emergency, I'm afraid. Can you check the connections for me?'

Dubiously: 'Yes, ma'am, but this is very short notice.'

'Well, please *check*,' Rachel said, her voice cracking a little. 'I'll take standby, anything.'

'All right, ma'am. Please hold.' The line became smoothly silent.

Rachel closed her eyes, and after a moment, she felt a cool hand on her arm. She opened her eyes and saw that Ellie had moved next to her. Irwin and Dory stood together, talking quietly and looking at them. *The way you look at people you suspect of being lunatics*, Rachel thought wearily. She mustered a smile for Ellie.

'Don't let them stop you, Mommy,' Ellie said in a low voice. 'Please.'

'No way, big sister,' Rachel said, and then winced – it was what they had called her ever since Gage had been born. But she was no one's big sister any more, was she?

'Thank you,' Ellie said.

'It's very important, isn't it?'

Ellie nodded.

'Honey, I believe that it is. But you could help me if you could tell me more. Is it just the dream?'

'No,' Ellie said. 'It's . . . it's everything now. It's running all through me now. Can't you feel it, Mommy? Something like a —'

'Something like a wind.'

Ellie sighed shakily.

'But you don't know what it is? You don't remember anything more about your dream?'

Ellie thought hard, then shook her head reluctantly. 'Daddy. Church. And Gage. That's all I remember. But I don't remember how they go together, Mommy!'

Rachel hugged her tightly. 'It will be all right,' she said. But the weight on her heart did not lessen.

'Hello, ma'am,' the reservations clerk said.

'Hello?' Rachel tightened her grip on both Ellie and the phone.

'I think I can get you to Bangor, ma'am – but you're going to be getting in very late.'

'That doesn't matter,' Rachel said.

'Do you have a pen? It's complicated.'

'Yes, right here,' Rachel said, getting a stub of pencil out of the drawer. She found the back of an envelope to write on.

Rachel listened carefully, writing down everything. When the airline clerk finished, Rachel smiled a little and made an O with her thumb and forefinger to show Ellie that it was going to work. *Probably* going to work, she amended. Some of the connections looked very, very tight . . . especially in Boston.

'Please book it all,' Rachel said. 'And thank you.'

Kim took Rachel's name and credit card number. Rachel hung up at last, limp but relieved. She looked at her father. 'Daddy, will you drive me to the airport?'

'Maybe I ought to say no,' Goldman said. 'I think I might have a responsibility to put a stop to this craziness.'

'*Don't you dare!*' Ellie cried shrilly. 'It's not crazy!' It's *not!*'

Goldman blinked and stepped back at this small but ferocious outburst.

'Drive her, Irwin,' Dory said quietly into the silence that followed. 'I've begun to feel nervous, too. I'll feel better if I know Louis is all right.'

Goldman stared at his wife, and at last turned to Rachel. 'I'll drive you, if it is what you want,' he said. 'I . . . Rachel, I'll come with you, if you want that.'

Rachel shook her head. 'Thank you, Daddy, but I got all the last seats. It's as if God saved them for me.'

Irwin Goldman sighed. At that moment he looked very old, and it suddenly occurred to Rachel that her father looked like Jud Crandall.

'You have time to pack a bag, if you want,' he said. 'We can be at the airport in forty minutes, if I drive the way I used to when your mother and I were first married. Find her your tote-bag, Dory.'

'Mommy,' Ellie said. Rachel turned toward her. Ellie's face was now sheened with light sweat.

'What, honey?'

'Be careful, Mommy,' Ellie said. 'Please be careful.'

CHAPTER FORTY-NINE

The trees were only moving shapes against the cloudy sky backlit by the glow from the airport not too far distant. Louis parked the Honda on Mason Street. Mason bordered Pleasantview on its south side, and here the wind was almost strong enough to rip the car door out of his hand. He had to push hard to shut it. The wind rippled at his jacket as he opened the Honda's hatch and took out the piece of tarpaulin he had cut and wrapped around his tools.

He was in a wing of darkness between two street lights, standing on the curb with the canvas-wrapped bundle cradled in his arms, looking carefully for traffic before crossing to the wrought-iron fence which marked the boundary of the graveyard. He did not want to be seen at all, if he could help it, not even by someone who would notice him and forget him the next second. Beside him, the branches of an old elm groaned restlessly in the wind, making Louis think of jackleg necktie parties. God, he was so scared. This wasn't wild work; it was the work of the mad.

No traffic. On the Mason Street side the street lamps marched away in perfect white circles, casting spotlights on the sidewalk where, during the days after Fairmount Grammar School let out, boys would ride bikes and girls would jump rope and play hopscotch, never noticing the nearby graveyard, except perhaps at Halloween, when it would acquire a certain spooky charm. Perhaps they would dare to cross their suburban street and hang a paper skeleton on the wrought-iron bars of the high fence, giggling at the old jokes: '*It's the most popular place in town, people are dying to get in. Why is it a sin to laugh in the graveyard? Because everyone who lives there is always in a grave mood.*

'Gage,' he muttered. Gage was in there, behind that wrought-iron fence, unjustly imprisoned under a blanket of dark earth. *Gonna break you out, Gage*, he thought. *Gonna break you out, big guy, or die trying.*

Louis crossed the street with his heavy bundle in his arms, stepped up on the other curb, glanced both ways again, and tossed the canvas roll over the fence. It clinked softly as it struck the ground on the far side. Dusting his hands, Louis walked away. He had marked the place in his mind. Even if he forgot, all he really had to do was follow the fence on the inside until he was standing opposite his Civic, and he would fall over it.

But would the gate be open this late?

He walked down Mason Street to the stop-sign, the wind chasing him and worrying his heels. Moving shadows danced and twined on the roadway.

He turned the corner on to Pleasant Street, still following the fence. Car headlights splashed up the street, and Louis stepped casually behind an elm tree. It wasn't a cop car, he saw, only a van moving toward Hammond Street and, probably, the turnpike. When it was well past him, Louis walked on.

Of course it will be unlocked. It's got to be.

He reached the gate, which formed a cathedral shape in wrought-iron, slim and graceful in the moving wind-shadows thrown by the street lights. He reached out and tried it.

Locked.

You stupid fool, of course it's locked — did you really think anyone would leave a cemetery inside the municipal city limits of any American city unlocked after eleven o'clock? No one is that trusting, dear man, not any more. So what do you do now?

Now he would have to climb, and just hope no one happened to glance away from the Carson Show long enough to see him monkeying up the wrought-iron like the world's oldest, slowest kid.

—Hey, police? I just saw the world's oldest, slowest kid climbing

into Pleasantview Cemetery. Looked like he was dying to get in. Yeah, looked like a grave matter to me. Kidding? Oh no, I'm in dead earnest. Maybe you ought to dig into it.

Louis continued up Pleasant Street and turned right at the next intersection. The high iron fence marched along beside him relentlessly. The wind cooled and evaporated the drops of sweat on his forehead and in the hollows of his temples. His shadow waxed and waned in the street lights. Every now and then he glanced at the fence, and then he stopped and forced himself to really *look* at it.

You're going to climb that baby? Don't make me laugh.

Louis Creed was a fairly tall man, standing a bit over six-two, but the fence was easily nine feet high, each wrought-iron stave ending in a decorative, arrow-like point. Decorative, that was, until you happened to slip while swinging your leg over and the force of your suddenly dropping two hundred pounds drove one of those arrow-points into your groin, exploding your testicles. And there you would be, skewered like a pig at a barbecue, hollering until someone called for the police and they came and pulled you off and took you to the hospital.

The sweat continued to flow, sticking his shirt to his back. All was silent except for the faint hum of late traffic on Hammond Street.

There had to be a way to get in there.

Had to be.

Come on, Louis, face the facts. You may be crazy, but you're not that crazy. Maybe you could shinny up to the top of that fence, but it would take a trained gymnast to swing over those points without sticking himself on them. And even supposing you can get in, how are you going to get yourself and Gage's body out?

He went on walking, vaguely aware that he was circling the cemetery but not doing anything constructive.

All right, here's the answer. I'll just go on home to Ludlow tonight and come back tomorrow, in the late afternoon. I'll go in through the gate around four o'clock and find a place to hole up until it's midnight

371

or a little later. I will, in other words, put off until tomorrow what I should have been smart enough to think of today.

Good idea, o great Swami Louis . . . and in the meantime, what do I do about that great big bundle of stuff I threw over the wall? Pick, shovel, flashlight . . . you might as well stamp GRAVEROBBING EQUIPMENT on every damn piece of it.

It landed in the bushes. Who's going to find it, for Christ's sake?

On measure, that made sense. But this was no sensible errand he was on, and his heart told him quietly and absolutely that he couldn't come back tomorrow. If he didn't do it tonight, he would never do it. He would never be able to screw himself up to this crazy pitch again. This was the moment, the only time for it he was ever going to have.

There were fewer houses up this way – an occasional square of yellow light gleamed on the other side of the street, and once he saw the gray-blue flicker of a black-and-white TV – and looking through the fence he saw that the graves were older here, more rounded, sometimes leaning forward or backward with the freezes and thaws of many seasons. There was another stop-sign up ahead, and another right turn would put him on a street roughly parallel to Mason Street, where he had begun. And when he got back to the beginning, what did he do? Collect two hundred dollars and go around again? Admit defeat?

Car headlights turned down the street, and Louis stepped behind another tree, waiting for it to pass. This car was moving very slowly, and after a moment a white spotlight stabbed out from the passenger side and ran flickering along the wrought-iron fence. His heart squeezed painfully in his chest. It was a police car, checking the cemetery.

He pressed himself tight against the tree, rough bark against his cheek, hoping madly that it was big enough to shield him. The spotlight ran toward him. Louis put his head down, trying to shield the white blur of his face. The spotlight reached the tree, disappeared for a moment, and then reappeared on Louis's right. He slipped around the tree a little to be out of the car's line of sight. He had a momentary glimpse of the dark bubbles on the cruiser's roof. He waited for the tail lights to flare a brighter red, for the doors to open, for the spotlight to suddenly turn back on its ball-joint, hunting for him like a big white finger. *Hey you! You behind that tree! Come on out where we can see you, and we want to see both hands empty! Come out NOW!*

The police car kept on going. It reached the corner, signalled with sedate propriety, and turned left. Louis collapsed back against the tree, breathing fast, his mouth sour and dry. He supposed they would cruise past his parked Honda, but that didn't really matter. Parking from six p.m. to seven a.m. was legal on Mason Street. There were plenty of other cars parked along it. Their owners would belong to the scattering of apartment buildings on the other side of the street.

Louis found himself glancing up at the tree he had hidden behind.

Just above his head, the tree forked. He supposed he could—

Without allowing himself to think about it further, he reached into the fork and pulled himself up, scrambling with his tennis shoes for purchase, sending a little shower of bark down to the ground. He got a knee up and a moment later he had one foot planted solidly in the crotch of the elm. If the police car should happen to come back, their spotlight would find an extremely peculiar bird in this tree. He ought to move quickly.

He pulled himself up to a higher branch, one which overhung the very top of the fence. He felt absurdly like the twelve-year-old he supposed he had once been. The tree was not still; it rocked easily, almost soothingly, in the steady wind. Its leaves rustled and murmured. Louis assessed the situation and then, before he could get cold feet, he dropped off into space, holding on to the branch with his hands laced together over it. The branch was perhaps a little thicker than a brawny man's forearm. Sneakers dangling about eight feet over the sidewalk, he pulled himself hand-for-hand toward the fence.

The branch dipped but showed no sign of breaking. He was faintly aware of his shadow following along on the cement sidewalk below him, an amorphous black ape-shape. The wind chilled his hot armpits, and he found himself shivering in spite of the sweat running down his face and neck. The branch dipped and swayed with his movements. The further out he moved, the more pronounced the dip became. His hands and wrists were getting tired now, and he was afraid that his sweat-greasy palms might slip.

He reached the fence. His tennis shoes dangled perhaps a foot below the arrow-tips. The tips did not look blunt at all from this angle. They looked very sharp. Sharp or not, he suddenly realized it was not just his balls that were at stake here. If he fell, and hit it dead on, his weight would be enough to drive one of those spears all the way up into his lungs. The returning cops would find an early and extremely grisly Halloween decoration on the Pleasantview fence.

Breathing fast, not quite gasping, he groped for the fence-points with his feet, needing a moment's rest. For a moment he hung there, feet moving in an air dance, searching but not finding.

Light touched him, and grew.

Oh Christ, that's a car, there's a car coming—!

He tried to shuffle his hands forward but his palms slipped. His interlaced fingers were coming apart.

Still groping for purchase, he turned his head to the left, looking under his straining arm. It was a car, but it shot through the intersection up the street without slowing. Lucky. If it had—

His hands slipped again. He felt bark sift down on to his hair.

One foot found purchase, but now his other pantsleg had caught on one of the arrow-points. And Christ, he wasn't going to be able to hang on much longer. Desperately, Louis jerked his leg. The branch dipped. His hands slipped again. There was a mutter of tearing cloth and then he was standing on two of the arrow-points. They dug into the soles of tennis shoes and the pressure quickly became painful, but Louis stood on them for a moment anyway. The relief in his hands and arms was greater than the pain in his feet.

What a figure I must cut, Louis thought with dim and dismal amusement. Holding the branch with his left hand, he wiped his right hand across his jacket. Then he wiped off the left while he held with the right.

He stood on the points for a moment longer and then slipped his hands forward along the branch. It was slim enough for him to be able to lace his fingers together comfortably now. He swung forward like Tarzan, feet leaving the arrow-points. The branch dipped alarmingly, and he heard an ominous cracking sound. He let go, dropping blindly.

He landed badly. One knee thudded against a gravestone, sending a sickening lance of pain up his thigh. He rolled over on the grass, holding it, lips pulled back in something like a grin, hoping that he hadn't shattered his kneecap. At last the pain began to fade a little, and he found that he could flex the joint. It would be all right if he kept moving and didn't allow it to stiffen up on him. Maybe.

He got to his feet and started to walk along the fence back toward Mason Street and his equipment. His knee was bad at first and he limped, but the pain smoothed out to a dull ache as he went. There was aspirin in the Honda's first-aid kit. He should have remembered to bring that with him. Too late now. He kept an eye out for cars and faded back deeper into the cemetery when one came.

On the Mason Street side, which was apt to be better travelled, he kept well back from the fence until he was opposite the Civic. He was about to trot down to the fence and pull his bundle out of the bushes when he heard footfalls on the sidewalk, and a woman's low laughter. He sat down behind a large grave marker – it hurt his knee too much to squat – and watched a couple walk up the far side of Mason Street. They were walking with their arms about each other's waists, and something about their movement from one white pool of light to the next made Louis think of some old TV show. In a moment he had it. *The Jimmy Durante Hour.* What would they do if he rose up now, a wavering shadow in this silent city of the dead, and cried hollowly across to them: 'Goodnight, Mrs Calabash, wherever you are!'

They stopped in the pool of light just beyond his car and embraced. Watching them, Louis felt a kind of sick wonder and self-loathing. Here he was, crouched behind a tombstone like a ghoulish, subhuman character in some cheap comic-book story, watching lovers. *Is the line so thin, then?* he wondered, and that thought also had a ring of familiarity. *So thin you can simply step over it with this little fuss, muss, and bother? Climb a tree, shinny along a branch, drop into a graveyard, watch lovers . . . dig holes? That simple? Is it lunacy? I spent eight years becoming a doctor, but I've become a grave-robber in one simple step – what I suppose people would call a ghoul.*

He crammed his fists against his mouth to stop some sound from coming out, and felt for that interior coldness, that sense of disconnection. It was there, and Louis drew it gratefully around him.

When the couple finally walked on, Louis watched them with nothing but impatience. They climbed the steps of one of the apartment buildings. The man felt for a key, and a moment later they were inside. The street was silent again except for the constant beat of the wind, rustling the trees and tumbling his sweaty hair over his forehead.

Louis ran down to the fence, bent low, and felt through the brush for his canvas bundle. Here it was, rough under his fingers. He picked it up, listening to the muffled clank from inside. He carried it over to the broad gravelled drive that led in through the gates and paused to orient himself. Straight up here, go left at the fork. No problem.

He walked along the edge of the drive, wanting to be able to go further into the shadow of the elms if there did happen to be a full-time caretaker and if he happened to be out. Louis did not really expect trouble from that quarter – it was, after all, a graveyard in a small city – but it would not be wise to take chances.

He bore left at the fork, approaching Gage's grave now, and suddenly, appallingly, realized he could not remember what his son had looked like. He paused, staring off into the rows of graves, the frowning façades of the monuments, and tried to summon him up. Individual features came to him – his blonde hair, still so fine and light, his slanting eyes, his small, white teeth, the little twist of scar on his chin from the time he had fallen down the back steps of their place in Chicago. He could see these things, but could not integrate them into a coherent whole. He saw Gage running toward the road, running toward his appointment with the Orinco truck, but Gage's face was turned away. He tried to summon up Gage as he had been in his crib on the night of the kite-flying day, and could see only darkness in his mind's eye.

Gage, where are you?

Have you ever thought, Louis, that you may not be doing your son any good service? Perhaps he's happy where he is . . . maybe all of that isn't the bullshit you always thought it was. Maybe he's with the angels, or maybe he's just sleeping. And if he's sleeping, do you really know what it is you want to wake up?

Oh Gage, where are you? I want you home with us.

But was he really controlling his own actions? Why couldn't he summon up Gage's face, and why was he going against everyone's warning – Jud's, the dream of Pascow, the trepidation of his own troubled heart?

He thought of the grave markers in the Pet Sematary, those rude circles, spiraling down into the Mystery, and then the coldness came over him again. Why was he standing here, trying to summon up Gage's face, anyway?

He would be seeing it soon enough.

The headstone was here now; it read simply GAGE WILLIAM CREED, followed by the two dates. Someone had been here today to pay his or her respects, he saw; there were fresh flowers. Who would that have been? Missy Dandridge?

His heart beat heavily but slowly in his chest. This was it, then; if he was going to do it, he had better start. There was only so much night ahead, and then the day would come.

Louis glanced into his heart one final time and saw that, yes, he did intend to go ahead with this. He nodded his head almost imperceptibly and fished in his pocket for his pocketknife. He had cinched his bundle with Scotch strapping tape, and now he cut it. He unrolled the tarp at the foot of Gage's grave like a bedroll and then arranged items in exactly the same way he would have arranged instruments to suture a cut or to perform a small in-office operation.

Here was the flashlight with its lens felted as the hardware store clerk had suggested. The felt was also secured with strapping tape. He had made a small circle in the middle by placing a penny on the felt and cutting around it with a scalpel. Here was the short-handled pick which he should not have to use – he had brought it only as a contingency. He would have no sealed cap to deal with, and he shouldn't run into any rocks in a newly filled grave. Here was the shovel, the spade, the length of rope, the work-gloves. He put the gloves on, grabbed the spade, and started.

The ground was soft, the digging easy. The grave's shape was well-defined, the dirt he was throwing out softer than the earth at the verge. His mind made a kind of automatic comparison between the ease of this dig and the rocky, unforgiving ground of the place where, if all went well, he would be reburying his son later on this night. Up there, he would need the pick. Then he tried to stop thinking altogether. It only got in the way.

He threw the dirt on the ground to the left of the grave, working into a steady rhythm that only became more difficult to maintain as the hole deepened. He stepped into the grave, smelling that dank aroma of fresh dirt, a smell he remembered from his summers with Uncle Carl.

Digger, he thought, and stopped to wipe sweat from his brow. Uncle Carl had told him that was the nickname for every graveyard sexton in America. Their friends called them Digger.

He started in again.

He stopped only once more, and that was to check his watch. It was twenty minutes past twelve. He felt time slipping through his fist like something that had been greased.

Forty minutes later, the spade gritted across the top of the grave-liner, and Louis's teeth came down on his upper lip hard enough to bring blood. He got the flashlight and shone it down. Here was more dirt, and scrawled across it in a diagonal slash, a grayish-silver line. It was the top of the grave-liner. Louis got the dirt off it as best he could, but he was wary of making too much noise, and nothing was much louder than a shovel scraping across concrete in the dead of night.

When he had gotten rid of as much of the dirt as he could, he climbed out of the grave and got the rope. This he threaded through the iron rings on one half of the segmented grave-liner top. He got out of the grave again, spread out the tarpaulin, lay down on it, and grasped the ends of the rope.

Louis, I think this is it. Your last chance.

You're right. It's my last chance and I'm damned well taking it.

He wound the ends of the rope around his hands and pulled. The square of concrete came up easily, gritting on the pivot end. It stood neatly upright over a square of blackness, now a vertical tombstone instead of a horizontal grave cover.

Louis pulled the rope out of the rings and tossed it aside. He wouldn't need it for the other half; he could stand on the sides of the grave-liner and pull it up.

He got down into the grave again, moving carefully, not wanting to overturn the cement slab he had already pulled up and mash his toes or break the damned thing, which was quite thin. Pebbles rattled down into the hole, and he heard several of them chip hollowly off Gage's coffin.

Bending, he grasped the other half of the grave-liner top

and pulled upward. As he did so, he felt something squelch coldly under his fingers. When he had this second half of the top standing on end (the two halves now resembled book-ends), he looked down at his hand and saw a fat earthworm wriggling feebly there. With a choked cry of disgust, Louis wiped it off on the earthen sidewall of his son's grave.

Then he shone his flashlight downward.

Here was the coffin he had last seen resting on chrome runners over the grave at the funeral service, surrounded by that ghastly green Astroturf. This was the safety-deposit box in which he was supposed to bury all his hopes for his son. Fury, clean and white-hot, the antithesis of his former coldness, rose up in him. Idiotic! The answer was no!

Louis groped for the spade and found it. He raised it over his shoulder and brought it down on the coffin's latch once, twice, a third time, a fourth. His lips were drawn back in a furious grimace.

Going to break you out, Gage, see if I don't!

The latch had splintered on the first stroke and probably no more were necessary, but he went on, not wanting just to open the coffin but to hurt it. Some kind of sanity returned – more quickly than it might have done under other circum- stances – and he stopped with the spade raised for another blow.

The blade was bent and scratched. He tossed it aside and scrambled out of the grave on legs that felt weak and rubbery. He felt sick to his stomach, and the anger had gone as quickly as it had come. In its place the coldness flooded back in and never in his life had his mind felt so alone and disconnected; it felt like an astronaut who has floated away from his ship during an EVA and now only drifts in a great blackness, breath- ing on borrowed time. *Did Bill Baterman feel like this?* he wondered.

He lay on the ground, on his back this time, waiting to see if he was under control and ready to proceed. When the rubbery feeling had left his legs, he sat up and slipped back down into the grave. He shone the flashlight on the latch and saw it was not just broken, but demolished. He had swung the spade in a blind fury, but every blow he had struck had gone directly there, bull's eye, as if guided. The wood around it had splintered.

Louis slipped the flashlight into his armpit. He squatted down slightly. His hands groped, like the hands of a catcher in a troupe of circus flyers, waiting to perform his part in a mortal docking.

He found the groove in the lid, and he slipped his fingers into it. He paused for a moment – one could not rightly call it a hesitation – and then he opened his son's coffin.

CHAPTER FIFTY

Rachel Creed almost made her flight from Boston to Portland. Almost. Her Chicago plane left on time (a kind of miracle in itself), was cleared straight into LaGuardia (another) and left New York only five minutes behind schedule. It got to the gate to Boston fifteen minutes late – at 11:12 p.m. That left her with thirteen minutes.

She still might have made her connecting flight, but the shuttle-bus which makes a circle around the Logan terminals was late. Rachel waited, now in a kind of constant low-grade panic, shifting from foot to foot as if she needed to go to the bathroom, switching the travel-bag her mother had loaned her from one shoulder to the other.

When the shuttle still hadn't come at 11:25, she began to run. Her heels were low but still high enough to cause her problems. One of her ankles buckled painfully and she paused long enough to take off the shoes. Then she ran on in her pantyhose, past Alleghany and Eastern Airlines, breathing hard now, getting the beginnings of a stitch in her side.

Her breath was hot in her throat, that tuck in her side deeper and more painful. Now she was running past the international terminal, and there, up ahead, was Delta's triangular sign. She burst in through the doors, almost dropped one shoe, juggled it, caught it. It was 11:37.

One of the two clerks on duty glanced up at her.

'Flight 104,' she panted. 'The Portland flight. Has it left?'

The clerk glanced behind him at the monitor. 'Still at the gate it says here,' he said, 'but they called for final boarding five minutes ago. I'll call ahead. Bags to check?'

'No,' Rachel gasped, brushing her sweaty hair out of her eyes. Her heart was galloping in her chest.

'Then don't wait for me to call. I will – but I advise you to run very fast.'

Rachel didn't run very fast – she was no longer able. But she did as well as she could. The escalator had been turned off for the night and she pounded up the stairs, tasting copper shavings in her mouth. She reached the security checkpoint and almost threw the tote-bag at the startled female guard, then waited for it to come through on the conveyor belt, her hands clenching and unclenching. It was barely out of the X-ray chamber before she had snatched it by the strap and ran again, the bag flying out behind her and then banging her on the hip.

She looked up at one of the monitors as she ran.

FLIGHT 104 PORTLAND SCHED 11:25PM GATE 31 BOARDING

Gate 31 was at the far end of the concourse – and even as she snatched her glance at the monitor, **BOARDING** in steady letters changed to **DEPARTING**, blinking rapidly.

A frustrated cry burst from her, and a black woman who was hoisting her son up to the drinking fountain looked around, startled. She ran into the gate area just in time to see the gate attendant removing the strips which read **FLIGHT 104 BOSTON-PORTLAND 11:25**.

'It's gone?' She asked incredulously. 'It's really *gone*?'

The attendant looked at her sympathetically. 'It rolled out of the jetway at 11:40. I'm sorry, ma'am. You made a helluva good try, if that's any consolation.' He pointed out the wide glass windows. Rachel could see a big 727 with Delta markings, its running-lights Christmas-tree bright, starting its take-off roll.

'Christ, didn't anyone tell you I was coming?' Rachel cried.

'When they called up here from downstairs, 104 was on an active taxiway. If I'd called her back, she would have gotten caught in the parade going out to Runway 30, and that pilot would have had my bee-hind on a platter. Not to mention the hundred or so passengers on board. I'm very sorry. If you'd been even four minutes sooner—'

She walked away, not listening to the rest. She was halfway back to the security checkpoint when waves of faintness rode over her. She stumbled into another gate area and sat down until the darkness had passed. Then she slipped her shoes back on, picking a squashed Lark cigarette butt off the tattered sole of one stocking first. *My feet are dirty and I don't give a fuck,* she thought disconsolately.

She walked back toward the terminal.

The security guard eyed her sympathetically. 'Missed it?'

'I missed it, all right,' Rachel said.

'Where were you headed?'

'Portland. Then Bangor.'

'Well, why don't you rent a car? If you really have to be there, that is? Ordinarily I'd advise a hotel close to the airport, but if I ever saw a lady who looked like she really had to be there, you are that lady.'

'I'm that lady, all right,' Rachel said. She thought about it. 'Yes, I suppose I could do that, couldn't I? If any of the agencies has a car.'

The security guard laughed. 'Oh, they'll have cars. Only time they don't have cars at Logan is when the airport's fogged in. Which is a lot of the time.'

Rachel barely heard him. In her mind, she was already trying to calculate it.

She couldn't get to Portland in time to catch her Bangor flight even if she bulleted up the turnpike at a suicidal pace. So figure driving straight through. How long? That depended on how far. Two hundred and fifty miles, that was the figure which came to mind. Something Jud had said, maybe. It was going to be at least quarter past twelve before she got going, probably closer to 12:30 a.m. It was all turnpike. She thought that her chances of going the whole distance at sixty-five without getting hauled down for speeding were reasonably good. She ran the figures quickly in her head, dividing sixty-

five into two hundred and fifty. Not quite four hours. Well
. . . say four even. She would have to stop once and go to the
bathroom. And although sleep seemed impossibly distant now,
she knew her own resources well enough to believe she would
also have to stop for a great big black coffee. Still, she could
be back in Ludlow before first light.

Mulling all this over, she started for the stairs – the car
rental desks were one level down from the concourses.

'Good luck, honey,' the security guard called. 'Take care.'

'Thanks,' Rachel said. She felt that she deserved some good
luck.

CHAPTER FIFTY-ONE

The smell hit him first, and Louis recoiled, gagging. He hung on the edge of the grave, breathing hard, and just when he thought he had his gorge under control, his entire big, tasteless meal came up in a grotesque spurt. He threw up on the far side of the grave and then put his head against the ground, panting. At last the nausea passed. Teeth clamped together, he took the flashlight out of his armpit and shone it down into the open coffin.

A deep horror that was very nearly awe stole over him — it was the sort of feeling usually reserved for the worst nightmares, the ones you can barely remember upon awakening.

Gage's head was gone.

Louis's hands were trembling so badly he had to hold the flashlight with both hands, gripping it the way a policeman is taught to grip his service revolver on the target range. Still the beam jittered back and forth and it was a moment before he could train the pencil-thin beam back into the grave.

It's impossible, he told himself, *just remember that what you thought you saw is impossible.*

He slowly moved the narrow beam up Gage's three foot length, from the new shoes to the suit pants, the little coat (ah, Christ, no two-year-old was ever meant to wear a suit), to the open collar, to—

His breath caught in a harsh sound that was too outraged to be a gasp, and all his fury at Gage's death came back in a rush, drowning fears of the supernatural, the paranatural, and his growing certainty that he had crossed over into the country of the mad.

Louis scrabbled in his back pocket for his handkerchief and

pulled it out. Holding the light in one hand, he leaned into the grave again, almost past the point of balance. If one of the segments of grave-liner had fallen now, it would have surely broken his neck. Gently, he used his handkerchief to wipe away the damp moss that was growing on Gage's skin – moss so dark that he had been momentarily fooled into thinking Gage's whole head was gone.

The moss was damp but no more than a scum. He should have expected it; there had been rain, and a grave-liner was not water-tight. Flashing his light to either side, Louis saw that the coffin was lying in a thin puddle. Beneath the light slime of growth he saw his son. The mortician, aware that the coffin could not be opened after such a terrible accident, had nonetheless done the best he could – morticians almost always did. Looking at his son was like looking at a badly made doll. Gage's head bulged in strange directions. His eyes had sunken deep behind closed lids. Something white protruded from his mouth like an albino tongue, and Louis thought at first it might be some kind of fluid extrusion. They had, perhaps, used too much embalming fluid. It was tricky stuff at best, and with a child it was next to impossible to tell how much was enough . . . or too much.

Then he realized it was only cotton. He reached in and plucked it out of the boy's mouth. Gage's lips, oddly lax and seeming somehow too dark and too wide, closed with a faint but audible *plip*! He threw it into the grave where it floated in the shallow puddle and gleamed a loathsome white. Now one of Gage's cheeks had a hollow old man's look.

'Gage,' he whispered. 'Going to take you out now, okay?'

He prayed no one would come along now, a caretaker making a 12:30 swing through the cemetery, something like that. But it was no longer a matter of not being caught; if someone else's flashlight beam speared him as he stood here in the grave going about his grim work, he would seize the bent, scarred spade and put it through the intruder's skull.

He worked his arms under Gage. The body lolled bonelessly

from side to side and a sudden, awful certainty came over him: when he lifted Gage, his body would break apart and he would be left with the pieces. He would be left standing with his feet on the sides of the grave-liner with the pieces, screaming. And that was how they would find him.

Go on, you chicken, go on and do it!

He got Gage under the arms, aware of the fetid dampness, and lifted him that way, as he had lifted him so often from his evening tub. Gage's head lolled backwards all the way to the middle of his back, and Louis gagged again as he saw the grinning circlet of stitches which held Gage's head on to his shoulders.

Somehow, panting, his stomach spasming from the smell and from the boneless loose feel of his son's miserably smashed body, Louis wrestled the body out of the coffin, then out of the grave. At last he sat on the verge of the grave with the body in his lap, his feet dangling in the hole, his face a horrible livid color, his eyes black holes, his mouth drawn down in a trembling bow of horror and pity and sorrow.

'Gage,' he said, and began to rock the boy in his arms. Gage's hair lay against Louis's wrist, as lifeless as wire. 'Gage, it will be all right, I swear, Gage, it will be all right, this will end, this is just the night, please, Gage, I love you, Daddy loves you.'

Louis rocked his son.

By quarter of two, Louis was ready to leave the cemetery. Actually handling the body had been the worst of it — that was the point at which that interior astronaut, his mind, seemed to float the furthest into the void. And yet now, resting, his back a throbbing hurt in which exhausted muscles jumped and twitched, he felt it might be possible to get back. All the way back.

He put Gage's body on the tarpaulin and wrapped it up. He cinched it with long strips of strapping tape, then cut the length of rope in two and tied off the ends neatly. Once more he might have had a rolled-up rug, no more. He closed the coffin, then after a moment's thought, he reopened it and put the bent spade in. Let Pleasantview have that relic; it would not have his son. He closed the coffin and then lowered half of the cement grave-liner top. He considered simply dropping the other half, but was afraid it would shatter. After a moment's consideration he threaded his belt through the iron rings and used it to lower the cement square gently into place. Then he used the shovel to fill in the hole. There was not enough dirt to bring it up even with the ground again. There never was. The grave's sway-backed look might be noticed. It might not. It might be noticed and disregarded. He would not allow himself to think about it, or worry about it tonight – too much still lay ahead of him. More wild work. And he was very tired.

Hey-ho, let's go.

'Indeed,' Louis muttered. The wind rose, shrieking briefly through the trees and making him look around uneasily. He laid the shovel, the pick he had yet to use, the gloves, and the flashlight beside the bundle. Using the light was a temptation, but he resisted it. Leaving the body and the tools, Louis walked back the way he had come and arrived at the high wrought-iron fence about five minutes later. There, across the street, was his Civic, parked neatly at the curb. So near and yet so far.

Louis looked at it for a moment and then struck off in a different direction.

This time he moved away from the gate, walking along the wrought-iron fence until it turned away from Mason Street at a neat right angle. There was a drainage ditch here, and Louis looked into it. What he saw made him shudder. There were masses of rotting flowers here, layer upon layer of them, washed down by seasons of rain and snow.

Christ.

No, not Christ. These leavings were made in propitiation of a much older God than the Christian one. People have called Him different things at different times, but Rachel's sister gave Him a perfectly good name, I think. Oz, the Gweat and Tewwible. God of dead things left in the ground to rot. God of the Mystery.

Louis stared down into the drainage ditch as if hypnotized. At last he dragged his gaze away with a little gasp – the gasp of one who has come to, or who has been called from a mesmerist's trance by the final number in a count of ten.

He went on. He hadn't walked far before he found what he was looking for, and he suspected that his mind had neatly stored this bit of information on the day of Gage's burial.

Here, looming in the windy dark, was the cemetery's crypt.

Coffins were stored there in the winter when it was too cold for even the payloaders to dig in the frozen earth. It was also used when there was a rush of business – a kind of cold-storage for people.

There were such rushes of what Uncle Carl had sometimes called 'cold custom' from time to time, Louis knew; in any given population there were times when, for no reason anyone could understand, lots of people died.

'It all balances out,' Uncle Carl told him. 'If I have a two-week period in May when nobody dies, Lou, I can count on a two-week period in November when I'll have ten funerals. Only it's rarely November, and it's never around Christmas, although people always think that's when a lot of people die. That stuff about Christmas depression is just a load of bullshit. Just ask any funeral director. Most people are real happy around Christmas, and they want to live. So they *do* live. It's usually February when we get a big bulge. The flu gets the old people, and pneumonia, of course – but that's not all. There'll be people who've been battling cancer like mad bastards for a year, sixteen months. Then bad old February comes around and it seems like they get tired and the cancer just rolls them up like a rug. January 31st they're in remission, and they feel like they're in the pink. February 24th, they're planted. People have heart attacks in February, strokes in February, renal failure in February. It's a bad month. People get tired in February.

We're used to it, in the business. But then, for no reason, the same thing will happen in June, or in October. Never in August. August's a slow month. Unless a gas main explodes or a city bus goes off a bridge, you never fill up the cemetery crypt in August. But there have been Februarys when we've had caskets stacked up three deep, hoping like hell for a thaw so we can plant some of them before we have to rent a frigging apartment.'

Uncle Carl had laughed. And Louis, feeling a party to a secret that not even his instructors in med school knew, had laughed, too.

The crypt's double doors were set into a grassy rise of hill, a shape as natural and as attractive as the swell of a woman's breast. This hill (which Louis suspected was landscaped rather than natural – that evenness was simply too suggestive) crested only a foot or two below the decorative arrow-tips of the wrought-iron fence, which remained even at the top rather than rising.

Louis glanced around, then scrambled up the slope. On the other side was an empty square of ground, perhaps two acres in all. No . . . not quite empty. There was a single outbuilding, like a disconnected shed. *Probably belongs to the cemetery*, Louis thought. That would be where they kept their grounds equipment.

The street lights shone through the moving leaves of a belt of trees – old elms and maples – that screened this area from Mason Street. Louis saw no other movement.

He slid back down on his butt, afraid of falling and re-injuring his knee, and returned to his son's grave. He almost stumbled over the roll of the tarpaulin. He saw he would have to make two trips, one with the body and another for the tools. He bent, grimacing at his back's protest, and got the stiff canvas roll in his arms. He could feel the shift of Gage's body within, and steadfastly ignored that part of his mind which whispered constantly that he had gone mad.

He carried the body over to the hill which housed

Pleasantview's crypt with its two steel sliding doors (they made it look queerly like a two-car garage). He saw what would have to be done if he were going to get his forty-pound bundle up that steep slope now that his rope was gone (he wished he had left it whole a while longer, but wish in one hand and spit in the other) and prepared to do it. He backed up and then ran at the slope, leaning forward, letting his forward motion carry him as far as it would. He got almost to the top before his feet skidded out from under him on the short, slick grass, and he tossed the canvas roll as far as he could as he came down. It landed almost at the crest of the hill. He scrambled the rest of the way up, looked around again, saw no one, and laid the rolled-up tarp against the fence. Then he went back for the rest of his things.

He gained the top of the hill again, put the gloves on, and piled the flashlight, pick and shovel next to the tarp. Then he rested, back against the staves of the fence, hands propped on his knees. The new digital watch Rachel had given him for Christmas informed him that it was now 2:01.

He gave himself five minutes to regroup and then tossed the shovel over the fence. He heard it thud in the grass. He tried to stuff the flashlight into his pants, but it just wouldn't go. He slipped it through two of the iron staves and listened to it roll down the hill, hoping it would not hit a stone and break. He wished he had worn a packsack.

Now he removed his dispenser of strapping tape from the pocket of his jacket and bound the business-end of the pick to the canvas roll, going around and around, drawing the tape tight over the pick's metal arms and tight under the canvas. He did this until the tape was gone, and then tucked the empty dispenser back in his pocket. He lifted the bundle and hoisted it over the fence (his back screamed in protest; he would pay for this night all the following week, he suspected) and then let it drop, wincing at the soft thud.

Now he swung one leg over the fence, grasped two of the decorative arrow-points, and swung his other leg over. He skidded down, digging in at the earth between the staves of the fence with the toes of his shoes, and dropped to the ground.

He made his way down the far side of the hill and felt through the grass. He found the shovel right away – muted as the glow from the street lights was through the trees, it reflected a faint gleam from the blade. He had a bad couple of moments when he was unable to find the flashlight – how far could it have rolled in this grass? He got down on his hands and knees and felt through the thick plush, his breath and heartbeat loud in his own ears.

At last he spotted it, a thin black shadow some five feet from where he had guessed it would be; like the hill masking the cemetery crypt, the regularity of its shape gave it away. He grabbed it, cupped a hand over its felted lens, and pushed the little rubber nipple on top that hid the switch. His palm lit up briefly, and Louis switched it off. The flashlight was okay.

He used his pocketknife to cut the pick free from the canvas roll, and took the tools through the grass to the trees. He stood behind the biggest, looking both ways along Mason Street. It was utterly deserted now. He saw only one light on the entire street – a square of yellow-gold in an upstairs room. An insomniac, perhaps, or an invalid.

Moving quickly but not running, Louis stepped out on to the sidewalk. After the dimness of the cemetery, he felt horribly exposed under the street lights; here he stood, only yards away from Bangor's second-largest boneyard, a pick, shovel and flashlight cradled in his arms. If someone saw him now, the inference would be too clear to miss.

He crossed the street rapidly, heels clicking. There was his Civic, only fifty yards down the street. To Louis, it looked like five miles. Sweating, he walked down to it, alert for the sound of an approaching car engine, footfalls other than his own, perhaps the rasp of a window going up.

He got to his Honda, leaned the pick and shovel against the side, and fumbled for his keys – they weren't there, not in either pocket, and fresh sweat began to break on his face. His heart began to run again, and his teeth were clenched together against the panic that wanted to leap free.

He had lost them, most likely when he had dropped from the tree-limb, hit the grave-marker with his knee, and rolled over. His keys were lying somewhere in the grass, and if he had had trouble finding his flashlight, how could he hope to recover his keys? It was over. One piece of bad luck and it was over.

Now wait, wait just a goddam minute. Go through your pockets again. Your change is there – and if your change didn't fall out, your keys didn't fall out, either.

This time he went through his pockets more slowly, removing the change, even turning the pockets themselves inside out.

No keys.

Louis leaned against the car, wondering what to do next. He would have to climb back in, he supposed. Leave his son where he was, take the flashlight, climb back in, and spend the rest of the night in a fruitless hunt for—

Light suddenly broke in his tired mind.

He bent down and stared into the Civic. There were his keys dangling from the ignition switch.

A soft grunt escaped him, and then he ran around to the driver's side, snatched the door open, and took the keys out. In his mind he suddenly heard the authoritative voice of that grim father-figure Karl Malden, he of the potato-nose and the archaic snap-brim hat: *Lock your car. Take your keys. Don't help a good boy go bad.*

He went around to the rear of the Civic and opened the hatchback. He put in the pick, shovel and flashlight, then slammed it. He had gotten twenty or thirty feet down the sidewalk when he remembered his keys. This time he had left them in the hatchback lock.

Stupid! He railed at himself. *If you're going to be so goddam stupid, you better forget the whole thing!*

He went back and got his keys.

★

He had gotten Gage in his arms and was most of the way back to Mason Street when a dog began to bark somewhere. No – it didn't just begin to bark. It began to howl, its gruff voice filling the street. *Auggggh-ROOOO! Auggggh-ROOOOOO!*

He stood behind one of the trees, wondering what could possibly happen next, wondering what to *do* next. He stood there expecting lights to start going on all up and down the street.

In fact, only one light did go on, at the side of a house just opposite where Louis stood in the shadows. A moment later a hoarse voice cried, 'Shut up, Fred!'

Auggggh-ROOOOOO! Fred responded.

'Shut him up, Scanlon, or I'm calling the police!' Someone yelled from the side of the street Louis was on, making him jump, making him realize just how false the illusion of emptiness and desertion was. There were people all around him, hundreds of eyes, and that dog was attacking sleep, his only friend. *Goddam you, Fred*, he thought. *Oh, goddam you.*

Fred began another chorus; he got well into the *Auggggh*, but before he could do more than get started on a good solid *ROOOOOO*, there was a hard whacking sound followed by a series of low whimpers and yips.

Silence followed by the faint slam of a door. The light at the side of Fred's house stayed on for a moment, then clicked off.

Louis felt strongly inclined to stay in the shadows, to wait; surely it would be better to wait until the rumpus had died down. But time was getting away from him.

'Let's go,' he muttered, and went.

He crossed the street with his bundle and walked back down to the Civic, seeing no one at all. Fred held his peace. He clutched his bundle in one hand, got his keys, opened the hatchback.

Gage would not fit.

Louis tried the bundle vertically, then horizontally, then diagonally. The Civic's back compartment was too small. He could have bent and crushed the bundle in there – Gage would not have minded – but Louis could simply not bring himself to do it.

Come on, come on, come on, let's get out of here, let's not push it any further.

But he stood, nonplussed, out of ideas, the bundle containing his son's corpse in his arms. Then he heard the sound of an approaching car, and without really thinking at all, he took the bundle around to the passenger side, opened the door, and slipped the bundle into the seat, bending it at the places where he believed Gage's knees and waist to be.

He shut the door, ran around to the rear of the Civic, and slammed the hatchback. The car went right through the intersection, and Louis heard the whoop of drunken voices. He got behind the wheel, started his car, and was reaching for the headlight switch when a horrible thought struck him. What if Gage were facing backwards, sitting there with those joints at knee and hip bending the wrong way, his sunken eyes looking toward the rear window instead of out through the windshield?

It doesn't matter, his mind responded with a shrill fury born of exhaustion. *Will you get that through your head? It just doesn't matter!*

But it does. It does matter. It's Gage in there, not a bundle of towels!

He reached over and gently began to press his hands against the canvas tarpaulin, feeling for the contours underneath. He looked rather like a blind man trying to determine what a specific object might be. At last he came upon a protuberance that could only be Gage's nose – facing in the right direction.

Only then could he bring himself to put the Civic in gear and start the twenty-five-minute drive back to Ludlow.

CHAPTER FIFTY-TWO

At one o'clock that morning, Jud Crandall's telephone rang, shrilling in the empty house, starting him awake. In his doze he was dreaming, and in the dream he was twenty-three again, sitting on a bench in the B&A coupling shed with George Chapin and Rene Michaud, the three of them passing around a bottle of Georgia Charger whiskey – jumped-up moonshine with a revenue stamp on it – while outside a nor'easter blew its randy shriek over the world, silencing all that moved, including the rolling stock of the B&A railroad. So they sat and drank around the potbellied Defiant, watching the red glow of the coals shift and change behind the cloudy isinglass, casting diamond-shaped flame-shadows across the floor, telling the stories which men hold inside for years like the junk treasures boys store under their beds, the stories they store up for nights such as this. Like the glow of the Defiant, they were dark stories with a glow of red at the center of each, and the wind to wrap them round. He was twenty-three, and Norma was very much alive (although in bed alone now, he had no doubt; she would not expect him home this wild night), and Rene Michaud was telling a story about a Jew peddler in Bucksport who—

That was when the phone began to ring and he jerked up in his chair, wincing at the stiffness in his neck, feeling a sour heaviness drop into him like a stone – it was, he thought, all those years between twenty-three and eighty, all fifty-seven of them, dropping into him at once. And on the heels of that thought: *You been sleepin', boyo. That's no way to run this railroad . . . not tonight.*

He got up, holding himself straight against the stiffness that had also settled into his back, and crossed to the phone.

It was Rachel.

'Hello?'

'Jud? Has he come home?'

'No,' Jud said. 'Rachel, where are you? You sound closer.'

'I am closer,' Rachel said. And although she *did* sound closer somehow, there was a distant humming on the wire. It was the sound of the wind, somewhere between here and wherever she was. The wind was high tonight. That sound that always made Jud think of dead voices, sighing in chorus, maybe singing something just a little too far away to be made out. 'I'm at the rest area at Biddeford on the Maine Turnpike.'

'Biddeford!'

'I couldn't stay in Chicago. It was getting to me, too . . . whatever it was that got Ellie, it was getting me, too. And you feel it. It's in your voice.'

'Ayuh.' He picked a Chesterfield out of his pack and slipped it into the corner of his mouth. He popped a wooden match alight and watched it flicker as his hand trembled. His hands hadn't trembled; not before this nightmare had commenced, anyway. Outside, he heard that dark wind gust. It took the house in its hand and shook it.

Power's growing. I can feel it.

Dim horror in his old bones. It was like spun glass, fine and fragile.

'Jud, please tell me what's going on!'

He supposed she had a right to know – a need to know. And he supposed he would tell her. Eventually he would tell her the whole story. He would show her the chain that had been forged link by link. Norma's heart attack, the death of the cat, Louis's question – has anyone ever buried a *person* up there? – Gage's death . . . and God alone knew what further link Louis might be forging right now. Eventually he would tell her. But not over the phone.

'Rachel, how come you to be on the turnpike instead of in a plane?'

She explained how she had missed her connecting flight at Boston. 'I got an Avis car, but I'm not making the time I thought I would. I got a little bit lost coming from Logan to the turnpike, and I've only got into Maine. I don't think I can get there until dawn. But Jud . . . please. Please tell me what's happening. I'm so scared, and I don't even know *why*.'

'Rachel, listen to me,' Jud said. 'You drive on up to Portland and lay over, do you hear me? Check into a motel there and get some —'

'Jud I can't do th —'

'— and get some sleep. Feel no fret, Rachel. Something may be happening here tonight, or something may not. If something is — if it's what I think — then you wouldn't want to be here anyway. I can take care of it, I think. I better be able to take care of it, because what's happening is my fault. If nothing's happening, then you get here this afternoon, and that will be fine. I imagine Louis will be real glad to see you.'

'I couldn't sleep tonight, Jud.'

'Yes,' he said, reflecting that he had believed the same thing — hell, Peter had probably believed the same thing on the night Jesus had been taken into custody. Sleeping on sentry duty. 'Yes, you can. Rachel, if you doze off behind the wheel of that damn rent-a-car and go off the road and get yourself killed, what's going to happen to Louis then? And Ellie?'

'Tell me what's going *on*! If you tell me that, Jud, maybe I'll take your advice. But I have to *know*!'

'When you get to Ludlow, I want you to come here,' Jud said. 'Not over to your house. Come here first. I'll tell you everything I know, Rachel. And I am watching for Louis.'

'*Tell* me,' she said.

'No, ma'am. Not over the phone. I won't. Rachel, I *can't*. You go on, now. Drive up to Portland and lay over.'

There was a long, considering pause.

'All right,' she said at last. 'I *have* had some trouble keeping my eyes open. Maybe you're right. Jud, tell me one thing. Tell me how bad it is.'

'I can handle it,' Jud said calmly. 'Things have got as bad as they're going to get.'

Outside the headlights of a car appeared, moving slowly. Jud half-stood, watching it, and then sat down again when it accelerated past the Creed house and out of sight.

'All right,' she said, 'I guess. The rest of this drive has seemed like a stone on my head.'

'Let the stone roll off, my dear,' Jud said. 'Please. Save yourself for tomorrow. Things here will be all right.'

'You promise you'll tell me the whole story?'

'Yes. We'll have us a beer and I'll tell you the whole thing.'

'Goodbye, then,' Rachel said. 'For now.'

'For now,' Jud agreed. 'I'll see you tomorrow, Rachel.'

Before she could say anything else, Jud hung up the telephone.

He thought there were caffeine pills in the medicine cabinet, but he could not find them. He put the rest of the beer back in the refrigerator – not without regret – and settled for a cup of black coffee. He took it back to the bay window and sat down again, sipping and watching.

The coffee – and the conversation with Rachel – kept him awake and alert for three quarters of an hour, but then he began to nod once more.

No sleeping on sentry duty, old man. You let it get hold of you; you bought something and now you have to pay for it. So no sleeping on sentry duty.

He lit a fresh cigarette, drew deep, and coughed an old man's rasping cough. He put the cigarette on the groove of the ashtray and rubbed his eyes with both hands. Outside a ten-wheeler blasted by, running lights glaring, cutting through the windy, uneasy night.

He caught himself dozing off again, snapped awake, and abruptly slapped himself across the face, forehand and backhand, causing his ears to ring. Now terror awakened in his heart, a stealthy visitor who had broken into that secret place.

It's puttin' me to sleep . . . hypnotizin' me . . . somethin'. It doesn't want me awake. Because he'll be comin' back pretty soon. Yeah, I feel that. And it wants me out of the play.

'No,' he said grimly. 'No way at all. You hear me? I'm puttin' a stop to this. This has gone far enough.'

The wind whined around the eaves, and the trees on the other side of the road shook their leaves in hypnotic patterns. His mind went back to that night around the Defiant stove in the coupling shed, which had stood right where the Evarts Furniture Mart stood in Brewer now. They had talked the night away, he and George and Rene Michaud, and now he was the only one left; Rene crushed between two boxcars on a stormy night in March of 1939, George Chapin dead of a heart attack just last year. Of so many, he was the only one left, and the old get stupid. Sometimes the stupidity masquerades as kindness, and sometimes it masquerades as pride – a need to tell old secrets, to pass things on, to pour from the old glass to the new one, to . . .

So dis Jew peddler comes in and he says I got something you never seen before. These pos'cards, dey jus look like wimmin in bathin' suits until you rub dem wit a wet cloth, and den—

Jud's head nodded. His chin settled slowly, gently, against his chest.

—dey's as nakid as the day dey was born! But when dey dry, the clo'es, dey come back on! And dat ain't all! I got—

Rene telling this story in the coupling shed, leaning forward, smiling, and Jud holds the bottle – he *feels* the bottle and his hand closes around it on thin air.

In the ashtray, the cigarette-ash on the end of the old man's cigarette grew longer. At last the cigarette tipped forward into the ashtray and burned out, its shape recalled in the neat roll of ash like a rune.

Jud slept.

And when the tail lights flashed outside and Louis turned the Honda Civic into his driveway some forty minutes later and drove it into the garage, Jud did not hear, nor stir, or awaken, any more than Peter awoke when the Roman soldiers came to take a tramp named Jesus into their custody.

CHAPTER FIFTY-THREE

Louis found a fresh dispenser of strapping tape in one of the kitchen drawers, and there was a coil of rope in the corner of the garage near last winter's snow tires. He used the tape to bind the pick and shovel together in a single neat bundle, and the rope to fashion a rough sling.

Tools in the sling. Gage in his arms.

He looped the sling over his back, then opened the passenger door of the Civic, pulling the bundle out. Gage was much heavier than Church had been. He might well be crawling by the time he got his boy up to the Micmac burying ground – and he would still have the grave to dig, fighting his way through that stony, unforgiving soil.

Well. He would manage. Somehow.

Louis Creed stepped out of his garage, pausing to thumb off the light switch with his elbow, and stood for a moment at the place where asphalt gave way to grass. Ahead of him he could see the path leading away to the Pet Sematary well enough in spite of the blackness; the path, with its short grass, glowed with a kind of luminescence.

The wind pushed and pulled its fingers through his hair, and for a moment the old, childlike fear of the dark rushed through him, making him feel weak and small and terrorized. Was he really going into the woods with this corpse in his arms, passing under the trees where the wind walked, from darkness into darkness? And alone this time?

Don't think about it. Just do it.

Louis got walking.

*

By the time he got to the Pet Sematary twenty minutes later, his arms and legs were trembling with exhaustion and he collapsed with the rolled-up tarpaulin across his knees, gasping. He rested there for another twenty minutes, almost dozing, no longer fearful – exhaustion had driven fear out, it seemed.

Finally he got to his feet again, not really believing he could climb the deadfall, only knowing in some numb sort of way that he must try. The bundle in his arms seemed to weigh two hundred pounds instead of forty.

But what had happened before happened again; it was like suddenly, vividly remembering a dream. No, not remembering; *reliving*. When he placed his foot on the first dead treetrunk, that queer sensation rushed through him again, a feeling that was almost exaltation. The weariness did not leave him, but it became bearable – unimportant, really.

Just follow me. Follow me and don't look down, Louis. Don't hesitate and don't look down. I know the way through, but it has to be done quick and sure.

Quick and sure, yes – the way Jud had removed the stinger. *I know the way through.*

But there was only one way through, Louis thought. Either it let you through or it did not. Once before he had tried to climb the deadfall by himself, and hadn't been able to. This time he mounted it quickly and surely, as he had on the night Jud had shown him the way.

Up and up, not looking down, his son's body in its canvas shroud cradled in his arms. Up until the wind funneled secret passages and chambers through his hair again, flipping it, parting it widdershins.

He stood on the top for a moment and then descended quickly, as if going down a set of stairs. The pick and shovel rattled and clinked dully against his back. In no more than a minute he was standing on the springy, needle-covered ground of the path again, the deadfall bulking behind him, higher than the graveyard fence had been.

He moved up the path with his son, listening to the wind moan in the trees. The sound held no terror for him now. The night's work was almost done.

CHAPTER FIFTY-FOUR

Rachel Creed passed the sign reading EXIT 8 KEEP RIGHT FOR PORTLAND WESTBROOK, put on her blinker, and guided the Avis Chevette toward the exit ramp. She could see a green Holiday Inn sign clearly against the night sky. A bed, sleep. An end to this constant, racking, sourceless tension. Also an end – for a little while, at least – to her grieving emptiness for the child who was no longer there. This grief, she had discovered, was like a massive tooth extraction. There was numbness at first, but even through the numbness you felt pain curled up like a cat switching its tail, pain waiting to happen. And when the Novocaine wore off, oh boy, you sure weren't disappointed.

He told her that he was sent to warn . . . but that he couldn't interfere. He told her he was near Daddy because they were together when his soul was discorporated.

Jud knows, but he won't tell. Something is going on. Something. But what?

Suicide? Is it suicide? Not Louis: I can't believe that. But he was lying about something. It was in his eyes . . . oh shit, it was all over his FACE, almost as if he wanted me to see the lie . . . see it and put a stop to it . . . because part of him was scared . . . so scared . . .

Scared? Louis is NEVER scared!

Suddenly she jerked the Chevette's steering wheel hard over to the left, and the car responded with the abrupt suddenness that small cars have, the tires wailing. For a moment she thought it was going to turn over. But it straightened and a moment later she was moving north again, Exit 8 with its comforting Holiday Inn sign slipping behind her. A new sign came in view, reflective paint twinkling eerily.

**NEXT EXIT   ROUTE 12   CUMBERLAND
CUMBERLAND CENTER   JERUSALEM'S LOT
FALMOUTH   FALMOUTH FORESIDE**

Jerusalem's Lot, she thought randomly, what an odd name. Not a pleasant name, for some reason. *Come and sleep in Jerusalem.*

But there would be no sleep for her tonight; Jud's advice notwithstanding, she now meant to drive straight through. Jud knew what was wrong and had promised her he would put a stop to it, but the man was eighty-some years old and had lost his wife only three months before. She would not put her trust in Jud. She should never have allowed Louis to bulldoze her out of the house the way he had, but she had been weakened by Gage's death. Ellie with her Polaroid picture of Gage and her pinched face – it had been the face of a child who has survived a tornado or a sudden dive-bombing from a clear blue sky. There had been times in the dark watches of the night when she had longed to hate Louis for the grief he had fathered inside her, and for not giving her the comfort she needed (or allowing her to give the comfort she needed to give), but she could not. She loved him too much still, and his face had been so pale . . . so watchful . . .

The Chevette's speedometer needle hung poised just a bit to the right of sixty miles an hour. A mile a minute. Two hours and a quarter to Ludlow, maybe. Maybe she could still beat the sunrise.

She fumbled with the radio, turned it on, found a rock and roll station out of Portland. She turned up the volume and sang along, trying to keep herself awake. The station began to fade in and out half an hour later and she re-tuned to an Augusta station, rolled the window down, and let the restless night air blow in on her.

She wondered if this night would ever end.

CHAPTER FIFTY-FIVE

Louis had rediscovered his dream and was in its grip; every few moments he looked down to make sure it was a body in a tarpaulin he was carrying, and not one in a green Hefty Bag. He remembered how on awakening the morning after Jud had taken him up there with Church he had been barely able to remember what they had done – but now he also remembered how vivid those sensations had been, how alive each of his senses had felt, how they had seemed to reach out, touching the woods as if they were alive, and in some kind of telepathic contact with himself.

He followed the path up and down, rediscovering the places where it seemed as wide as Route 15, the places where it narrowed until he had to turn sideways to keep the head and foot of his bundle from getting tangled in the underbrush, the places where the path wound through great cathedral stands of trees. He could smell the clear tang of pine resin, and he could hear that strange crump-crump of the needles underfoot – a sound that is really more feeling than sound.

At last the path began to slant downward more steeply and constantly. A short time later one foot splashed through thin water and became mired in the sludgy stuff underneath ... the quicksand, if Jud was to be believed. Louis looked down and could see the standing water between growths of reeds and low, ugly bushes with leaves so broad they were almost tropical. He remembered that the light had seemed brighter that other night, too. More electrical.

This next bit is like the deadfall – you got to walk steady and easy. Just follow me and don't look down.

Yes, okay ... and just by the by, have you ever seen plants like

408

these in Maine before? In Maine or anywhere else? What in Christ's name are they?

Never mind, Louis. Just . . . let's go.

He began to walk again, looking at the wet, marshy under-growth just long enough to sight the first tussock and then only looking ahead of himself, his feet moving from one grassy hump to the next – *faith is accepting gravity as a postulate*, he thought; nothing he had been told in a college theology or philosophy course, but something his high school physics instructor had once tossed off near the end of a period . . . something Louis had never forgotten.

He accepted the ability of the Micmac burying ground to resurrect the dead and walked into Little God Swamp with his son in his arms, not looking down or back. These marshy bottoms were noisier now than they had been at the tag-end of autumn. Peepers sang constantly in the reeds, a shrill chorus which Louis found alien and uninviting. An occasional frog twanged a deep elastic somewhere in its throat. Twenty paces or so into Little God Swamp he was buzz-bombed by some shape . . . a bat, perhaps.

The ground mist began to swirl around him, first covering his shoes, then his shins, finally enclosing him in a glowing white capsule. It seemed to him that the light was brighter, a pulsing effulgence, like the beat of some strange heart. He had never before felt so strongly the presence of nature as a kind of coalescing force, a real being . . . possibly sentient. The swamp was alive, but not with the sound of music. If asked to define either the sense or the nature of that aliveness, he would have been unable. But it was rich with possibility, and textured with strength. Inside it, Louis felt very small and very mortal.

Then there *was* a sound, and he remembered this from the last time, as well: a high, gobbling laugh that became a sob. There was silence for a moment and then the laugh came again, this time rising to a maniacal shriek that froze Louis's blood. The mist drifted dreamily around him. The laughter faded, leaving only the drone of the wind, heard but no longer felt. Of course not; this had to be some sort of geological cup in the earth. If the wind could have penetrated here, it would have torn this mist to tatters ... and Louis wasn't sure he would want to see what might have been revealed.

You may hear sounds like voices, but they are the loons down south toward Prospect. The sound carries. It's funny.

'Loons,' Louis said, and barely recognized the cracked, somehow ghastly sound of his own voice.

He hesitated briefly, then moved on again. As if to punish him for his brief pause, his foot slipped from the next tussock, and he almost lost his shoe, pulling it free from the grasping ooze under the shallow water.

The voice – if that was what it was – came again, this time from the left. Moments later it came from behind him ... from *directly* behind him, it seemed, as if he could have turned and seen some blood-drenched thing less than a foot from his back, all bared teeth and glittering eyes ... but this time Louis did not slow. He looked straight ahead and kept walking.

Suddenly the mist lost its light and Louis realized that a face was hanging in the air ahead of him, leering and gibbering. Its eyes, tilted up like the eyes in a classical Chinese painting, were a rich yellowish-gray, sunken, gleaming. The mouth was drawn down in a rictus; the lower lip was turned inside out, revealing teeth stained blackish-brown and worn down almost to nubs. But what struck Louis were the ears, which were not ears at all, but curving horns ... they were not like devil's horns; they were ram's horns.

This grisly, floating head seemed to be speaking – laughing. Its mouth moved, although that turned-down lower lip never came back to its natural shape and place. Veins in there pulsed black. Its nostrils flared, as if with breath and life, and blew out white vapors.

As Louis drew closer, the floating head's tongue lolled out. It was long and pointed, dirty yellow in color. It was coated with peeling scales and as Louis watched, one of these flipped up and over like a manhole cover and a white worm oozed out. The tongue's tip skittered lazily on the air somewhere below where its adam's apple should have been . . . it was laughing.

He clutched Gage closer to him, hugging him, as if to protect him, and his feet faltered and began to slip on the grassy tussocks where they held slim purchase.

You might see St Elmo's fire, what the sailors call foo-lights. It can make funny shapes, but it's nothing. If you should see some of those shapes and they bother you, just look the other way . . .

Jud's voice in his head gave him a measure of resolve. He began to move steadily forward again, lurching at first, then finding his balance. He didn't look away, but noticed that the face – if that was what it was and not just a shape made by the mist and his own mind – seemed to always remain the same distance away from him. And seconds or minutes later, it simply dissolved into drifting mist.

That was not St Elmo's fire.

No, of course it wasn't. This place was alive with spirits; it was tenebrous with them. You could look around and see something that would send you raving mad. He would not think about it. There was no need to think about it. There was no need to——

Something was coming.

Louis came to a total halt, listening to that sound . . . that inexorable, approaching sound. His mouth fell open, every tendon that held his jaw shut simply giving up.

It was a sound like nothing he had ever heard in his life – a living sound; a *big* sound. Somewhere nearby, growing closer, branches were snapping off. There was a crackle of underbrush breaking under unimaginable feet. The jelly-like ground under Louis's feet began to shake in sympathetic vibration. He became aware that he was moaning

(oh my God oh my dear God what is that what is coming through this fog?)

and once more clutching Gage to his chest; he became

aware that the peepers and frogs had fallen silent, he became aware that the wet, damp air had taken on an eldritch, sickening smell like warm, spoiled pork.

Whatever it was, it was huge.

Louis's wondering, terrified face tilted up and up, like a man following the trajectory of a launched rocket. The thing thudded toward him, and there was the ratcheting sound of a tree – not a branch, but a whole tree – falling over somewhere close by.

Louis saw something.

The mist stained to a dull slate-gray for a moment, but this diffuse, ill-defined watermark was better than sixty feet high. It was no shade, no insubstantial ghost; he could feel the displaced air of its passage, could hear the mammoth thud of its feet coming down, the suck of mud as it moved on.

For a moment he believed he saw twin yellow-orange sparks high above him. Sparks like eyes.

Then the sound began to fade. As it went away, a peeper called hesitantly – one. It was answered by another. A third joined the conversation; a fourth made it a bull-session; a fifth and sixth made it a peeper convention. The sounds of the thing's progress (slow, but not blundering; perhaps that was the worst of it, that feeling of sentient progress) were moving away to the north. Little . . . less . . . gone.

At last Louis began to move again. His shoulders and back were a frozen ache of torment. He wore an undergarment of sweat from neck to ankles, close-fitting and hot. The season's first mosquitoes, new-hatched and hungry, found him and sat down to a late snack.

The Wendigo, dear Christ, that was the Wendigo – the creature that moves through the north country, the creature that can touch you and turn you into a cannibal. That was it. The Wendigo has just passed within sixty yards of me.

He told himself not to be ridiculous, to be like Jud and avoid ideas about what might be seen or heard beyond the Pet Sematary – they were loons, they were St Elmo's fire, they were the members of the New York Yankees' bullpen. Let them be anything but the creatures which leap and crawl and slither and shamble in the world between. Let there be God, let there be Sunday morning, let there be smiling Episcopalian ministers in shining white surplices . . . but let there not be these dark and draggling horrors on the nightside of the universe.

Louis walked on with his son, and the ground began to firm up again under his feet. Only moments later he came to a felled tree, its crown visible in the fading mist like a gray-green feather duster dropped by a giant's housekeeper.

The tree was broken off – splintered off – and the break was so fresh that the yellowish-white pulp still bled sap that was warm to Louis's touch as he climbed over . . . and on the other side was a monstrous indentation out of which he had to scramble and climb, and although juniper and low pump-laurel bushes had been stamped right into the earth, he would not let himself believe it was a footprint. He could have looked back to see if it had any such configuration once he had climbed beyond and above it, but he would not. He only walked on, skin cold, mouth hot and arid, heart flying.

The squelch of mud under his feet soon ceased. For a while there was the faint cereal-sound of fir needles again. Then there was rock. He had nearly reached the end.

The ground began to rise faster. He barked his shin painfully on an outcropping. But this was not *just* a rock. Louis reached out clumsily with one hand (the strap of his elbow, which had grown numb, screamed briefly) and touched it.

Steps here. Cut into the rock. Just follow me. We get to the top and we're there.

So he began to climb and the exhilaration returned, once more beating exhaustion back . . . at least a little way. His mind tolled off the steps as he rose into the chill, as he climbed back into that ceaseless river of wind, stronger now, rippling his clothes, making the piece of canvas tarp in which Gage was wrapped stutter gunshot sounds like a lifted sail.

He cocked his head back once and saw the mad sprawl of the stars. There were no constellations he recognized, and he looked away again, disturbed. Beside him was the rock wall, not smooth but splintered and gouged and friable, taking here the shape of a boat, here the shape of a badger, here the shape of a man's face with hooded, frowning eyes. Only the steps that had been carved from the rock were smooth.

Louis gained the top and stood there with his head down, swaying, sobbing breath in and out of his lungs. They felt like cruelly punched bladders, and there seemed to be a large splinter sticking into his side.

The wind ran through his hair like a dancer, roared in his ears like a dragon.

The light was brighter this night; had it been overcast the other time, or had he just not been looking? It didn't matter. But he could see, and that was enough to start another chill worming down his back.

It was just like the Pet Sematary.

Of course you knew that, his mind whispered as he surveyed the piles of rocks that had once been cairns. *You knew that — or should have known it; not concentric circles but the spiral—*

Yes. Here on top of this rock table, its face turned up to cold starlight and to the black distances between the stars, was a gigantic spiral, made by what the oldtimers would have called Various Hands. But there were no cairns, Louis saw; every one of them had been burst apart as something buried beneath returned to life . . . and clawed its way out. Yet the rocks themselves had fallen in such a way that the shape of the spiral was apparent.

Has anyone ever seen this from the air? Louis wondered randomly, and thought of those desert-drawings that one tribe of Indians or another had made in South America. *Has anyone ever seen it from the air, and if they did, what did they think, I wonder?*

He knelt and set Gage's body on the ground with a groan of relief.

At last his consciousness began to come back. He used his pocket knife to cut the tape holding the pick and shovel slung over his back. They fell to the ground with a clink. Louis rolled over and lay down for a moment, spread-eagled, staring blankly at the stars.

What was that thing in the woods? Louis, Louis, do you really think anything good can come at the climax of a play where something like that is among the cast of characters?

But now it was too late to back out, and he knew it . . .

Besides, he gibbered to himself, *it may still come out all right, there is no gain without risk, perhaps no risk without love. There's still my bag, not the one downstairs but the one in our bathroom on the high shelf, the one I sent Ellie for the night Norma had her heart attack. There are syringes, and if something happens . . . something bad . . . no one has to know but me.*

His thoughts dissolved into the inarticulate, droning mutter of prayer even as his hands groped for the pick . . . and still on his knees, Louis began to dig into the earth. Each time he brought the pick down he collapsed over the end of it, like an old Roman falling on his sword. Yet little by little the hole took shape and deepened. He clawed the rocks out, and most he simply pushed aside along with the growing pile of stony dirt. But some of them he saved.

For the cairn.

CHAPTER FIFTY-SIX

Rachel slapped her face until it began to tingle, and still she kept nodding off. Once she snapped fully awake (she was in Pittsfield now, and had the turnpike all to herself) and it seemed to her for a split second that dozens of silvery, merciless eyes were looking at her, twinkling like cold, hungry fire.

Then they resolved themselves into the small reflectors on the guardrail posts. The Chevette had drifted far over into the breakdown lane.

She wrenched the wheel to the left again, the tires wailing, and she believed she heard a faint *tick!* that might have been her right front bumper just kissing off one of those guardrail posts. Her heart leaped in her chest and began to bang so hard between her ribs that she saw small specks before her eyes, growing and shrinking in time with its beat. And yet a moment later, in spite of her close shave, her scare, and Robert Gordon shouting 'Red Hot' on the radio, she was drowsing off again.

A crazy, paranoid thought came to her. It was just the weariness, undoubtedly the weariness, but she began to feel that something was trying to keep her from getting to Ludlow tonight.

'Paranoid, all right,' she muttered under the rock-and-roll. She tried to laugh – but she couldn't laugh. Not quite. Because the thought remained, and in the eye of the night it gained a spooky kind of credibility. She began to feel like a cartoon figure who has run into the rubber band of a gigantic slingshot. Poor guy finds forward motion harder and harder, until at last the potential energy of the rubber band equalizes the actual energy of the runner ... inertia becomes ... what? ... elementary physics ... something trying to hold her back ...

stay out of this, you . . . and a body at rest tends to remain at rest . . . *Gage's body, for instance* . . . once set in motion . . .

This time the scream of tires was louder, the shave a lot closer; for a moment there was the squealing, grailing sound of the Chevette running along the guardrail cables, scraping paint down to the twinkling metal, and for a moment the wheel didn't answer, and then Rachel was standing on the brake, sobbing, she had been asleep this time, not just dozing but *asleep and dreaming* at sixty miles an hour, and if there had been no guardrail . . . or if there had been an overpass stanchion . . .

She pulled over and put the car in park and wept into her hands, bewildered and afraid.

Something is trying to keep me away from him.

When she felt she had control of herself, she began to drive again – the little car's steering did not seem impaired, but she supposed the Avis company would have some serious questions for her when she returned their car to BIA tomorrow.

Never mind. One thing at a time. Got to get some coffee into me, that's the first thing.

When the Pittsfield exit came up, Rachel took it. About a mile down the road she came to bright arc-sodium lights and the steady mutter-growl of diesel engines. She pulled in, had the Chevette filled up ('Somebody put a pretty good ding along the side of her,' the gas-jockey said in an almost admiring voice), and then went into the diner, which smelled of deep-fat grease, vulcanized eggs . . . and, blessedly, of good strong coffee.

Rachel had three cups, one after another, like medicine – black, sweetened with a lot of sugar. A few truckers sat at the counter or in the booths, kidding the waitresses, who somehow all managed to look like tired nurses filled with bad news under these fluorescents burning in the night's little hours.

She paid her check and went back out to where she had parked the Chevette. It wouldn't start. The key, when turned, would cause the solenoid to utter a dry click, but that was all.

Rachel began to beat her fists slowly and forcelessly against the steering wheel. Something was trying to stop her. There was no reason for this car, brand-new and with less than five thousand miles on its odometer, to have died like this, but it had. Somehow it had, and here she was, stranded Pittsfield, still almost fifty miles from home.

She listened to the steady mutter-drone of the big trucks, and it came to her with a sudden, vicious certainty that the truck which had killed her son was here among them . . . not muttering but chuckling.

Rachel lowered her head and began to cry.

CHAPTER FIFTY-SEVEN

Louis stumbled over something and fell full-length on the ground. For a moment he didn't think he would be able to get up – getting up was far beyond him – he would simply lie here, listening to the chorus of peepers from Little God Swamp somewhere behind him and feeling the chorus of aches and pains inside his own body. He would lie here until he went to sleep. Or died. Probably the latter.

He could remember slipping the canvas bundle into the hole he had dug, and actually pushing most of the earth back into the hole, with his bare hands. And he believed he could remember piling the rocks up, building from a broad base to a point . . .

From then to now he remembered very little. He had obviously gotten back down the steps again or he wouldn't be here, which was . . . where? Looking around, he thought he recognized one of the groves of great old pines not far beyond the deadfall. Could he have made it all the way back through Little God Swamp without knowing it? He supposed it was possible. Just.

This is far enough. I'll just sleep here.

But it was that thought, so falsely comforting, that got him to his feet and moving again. Because if he stayed here, that thing might find him . . . that thing might be in the woods and looking for him right this moment.

He scrubbed his hand up to his face, palm first, and was stupidly surprised to see blood on his hand . . . at some point he'd given himself a nosebleed. 'Who gives a fuck?' he muttered hoarsely, and grubbed apathetically around him until he had found the pick and shovel again.

Ten minutes later the deadfall loomed ahead. Louis climbed it, stumbling repeatedly but somehow not falling until he was almost down. Then he glanced at his feet, a branch promptly snapped (don't look down, Jud had said), another branch tumbled, spilling his foot outward, and he fell with a thud on his side, the wind knocked out of him.

I'll be goddamned if this isn't the second graveyard I've fallen into tonight . . . and I'll be goddamned if two isn't enough.

He began to feel around for the pick and shovel again, and laid his hands on them at last. For a moment he surveyed his surroundings, visible by starlight. Nearby was the grave of SMUCKY. He was obedient, Louis thought wearily. And TRIXIE, KILLED ON THE HIGHWAY. The wind still blew strongly, and he could hear the faint *ting-ting-ting* of a piece of metal – perhaps once it had been a Del Monte can, cut laboriously by a grieving pet-owner with his father's tin-snips and then flattened out with a hammer and nailed to a stick – and that brought the fear back again. He was too tired now to feel it in that dry, blazing way; it was more like a low and somehow sickening pulsebeat. He had done it. Somehow that steady *ting-ting-ting* sound coming out of the darkness brought it home to him more than anything else.

He walked through the Pet Sematary, past the grave of MARTA OUR PET RABIT who had DYED MARCH 1 1965 and near the barrow of GEN. PATTON; he stepped over the ragged chunk of board that marked the final resting place of POLYNESIA. The tick of metal was louder now, and he paused, looking down. Here, atop a slightly leaning board that had been driven into the ground, was a tin rectangle, and by starlight Louis read: RINGO OUR HAMPSTER 1964–1965. It was this piece of tin that was ticking repeatedly off the boards of the Pet Sematary's entry arch. Louis reached down to bend the piece of tin back . . . and then froze, scalp crawling.

Something was moving back there. Something was moving on the other side of the deadfall.

What he heard was a stealthy kind of sound — the furtive crackle of fir needles, the dry pop of a twig, the rattle of underbrush. They were almost lost under the sough of the wind through the firs.

'Gage?' Louis called hoarsely.

The very realization of what he was doing — standing here in the dark and calling his dead son — pulled his scalp stiff and brought his hair up on end. He began to shudder helplessly and steadily, as if with a sick and killing fever.

'Gage?'

The sounds had died away.

Not yet; it's too early. Don't ask me how I know, but I do. That isn't Gage over there. That's ... something else.

He suddenly thought of Ellie telling him: *He called 'Lazarus, come forth' ... because if He hadn't called for Lazarus by name, everyone in that graveyard would have risen.*

On the other side of the deadfall, those sounds had begun again. On the other side of the barrier. Almost — but not quite — hidden under the wind. As if something blind were stalking him with ancient instincts. His dreadfully overstimulated brain conjured horrible, sickening pictures: a giant mole; a great bat that flopped through the underbrush rather than flying.

Louis backed out of the Pet Sematary, not turning his back to the deadfall — that ghostlike glimmer, a livid scar on the dark — until he was well down the path. Then he began to hurry, and perhaps a quarter of a mile before the path ran out of the woods and into the field behind his house, he found enough left inside him to run.

Louis slung the pick and shovel indifferently inside the garage and stood for a moment at the head of his driveway, looking first back the way he had come, and then up at the sky. It was quarter past four in the morning, and he supposed dawn could not be so far away. Light would already be three-quarters of the way across the Atlantic, but for now, here in Ludlow, the night held hard. The wind blew steadily.

He went into the house, feeling his way along the side of the garage and unlocking the back door. He went through the kitchen without turning on a light and stepped into the small bathroom between the kitchen and the dining room. Here he did snap on a light, and the first thing he saw was Church, curled up on top of the toilet tank, staring at him with those muddy yellow eyes.

'Church,' he said. 'I thought someone put you out.'

Church only looked at him from atop the toilet tank. Yes, someone had put Church out; he had done it himself. He remembered that very clearly. Just as he remembered replacing the windowpane down the cellar that time and then telling himself that had taken care of the problem. But exactly whom had he been kidding? When Church wanted to get in, Church got in. Because Church was different now.

It didn't matter. In this dull, exhausted aftermath, nothing seemed to matter. He felt like something less than human now, one of Romero's stupid, lurching zombies, or maybe someone who had escaped from Eliot's poem about the hollow men. *I should have been a pair of ragged claws, scuttling through Little God Swamp and up to the Micmac burying ground*, he thought, and uttered a dry chuckle.

'Headpiece full of straw, Church,' he said in his croaking voice. He was unbuttoning his shirt now. 'That's me. You better believe it.'

There was a nice bruise coming on his left side, about halfway up his ribcage, and when he shucked his pants he saw that the knee he had banged on the gravestone was swelling up like a balloon. It had already turned a rotten purple-black, and he supposed that as soon as he stopped flexing it, the joint would become stiff and painfully obdurate – as if it had been dipped in cement. It looked like one of those injuries that might want to converse with him on rainy days for the rest of his life.

He reached out a hand to stroke Church, wanting some sort of comfort, but the cat leaped down from the toilet tank, staggering in that drunken and weirdly unfeline way, and left for some other place. It spared Louis one flat, yellow glance as it went.

There was Ben-Gay in the medicine cabinet. Louis lowered the toilet seat, sat down, and smeared a gob on his bad knee. Then he rubbed some more on the small of his back — a clumsy operation.

He left the toilet and walked into the living room. He turned on the hall light and stood there at the foot of the stairs for a moment, looking stupidly around. How strange it all seemed! Here was where he had stood on Christmas Eve when he had given Rachel the sapphire. It had been in the pocket of his robe. There was his chair, where he had done his best to explain the facts of death to Ellie after Norma Crandall's fatal heart attack — facts he had found ultimately unacceptable to himself. The Christmas tree had stood in that corner, Ellie's construction-paper turkey — the one that had reminded Louis of some sort of futuristic crow — had been Scotch-taped in that window, and much earlier the entire room had been empty except for the United Van Lines boxes, filled with their family possessions and trucked across half the country from the Midwest. He remembered thinking that their things looked very insignificant, boxed up like that; small enough bulwark between his family and the coldness of all the outer world where their names and their family customs were not known.

How strange it all seemed . . . and how he wished they had never heard of the University of Maine, or Ludlow, or Jud and Norma Crandall, or any of it.

He went upstairs in his skivvies, and in the bathroom at the top he got the stool, stood on it, and took down the small black bag from on top of the medicine cabinet. He took this into the master bedroom, sat down, and began to rummage through it. Yes, there were syringes in case he needed one, and amid the rolls of surgical tape and surgical scissors and neatly wrapped papers of surgical gut were several ampoules of very deadly stuff.

If needed.

Louis snapped the bag shut and put it by the bed. He turned off the overhead light, then lay down, hands behind his head. To lie here on his back, at rest, was exquisite. His thoughts turned to Disney World again. He saw himself in a plain white uniform, driving a white van with the mouse-ears logo on it – nothing to indicate it was a rescue unit on the outside, of course, nothing to scare the paying customers.

Gage was sitting beside him, his skin deeply tanned, the whites of his eyes bluish with health. Here, just to the left, was Goofy, shaking hands with a little boy; the kid was in a trance of wonder. Here was Winnie the Pooh posing with two laughing grandmas in pants suits so a third laughing grandma could snap their pictures; here was a little girl in her best dress crying: 'I love you, Tigger! I love you, Tigger!'

He and his son were on patrol. He and his son were the sentries in this magic land, and they cruised endlessly in their white van with the red dashboard flasher neatly and sensibly covered. They were not looking for trouble, not they, but they were ready for it should it show its face. That it was lurking even here, in a place dedicated to such innocent plea-sures, could not be denied; some grinning man buying film along Main Street could clutch his chest as the heart attack struck, a pregnant woman might suddenly feel the labor-pains start as she walked down the steps from the Sky Chariot, a teenage girl as pretty as a Norman Rockwell cover would suddenly collapse in a flopping epileptic fit, loafers rattling out a jagged back-beat on the cement as the signals in her brain suddenly jammed up. There was sunstroke and heatstroke and brainstroke and perhaps at the end of some sultry summer Orlando afternoon there might even be a stroke of lightning; there was, even, Oz the Gweat and Tewwible himself here – he might be glimpsed walking around near the monorail's point of egress into the Magic Kingdom, or peering down from one of the flying Dumbos with his flat and stupid gaze – down here Louis and Gage had come to know him as just

another amusement park figure like Goofy or Micky or Tigger
or the estimable Mr D. Duck. He was the one, however, with
whom no one wanted his or her picture taken, the one to
whom no one wanted to introduce his son or daughter. Louis
and Gage knew him; they had met him and faced him down
in New England, some time ago. He was waiting to choke
you on a marble, to smother you with a dry-cleaning bag, to
sizzle you into eternity with a fast and lethal boogie of electricity – Available at Your Nearest Switchplate or Vacant
Light-Socket Right Now. There was death in a quarter bag
of peanuts, an aspirated piece of steak, the next pack of cigarettes. He was around all the time, he monitored all the check-
points between the mortal and the eternal. Dirty needles,
poison beetles, downed live wires, forest fires. Whirling roller
skates that shot nurdy little kids into busy intersections. When
you got into the bathtub to take a shower, Oz got right in
there too – Shower with a Friend. When you got on an
airplane, Oz took your boarding pass. He was in the water
you drank, the food you ate. *Who's out there?* you howled into
the dark when you were frightened and all alone, and it was
his answer that came back: Don't be afraid, it's just me. Hi,
howaya? You got cancer of the bowel, what a bummer, so
solly, Cholly! Septicemia! Leukemia! Arteriosclerosis! Coronary thrombosis! Encephalitis! Osteomyelitis! Hey-ho, let's go!
Junkie in a doorway with a knife. Phone call in the middle
of the night. Blood cooking in battery acid on some exit ramp
in North Carolina. Big handfuls of pills, munch 'em up. That
peculiar blue cast of the fingernails following asphyxiation –
in its final grim struggle to survive the brain takes all the
oxygen that is left, even that in those living cells under the
nails. Hi, folks, my name's Oz the Gweat and Tewwible, but
you can call me Oz if you want, hell, we're old friends by
now. Just stopped by to whop you with a little congestive
heart failure or a cranial blood-clot or something, can't stay,
got to see a woman about a breach birth, then I've got a little
smoke-inhalation job to do in Omaha.

And that thin voice is crying, 'I love you, Tigger! I love you! I believe in you, Tigger! I will always love you and believe in you, and I will stay young, and the only Oz to ever live in my heart will be that gentle faker from Nebraska! I love you . . .'

We cruise . . . my son and I . . . because the essence of it isn't war or sex but only that sickening, noble, hopeless battle against Oz the Gweat and Tewwible. He and I, in our white van under this bright Florida sky, we cruise. And the red flasher is hooded, but it is there if we need it . . . and none need know but us. Because the soil of a man's heart is stonier; a man grows what he can . . . and tends it.

Thinking such troubled half-dreaming thoughts, Louis Creed slipped away, unplugging his connections to waking reality line by line, until all thoughts ceased and exhaustion dragged him down to black dreamless unconsciousness.

Just before the first signs of dawn touched the sky in the east, there were footsteps on the stairs. They were slow and clumsy, but purposeful. A shadow moved in the shadows of the hall. A smell came with it – a stench. Louis, even in his thick sleep, muttered and turned away from that smell. There was the steady pull and release of respiration.

The shape stood outside the master bedroom door for some little time, not moving. Then it came inside. Louis's face was buried in his pillow. White hands reached out and there was a click as the black doctor's bag by the bed was opened.

The low clink and shift as the things inside were moved.

The hands explored, pushing aside drugs and ampoules and syringes with no interest at all. Now they found something and held it up. In the first dim light there was a gleam of silver.

The shadowy thing left the room.

PART THREE:

OZ THE GWEAT AND TEWWIBLE

Jesus therefore, groaning inside of himself and full of trouble, came to the grave. It was a cave, and a stone had been raised against the mouth. 'Roll away the stone,' Jesus said.

Martha said, 'Lord, by this time he will have begun to rot. He has been dead four days.' . . .

And when he had prayed a while, Jesus raised his voice and cried: 'Lazarus, come forth!' And he that was dead came forth, bound hand and foot with graveclothes: and his face was bound about with a napkin.

Jesus said to them, 'Loose him and let him go.'

— John's Gospel (paraphrase)

'I only just thought of it,' she said hysterically. 'Why didn't I think of it before? Why didn't you think of it?'

'Think of what?' he questioned.

'The other two wishes,' she replied rapidly. 'We've only had one.'

'Was that not enough?' he demanded fiercely.

'No,' she cried triumphantly: 'we'll have one more. Go down and get it quickly, and wish our boy alive again.'

— W. W. Jacobs (The Monkey's Paw)

CHAPTER FIFTY-EIGHT

Jud Crandall came awake with a sudden jerk, almost falling out of his chair. He had no idea how long he had slept; it could have been fifteen minutes or three hours. He looked at his watch and saw that it was five minutes of five. There was a feeling that everything in the room had been subtly shifted out of position, and there was a line of pain across his back from sleeping sitting up.

Oh you stupid old man, look what you gone and done!

But he knew better; in his heart, he knew better. It wasn't just him. He hadn't simply fallen asleep on watch; he had been *put* to sleep.

That frightened him, but one thing frightened him more: what had awakened him? He was under the impression that there had been some sound, some—

He held his breath, listening over the papery rustle of his heart.

Here was a sound; not the same one that had awakened him, but something. The faint creak of hinges.

Jud knew every sound in this house – which floorboards creaked, which stair-levels squeaked, where along the gutters the wind was apt to hoot and sing when it was drunkenly high, as it had been last night. He knew this sound as well as any of those. The heavy front door, the one that communicated between his porch and the front hall, had just swung open. And with that information to go on, his mind was able to remember the sound that had awakened him. It had been the slow expansion of the spring on the screen door communicating between the porch and the front walk.

'Louis?' he called, but with no real hope. That wasn't Louis

429

out there. Whatever was out there had been sent to punish an old man for his pride and vanity.

Footsteps moved slowly up the hall toward the living room.

'Louis?' he tried to call again, but only a faint croak actually emerged, because now he could smell the thing which had come into his house here at the end of the night. It was a dirty, low smell like the smell of poisoned tidal flats.

Jud could make out bulking shapes in the gloom – Norma's *armoire*, the Welsh dresser, the highboy – but no details. He tried to get to his feet on legs that had gone to water, his mind screaming that he needed more time, that he was too old to face this again without more time, Timmy Baterman had been bad enough and then he had been young.

The swing door opened and let in shadows. One of the shadows was more substantial than the others.

Dear God, that stink.

Shuffling steps in the darkness.

'Gage?' Jud gained his feet at last. From one corner of his eye he saw the neat roll of cigarette ash in the Jim Beam ashtray. 'Gage, is that y—'

A hideous mewing sound now arose, and for a moment all of Jud's bones turned to white ice. It was not Louis's son returned from the grave but some hideous demon—

No. It was neither.

It was Church, crouched in the hall doorway, making that sound. The cat's eyes flared like dirty lamps. Then his eyes moved in the other direction and fixed on the thing which had come in with the cat.

Jud began to back up, trying to catch at his thoughts, trying to hold on to his reason in the face of that smell. Oh, it was cold in here – the thing had brought its chill with it.

Jud rocked unsteadily on his feet – it was the cat, twining around his legs, making him totter. It was purring. Jud kicked at it, driving it away. It bared its teeth at him and hissed.

Think! Oh, think, you stupid old man, it mayn't be too late, even yet it mayn't be too late . . . it's back but it can be killed again . . . if you can only do it . . . if you can only think . . .

He backed away toward the kitchen, and he suddenly remembered the utensil drawer beside the sink. There was a meat-cleaver in that drawer.

His thin shanks struck the swinging door that led into the kitchen and he pushed it open. The thing that had come into his house was still indistinct, but Jud could hear it breathing. He could see one white hand swinging back and forth – there was something in that hand, but he could not make out what. The door swung back as he entered the kitchen, and Jud at last turned his back and ran to the utensil drawer. He jerked it open and found the cleaver's worn hardwood handle. He snatched it up and turned toward the door again; he even took a step or two toward it. Some of his courage had come back.

Remember, it ain't a kid. It may scream or somethin' when it sees you've got its number; it may cry. But you ain't gonna be fooled. You been fooled too many times already, old man. This is your last chance.

The swing door opened again, but at first only the cat came through. Jud's eye followed it for a moment and then he looked up again.

The kitchen faced east, and dawn's first light came in through the windows, faint and milky-white. Not much light, but enough. Too much.

Gage Creed came in, dressed in his burial suit. Moss was growing on the suit's shoulders and lapels. Moss had fouled his white shirt. His fine blonde hair was caked with dirt. One eye had gone to the wall; it stared off into space with terrible concentration. The other was fixed on Jud with glittery, blank intensity.

Gage was grinning at him.

'Hello, Jud,' Gage piped in a babyish but perfectly understandable voice. 'I've come to send your rotten, stinking old soul straight to hell. You fucked with me once. Did you think I wouldn't come back sooner or later and fuck with you?'

Jud raised the cleaver. 'Come on and get your pecker out then, whatever you are. We'll see who fucks with who.'

'Norma's dead and there'll be no one to mourn you,' Gage said. 'What a cheap slut she was. She fucked every one of your friends, Jud. She let them put it up her ass. That's how she liked it best. She's burning down in hell, arthritis and all. I *saw* her there, Jud. I *saw* her there.'

It lurched two steps toward him, shoes leaving muddy tracks on the worn linoleum. It held one hand out in front of it as if to shake with him; the other hand was curled behind its back.

'Listen, Jud,' it whispered – and then its mouth hung open, baring small milk-teeth, and although the lips did not move, Norma's voice issued forth.

'Cuckold! Miserable cuckold! I always hated you! I laughed at you! We all laughed at you! How we laaaaaauuughed—'

'Stop it!' The cleaver jittered in his hand.

'We did it in our bed. Herk and I did it, I did it with George. I did it with all of them. I knew about your whores but you never knew you married a whore and how we laughed, Jud! We rutted together and we laaaaaaaaaughed at—'

'*STOP IT*' Jud screamed. He sprang at the tiny, swaying figure in its dirty burial suit, and that was when the cat arrowed out of the darkness under the butcher block where it had been crouched. It was hissing, its ears laid back along the bullet of its skull, and it tripped Jud up just as neat as you please. The cleaver flew out of his hand. It skittered across the humped and faded linoleum, blade and handle swiftly changing places as it whirled. It struck the baseboard with a thin clang and slid under the refrigerator.

Jud realized that he had been fooled again, and the only consolation was that it was for the final time. The cat was on his legs, mouth open, eyes blazing, hissing like a tea kettle. And then Gage was on him, grinning a happy black grin, moon-eyes rimmed with red, and his right hand came out from behind his back, and Jud saw that what he had been holding when he came in was a scalpel from Louis's black bag.

'Oh m' dear Jesus,' Jud managed, and put his right hand up to block the blow. And here was an optical illusion; surely his mind had snapped, because it appeared that the scalpel was on both sides of his palm at the same time. Then something warm began to drizzle down on his face and he understood that it was no illusion.

'I'm gonna fuck with *you*, old man!' The Gage-thing chortled, blowing its poisoned breath in his face. 'I'm gonna fuck with *you*! I'm gonna fuck with *you* all . . . I . . . *want*!'

Jud flailed and got hold of Gage's wrist. Skin peeled off like parchment in his hand.

The scalpel was yanked out of his hand, leaving a vertical mouth.

'*All . . . I . . . WANT!*'

The scalpel came down again. And again. And again.

CHAPTER FIFTY-NINE

'Try it now, ma'am,' the truckdriver said. He was looking into the engine cavity of Rachel's rented car.

She turned the key. The Chevette's engine roared into life. The truckdriver slammed the hood down and came around to her window, wiping his hands on a big blue handkerchief. He had a pleasant, ruddy face. A Dysart's Truck-Stop cap was tilted back on his head.

'Thank you so much,' Rachel said, on the verge of tears. 'I just didn't know what I was going to do.'

'Aw, a kid could have fixed that,' the trucker said. 'But it was funny. Never seen something like that go wrong on such a new car, anyway.'

'Why? What was it?'

'One of your battery cables come right off. Wasn't nobody frigging with it, was there?'

'No,' Rachel said, and she thought again of that feeling she'd had, that feeling of running into the rubber band of the world's biggest slingshot.

'Must have jogged her loose just ridin' along, I guess. But you won't have no more trouble with your cables, anyway. I tightened her up real good.'

'Could I give you some money?' Rachel asked timidly.

The trucker roared laughter. 'Not me, lady,' he said. 'Us guys are the knights of the road, remember?'

She smiled. 'Well . . . thank you.'

'More'n welcome.' He gave her a good grin, incongruously full of sunshine at this hour of the morning.

Rachel smiled back and drove carefully across the parking lot to the feeder road. She glanced both ways for traffic, and five minutes later was back on the turnpike again, headed north. The coffee had helped more than she would have believed. She felt totally awake now, not the slightest bit dozy, her eyes as big as doorknobs. That feather of unease touched her again, that absurd feeling that she was being manipulated. The battery cable coming off the terminal post like that . . .

So she could be held up just long enough for . . .

She laughed nervously. Long enough for what?

For something irrevocable to happen.

That was stupid. Ridiculous. But Rachel began to push the little car along faster nonetheless.

At five o'clock, as Jud was trying to ward off a scalpel stolen from the black bag of his good friend Dr Louis Creed, and as her daughter was awakening bolt-upright in bed, screaming in the grip of a nightmare which she could mercifully not remember, Rachel left the turnpike, drove the Hammond Street Cutoff close to the cemetery where a spade was now the only thing buried in her son's coffin, and crossed the Bangor-Brewer Bridge. By quarter past five, she was on Route 15 and headed for Ludlow.

She had decided to go directly to Jud's, and she would make good on at least that much of her promise. The Civic was not in their driveway, anyway, and although she supposed it might be in the garage, their house had a sleeping, unoccupied look. No intuition suggested to her that Louis might be home.

Rachel parked behind Jud's pickup and got out of the Chevette, looking around carefully. The grass was heavy with dew, sparkling in this clear, new light. Somewhere a bird sang and then was silent. On the few occasions since her pre-teenage years when she had been awake and alone at dawn without some responsibility to fulfil as the reason, she had a lonely but somehow uplifted feeling – a paradoxical sense of newness and continuity. This morning she felt nothing so clean and good. There was only a dragging sense of unease which she could not entirely charge off to the terrible twenty-four hours just gone by and her recent bereavement.

She mounted the porch steps and went in through the screen door, meaning to use the old-fashioned bell on the front door. She had been charmed by that bell the first time she and Louis came over together; you twisted it clockwise and it uttered a loud but musical cry that was anachronistic but delightful.

She reached for it now, then glanced down at the porch floor and frowned. There were muddy tracks on the mat. Looking around, she saw that they led from the screen door to this one. Very small tracks. A child's tracks, by the look of them. But she had been driving all night, and there had been no rain. There hadn't even been a ground mist.

She looked at the tracks for a long time – too long, really – and discovered she had to force her hand back to the turn-bell. She grasped it . . . and then her hand fell away again.

I'm anticipating, that's all. Anticipating the sound of that bell in this stillness. He's probably gone to sleep after all and it will startle him awake . . .

But that wasn't what she was afraid of. She had been nervous, scared in some deep and diffuse way ever since she had found it so hard to stay awake, but this sharp fear was something new, something which had solely to do with those small tracks. *Tracks that were the size—*

Her mind tried to block this thought, but it was too tired, too slow.

—of Gage's feet.

Oh stop it, can't you stop it?

She reached out and twisted the bell.

Its sound was even louder than she remembered, but not so musical – it was a harsh, choked scream in the stillness. Rachel jumped back, uttering a nervous little laugh that had absolutely no humor in it at all. She waited for Jud's footsteps, but his footsteps did not come. There was silence, and silence, and she was beginning to debate in her own mind whether or not she could bring herself to twist that iron butterfly shape again, when a sound did come from behind the door, a sound she would not have expected in her wildest surmises.

Waow! . . . Waow! . . . Waow!

'Church?' she asked, startled and puzzled. She bent forward but it was of course impossible to see in; the door's large glass panel had been covered with a neat white curtain. Norma's work. 'Church, is that you?'

Waow!

Rachel tried the door. It was unlocked. Church was there, sitting in the hallway with his tail coiled neatly around his feet. The cat's fur was streaked with something dark. *Mud*, Rachel thought, and then saw that the beads of liquid caught in Church's whiskers were red.

He raised one paw and began to lick it, his eyes never leaving her face.

'Jud?' she called out, really alarmed now. She stepped just inside the door.

The house gave back no answer; only silence.

Rachel tried to think, but all at once images of her sister Zelda had begun to creep into her mind, blurring thought. How her hands had twisted. How she used to slam her head against the wall sometimes when she was angry – the paper had been all torn there, the plaster beneath torn and broken. This was no time to think of Zelda, not when Jud might be hurt. Suppose he had fallen down? He was an old man.

Think about that, not about the dreams you had as a kid, dreams of opening the closet and having Zelda spring out at you with her blackened, grinning face, dreams of being in the bathtub and seeing Zelda's eyes peering out of the drain, dreams of Zelda lurking in the basement behind the furnace, dreams—

Church opened his mouth, exposing his sharp teeth and cried: *Waow!* again.

Louis was right, we never should have had him fixed, he's never seemed right since then. But Louis said it would take away all of his aggressive instincts. He was wrong about that, anyway; Church still hunts. He—

Waow! Church cried again, then turned and darted up the stairs.

'Jud?' she called again. 'Are you up there?'

Waow! Church cried from the top of the stairs, as if to confirm the fact, and then he disappeared down the hall.

How did he get in, anyway? Did Jud let him in? Why?

Rachel shifted from one foot to the other, wondering what to do next. The worst of it was that all of this seemed . . . seemed somehow *managed*, as if something wanted her to be here, and—

And then there was a groan from upstairs, low and filled with pain – Jud's voice, surely Jud's voice. He had fallen in the bathroom or maybe tripped, broken a leg or sprained his hip, maybe, the bones of the old were so brittle, and what in the name of God are you thinking of, girl, standing down here and shifting back and forth like you had to go to the bathroom, that was blood on Church, *blood*, Jud's hurt and you're just standing here! What's *wrong* with you?

'Jud!' The groan came again and she ran up the stairs.

She had never been up here before, and because the hall's only window faced west, toward the river, it was still very dark. The hallway ran straight and wide beside the stairwell and toward the back of the house, the cherrywood rail gleaming with a mellow elegance. There was a picture of the Acropolis on the wall and

(it's Zelda all these years she's been after you and now it's her time open the right door and she'll be there with her humped and twisted back smelling of piss and death it's Zelda it's her time and finally she caught up with you)

the groan came again, low, from behind the second door on the right.

Rachel began to walk toward that door, her heels clacking on the boards. It seemed to her that she was going through some sort of warp – not a time-warp or a space-warp, but a size-warp. She was getting smaller. The picture of the Acropolis was floating higher and higher, and that cut-glass doorknob would soon be at eye-level. Her hand stretched out for it . . . and before she could even touch it, the door was snatched open.

Zelda stood there.

She was hunched and twisted, her body so cruelly deformed that she had actually become a dwarf, little more than two feet high; and for some reason Zelda was wearing the suit they had buried Gage in. But it was Zelda, all right, her eyes alight with an insane glee, her face a raddled purple; it was Zelda screaming, '*I finally came back for you, Rachel, I'm going to twist your back like mine and you'll never get out of bed again never get out of bed again NEVER GET OUT OF BED AGAIN—*'

Church was perched on one of her shoulders and Zelda's face swam and changed, and Rachel saw with spiraling, sickening horror that it really wasn't Zelda at all, how could she have made such a stupid mistake? It was Gage. His face was not black but dirty, smeared with blood. And it was swollen, as if he had been terribly hurt and then put back together again by crude, uncaring hands.

She cried his name and held her arms out. He ran to her and climbed into them, and all the time one hand remained behind his back, as if with a bunch of posies picked in someone's back meadow.

'*I brought you something, Mommy!*' he screamed. '*I brought you something, Mommy! I brought you something, I brought you something!*'

CHAPTER SIXTY

Louis Creed woke up with the sun blazing full in his eyes. He tried to get up and grimaced at the stab of pain in his back. It was huge. He fell back on the pillow and glanced down at himself. Still fully dressed. Christ.

He lay there for a long moment, steeling himself against the stiffness that had settled into every muscle, and then he sat up.

'Oh, shit,' he whispered. For a few seconds the room see-sawed gently but perceptibly. His back throbbed like a bad tooth, and when he moved his head it felt as if the tendons in his neck had been replaced by rusty bandsaw blades. But his knee was really the worst. The Ben-Gay hadn't done a thing for it. He should have given himself a fucking cortisone shot. His pants were drawn tightly against the knee by the swelling; it looked like there was a balloon under there.

'Really jobbed it,' he muttered. 'Boy, oh boy, did I ever.'

He bent it very slowly so he could sit on the edge of the bed, lips pressed so tightly together that they were white. Then he began to flex it a bit, listening to the pain talk, trying to decide just how bad it really was, if it might be—

Gage! Is Gage back?

That got him on his feet in spite of the pain. He lurched across the room like Matt Dillon's old sidekick Chester. He went through the door and across the hall into Gage's room. He looked around wildly, his son's name trembling on his lips. But the room was empty. He limped down to Ellie's room, which was also empty, and then into the spare room. That room, which faced the highway, was also empty. But—

440

There was a strange car across the road. Parked behind Jud's truck.

So what?

So a strange vehicle over there could mean trouble, that was so what.

Louis drew the curtain aside and examined it more closely. It was a small blue car, a Chevette. And curled up on top of it, apparently sleeping, was Church.

He looked for a long time before letting the curtain go. Jud had company, that was all, so what? And it was maybe too early to worry about what was or was not going to happen with Gage; Church hadn't come back until noon or a little after, and it was only nine o'clock now. Nine o'clock of a beautiful May morning. He would simply go downstairs and make some coffee, get out the heating pad and wrap it around his knee and—

—and what's Church doing on top of that car?

'Oh, come on,' he said aloud, and began to limp back down the hall. Cats sleep anywhere and everywhere, it's the nature of the beast—

Except Church doesn't cross the road any more, remember?

'Just forget it,' he muttered, and paused halfway down the stairs (which he was working his way down almost sidesaddle). Talking to himself, that was bad. That was—

What was that thing in the woods last night?

The thought came to him unbidden, making him tighten his lips the way the pain in his knee had done when he swung it out of bed. He had dreamed about the thing in the woods last night. His dreams of Disney World had seemed to blend naturally and with a deadly ease into dreams of that thing. He dreamed that it had touched him, spoiling all good dreams for ever, rotting all good intentions. It was the Wendigo, and it had turned him into not just a cannibal but the father of cannibals. In his dream he had been in the Pet Sematary again, but not alone. Bill and Timmy Baterman had been there. Jud had been there, looking ghostly and dead, holding his dog

Spot on a clothesrope leash. Lester Morgan was there with Hanratty the bull on a length of car towing chain. Hanratty was lying on his side, looking around with a stupid, drugged fury. And for some reason Rachel was there, too, and she'd had some sort of accident at the dinner table – spilled a bottle of catsup or maybe dropped a dish of cranberry jelly, maybe, because her dress was splattered with red stains.

And then, rising behind the deadfall to a titanic height, its skin a cracked reptilian yellow, its eyes great hooded foglamps, its ears not ears at all but massive curling horns, was the Wendigo, a beast that looked like a lizard born of a woman. It pointed its horny, nailed finger at all of them as they craned their necks up and up to watch it . . .

'Stop it,' he whispered, and shuddered at the sound of his own voice. He would go out into the kitchen, he decided, and make himself breakfast just as if it were any ordinary day. A bachelor breakfast, full of comforting cholesterol. A couple of fried egg sandwiches with mayo and a slice of Bermuda onion on each one. He smelled sweaty and dirty and cruddy, but he would save the shower for later; right now getting undressed seemed like too much work, and he was afraid he might have to get the scalpel out of his bag and actually cut the leg of the pants open in order to allow his bloated knee to escape. A hell of a way to treat good instruments, but none of the knives in the house would cut the heavy jeans fabric, and Rachel's sewing scissors certainly would not do the trick.

But first, breakfast.

So he crossed the living room and then detoured into the front entry and looked out at the small blue car in Jud's driveway. It was covered with dewfall, which meant it had been there for some time. Church was still on the roof, but not sleeping. He appeared to be staring right at Louis with his ugly yellow eyes.

Louis stepped back hurriedly, as if someone had caught him peeking.

He went into the kitchen, rattled out a frying pan, put it

on the stove, got eggs from the fridge. The kitchen was bright and crisp and clear. He tried to whistle, a whistle would bring the morning into its proper focus, but he could not. Things looked right, but they weren't right. The house seemed dreadfully empty, and last night's work weighed on him like a millstone. Things were wrong, awry; he felt a shadow hovering, and he was afraid.

He limped into the bathroom and took a couple of aspirin with a glass of juice. He was working his way back to the stove when the telephone rang.

He did not answer it immediately but turned and looked at it, feeling slow and stupid, a sucker in some game which he was only now realizing he did not understand in the least.

Don't answer that, you don't want to answer that because that's the bad news, that's the end of the leash that leads around the corner and into the darkness, and I don't think you want to see what's on the other end of that leash, Louis, I really don't think you do, so don't answer that phone, run, run now, the car's in the garage, get in it and take off but don't answer that phone—

He crossed the room and picked it up, standing there with one hand on the dryer as he had so many times before, and it was Irwin Goldman, and even as Irwin said hello he saw the tracks crossing the kitchen, small, muddy tracks, and his heart seemed to freeze in his chest and he believed he could feel his eyeballs swelling in his head, starting from their sockets; he believed that if he could have seen himself in a mirror at that moment he would have seen a face from a cheap pulp comic book. They were Gage's tracks, Gage had been here, *he had been here in the night*, and so where was Gage now?

'It's Irwin, Louis . . . Louis? Are you there? Hello?'

'Hello, Irwin,' he said, and already he knew what Irwin was going to say. He understood the blue car. He understood everything. The leash . . . the leash going into the darkness . . . he was moving fast along it now, hand over hand. Ah, if he could drop it before he saw what was at the end! But it was his leash. He had bought it.

'For a moment I thought we'd been cut off,' Goldman was saying.

'No, the phone slipped out of my hand,' Louis said. His voice was calm.

'Did Rachel make it home last night?'

'Oh yes,' Louis said, thinking of the blue car, Church perched on top of it, the blue car that was so still. His eye traced the muddy footprints on the floor.

'I ought to speak to her,' Goldman said. 'Right away. It's about Ellie.'

'Ellie? What about Ellie?'

'I really think Rachel—'

'Rachel's not here right now,' Louis said harshly. 'She's gone to the store for bread and milk. What about Ellie? Come on, Irwin!'

'We had to take her to the hospital,' Goldman said reluctantly. 'She had a bad dream, or a whole series of them. She was hysterical, and wouldn't come out of it. She—'

'Did they sedate her?'

'What?'

'Sedation,' Louis said impatiently. 'Did they give her sedation?'

'Yes, oh yes. They gave her a pill and she went back to sleep.'

'Did she say anything? What scared her so badly?' He was gripping the phone white-knuckled now.

Silence from Irwin Goldman's end – a long silence. This time Louis did not interrupt, much as he would have liked to.

'That was what scared Dory so badly,' Irwin said finally. 'She babbled a lot before she got . . . before she was crying too hard to understand. Dory herself was almost . . . you know.'

'What did she say?'

'She said Oz the Great and Terrible had killed her mother. Only she didn't say it that way. She said . . . she said "Oz the Gweat and Tewwible," which was the way our other daughter always used to say it. Our daughter Zelda. Louis, believe me when I say I would much rather have asked Rachel this question, but how much have you and she told Ellie about Zelda, and how she died?'

Louis had closed his eyes; the world seemed to be rocking gently under his feet, and Goldman's voice had the lost quality of a voice coming through thick mists.

You may hear sounds like voices, but they are only the loons down south toward Prospect. The sound carries.

'Louis, are you there?'

'Is she going to be all right?' Louis asked, his own voice distant. 'Is Ellie going to be all right? Did you get a prognosis?'

'Delayed shock from the funeral,' Goldman said. 'My own doctor came. Lathrop. A good man. Said she had a degree of fever and that when she woke up this afternoon, she might not even remember. But I think Rachel should come back. Louis, I am frightened. I think you should come back, too.'

Louis did not respond. The eye of God was on the sparrow; so said good King James. He, however, was a lesser being, and his eye was on those muddy footprints.

'Louis, Gage is dead,' Goldman was saying. 'I know that must be hard to accept – for you and Rachel both – but your daughter is very much alive, and she needs you.'

Yes, I accept that. You may be a stupid old fart, Irwin, but perhaps the nightmare that passed between your two daughters on that April day in 1963 taught you something about sensitivity. She needs me, but I can't come, because I'm afraid – so terribly afraid – that my hands are filthy with her mother's blood.

Louis regarded those hands. Louis regarded the dirt under his nails, which was so like the dirt which comprised those footprints on the kitchen floor.

'All right,' he said, 'I understand. We'll be there as soon as we can, Irwin. By tonight, if that's possible. Thank you.'

'We did the best we could,' Goldman said. 'Maybe we're too old. Maybe, Louis, maybe we always were.'

'Did she say anything else?' Louis asked.

Goldman's reply was like the toll of a funeral bell against the wall of his heart. 'A lot, but only one other thing I could make out. "Paxcow says it's too late." '

He hung up the telephone and moved back toward the stove in a daze, apparently meaning to continue on with breakfast or put the things away, he didn't know which, and about halfway across the kitchen a wave of faintness poured over him, floating gray overcame his sight and he swooned to the floor – swoon was the right word because it seemed to take forever. He fell down and down through cloudy depths; it seemed to him that he turned over and over, looped the loop, did a dipsy-doodle or two, slipped an Immelmann. Then he struck on his bad knee and the chromium bolt of pain through his head brought him back with a scream of agony and for a moment he could only crouch, the tears starting from his eyes.

At last he made it back to his feet and stood there, swaying. But his head was clear again. That was something. Wasn't it?

That urge to flee came on him again, for the last time, stronger than ever – he actually felt the comforting bulge of his car keys in his pocket. He would get in the Civic and drive to Chicago. He would get Ellie and go on from there. Of course by then Goldman would know something was wrong, that something was dreadfully amiss, but he would get her anyway . . . snatch her, if he had to.

Then his hand fell away from the bulge of the keys. What killed the urge was not a sense of futility, not guilt, not despair or the deep weariness inside him. It was the sight of those muddy footprints on the kitchen floor. In his mind's eye he could see them tracing a path across the entire country – first to Illinois, then to Florida – across the entire world, if necessary. What you bought, you owned, and what you owned eventually came home to you.

There would come a day when he opened a door and there would be Gage, a demented parody of his former self, grinning a sunken grin, his clear blue eyes gone yellow and smart-stupid.

Or Ellie would open the bathroom door for her morning shower and there would be Gage in the tub, his body criss-crossed with the faded scars and bulges of his fatal accident, clean but stinking of the grave.

Oh yes, that day would come – he didn't doubt it a bit.

'How could I have been so stupid?' he said to the empty room, talking to himself again, not caring. 'How?'

Grief, not stupidity, Louis. There is a difference . . . small, but vital. The battery that burying ground survives on. Growing in power, Jud said, and of course he was right – and you're part of its power now. It has fed on your grief . . . no, more than that. It's doubled it, cubed it, raised it to the nth power. And it isn't just grief it feeds on. Sanity. It's eaten your sanity. The flaw is only the inability to accept, not uncommon. It's cost you your wife and it's almost surely cost you your best friend as well as your son. This is it. What comes when you're too slow wishing away the thing that knocks on your door in the middle of the night is simple enough. Total darkness.

I would commit suicide now, he thought, *and I suppose it's in the cards, isn't it? I have the equipment in my bag. It has managed everything, managed it from the first. The burying ground, the Wendigo, whatever it is. It forced our cat into the road, and perhaps it forced Gage into the road as well, it brought Rachel home, but only in its own good time. Surely I'm meant to do that . . . and I want to.*

But things have to be put right, don't they?

Yes. They did.

There was Gage to think about. Gage was still out there. Somewhere.

He followed the footprints through the dining room and the living room and back up the stairs. They were smudged there, because he had walked over them on his way down without seeing them. They led into the bedroom. *He was here*, Louis thought wonderingly, *he was right here*, and then he saw that his medical bag was unsnapped.

The contents inside, which he always arranged with careful

neatness, were now in jumbled disorder. But it did not take Louis long to see that his scalpel was missing, and he put his hands over his face and sat that way for some time, a faint, despairing noise coming from his throat.

At last he opened the bag again and began to look through it.

Downstairs again.

The sound of the pantry door being opened. The sound of a cupboard being opened, then slammed shut. The busy whine of the can-opener. Last, the sound of the garage door opening and closing. And then the house stood empty in the May sunshine, as it had stood empty on that August day the year before, waiting for the new people to arrive ... as it would wait for other new people to arrive at some future date, a young married couple, perhaps, with no children (but hopes and plans). Bright young marrieds with a taste for Mondavi wine and Lowenbrau beer; he would be in charge of the Northeast Bank's credit department, perhaps, she with a dental hygienist's credential or maybe three years' experience as an optometrist's assistant. He would split half a cord of wood for the fireplace, she would wear high-waisted corduroy pants and walk in Mrs Vinton's field, collecting November's fall grasses for a table centerpiece, her hair in a ponytail, the brightest thing under the gray skies, totally unaware that an invisible Vulture rode the aircurrents overhead. They would congratulate themselves on their lack of superstition, on their hardheadedness in snaring the house in spite of its history – they would tell their friends that it had been fire-sale priced and joke about the ghost in the attic and all of them would have another Lowenbrau or another glass of Mondavi and perhaps they would play backgammon or Mille Bourne.

And perhaps they would have a dog.

CHAPTER SIXTY-ONE

Louis paused on the soft shoulder to let an Orinco truck loaded with chemical fertilizer blast by him, and then he crossed the street to Jud's house, trailing his shadow to the west behind him. He held an open can of Calo catfood in one hand.

Church saw him coming and sat up, his yellow eyes watchful.

'Hi, Church,' Louis said, surveying the silent house. 'Want some grub?'

He put the can of catfood down on the trunk of the Chevette and watched as Church leaped lightly down from its roof and began to eat. Louis put his hand in his jacket pocket. Church looked around at him, tensing, as if reading his mind, Louis smiled and stepped away from the car. Church began to eat again, and Louis took a syringe from his pocket. He stripped the paper covering from it and filled it with 75 milligrams of morphine. He put the multi-dose phial back in his jacket and walked over to Church, who looked around again mistrustfully. Louis smiled at the cat and said, 'Go on, eat up, Church. Hey-ho, let's go, right?' He stroked the cat, felt its back arch, and when Church went back to his meal again, Louis seized it around its stinking guts and sank the needle deep into its haunch.

Church went electric in his grip, struggling against him, spitting and clawing, but Louis held on and depressed the plunger all the way. Only then did he let go. The cat leaped off the Chevette, hissing like a tea kettle, yellow eyes wild and baleful. The needle and syringe dangled from its haunch as it leaped, then fell out and broke. Louis was indifferent. He had more.

The cat started for the road, then turned back toward the house, as if remembering something. It got halfway there and then began to weave drunkenly. It made the steps, leaped up to the first one, then fell off. It lay on the bare patch at the foot of the porch steps on its side, breathing weakly.

Louis glanced into the Chevette. If he had needed more confirmation than the stone that had replaced his heart, he had it: Rachel's purse on the seat, her scarf, and a clutch of plane tickets spilling out of a Delta Airlines folder.

When he turned around again to walk to the porch, Church's side had ceased its rapid, fluttery movement. Church was dead. Again.

Louis stepped over it and mounted the porch steps.

'Gage?'

It was cool in the front hall. Cool and dark. The single word fell into the silence like a stone down a deep-drilled well. Louis threw another.

'Gage?'

Nothing. Even the tick of the clock in the parlor had ceased. This morning there had been no one to wind it.

But there were tracks on the floor.

Louis went into the living room. There was the smell of cigarettes, stale and long since burned out. He saw Jud's chair by the window. It was pushed askew, as if he had gotten up suddenly. There was an ashtray on the windowsill, and in it a neat roll of cigarette ash.

Jud sat here watching. Watching for what? For me, of course; watching for me to come home. Only he missed me. Somehow he missed me.

Louis glanced at the four beer cans lined up in a neat row. Not enough to put him to sleep, but maybe he had gotten up to go to the bathroom. However it had been, it was just a little bit too good to have been perfectly accidental, wasn't it?

The muddy tracks approached the chair by the window.

Mixed among the human tracks were a few faded, ghostly catprints. As if Church had walked in and out of the grave-dirt left by Gage's small shoes. Then the tracks made for the swinging door leading into the kitchen.

Heart thudding, Louis followed the tracks.

He pushed the door open and saw Jud's splayed feet, his old green workpants, his checked flannel shirt. The old man was lying sprawled in a wide pool of drying blood.

Louis clapped his hands to his face, as if to blight his own vision. But there was no way to do that; he saw eyes, Jud's eyes, open, accusing him, perhaps even accusing himself for setting this in motion.

But did he? Louis wondered. *Did he really do that?*

Jud had been told by Stanny B., and Stanny B. had been told by his father, and Stanny B.'s father had been told by his father, the last trader to the Indians, a Frenchman from the Northcountry in the days when Franklin Pierce had been a living President.

'Oh Jud, I'm so sorry,' he whispered.

Jud's blank eyes stared at him.

'So sorry,' Louis repeated.

His feet seemed to move by themselves, and he was suddenly back to last Thanksgiving in his mind, not that night when he and Jud had taken the cat up to the Pet Sematary and beyond, but at the turkey dinner Norma had put on the table, all of them laughing and talking, the two men drinking beer and Norma with a glass of white wine, and she had taken the white lawn tablecloth from the lower drawer as he was taking it now, but she had put it on the table and then anchored it with lovely pewter candlestick holders, while he—

Louis watched it billow down over Jud's body like a collapsing parachute, mercifully covering that dead face. Almost immediately, tiny rosepetals of deepest, darkest scarlet began to stain the white lawn.

'I'm sorry,' he said for a third time. 'So so—'

Then something moved overhead, something scraped, and

the word broke off between his lips. It had been soft, it had been stealthy, but it had been *deliberate*. Oh yes, he was convinced of that. A sound he had been meant to hear.

His hands wanted to tremble, but he would not allow them. He stepped over to the kitchen table with its checkered oilcloth covering, and reached into his pocket. He removed three more Becton-Dickson syringes, stripped them of their paper coverings, and laid them out in a neat row. He removed three more multi-dose phials and filled each of the syringes with enough morphine to kill a horse – or Hanratty the bull, if it came to that. He put them in his pocket again.

He left the kitchen, crossed the living room, and stood at the base of the stairs.

'Gage?' he called.

From somewhere in the shadows above, there came a giggling – a cold and sunless laughter that made the skin on Louis's back prickle.

He started up.

It was a long walk to the top of those stairs. He could well imagine a condemned man taking a walk almost as long (and as horribly short) to the platform of a scaffold with his hands tied behind his back, knowing that he would piss when he could no longer whistle.

He reached the top at last, one hand in his pocket, staring only at the wall. How long did he stand that way? He did not know. He could now feel his sanity beginning to give way. This was an actual sensation, a true thing. It was interesting. He imagined a tree overloaded with ice in a terrible storm would feel this way – if trees could feel anything – shortly before toppling.

'Gage, want to go to Florida with me?' he called at last.

That giggle again.

Louis turned and was greeted by the sight of his wife, to whom he had once carried a rose in his teeth, lying halfway down the hall, dead. Her legs were splayed out as Jud's had been. Her back and head were cocked at an angle against the wall. She looked like a woman who has gone to sleep while reading in bed.

He walked down toward her.

Hello, darling, he thought, *you came home.*

Blood had splashed the wallpaper in idiot shapes. She had been stabbed a dozen times, two dozen, who knew? His scalpel had done this work.

Suddenly he saw her, really *saw* her, and Louis Creed began to scream.

His screams echoed and racketed shrilly through this house where now only death lived and walked. Eyes bulging, face livid, hair standing on end, he screamed; the sounds came from his swollen throat like the bells of hell, terrible shrieks that signalled the end not of love but of sanity; in his mind all the hideous images were suddenly unloosed at once. Victor Pascow's dying on the infirmary carpet, Church coming back with bits of green plastic in his whiskers, his son's baseball cap lying in the road, full of blood, but most of all that thing he had seen near Little God Swamp, the thing that had pushed the tree over, the thing with the yellow eyes, the Wendigo, creature of the Northcountry, the dead thing whose touch awakens unspeakable appetites.

Rachel had not just been killed.

Something had been . . . something had been at her.

(! CLICK !)

That click was in his head. It was the sound of some relay fusing and burning out for ever, the sound of lightning stroking down in a direct hit, the sound of a door opening.

He looked up numbly, the scream still shivering in his throat and here was Gage at last, his mouth smeared with blood, his chin dripping, his lips pulled back in a hellish grin. In one hand he held Louis's scalpel.

As he brought it down, Louis pulled back with no real thought at all. The scalpel whickered past his face, and Gage overbalanced. *He is as clumsy as Church,* Louis thought. Louis kicked his feet from under him. Gage fell awkwardly and Louis was on him before he could get up, straddling him, one knee pinning the hand which held the scalpel.

'*No,*' the thing under him panted. Its face twisted and writhed. Its eyes were baleful; insectile in their stupid hate. '*No, no, no —*'

Louis clawed for one of the hypos, got it out. He would have to be quick. The thing under him was like a greased fish and it would not let go of the scalpel no matter how hard he bore down on its wrist. And its face seemed to ripple and change even as he looked at it: it was Jud's face, dead and staring; it was the dented, ruined face of Victor Pascow, eyes rolling mindlessly; it was, mirrorlike, Louis's own, so dreadfully pale and lunatic. Then it changed again and became the face of that creature in the woods – the low brow, the dead yellow eyes, the tongue long and pointed and bifurcated, grinning and hissing.

'*No, no, no-no-no —*'

It bucked beneath him. The hypo flew out of Louis's hand and rolled a short way down the hall. He groped for another, brought it out, and jammed it straight down into the small of Gage's back.

It screamed beneath him, body straining and sunfishing, nearly throwing him off. Grunting, Louis got the third syringe and jammed this one home in Gage's arm, depressing the plunger all the way. He got off then and began to back slowly down the hallway. Gage got slowly to his feet and began to stagger toward him. Five steps and the scalpel fell from its hand. It struck the floor blade first and stuck itself in the wood, quivering. Ten steps and that strange yellow light in its eyes began to fade. A dozen and it fell to its knees.

Now Gage looked up at him and for a moment Louis saw his son – his real son – his face unhappy and filled with pain.

'*Daddy!*' he cried, and then fell forward on his face.

Louis stood there for a moment, then went to Gage, moving carefully, expecting some trick. But there was no trick, no sudden leap with clawed hands. He slid his fingers expertly down Gage's throat, found the pulse, and held it. He was then a doctor for the last time in his life, monitoring the pulse, monitoring until there was nothing, nothing inside, nothing outside.

When it was gone at last, Louis got up and sauntered down the hall to a far corner. He crouched there, pulling himself into a ball, cramming himself into the corner, tighter and tighter. He found he could make himself smaller if he put a thumb in his mouth and so he did that.

He remained that way for better than two hours . . . and then, little by little, a dark and oh-so-plausible idea came to him. He pulled his thumb from his mouth. It made a small pop. Louis got himself
(*hey-ho, let's go*)
going again.

In the room where Gage had hidden, he stripped the sheet from the bed and took it out into the hall. He wrapped his wife's body in it, gently, with love. He was humming but did not realize it.

He found gasoline in Jud's garage. Five gallons of it in a red can next to the Lawnboy. More than enough. He began in the kitchen where Jud still lay under the Thanksgiving tablecloth. He drenched that, then moved into the living room with the can still upended, spraying amber gas over the rug, the sofa, the magazine rack, the chairs, and so out into the downstairs hall and toward the back bedroom. The smell of gas was strong and rich.

Jud's matches were on top of his cigarettes by the chair where he had kept his fruitless watch. Louis took them. At the front door he tossed a lighted match back over his shoulder and stepped out. The blast of the heat was immediate and savage, making the skin on his neck feel too small. He shut the door neatly and only stood on the porch for a moment, watching the orange flickers behind Norma's curtains. Then he crossed the porch, pausing for a moment, remembering the beers he and Jud had drunk here a million years ago, listening to the soft, gathering roar of fire within the house.

Then he stepped out.

CHAPTER SIXTY-TWO

Steve Masterton came around the final curve just before Louis's house and saw the smoke almost immediately – not from Louis's place, but from the house of the old duck across the street.

He had come out this morning because he had been worried about Louis – deeply worried. Charlton had told him about Rachel's call of the day before, and that had set him to wondering just where Louis was . . . and what he was up to.

His worry was vague, but it itched at his mind – he wasn't going to feel right until he had gone out there and checked to see if things were okay . . . or as okay as they could be, under the circumstances.

The spring weather had emptied the infirmary like white magic, and Surrendra had told him to go ahead; he could handle whatever came up. So Steve had jumped on to his Honda, which he had liberated from the garage only last weekend, and headed out for Ludlow. He maybe pushed the cycle a little faster than was strictly necessary, but the worry was there; it gnawed. And with it came the absurd feeling that he was already late. Stupid, of course, but in the pit of his stomach there was a feeling similar to the one he'd had there last fall when that Pascow thing cropped up – a feeling of miserable surprise and almost leaden disillusion. He was by no means a religious man (in college Steve had been a member of the Atheists' Society for two semesters and had dropped out only when his advisor had told him – privately and very much off the record – that it might very well hurt his chances to obtain a med school scholarship later on), but he supposed he fell as much heir to whatever biological or biorhythmic conditions

457

passed for premonitions as any other human being, and the death of Pascow had seemed to set a tone for the year which followed, somehow. Not a good year, by any means. Two of Surrendra's relatives had been clapped in jail back home, some political thing, and Surrendra had told him that he believed one of them – an uncle he cared for very much – might well now be dead. Surrendra had wept, and the tears from the usually benign Indian had frightened Steve. And Charlton's mother had had a radical mastectomy. The tough nurse was not very optimistic about her mother's chances for joining the Five Year Club. Steve himself had attended four funerals since the death of Victor Pascow – his wife's sister, killed in a car crash, a cousin, killed in a freak accident as the result of a bar-room bet (he had been electrocuted while proving he could shinny all the way to the top of a power pole), a grandparent, and, of course, Louis's little boy.

And he liked Louis. He wanted to make sure Louis was all right. Louis had been through hell lately.

When he saw the billows of smoke, his first thought was that this was something else to lay at the door of Victor Pascow, who seemed, in his dying, to have removed some sort of crash-barrier between these ordinary people and an extraordinary run of bad luck. But that was stupid, and Louis's house was the proof. It stood calm and white, a little piece of clean-limbed New England architecture in the mid-morning sun.

People were running toward the old duck's house, and as Steve banked his bike across the road and pulled into Louis's driveway, he saw a man dash up on to the old duck's porch, approach the front door, and then retreat. It was well that he did; a moment later the glass pane in the center of the door blew out and flames boiled through the opening. If the fool actually had gotten the door open, the blow-out would have cooked him like a lobster.

Steve dismounted and put the Honda on its kickstand, Louis momentarily forgotten. He was drawn by all the old mystery of fire. Maybe half a dozen people had gathered; except for the would-be hero, who lingered on the Crandalls' lawn, they kept a respectful distance. Now the windows between the porch and the house blew out. Glass danced in the air. The would-be hero ducked and ran for it. Flames ran up the inner wall of the porch like groping hands, blistering the white paint. As Steve watched, one of the rattan easy-chairs smouldered and then exploded into flame.

Over the crackling sounds, he heard the would-be hero cry out with a shrill and absurd sort of optimism: 'Gonna lose her! Gonna lose her sure! If Jud's in there, he's a gone goose! Told 'im about the creosote in that chimbly a hunnert times!'

Steve opened his mouth to holler across and ask if the fire department had been called, but just then he heard the faint wail of sirens approaching. A lot of them. They had been called, but the would-be hero was right: the house was going. Flames probed through half a dozen broken windows now, and the front eave had grown an almost transparent membrane of fire over its bright green shingles.

He turned back, then, remembering Louis – but if Louis were here, wouldn't he be with the others across the street?

Steve caught something then, just barely caught it with the tail of his eye.

Beyond the head of Louis's hot-topped driveway there was a field, a field that stretched up a long, gently rising hill. The timothy, although still green, had grown high already this May, but Steve could see a path, almost as neatly mowed as a putting green on a golf course. It wound and meandered its way up the slope of the field, rising to meet the woods that began, thick and green, just below the horizon. It was here, where the pale green of the timothy grass met the thicker, denser green of the woods, that Steve had seen movement – a flash of bright white that seemed to be moving. It was gone almost as soon as his eye registered it, but it had seemed to him for that brief moment that he had seen a man carrying a white bundle.

That was Louis, his mind told him with sudden irrational

certainty. *That was Louis, and you better get to him quick, because something damn bad has happened and pretty quick something even more damn bad is going to happen. If you don't stop him.*

He stood indecisively at the head of the driveway, shifting one foot for the other, his weight jittery between two of them.

Steve baby, you're scared shitless just about now, aren't you?

Yes. He was. He was scared shitless, and for no reason at all. But there was also a certain . . . a certain

(*attraction*)

yes, a certain attraction here, something about that path, that path leading up the hill and perhaps continuing on into the woods, surely that path had to go somewhere, didn't it? Yes, of course it did. All paths eventually went somewhere.

Louis. Don't forget about Louis, you dummy! Louis was the man you came out to see, remember? You didn't come out to Ludlow to go exploring the goddam woods.

'What you got there, Randy?' the would-be hero cried. His voice, still shrill and somehow optimistic, carried well.

Randy's reply was almost but not quite obscured by the growing wail of the fire sirens: 'Dead cat.'

'Burnt up?'

'Don't look burnt,' Randy returned. 'Just looks dead.'

And Steve's mind returned implacably, as if the exchange across the street had something to do with what he had seen – or what he thought he had seen: That *was* Louis.

He started to move then, trotting up the path toward the woods, leaving the fire behind him. He had worked up a good sweat by the time he reached the edge of the woods, and the shade felt cool and good. There was the sweet aroma of pine and spruce, bark and sap.

Once into the woods he broke into an all-out run, not sure why he was running, not sure why his heart was beating double-time. His breath whistled in and out. He was able to lengthen his run to a sprint going downhill – the path was admirably clear – but he reached the arch that marked the entrance to the Pet Sematary at little more than a fast walk.

There was a hot stitch high in his right side, just under the armpit.

His eyes barely registered the circles of graves, the beaten tin squares, the bits of board and slate. His gaze was fixed on the bizarre sight at the far side of the circular clearing. It was fixed on Louis, who was climbing a deadfall, seemingly in outright defiance of gravity. He mounted the steep fall step by step, his eyes straight ahead, like a man who has been mesmerized or who is sleepwalking. In his arms was the white thing that Steve had seen from the tail of his eye. This close, its configuration was undeniable – it was a body. One foot, clad in a black shoe with a low heel, protruded. And Steve knew with a sudden and sickening certainty that Louis was carrying Rachel's body.

Louis's hair had gone white.

'*Louis!*' Steve screamed.

Louis didn't hesitate, didn't pause. He reached the top of the deadfall and began down the far side.

He'll fall, Steve thought incoherently. *He's been damned lucky, incredibly lucky, but pretty soon he's going to fall and if his leg's the only thing he breaks—*

But Louis did not fall. He reached the other side of the deadfall, was temporarily out of Steve's sight, and then reappeared as he walked toward the woods again.

'Louis!' Steve yelled again.

And this time Louis stopped, and turned back.

Steve was struck dumb by what he saw. Besides the white hair, Louis's face was that of an old, old man.

At first there was no recognition at all in Louis's face. It dawned little by little, as if someone was turning a rheostat up in his brain. Louis's mouth was twitching. After a while Steve realized Louis was trying to smile.

'Steve,' he said in a cracked, uncertain voice. 'Hello, Steve. I'm going to bury her. Have to do it with my bare hands, I guess. It may take until dark. The soil up there is very stony. I don't suppose you'd want to give me a hand?'

Steve opened his mouth, but no words came out. In spite of his surprise, in spite of his horror, he *did* want to give Louis a hand. Somehow, up here in the woods, it seemed very right, very . . . very natural.

'Louis,' he managed to croak at last. 'What happened? Good Christ, what happened? Was she . . . was she in the fire?'

'I waited too long with Gage,' Louis said. 'Something got into him because I waited too long. But it will be different with Rachel, Steve. I know it will.'

He staggered a little, and Steve saw that Louis had gone insane – he saw this quite clearly. Louis was insane and abysmally weary. But somehow, only the latter seemed to carry weight in his own bewildered mind.

'I could use some help,' Louis said.

'Louis, even if I wanted to help you, I couldn't climb over that pile of wood.'

'Oh yes,' Louis said. 'You could. If you just move steadily and don't look down. That's the secret, Steve.'

He turned then, and although Steve called his name, Louis moved off into the woods. For a few moments Steve could see the white of the sheet flickering through the trees. Then it was gone.

He ran across to the deadfall and began to climb it with no thought at all, at first feeling with his hands for good holds, attempting to crawl up it, and then gaining his feet. As he did so, a crazy sort of daredevil exhilaration swept over him – it was like hitting on pure oxygen. He *believed* he could do it – and he did. Moving swiftly and surely, he reached the top. He stood there for a moment, swaying, watching Louis move along the path – the path which continued on the far side of the deadfall.

Louis turned and looked back at Steve. He held his wife, wrapped in a bloody sheet, in his arms.

'You may hear sounds,' Louis said. 'Sounds like voices. But they are just the loons, down south toward Prospect. The sound carries. It's funny.'

'Louis—'

But Louis had turned away.

For a moment Steve almost followed him — it was very, very close.

I could help him, if that's what he wants . . . and I want to help him, yes. That's the truth, because there's more going on here than meets the eye and I want to know what it is. It seems very . . . well . . . very important. It seems like a secret. Like a mystery.

Then a branch snapped under one of his canted feet. It made a dry, dusty sound like a track-starter's gun. It brought him back to exactly where he was, and what he was doing. Terror leaped into him and he turned around in a clumsy circle, arms held out for balance, his tongue and throat oily with fright, his face bearing the dismayed grimace of a man who wakes up only to find he has sleepwalked his way on to a high skyscraper ledge.

She's dead and I think that maybe Louis has killed her, Louis has gone mad, utterly mad, but—

But there was something worse than madness here; something much, much worse. It was as if there was a magnet somewhere out in those woods and he could feel it pulling at something in his brain. Pulling him toward that place where Louis was taking Rachel.

Come on, man, walk the path . . . walk the path and see where it goes. We got stuff to show you out here, Steverino, stuff they never told you about in the Atheists' Society back in Lake Forest.

And then, perhaps simply because it had enough for one day to feed on and lost interest in him, the call of the place in his mind simply ceased. Steve took two plunging, drunken steps back down the side of the deadfall. Then more branches let go with a grinding rattle and his left foot plunged into the tangled deadwood; harsh sharp splinters pulled off his sneaker and then tore into his flesh as he yanked free. He fell forward into the Pet Sematary, barely missing a piece of orange-crate that could easily have punched into his stomach.

He got to his feet, staring around, bewildered, wondering

what had happened to him . . . or if *anything* had happened to him. Already it had begun to seem like a dream.

Then, from the deep woods behind the deadfall, woods so deep that the light looked green and tarnished even on the brightest days, a low, chuckling laugh arose. The sound was huge. Steve could not even begin to imagine what sort of creature could have made such a sound.

He ran, one shoe off and one shoe on, like the boy in the nursery rhyme, trying to shriek, but unable. He was still running when he reached Louis's house, and still trying to shriek when he finally got his bike started and slued out on to Route 15. He very nearly sideswiped an arriving fire engine from Brewer. Inside his Bell helmet, his hair was standing on end.

By the time he got back to his apartment in Orono, he could not precisely remember having gone to Ludlow at all. He called in sick at the infirmary, took a pill, and went to bed.

Steve Masterton never really remembered that day . . . except in deep dreams, those that come in the small hours of the morning. And in these dreams he would sense that something huge had shrugged by him – something which had reached out to touch him . . . and had then withdrawn its inhuman hand at the very last second.

Something with great yellow eyes which gleamed like fog lamps.

Steve sometimes awoke shrieking from these dreams, his eyes wide and bulging, and he would think: *You think you are screaming, but it's only the sound of the loons, down south, in Prospect. The sound carries. It's funny.*

But he did not know, could not remember, what such a thought might mean. The following year he took a job halfway across the country, in St Louis.

In the time between his last sight of Louis Creed and his departure for the Midwest, Steve never went into the town of Ludlow again.

EPILOGUE

The police came late that afternoon. They asked questions but voiced no suspicions. The ashes were still hot; they had not yet been raked. Louis answered their questions. They seemed satisfied. They spoke outside and he wore a hat. That was good. If they had seen his gray hair, they might have asked more questions. That would have been bad. He wore his gardening gloves, and that was good, too. His hands were bloody and ruined.

He played solitaire that night until long after midnight.

He was just dealing a fresh hand when he heard the back door open.

What you buy is what you own, and sooner or later what you own will come back to you, Louis Creed thought.

He did not turn around but only looked at his cards as the slow, gritting footsteps approached. He saw the Queen of Spades. He put his hand on it.

The steps ended directly behind him.

Silence.

A cold hand fell on Louis's shoulder. Rachel's voice was grating, full of dirt.

'*Darling,*' it said.

465

Don't miss the following
iconic chillers